Broken but... Mending

by
Dale Mayer

Book in this series:

Skin
Scars
Scales (of Justice)
Broken but… Mending 1-3

BROKEN BUT... MENDING
Dale Mayer
Valley Publishing

Copyright © 2011, 2015

All rights reserved. Except for use in any review, the reproduction or utilization of this work in whole or in part by any electronic, mechanical or other means, now known or hereafter invented, including xerography, photocopying and recording, or in any information storage or retrieval system, is forbidden without the written permission of the publisher.

This is a work of fiction. Names, characters, places, brands, media, and incidents are either the product of the author's imagination or are used fictitiously. Any resemblance to actual events, locales, or persons, living or dead, is entirely coincidental.

ISBN-13: 978-1-988315-37-9
Print Edition

Back Cover

Skin
A journey of exploration…
A journey of healing…
A journey of love…

Two people are forced by circumstances into a therapy class to help them deal with their problems. They are strangers. Forced to be partners. Naturally opposites.

Kane is dealing with anger of betrayal at the deepest level, needing to find his way back to forgiveness. Tania is a previous rape victim hoping to deal with her fear of intimacy so she can have a loving relationship.

Tania's medium of expression – her camera.

Her subject – the human body – Kane's physical body.

Looking through the lens of a camera, she learns to find beauty and compassion…and the strength to find wholeness…with him.

Scars
Some scars are visible…
Some scars are hidden…
The worst scars are buried deep inside…

Robin and Sean are existing in their private worlds. Hiding in plain sight, not really living, definitely not thriving. They both need to move forward… if they can.

Yet the price of success is pain as they confront issues that have plagued them for years. They're so different, with such opposite problems. Yet they complement each other – or at least they will, if they can work through their issues and find each other.

This is a story of pain and sorrow, joy and success… and… love.

Scales (of Justice)

She thinks she escaped Justice

He is still waiting for Justice to happen.

She's afraid her day of reckoning is near.

He's afraid his day of reckoning will never arrive.

Will love balance the scales of Justice?

Sign up to be notified of all Dale's releases here!

http://dalemayer.com/category/blog/

Your Free Book Awaits!

KILL OR BE KILLED

Part of an elite SEAL team, Mason takes on the dangerous jobs no one else wants to do – or can do. When he's on a mission, he's focused and dedicated. When he's not, he plays as hard as he fights.

Until he meets a woman he can't have but can't forget. Software developer, Tesla lost her brother in combat and has no intention of getting close to someone else in the military. Determined to save other US soldiers from a similar fate, she's created a program that could save lives. But other countries know about the program, and they won't stop until they get it – and get her.

Time is running out… For her… For him… For them…

DOWNLOAD a *complimentary* copy of MASON? Just tell me where to send it!

http://dalemayer.com/sealsmason/

Skin

by
Dale Mayer

Chapter 1

TANIA TOOK HER seat in the small room. She was early, and the seminar room was empty. She liked to arrive early in class because it gave her time to settle before things got started.

She'd been in similar scenarios before. She could do this, again and again, if she had to. Using the meditation tricks she learned, she practiced her deep-breathing techniques to ease back the stress threatening to choke the breath from her body. Therapy was good for her. She was getting better. She could do this.

This particular program was special, a university workshop type of thing. Intensive, invasive, and guaranteed to help bring about change.

She could do this.

Liar. She so sucked at this.

She stared out the large windows, her nerves raw, hot. Morning sunshine shone through the curtains, giving a muted look to the bright light. Kind of like her own life. As if she was living only a shade of the life she could be.

That was precisely what she was doing.

Several other attendees entered and took their seats. Special group, special problems, and they'd all signed up to do this willingly; had even paid for it. More than that, once committed there was no quitting. They were all students here at the University of British Columbia in Vancouver. They were all associated in one way or another with the professor who'd be leading this weeklong session. She was friends with one of the participants and recognized most of the others from Jenna's lectures on internal healing.

In her case, her best friend had paid the hefty deposit to hold Tania's place while she convinced her to get help. Five days in a hotel at the edge of campus. Workshops in the mornings, assignments in the afternoons, and therapy sessions dotted the rest of the evening. Even those who lived locally weren't allowed to leave at the end of the day; it was all-inclusive. She wished it were otherwise, then she could return to her normal life instead of this intensive, no-hiding type of session. Which was, of course, the purpose of the seminar.

She was scared, but she was more scared of staying caught in this limbo forever.

It was stupid. She shouldn't need help, not after all this time. It had happened years ago. She should be over this.

But the sad fact was, she wasn't. And if she didn't do something about it, her life would never go in the direction she wanted it to go. Her dream of a small house and white picket fence with the perfect two kids was never going to happen if she didn't find a way to let a man into her bedroom. *Sure*, she thought moodily, *I could adopt*. She had seriously considered it.

But she wanted the loving relationships she saw so many of her friends enjoying and to get there, she had to heal herself first. So not easy.

She smiled as her friend, Robin, came in and sat down beside her. Robin said, "Hi. How are you doing this week?"

Tania smiled wider. "Fine. As long as I avoid men, as usual."

"Ha." Robin grinned. "Defeats the purpose, doesn't it?"

"It's what I can do." Tania shrugged. "Leaving the safety net is not easy."

"I hear you." Robin settled in beside her. Tania's scars were inside, but Robin's were outside. She had been in a horrible accident and was dealing with reconstructive surgery and the fact she might never be 'normal'. She had trouble going out in public and had barricaded herself in a secular life of school. Robin was here to deal with her fears and how she looked now, and to find the strength to get out in public where she'd be ridiculed and stared at. After children had run from her screaming in a park almost a year ago, she'd gone home and stayed home. It had become the safe haven she didn't want to leave, but that also made it a prison. She had to force herself to go to class. Had to force herself to come to this seminar.

Tania understood.

They were all here to deal with issues – big issues. Whatever issues stopped them from living full lives. Their professor was a special woman who'd walked their path and had healed herself. Now, she was on a journey to help others do the same.

Just then, several men walked in, loud and boisterous. There was just something about that big, dominant energy as it filled the small, casual lounge. It was the same three men who arrived as a group last night. It was the same way they arrived at Jenna's classes on campus. Every week the quiet disappeared, and Tania and Robin became even quieter. This wasn't a normal therapy group – she'd been to those. This one demanded a commitment to complete the session and participation at all times. There was homework, assignments that forced participants to step out of their comfort zone.

Everyone knew something about each other, but the details had been offered at the discretion of the person. They were all here for a week. One week. Working together, pairing up for various assignments.

She *could* do this.

Then *he* walked in and sat down beside her.

Her stomach dropped and her blood heated. She could hardly breathe. She straightened and shifted ever so slightly closer to Robin like she always did. Like a moth to a flame, she knew better than to get any closer to Kane, a huge muscled guy who seemed too rough and…angry for her to be safe. But, just like the moth, the attraction was at the cellular level and she was helpless to resist.

God, she wanted him.

And she'd never wanted a man in her life.

He terrified her. She wanted to want a small man, someone her size. Someone…she'd have a chance to escape from if he turned abusive. Someone gentle, tender, and understanding.

Kane oozed strength, power, and bitterness.

Not at all what she wanted or needed.

Kane crossed his arms, his muscles bulging beside her. She shuddered. How could she want to stroke her fingers across his skin at the same time that she wanted to run away from him? He could pound her into the ground with one punch. Why? Why would her body want anything to do with him? It made no sense.

It only reinforced that she was crazy.

"Ah, Tania? Can you move back over slightly?" Robin gave her a concerned look then nudged her shoulder and, using her chin, pointed to Tania's half-empty seat.

Tania realized she'd damn near crawled into Robin's chair with her; she was that close. With a sideways glance at Kane,

Tania flushed and settled back into place. "Sorry," she whispered to Robin.

"Don't worry about it."

Two voices said the same thing.

She wanted to yell 'snap', that silly remnant from her childhood, but was too busy staring in surprise at Kane. He gave her a stone-faced look. She'd never considered how her constant avoidance of him must look. He was no monster; in fact, he was stunning – to her. He had a lean face full of angles and planes. She thought of granite when she contemplated him. Strong. Infallible. Unyielding.

She had no basis for such an assessment. She didn't know him outside of seeing him once in a while in Jenna's classes. They were of a similar age, she thought, but he seemed older. It was his demeanor, slightly off-putting as he almost always had a sneer on his face. As if he was here under duress, but he didn't truly belong.

But then, she'd had a similar attitude in her last therapy class. That she didn't now meant she'd grown a little. Maybe he just needed a bit more time. Accepting one had a problem was a hell of a start – and often the most difficult step.

He might not want to see himself as one of the participants here who needed help, but that was what he was. And being here meant he had issues regardless of his attitude, so he was no better than she was.

But his attitude needed some adjusting if he was going to get any benefit from the class. And considering the money he'd dumped into this, he'd better.

She couldn't help but wonder at his story. He had a chip on his shoulder obviously, and there was a thin layer of bitterness just below the surface. She had to think relationships were involved. From what she'd seen, there were some pretty screwed-up people in the world, and those here for this session had taken a hit from some of the worst.

It had been good for her to come here and see she wasn't alone in dealing with her problems, or that her problems were by no means the worst. One of the men was young, like nineteen…maybe or possibly younger, considering the sparse bristles on his chin. He had a raunchy humor and dead eyes. Another, Sean, was tall and lanky and seemed seriously old on the inside. He both scared her and struck a deep cord of sympathy inside. His mother had horribly abused him for years before she finally OD'd on drugs, and he'd been left with a legacy of pain.

And like so many others here, he'd been working on his healing for years. He hoped this retreat would get rid of his last stumbling block.

Tania wasn't so sure it could be possible. That look in his eye…

She shuddered, grateful she'd come as far as she had.

Now if only she could kick this fear and go all the way. Yet another school idiom that made her want to chuckle. What was wrong with her? It was as if she had a delayed teenage-hood. Maybe she had. She certainly hadn't spent it dreaming over movie stars or giggling in groups waiting for the special guys to walk by.

The door opened, admitting Jenna Price, their professor and therapist. She was a mix of ruthless compassion and steely resolve. She was determined that everyone here get something useful from this session. They weren't randomly accepted into this workshop; there had been a long list, which grew even longer every term, apparently. Money hadn't been the only criteria. The problems you were dealing with had to be something she felt would work in a group setting and she could help you move past, and so the other participants could help you to deal with your issues, too. She wasn't about everyone getting along, more about how the interaction would work to benefit everyone involved.

Jenna walked to the empty chair, her hand wrapped around a large china mug with a lid. She was a tea drinker. Apparently, at any time and any place she could always be seen with the mug. She was a stately woman, anywhere from her late thirties to mid-forties. Tania had no idea – just that she appeared to be competent. Now if only she held that magical key to getting Tania's life back on track.

"Good morning." Jenna placed the mug on the floor beside her. "Last night was basic. Today, we are going to get into the nitty-gritty stuff, and you are going to hurt. It's hard dealing with the issues we don't want to look at. It's painful to step out of our padded cloud and deal honestly and openly with what needs to be dealt with." She cast her warm but determined gaze around the room. "Remember, none of you are here by accident. You came because you want to deal with something, and you want change for yourself. Today is Day 1. You will have changed by Day 5; I guarantee it." Her gaze landed on Tania and Robin, a slight softening warming her chocolate-brown eyes. "We'll be working together as a group all morning. But after lunch, you will be put into groups of two with your weeklong assignment."

Weeklong assignment? That was the first Tania had heard anything about it. As long as it was in pairs, she was probably okay. She could work with Robin. That would most likely suit both of them.

Taking a deep breath, Tania turned her attention back to the morning's work.

A long time later, Jenna opened a folder she'd brought

with her and handed out sheets of paper to everyone. "This is the outline of the assignment. You will be given all afternoon every day for the rest of the week to work on this, with my help if need be, but let's make no mistake here: the assignment is not a cerebral one. Each of you must deal with people, the public, and yourselves for this to work."

A small knot of dread formed in Tania's stomach as she comprehended how very difficult such an assignment could be. Poor Robin; she'd have the worst time with this. Already Tania's mind was wandering, looking for ways to make it easier on her, and came to a full stop. No. That was not the answer. She'd be enabling Robin. Better for her to deal with her issues than to have Tania automatically assume she couldn't do it.

Tania would have her hands full herself.

She accepted the sheet of paper from Robin and handed the last one over to the silent Kane. At least he'd lost the bored look. She studied his body language, noticing that he sat a little straighter and locked his jaw. He wasn't as comfortable as he was letting on.

Interesting. So control was important to him. She filed the tidbit away and turned her attention back to class. Jenna had been taking pairs of people off to one side and speaking with them privately. She watched as Robin and the abused young male walked out of the room together. Tania was surprised at the compassion on Robin's face and on Sean's. What was going on?

She turned her attention back to the paper in her hand. The project was intended to push her out of her comfort zone while being within the scope of what she needed to learn to do. Given the private nature of her problem, she really didn't want to have to do anything really uncomfortable. It would be embarrassing and potentially crippling. As another pair of attendees left the room, she realized Jenna was speaking to two more, leaving her and Kane.

Her insides twisted in on themselves. Please, let her be wrong. She wanted Robin as a partner, not Kane. Maybe this had nothing to do with the project. But God, it really felt like it did. The longer she sat there waiting for her turn, the harder her fingers clenched the paper in her lap and the tighter the steel band around her chest constricted. She stared almost blindly as her knuckles turned white and her chest struggled to relax enough to let air in.

Oh God!

If she had to be partners with a man, let it be with a small one. Not Kane. Please, not the six-foot-four, 240-pound man who looked like he belonged with his mitts wrapped around a jackhammer all day.

She had nothing against construction workers, but she so didn't want anything to do with Kane where her problems were concerned. She was looking for so much less of a man.

And her mind called her on it. *Liar. You so want to have something to do with him.*

She had to correct herself. *No, I want to be able to do something with him, but I'm not there yet.* She slid a sideways glance at his massive thighs encased in tight jeans as he sat relaxed in the chair beside her. *And,* she repeated, *I might never get there.*

Then it was her turn.

"Tania and Kane." Jenna walked over to them and tugged a chair forward so she sat in front, making a triangle of their positions. "Sorry for making you wait."

It was on the tip of Tania's tongue to say 'no problem', but she couldn't get the words out. Feeling like a mouse caught in a horrible sense of knowing it was about to get pounced on, she sat, frozen…and waited.

She knew her fate was as bad as the mouse when Jenna said, "Let's discuss your project."

Tania felt more than saw Kane glance her way, but she heard his comment clear enough. "Are you sure this is a good idea? Maybe Tania would do better with someone else."

His smooth-as-chocolate voice sent waves of want through her, but the actual meaning sent rods of steel down her back, making her straighten in outrage.

"I'll be fine," she snapped and widened her gaze as she understood she'd just agreed to work with him. Oh, shit. That damn stubborn temper of hers.

"Good. I think you'll do just fine. Besides, your partnership isn't a spur-of-the-moment decision. I've been working on these pairings since you both confirmed you'd be here, and I think you'll work perfectly together." She studied the papers in her hand for a moment, as if unconcerned at the reception of the other two.

Tania knew she had to be perceptive to the change in the air, the tension. She also had to assume the woman knew what she was about, except Tania had been to some crazy therapists who should have dealt with their own crap before trying to counsel others.

She didn't *think* Jenna fell into the same category.

But who could know?

Hunkering down in the chair, she tried to open her mind to the concept of a team project, actually managing to laugh at herself. It was just for a few days. *Like, how hard could this be?*

Then she listened in growing horror to Jenna's explanation.

When Jenna fell silent, Tania could only stare at her in shock.

Thankfully, Kane appeared to have a handle on this and blasted Jenna with her sentiments exactly. "You want us to what?"

He stood up and stormed around the room. "Are you nuts?"

Tania couldn't agree more.

With his hands out, he said, "Look, I'm here and willing to do the work to deal with my stuff, but you're putting Tania in danger."

She what? Tania straightened. "Excuse me? What kind of danger?" Because she wasn't up for any, not in any way. She wanted a safe, controlled project so she could open the door to her comfort zone and put her big toe in to test the water; that was it.

Danger? Hell no. She'd had more than enough when she'd been raped over twelve years ago.

She wasn't going to be in any kind of danger – ever again.

KANE HAD SAT through enough today. Watching Tania's tiny body shift away from him from the moment he'd sat down – hell, probably from the moment he walked into the room, he knew she had some big-time man issues. He didn't get man-hater vibes from her, but a tiny woman would be easy prey for the wrong man. Unless she was a black belt in something, she had no protection from a man's anger. That she was here in therapy, he'd bet his years of experience she'd been in an abusive relationship. She was a creampuff for any guy over sixteen. For someone like him, hell, no way could he be around her.

He felt like he'd be slamming a teacup against the wall if he said anything in a harsh tone.

She was way too delicate for this class, for him, and for this project. The damn shrink had this one wrong.

There was no way anyone with his anger issues, his hatred of his ex, should be around someone who he could break in half with two fingers.

As he realized Tania was nodding in emphatic agreement, a tiny part of him was sorry for it. In the old days, he'd have loved to have been the knight in shining armor and help her deal with whatever issues she had. He'd seen enough sad cases in his years in law enforcement that he had some idea of what she might have gone through. It could be something completely different…but his instincts said he was close. Damn close.

The shrink smiled at them both, with that damn compassionate warmth that made him wonder if she lived with sunshine and pussycats all her life to have given her outlook a rosy tinge. Because that wasn't the reality as he knew it.

She had to know about him. They all interviewed to come here. Every one of them had spoken to her privately about their issues, and then they'd all attended her lectures at the university alongside their regular classes. While he might not know all of Tania's issues, he knew Jenna did.

And still she'd paired them together. Wondering what she could possibly be thinking, he slowly sat back down.

And wondered why.

Chapter 2

Tania watched silently and a bit regretfully as Kane blew through his temper and back into calm. Her father used to do that: blow up, cool down, and then refuel for the next blow. Her mother had always loved to get him going. They'd fought like cats and dogs all the time, but it hadn't weakened their relationship. They'd argued, debated, and made up with the same passion. Because they blew up often, bad feelings and irritations didn't build up to the point where they caused damage. They shared what they felt all the time – good and bad. It hadn't been the easiest childhood, but she'd always known where she stood on any issue. Bottom line – they loved each other and her.

Even after their divorce, she'd never doubted it. They were still friends today.

Kane looked to be of similar ilk.

It made him a little easier to understand. Except, in this instance, she wished he'd blow a little harder, a little louder. And get them out of this.

"It's only a project," Jenna was saying in her smooth, what-could-you-possibly-be-worried-about tone of voice.

That terrified Tania. She'd been through too much therapy to believe that tone of voice. And from the looks of him, Kane hadn't been through enough. He appeared to be falling for Jenna's line of bullshit.

Tania wasn't so easily swayed. She leaned forward. "Jenna, you know our history. I'm not sure what Kane's issue is, but you know mine."

Jenna smiled warmly at her and waited for her to continue, expectancy on her face for a favorite student about to give the right answer. That should have been enough warning, but just in case Jenna really didn't get it... "Surely," Tania added, "I could work with Robin. I'd love that." She beamed with relief at the smile on Jenna's face. This would work. Tania had always managed to get things to work at university and at work. People were accommodating; no one wanted discord.

Then she saw the look in Jenna's eyes and recognized there was to be no easy exit from this one.

"Fine. How hard can this be?" Tania glared at Kane, who just raised an eyebrow at her. He flicked something off his thigh, but it was the mocking look that made her ask. "What?"

"Oh, nothing; just flicking away an irritating mosquito."

She shot him a narrow-eyed look before turning her back on him to glare at Jenna. "This is a really bad idea," she said in a dark tone.

But Jenna was laughing. "Maybe and maybe not. So let's go over what you are going to do."

That was when Tania understood she was getting a camera.

A smile broke free, relieved laughter rippling throughout the room. "Oh my God! You should have said something in the beginning." She laughed and laughed.

When she could stop the giggles, only the odd hiccupping laugh still escaping, she realized Jenna had a wry smile on her face. Kane wore a thundercloud.

"I'm glad this isn't quite as impossible as you'd first been afraid it was," Jenna said gently.

And that, of course, had been the crux of the issue. Settling down, Tania relaxed, realizing she'd let her fears completely override rational thought here.

She loved photography, and of course Jenna knew that. They'd discussed it several times. She wasn't sure why or how, or if the sensation was real or just another mirage she put up in her world to make something doable, but being behind a camera put distance between her and a situation. It gave her a buffer from the uncomfortable, the too-intense insights, and the world at large.

It gave her a sense of security and of safety.

Jenna was seriously bright to have done this. Relief let Tania sit down and let herself settle inside. She was safe. This wasn't going to be something super scary or super intimate. In fact, she had to wonder if it would do anything for her at all, but her mind immediately clutched at the straw offered and said she could deal with the other stuff later down the road, like in ten years' time.

"Okay. I'm really going to love this project." Her mind wandered to the camera gear she'd brought with her, wondering what to use first. It all depended on what they had to photograph. Then another tidbit fell into place. "That's why you told me to be sure to bring my camera gear, isn't it?"

"Yes, it is." Jenna nodded, but she didn't look at Tania. Instead, she kept her gaze on Kane.

Realizing she'd been awash in her own satisfaction and joy at what she would be doing, she'd put no thought to Kane's role in all of this. It wasn't as if she needed him to carry stuff. It was all lightweight, and she'd been packing her gear for a long time.

She frowned as she took in the hard gaze between Jenna

and Kane, realizing she'd missed something.

"Uhm, what's going on?" She studied the tick on Kane's jaw and recognized that instead of a blow-up, he'd gone super quiet. In her dad's case, it meant he was seriously pissed. She winced. Kane was going to have a monster of a headache after this. Clenching his jaw, his neck was corded, and as her gaze slipped down his chest, she realized his fists were almost white at the knuckles.

"Jenna?" No one could miss the signals in the room right now. She cleared her throat and tried again. "Maybe you could tell me what Kane and I are going to photograph?"

Kane, his voice like silken steel, answered instead. "Go ahead, Jenna." His voice deepened dangerously. "Tell us."

Shit. Tania's gaze raced from the one so furious she couldn't believe he was holding back to Jenna, who sat calmly, returning his stare in apparent unconcern. But Jenna was no fool; everyone knew you didn't turn your back on a dangerous animal.

And right now Kane was one hell of a dangerous animal.

"Why don't you tell her, if you think you know," Jenna said smoothly.

"Kane?" Tania wanted this tension to break. Even tensile strength had a breaking point.

"It's not what you're going to photograph," he snapped. "It's who."

Tania didn't understand, but at the approving curl on Jenna's lips, she figured Kane just got the favorite student award.

"Who am I supposed to photograph?" she asked, bewildered.

"Me."

KANE CLOSED THE door to his room with a very controlled click. He stood stock-still and let the anger ripple through him. He didn't dare let loose or there'd be a hole in the door. He splayed his fingers wide with as much force as he could manage. When the tension finally drained, he relaxed slightly. Then he took several steps toward the bed, where he threw himself down on the cushy surface. He leaned his head back and groaned out loud.

"What the hell am I doing here?" He could blame his brother for this damn session, but that wasn't fair. Sure, Jerry had pushed and prodded to get Kane to sign up, and it had been a good idea initially. Sounded like just what he needed. He'd been nursing his grudge for far too long.

It was time to move on before he screwed up other relationships.

He groaned again, lifting both hands and scrubbing his face. He only had an hour's lunch break. Everyone had split immediately after their meetings with Jenna, taking off for their own silent spaces. He needed food, but he'd needed space and time to regroup more. He could do a stupid camera project with Tania.

So what if she took a picture of him? Big deal.

Then why was he damn near shaking? It's as if he was stressed to the max and if that was the case, why? He'd been fine first thing this morning. Fine since he'd arrived. He'd been disdainful as the process started. It gave him a bit of buffer in case he started to feel too involved, or they got too dangerously close to his own hurts.

It was easier to come to something like this if he kept himself separate from the others. And of course, the therapist's purpose was to stop him. He didn't know when he'd started to feel a fine edge of anger or bitterness to put more distance between them, but it was somewhere around the time he noticed Tania flinching away from him. This morning, she'd damned near crawled into Robin's lap.

It made for a tough few hours when every time he shifted, he felt her respond like a scared rabbit. He'd wanted to reassure her he wasn't planning on hitting her or hitting on her, but he'd known that would have made it all worse.

It was too bad.

She was tiny, delicate-featured, and curvy. He hadn't been able to stop thinking about her. Then with every breath he took, he was intimately aware of her reaction – just as she was aware of his every action.

To have that level of awareness with someone, someone who was terrified of him, was just wrong. No, he hadn't gotten the impression she was terrified of him…she didn't know him. He was a stranger to her. It was more she was terrified of what he represented.

His mind played with that.

What did he represent? Maleness. Strength. Power. He'd caught her gaze on his biceps. His thighs. He studied his arms; he kept in shape, worked out, and had a stocky build. No one would ever call him a toothpick.

From any other woman, he'd take her glances as interest. There could be a touch of that here, but he knew it wasn't the main part. Given they were in therapy, chances were good she'd been beaten up by someone bigger and stronger than her and most likely someone like himself – male.

It made it tough to sit beside her.

Because he didn't have the same issues. At least not over sex. He *was* interested. Then again, he was male, so of course he was interested.

He grinned, his good humor restored. It would be a cold day in Hell before any healthy male wasn't interested in Tinkerbelle.

But to put the two of them together for hours on end was just asking for trouble. He wasn't sure he could stay calm and cool around her like she needed him to be, and he didn't want to terrorize her by blowing up in front of her.

She didn't need that.

He just didn't know what she did need, and it was none of his business. Jenna would have to sort that out. He needed to tell her privately to forget about this project.

Feeling better, he hopped up to his feet, prepared to go down to the restaurant for a quick bite, when it hit him. He was making a big deal over nothing.

This was a class project, just a few hours when he had to be in control, calm, and detached. Even cop-like would work. He was a cop. He was just back in school finishing his degree so he could move up the ranks.

She could take a few pictures, he'd learn a little patience, and he could go home.

Feeling better, he ran down the stairs, hoping to get a bite to eat after all.

Surprisingly, his appetite had returned.

Chapter 3

While working her way through her lunch, Tania realized it was stupid to feel so relieved. She was here to face the parts of her she'd been keeping locked away. Finding out she got to hide behind the lens of a camera made this an easier assignment than she expected.

That Kane was going to be her subject filled her with mixed feelings. She adored playing with light and dark. The camera would love him; his muscles, that build. So much about him excited her to be able to do this.

And with the camera, she didn't feel in danger. He was no threat to her. She'd be able to keep a lens between them.

She knew photography. She understood images.

But she didn't know him. But she *would* know him by the time this assignment was over. There was no way she couldn't. Photography was a tool to study something. To learn about something she hadn't been able to access before. The lens brought her closer, highlighted the focus, and forced everything to drop away yet lifted the subject for closer inspection. It was almost as if he was standing naked. Alone, Vulnerable. Reachable.

She laid the fork back down beside her plate and stared off in the distance. Was it coincidental? Or had Jenna understood this could help Tania in a big way?

"Something wrong?" Robin asked across from her.

Tania shook her head. "Not really, just thinking about the assignments."

"Oh. Those." Robin sighed heavily. "Yeah, so not sure about that."

Part of the assignment instructions had been to keep the assignments private from the rest of the group so as not to be influenced by anyone else's thinking.

Robin attacked her fries with more force than necessary. She'd sat where her scarred face would be out of the public eye. The restaurant rumbled in a nice enough way to say it was busy but lacked the overpowering-noise element of being bustling.

It suited Tania fine. She could be lost in her own thoughts without anyone noticing.

Then Kane walked in. No, Kane didn't walk anywhere. He strode in, determined, loose-gaited, and ready for anything. Her photographer instincts kicked in. Kane definitely had presence. She could imagine screen producers loving him. He didn't just take over a space; he owned it.

Her fingers itched to run to her room for her camera.

Her hands actually clenched the table to hold herself back. With an inward shudder, she dragged her gaze away and caught Robin's wide-eyed stare.

She flushed as heat raced up her cheeks. "Sorry," she muttered.

"Oh, don't be. I would love an explanation though." Robin looked at her expectantly.

Tania shook her head. "Wish I could. It's part of the assignment we're doing."

"Uh-huh." Robin snorted lightly and dove back into her french fries. "Must be one hell of an assignment."

The teasing tone made Tania's cheeks heat up again. She

stuffed her mouth with salad so as to not have to answer. Lunch finished quickly. By the time they made their way back to the seminar room, Jenna was already getting the first groups started.

When it was Tania's turn, Jenna said, "Kane is going to maintain what would be his usual routine for the afternoon. This is where you will start. You need to come up with a title, a theme, and a series you can explain to me – if an explanation is necessary – of what and why and how."

Kane snorted. Tania spun around in surprise. She hadn't heard him come in. She frowned up at him, and he stared back, one eyebrow raised.

She wanted to ask what the hell he'd be doing for his half of this assignment besides lazing around all afternoon while she worked but held back. She had to trust that Jenna, who knew why Kane was here, had plans that would help him, too.

"We'll check back here at four. If you need any help, you can text or call me. I'll be in the morning room working." Jenna gave them a bright smile and walked away.

Damn.

Kane never said a word. Actually, she rarely heard him speak at all. She cleared her throat and said, "I have to get my camera from my room. What are you going to do?"

He stared at her then looked around. "If I were at home, I would be doing yard work. Here at a hotel, I might do a bit of sightseeing, watch a movie, go to the gym…"

"And your choice right now?"

He ran his fingers through his short, wavy hair and sighed. "I think I'd like to get the hell out. So a walk around the university sounds about right."

She brightened. "I love the university grounds. Perfect. I'll go get my camera and meet you in the lobby." She took off.

KANE WATCHED HER run away. She was brighter, happier than he'd seen her yet. How bad could wasting a few hours pretending to be a tourist be? Especially with Tinkerbelle at his side?

He had no idea how this assignment was going to help him.

As he turned to stare at the empty room, he recognized Jenna standing off to the side watching him, waiting, as if she knew.

What the hell was he doing here? He looked at her. "How does being a model help me?" The derision in his voice brought a smile to her face, which was not quite the reaction he was hoping for.

"I think it's going to help a lot, actually." The serious tone surprised him.

"So me going out and being a tourist is going to help me deal with my anger issues?" He shook his head and started to walk away in disgust. "What a waste of time."

"Really? Except look at where your anger issues sprang from."

He stalled and leaned his head back to stare at the ceiling. "I prefer to *not* think about that time of my life, thank you."

"And that's why the anger. You need to examine it. The pain is more painful because you keep it alive…whereas the anger is a blind…for something else." She paused then added gently, "Maybe for fear."

He spun around, feeling the familiar anger vibrating through his system. He glared at her. "I have to keep it alive, or else I will forget."

"No," she said, her voice gentle but determined. "You

need to understand you are keeping the anger as justification for not letting anyone else get close. Never again."

He stared at her, hating the resonating truth to her words. "Easier said than done," he muttered.

"Not easy. None of this is easy. But for a full life you can enjoy again, it's necessary."

"And playing the tourist is going to do that?"

"Interesting you chose being a tourist. Casual. Distant. Disconnected."

He reared back. "What? You said to do what you would normally do. I can hardly go mow the lawn now, can I?"

Those all-too-knowing eyes studied him. He wanted to squirm and held himself strong against it. He was no schoolboy.

"There are other activities you could choose, and you don't have to play tourist all afternoon."

She reached out and patted him on the shoulder "You'll figure it out." And she walked away, leaving him wondering what the hell she was up to.

He pulled out his phone and texted his brother. *Waste of time and money.*

As he closed his phone, an overly bright, I'm-determined-to-do-this voice called out to him, "Are you ready?"

Knowing she couldn't see him, he rolled his eyes and turned around to face her. He could only hope she wasn't going to be wearing half-dozen cameras around her neck, or they'd really look like a pair of damn tourists.

Instead, she had a single black fanny pouch on her tiny waist and a single camera around her neck. He knew nothing about cameras, but it didn't look to be a cheap, casual deal. She just might be a serious photographer, and for some reason, that made him feel better. He didn't know what she did for a living or what her education program was. He'd never seen her on campus except at Jenna's lectures. Still, she put her money into good equipment, and he could respect that.

If he had to play the gallant knight for a couple of days, whatever. And if a part of him wanted to give the no-refund policy of the damn contract a closer look, he pushed it to the back of his mind. What Jenna asked was impossible, but his pain didn't have to dim whatever problem Tinkerbelle was working on. He'd always been good at playing the stoic role. He could do this.

He nodded. "Let's go."

Chapter 4

Tania understood the camera, just not the subject. Kane was difficult; a man of secrets. Getting him to be natural was the key. He was doing the posing-tourist role, and she wanted nothing to do with it. Still, it would take some time to find the real him inside.

She let him walk ahead on the cobblestone. There were intricate patterns worked into the street, and her camera loved them. Whenever he looked away or something caught Kane's eye, she tried to capture him.

But she didn't like the results. She'd have to ditch most of them at this rate.

"Coffee?" he asked hopefully, pointing to a small bistro off to the side.

"Tea?" she suggested, not knowing what they'd talk about.

He shrugged and led the way over. "I'll go in and order."

Happy to let him take charge, she nodded and took pictures of him walking into the tiny shop. He had a hell of a butt. What she wouldn't do to get him in tight boxers. The magic her camera could work then… Her thought was immediately followed by shock. Had she really just thought that? About a perfect stranger?

He returned in a few minutes with two mugs. "Hope this is okay. Black tea and black coffee."

She fished the tea bag out quickly, not wanting to have it too strong if there wasn't milk and not wanting to go in and get milk even if it was available. For a therapy seminar, so far she'd cried no tears and had yet to feel under the gun with questions or swamped by emotions. She felt odd, not herself. Normally, she'd have just asked him to get the tea the way she liked it, but not this time.

Was it doing any good?

As if reading her thoughts, Kane said, "Weirdest therapy session I've ever done."

She laughed. "Exactly what I was thinking. I feel like this assignment is supposed to do something, but we are completely missing the mark."

"Are we?" Moodily, he stared into the deepest, blackest mug of coffee she'd ever seen. "Seems like a complete waste of time so far."

She leaned forward. "That's what I mean. We're out here sightseeing when we should be working on healing."

He leaned back at her emphatic comment. "You think we shouldn't be out here."

She shrugged and looked around. "I can't help but feel like we are deliberately avoiding something. Or aren't ready yet to get too close to the real issues."

"Really?" he snorted. "What real issues? I highly doubt you want to share your issues with me. And I know I'm not going to. So what else are we supposed to be doing here?"

She stared at him, realizing she *could* share, but she didn't want to. And he was right; if they weren't going to help each other, what was the point? Unless one of them could help the other, and maybe in the helping, the other could be healed a little as well.

"Did you research Jenna's seminar?" She smiled at his

emphatic nod.

"Hell yes."

"And read the comments, reviews people had left?" When he nodded again, she said, "And do you recognize our conversation is similar to many that were written on her website? And I quote, 'I started the journey expecting to find the opposite of what I got. Thank God.' Or 'When I first started this seminar, I thought I'd signed up for the wrong one. It was nothing like what I'd expected.'"

He stared at her then leaned back, dropping his gaze to his cup. Speaking slowly, he said, "The one that resonated with me was, 'I don't understand the how or the why or the process that happened, but healing has started…'"

"Oh, I like that." Contemplative, she stared around as the traffic picked up slightly as more people came looking for sustenance. "I'm supposed to find a journey with you as my subject. I don't understand really, but I'm willing to trust a little here. Outside, it feels like it's an impersonal journey." She stopped and frowned. "I'm not really sure where I'm going with this, but say we were at home and you had the week off – what would you be doing?"

"Refinishing my bathroom."

The answer came so fast it surprised her.

He grinned with real humor, and his face came alive. She stared, entranced, as he spoke. "It's been the plan for a while. Now if you were to say, if I had a couple days off, what I would be doing, I guess I'd be working out, catching up on yard work, lazing around the house, and watching some classic movies."

As his mouth moved, her eyes caught on the lean muscles that formed and reformed in perfect symmetry. He was lean and hard and spoke about a world she didn't understand. And she was suddenly afraid she just might know what Jenna had been thinking.

And hoped not.

She raised her gaze to Kane's and watched light play across his features as his eyes darkened. He leaned closer, his whole body language shifting, softening. Damn, she wanted to photograph him.

"What's up, Tinkerbelle?"

That startled a laugh out of her. "Tinkerbelle?"

He waved an arm at her. "You're tiny, delicate, and look like a good wind would blow you away." He shrugged. "It just came to me."

And something just came to me, she thought. Sending up a prayer that she had this right and Kane wouldn't find her off the wall, she said, "I know this might sound a bit weird, but..." she took a deep breath, and then added, "You have a very photogenic face." She motioned to his biceps. They bulged and relaxed almost as if he was bunching to a tune in his mind. "In fact, your muscles are really interesting." As his eyebrows shot up to his hairline, she quickly corrected, "For the camera, I mean."

She looked away for a moment before forcing herself back on target. "I guess what I meant to say is that skin and muscles, how people move, have always fascinated me. If you are okay with it," she took a deep breath before she dropped her gaze to the table, wishing it were wider, deeper, higher – anything to increase that barrier – and said in a rush, the words tripping over themselves before she could take them back, "I'd like to take pictures as you work out."

Her shoulders and chest collapsed, completely empty. There, she'd done it, and he hadn't laughed yet. She peeked at him from under her lashes to see him still staring at her. Shock turned to consideration, then to contemplation. She watched him throw down the napkin clenched in his fists. "Sure. Whatever."

Whatever? Did that mean he didn't mind? Or he was okay with her off-the-wall request? Or that he'd do anything to get through this assignment so he could go home? And did any of his reasons matter?

He did need to be comfortable with her doing this, or else it wouldn't work. The camera would pick up every nuance of his moods, his emotions. That was the thing about the images. They didn't lie.

Raw footage caught the truth. Sometimes more truth than anyone cared to have revealed. "I wouldn't want to make you uncomfortable, so if it's not okay, I'd rather hear the truth now."

He was watching the coffee swirl in his mug. After a moment, he raised his gaze to hers. There was a blind over his feelings, a sense of detached mockery coming through. She winced. "Okay, so it's not a good idea. Forget I mentioned it."

"No." He reached out to stop her as she'd instinctively pushed her chair back. "Wait."

She stilled as the heat of his hand soaked into her chilled skin, and she slowly sat back down. "I'm not trying to push your boundaries. I just thought this would be something I could do that would be within the parameters of the assignment and be something I would like to do. But I don't want to make you do something you don't want to do."

"And you can't." The corner of his mouth lifted. "But isn't doing what we're uncomfortable doing part of why we're here?"

"True."

"Are you taking an easy way out by doing something like

this?" he asked. "Where's the uncomfortable part in all this for you if you want to do it?"

"I don't know. I hadn't actually realized I'd enjoy documenting the process until I recognized how much my eye was caught by your muscles." She reached out and laid her finger on the cord, tightening and relaxing on the back of his hand as he tapped the top of the table. "You're very mobile. I mean muscles shift, skin moves, light plays over all of you in different ways." She gave herself a mental nudge to pull back.

She was fascinated by what she was seeing, and she desperately wanted to do this project now she had a topic she could hold on to. She hated to admit it, but there was a solid chance she needed to do this. Maybe Jenna was right. "But it's your body, and it's your personal space. I didn't mean to intrude." That she had was already incredible. She was normally the mouse at the door waiting to run at the first hint of discord. Instead, here she was actually asking this supermale physique to do something he didn't likely want to do.

"It's a stupid idea," she said suddenly. "Forget it."

"No, I won't forget it." He motioned to her tea. "Settle down and drink your tea while I mull it over."

She picked up her cup and waited impatiently.

KANE STUDIED THE disgruntled look on Tania's face. Tinkerbelle had a temper. Well, so did he. She'd seen him blow at Jenna earlier, but that had merely been a trickle of what it could be. Still, she hadn't seemed phased by it. He'd half-expected her to have run from the room screaming, but instead, she'd sat there with a grin on her face.

Someone around her had a temper for her to be so blasé. Interesting.

Now, did he have a problem with her taking pictures while he lifted weights? He couldn't think of a decent reason to stop her, especially when she'd lit up at the idea like she'd been covered in fairy dust. He hadn't ever been photographed working out. It was hot, hard, and sweaty work. He didn't go to the gym to look for girls. He went with a trainer for some serious, anger-releasing work until he was dead-tired from the workouts, and there was nothing pretty about that.

He stared morosely into his empty mug. There was nothing pretty about any of this bullshit. As much as he couldn't say he was comfortable with the concept, he'd had a few friends who had participated in similar photo shoots, so it was more his comfort level at question here.

"As long as you don't post these pictures online and they are only for the project, then I am good with it." He looked up to stare into her eyes. "That goes for all the pictures you're taking. I'm the model, but I'm not giving you the rights to the images beyond the scope of this class."

She smiled, and the relief in her eyes was obvious.

She said, "I won't. These pictures are just for the project, and if there are one or two I really like, I'll ask you for permission if there is anything I want to use them for." She laughed. "What am I talking about? I don't do anything with my photography. I don't post them online at all." She pursed her lips. "Maybe it's something I should consider."

"I'm surprised you haven't. You appear to be serious about it."

Her hand instinctively went to the camera around her neck. "It's just a hobby, something to keep my mind and hands active."

He stood up. "Kind of like my workouts. Come on, let's hit the gym at the hotel. You can take pictures, and I can work on some of this restlessness."

She bounced to her feet and dashed ahead of him.

Eager much? Still, there were worse things in life than having a beautiful woman sit there and watch him lift weights.

Chapter 5

INSIDE THE HOTEL lobby, Tania stopped her headlong rush. Belatedly, she realized how it must have looked. She'd raced back to the hotel as he'd strolled behind her. She turned her head to see him just now approaching the front doors. How idiotic.

On the other hand, she couldn't remember the last time she'd been this excited. And it was photography related the last time, too. Too bad she couldn't make a living that way.

Working part time with preschool children had brought her from the dark ages into the light. The laughter and light of the little children reminded her of the good things in life, the joys in the mundane, the reason for living.

It also reminded her why she was here. So she could heal to the point of having a relationship and having children of her own. Just the thought of those tiny chubby arms wrapped around her neck and snuggling close brought tears to her eyes.

Kane moved past her toward the elevator. When she didn't fall into step behind him, he turned and asked, "Have you changed your mind?"

"No."

"Then come on. I have to get changed, and the gym is on a different floor."

She ran into the elevator behind him, hating how stupid she must have looked. Of course, the fitness room was on a different floor, as were the other amenities. She stayed quiet until the door opened, then followed him into the hallway. He unlocked his room and pushed it open. She leaned back against the hallway and said, "I'll wait for you here."

"You can come in. I won't be a moment." He motioned for her to enter.

It felt stupid, but for some reason, her feet were obeying her mind and not her heart. She entered a man's bedroom for the first time in her life. Sure, it was a hotel bedroom, but it still counted…

"I'll get a few things."

And he disappeared from view, which gave her a chance to look around. Essentially, it was the same as her room, but slightly larger. There was a similar layout and look to the two rooms, but that was where the differences lay. His room had a suitcase and a large gym bag open on the bed, a few casual pieces of clothing lying around. He rummaged in the gym bag and pulled out a few things, including what looked like a pair of gloves that startled her, then an outfit. "Back in a moment." And he disappeared into the bathroom. She sat down on the edge of the single spare seat and lifted her camera to look through the lens.

Immediately, she felt better. The slight distance eased the discomfort of a new and uncomfortable situation. Inside, she was exultant. If only her friend, Jillian, could see her now. In fact, she'd take a few photos as proof. Quickly, she snapped a couple of shots of the male domain before he returned.

When the door opened, she'd retaken her seat and was making adjustments to the zoom. Looking around, she caught sight of him.

Her breath caught in her throat. Muscle shirts had been designed for men like him. Holy Hannah.

And she might be afraid of having sex, but apparently there was nothing wrong with her libido. His pants clung to his massive thighs and as he walked past her, she barely restrained her hand from reaching out and grabbing his ass to see if it was as rock-hard as it appeared. She shuddered.

He was to die for.

He pulled open the door, sighed, turned back her way, and said, "Are you coming?"

Heat swept through her. Her mind screamed, *I wish!* Her mouth mumbled, "Sorry. Lost in my thoughts."

"Whatever."

She scooted past him, careful not to touch him.

He shook his head slightly and locked the door behind her. "This way."

She followed along, lost in the rosy haze of lust, and wondered how people survived days of this. She'd never been one to moan over men in any size or shape, and now all she wanted to do was crawl up his frame.

Except, as soon as she touched him or he touched her, the situation would all change. There was no way it wouldn't.

And that was a sobering thought.

Cooler and more composed, she walked beside him, happy when he chose to take the stairs. He ran down lightly and she followed. She was in good shape, but she wasn't fit as in *fit* fit. She didn't work out, and she didn't do any crazy spin classes. She walked a lot and did yoga for stress relief. For some reason, twisting her body into crazy-ass positions always loosened her muscles. Probably because she stretched them past the point they'd normally go, so when she finally released them, they were like rubber and sagged in relief.

He pushed open the door to a lower level and led the way inside. It was a small but perfectly acceptable space as far as she was concerned. From the disgusted look on his, she figured the amenities were not up to his standards. Then again, a heavy fitness enthusiast probably needed more than the bits and pieces of equipment here. For her, it was fine. There were a few decent-sized mats leaning on one corner. She wouldn't mind doing a few yoga poses while she was here. She glanced down at her sandals and Capri pants. Not good. She wouldn't be able to maneuver in these clothes. Why hadn't she thought to get changed herself?

Stepping back to give him room, she watched him open the bag he'd brought down with him. There was a tub of chalk in the bag, and with a cloud of dust in the air, he pulled on his gloves.

He started with a few simple stretches to loosen up. She used the time to walk the room and change her settings for the interior light. There were no natural windows, and from the number of stairs they'd walked down, she had to assume they were below ground level. In spite of its location, the room was bright and open and boasted a full wall of mirrors. She took several pictures and adjusted the settings again. She shifted to a different lens, was unhappy with the results, and switched to another one. Finally satisfied, she turned back to Kane, watching as he performed a series of sit-ups, followed by pushups before locking into a nice, steady plank.

She might not work out, but she could certainly appreciate the ease and smoothness by which he switched from exercise to exercise. By the time she walked back over, she could see a thin shimmer of sweat on his skin. She immediately lifted her camera and clicked – then again and again. She was lost as she tried to zoom in and capture that sheen to his skin, the effervescent glow that made his muscles shine. She shifted around him, moving carefully as he worked just as hard at what he was doing.

She hoped she wasn't disturbing him. He was a serious machine in motion. His gaze was inward, as if working on controlling his breathing and counting his movements. His muscles shifted and rippled as they answered his demands.

And boy, was he demanding.

He was doing different reps of different intensities in the floor-exercise portion. She almost laughed. She was good at sitting down and doing reps of eating cupcakes just as seriously. This man was definitely working out!

She was lost in bemusement as he crunched and lifted and flipped and did it all over again. She was exhausted just watching him.

Then she watched a bead of sweat roll down his forehead, and she went into action. She stared from where she stood and zoomed in as many stages as she could go, trying to capture that single drop as it stood poised on the pulsating cords lifted along his temple. Then it dropped.

She couldn't stop. She moved as close as she dared, clicking away as his jaw twitched and clenched and that chin firmed and the cheekbone locked down.

"He's something," she murmured to herself.

Then realized he'd stopped and was staring at her.

She lowered the camera, tilted her head slightly, and asked, "Is there a problem?"

He stared at her as if she'd asked a seriously stupid question, then shook his head and silently went back to work.

She was left wondering what she'd done, or what he'd thought she'd done.

REALLY? SHE THOUGHT he was something. That was

intriguing. Tinkerbelle just might be interested. Except he wasn't sure she even knew what she was doing. She certainly hadn't appeared to recognize that she'd spoken her thought out loud. Most women he knew would never be so honest.

And he suspected she hadn't meant to be.

Sure, she was comfortable around a camera, but he had to wonder if she'd ever been around a man – not a boy but a full-grown, adult male – because she certainly wasn't acting like it. For someone her age, she appeared damn innocent.

At first, he'd managed to block her out as he got into the swing of it. He loved setting a rhythm and working his body through the paces. It felt good. It felt natural. It felt right.

And he managed to get through most of his warm-up until she fixated on his face. What the hell was she doing? She'd been quiet, taking the odd picture before she had suddenly gone click-happy, her fingers moving at a speed he could only guess at. Then she'd moved closer, and he understood she'd locked onto his face. And she appeared to be studying his forehead. It completely disconcerted him when he realized a drop of sweat had fallen from his brow to the padded floor and she dove after it to take a picture.

What was that about?

Why would she even think to focus on such a thing? He always worked up a sweat. Had she been taking pictures of his shirt as it slowly soaked up, too? He wanted to make a sarcastic remark then figured he better not bring attention to it – just in case she hadn't seen it yet.

He couldn't imagine what interest any of this would have for her, but she appeared enthralled. He closed his eyes and pushed his body through several more reps. The whirling click quickly became background noise. Then he stopped and rested. His body thrummed with energy, and fatigue had hit the muscles – that was a good thing. He stretched his arms up over his head and sighed gently.

"Feel good?" Her voice held an odd note. If he didn't know better, he'd say she was sending out mixed signals. He also couldn't get rid of the feeling that she had no idea what she was projecting. Or what she thought she was projecting.

She was like Tinkerbelle in the innocence department, too. He had to wonder if she could be, but her age and university status made it hard to believe. She wasn't model beautiful, but those huge, haunted eyes were enough to bring any man to his knees. It certainly brought out his protective instincts.

Another guy could easily use her as a punching bag. He'd assumed from her original trepidation around him that that had been her problem, but the camera had completely changed her.

It fascinated him.

He also assumed it was a surface change only, and that if he made a move on her, she'd bolt like lightning in the opposite direction.

There was a part of him really wanting to push the issue, too. Make her fess up to being as terrified as she really was. He knew it would be a shitty thing to do. He really wasn't that kind of guy, unless he was fucking pissed.

Then everyone was that kind of guy.

CHAPTER 6

SHE UNDERSTOOD SHE'D done something off, but for the first time in a long time, she was able to brush it away. She was doing something she loved with a subject that was fascinating. Even better, this activity was encouraged, necessary even.

A part of her wanted to squeal with joy. She'd wanted to take pictures of people for a long time, but there were rules and regulations and laws and…of course who she'd been interested in taking photos of versus the ones who were willing weren't the same, either.

Kane fascinated her.

And he was male. In the beginning – *was that only last night?* – he'd been imposing, scary, and forceful. She knew he could break her in two within seconds. She'd done a mess of self-defense courses and she'd have an edge if he tried anything, but there was no doubt that strength won out.

She'd spent the better part of the day capturing who he was, and although those fingers clenched into fists and his jaw clenched into stone, there was an element of control to him. As if he was afraid he'd cross the line…one day…but hadn't yet.

Not for the first time, she wondered at his story. Curiosity ate at her, but she didn't dare ask. Everyone struggled with personal boundaries in therapy. Some stories were meant to be told, others were told in parts, and even more would never see the light of day.

Hers was in the middle category. They used to be at the end. Progress.

In Kane's case, he was a cop back in university to finish his degree so he could move up and do more. There was an awareness, an alertness to everything going on around him at all times, as if he never rested. Never relaxed his guard. When they were at the coffee shop, there'd been a softening in his gaze a few times. She tried to capture it, but she wouldn't be able to tell if she'd succeeded unless she could take a closer look on her laptop.

The first time, he'd been looking across the harbor at a group of colorful sailboats drifting by, their sails billowing in the wind. A lazy afternoon on the water. There'd been something wistful in his gaze. She hoped she'd caught it, and also hoped she'd caught what she'd understood of him in that moment – the dreamer in him.

As they'd been getting ready to leave, there'd been an older couple walking on the street. They'd been holding hands. She'd instinctively taken pictures of the couple, although she had hundreds already. It was her dream future. She wanted to grow old together with someone special. She couldn't think of anything nicer than to sit on a veranda with her partner, together in rocking chairs, enjoying the passage of time, full of memories of their life together.

She'd caught sight of Kane's gaze on the same couple as they walked away. Sure, there was a bit of wistfulness there, but his gaze held more than a hint of regret for something just out of his reach. She'd been unable to resist taking several shots. A man like him had to have had a full and rich relationship history, but chances were also good that something had gone wrong with one of them. And that whatever had gone wrong was the major reason he was here.

There was a fury inside this man, but not against everyone. She definitely felt like it was directed at one particular person, most likely at his last relationship.

Or possibly...at himself.

As she sat there waiting for him to walk around and cool down from his last set of exercises, she wondered what could have gone so wrong as to send him to this place. It wasn't exactly AA therapy, but it was a specialized type of session for those who needed a different approach. As she hadn't been able to see the benefit for herself and had needed Jillian, her best friend, to point out how this could be her answer, she wondered who had shown Kane this next step in his journey.

Because he didn't look like he could see it for himself – especially not here and now.

She was due for a one-on-one session with Jenna this evening. She had to admit, she was looking forward to it. She had something to say, some new insight into her life, her mind, her way of looking at the world. And as much as she didn't want to dwell on Kane, some mention of her inscrutable partner was inevitable. She didn't want Jenna to know there was a definite physical attraction to Kane but thought the therapist would be able to figure it out within a few moments of Tania opening her mouth.

And that would be embarrassing.

She could feel her cheeks heating up at the thought of trying to explain herself. Now her friend Jillian would be screaming for joy, and she was tempted to text her friend and mention the hottie partner, but that would also start a long string of questions demanding answers.

And she didn't want to go there right now.

Or ever.

This was special, kinda like the first stirrings of long-dead hormones. Tania had tried to find other men attractive, but one couldn't force something like that. She didn't know why now. She couldn't submerge the constant need to look Kane's way and see what he was doing; the need to wonder about his story, his life, or any number of other issues going on. That awareness…that heat…that instinctive knowing where he was at any given time.

This was new for her, and she felt rubbed raw, super-sensitized to his presence. He must know. Maybe he could sense it. How humiliating. She felt like an overgrown teenager with awakening awareness of him.

She knew it had to be the circumstances. The setting. The project throwing them together in close proximity. It couldn't be real. She shook her head.

She smiled, feeling a release of tension across her shoulders.

This was just a moment in time. A passing thought.

"What's up?"

Startled, she looked over at Kane, now with a towel around his neck and wiping the sweat off his red face. He'd been working out while she'd been lost in thought.

She hopped to her feet. "I am so sorry. I was daydreaming."

"Yeah?" He tilted his head to study her. "About what?"

Willing the heat to stop its rapid climb up her neck, she stood up and fiddled with her camera. "Just life. The issues that brought me here. Things I want to take away from here."

He raised an eyebrow. "Glad you're getting something out of this."

"So are you." She grinned. "You're getting fit."

"Ha." He dropped the towel. "I am fit. There's no *getting* in this equation."

"Yeah, well, it seems to me you missed one rep on that last round."

He stared at her in mock outrage. "How would you know? You were sitting there like some kind of decoration, daydreaming. I'm the one working out here."

"And you'd better get back to it and make up your set," she said smoothly. She lifted her camera. "And this time, I'll be sure to catch every grunt and muscle movement."

He froze, a look of horror on his face. "You don't have audio on, do you?"

She laughed. "Nope. Just kidding. But I run a mean camera, which means I'll catch every little trick you try to avoid getting your full workout."

Good-naturedly, he returned to the huge set of weights and, starting with his right arm, he lifted a barbell she'd never be able to lift with two hands and started bicep curls.

She grabbed her camera and went to work herself.

When he stopped the next time, she noticed a change in his attitude. The look on his face. She bent closer, not quite understanding but wanting to – at least from behind the camera. It was as if he was exhausted but determined to continue. To force his body past this wall.

She didn't understand the will to do this. Why? Why would anyone, male or female, *want* so much physical pain and do yet more damage? She didn't understand how muscle building worked at this level. She understood it had something to do with creating tears in the fibers and having your body rebuild bigger, better, stronger.

But at this point...no, way earlier...she'd have walked away.

Instead, he was heading into this next set as if this was now...finally...serious business! As if everything else was a warm-up to this.

She leaned closer.

His face twisted with concentration, and his gaze flattened — those don't-mess-with-me cop eyes she'd seen flickered in the dark-chocolate depths. And he reached deep inside and pulled those damn weights up again.

She could see his pain. Hear his pain. Feel his pain, yet still he pushed himself to reach for that goal.

In the end, she was so absorbed in the intensity of his own moment that she completely forgot to take pictures at the final point before he hit the wall...and went over it. She lost her balance and fell on her butt, camera in hand, mouth open as she stared at him.

He ever so slowly lowered the massive weight as if everything in him wanted to drop it and he wouldn't give in to it.

He was all about control.

And goals.

And making them.

Pushing himself, forcing himself to face his own weakness was everything to him.

And she knew in that moment, in ways she couldn't understand, that this man would never allow himself to hurt another person through a moment of weakness. It was not to say that in an equal fight in a boxing ring he wouldn't enjoy pulverizing his opponent, because she thought he would love that.

But he'd never take advantage. Never hit a woman, a child, or another man in anger.

She knew he'd never abuse someone or take advantage of his superior strength.

But she wasn't sure *he* knew it. That when he lost it, when red took over his emotions and rage replaced the blood in his veins, he might shove his fist through a wall, but he'd never mistake a woman's face for that wall.

And he'd never, ever use force on a woman in other ways. He wouldn't have to. He would naturally see a lot of action, if he wanted it, but he wouldn't force a woman. He was a protector, not a predator.

With that thought, a band loosened around her chest, and the tension from just being this close to him eased back into the realm of normalcy. She'd been keeping a safe distance between them, being sure to avoid his touch, even accidentally. Something she'd done for years. Something she wasn't consciously aware of doing.

She sat quietly, contemplatively, while he collapsed and worked to regain his breathing.

How foolish she'd been. Walking the safe road may have been the way to go in the past, but she'd hit a turning point. She could trust her instincts that said he was safe to be around, or she could continue on this safe pathway and not give herself a chance to get a little closer to a strong, sexual male.

Her body said to jump his bones, but she was light years away from something so obvious. And so was he. He'd given no sign he was interested in her at all, and he had a lot more experience with sexual attraction than she had. He didn't seem to notice she was acting any differently.

So maybe she wasn't.

She lifted the camera and captured the sense of satisfaction, glowing exhaustion…pride.

Click. Click. *Click.*

WHAT COULD SHE possibly find to take pictures of after so many shots? She'd been going crazy with her damn camera. He'd blocked her out as he put himself through the pacing. He needed this workout, and all the more now because of her bouncing around. She'd gotten quiet once or twice. She'd called it daydreaming. He wasn't so sure, but it was weird.

Still, he needed to focus, needed this release of tension, of the uncomfortable situation. He wanted to be home in his space, in his gym…and work.

He had homework to do, cop work to do, getting his degree to do. He loved being a cop. He just wanted to do more. That's why he was here. Right? No, it was *one* of the reasons. His temper had been blowing louder and hotter. His personal issues had bled over into his work life, and that was when he'd understood he couldn't hold off doing something about this. He wanted a personal life, but he needed to work. And he couldn't afford to give his personal issues any more time to do their own thing on their own time – not once it had crossed into his work arena.

Then there was his brother.

Jessie had convinced him to take this step, to commit the time, energy, and intention to make this happen.

No one had warned him about the other people in the session – like Tania.

Then again, how did one prepare for such a thing?

He reached up and rubbed his face. The workout had done its job. He was exhausted. He was mentally and physically done; he was at the calm place where he was fine. Everything in his life was going to be okay. God, he loved this space.

It felt like home.

Centered. Balanced.

Peaceful.

Some people would say he was a gym junkie. That it was an addiction. If it was, he didn't want to get over it. There were truly few places he could go to and get this feeling, and even fewer ways to get there.

He needed this.

And now he felt like he could handle the world again.

Even Tinkerbelle.

"Surely you have enough pictures by now?"

She froze. "If you're done, then I do." She straightened and busied herself putting away her gear.

"Well, I need a shower," he joked. "So unless you're planning to document that..."

There was a tiny gasp. He spun around and realized she'd frozen in place, her eyes huge. But it was what churned in the back of those eyes that made him add, "Hey, I was just joking."

She blinked once again...and then she started babbling. "Sorry, I'm late. Need to go...back to my room. It's almost dinnertime." The whole time the words tumbled out of her mouth, she was backing up to the door, putting as much distance between them as she could.

At the door, she opened it and turned around as if to say something. Her face worked while he stood there with his mouth open, then she closed her lips and bolted.

The door slammed closed behind her.

Chapter 7

Panic drove Tania to the stairwell. She sprinted up the first flight of stairs and turned the corner to the next. When she remembered she and Kane had rooms on the same floor and he could be coming behind her, she could hardly breathe.

She hated being a fool, and after that crazed exit, how could he see her as anything but?

Moving as fast as she could force her body, she raced up the stairs, desperately wanting to make the safety of her room before meeting him again.

Two flights up, she barreled into the middle of a group of older people as they bunched up at a landing.

"Sorry, excuse me." She apologized and tried to get through them.

They were laughing and trying to move but as one moved away to make space for her, another accidentally blocked her way. Finally, she stopped, blew her errant strand of hair out of her eyes, and waited until they'd all moved past her down the stairs. After a long moment, she resumed her upward climb at a slower, steady pace.

The jolt of meeting those people somehow made her see her actions for what they were: silly fears. So what if she did see Kane on the way?

If he thought she was panicked at the idea of her taking

pictures of him in a shower, then fine. What did it matter to her? Besides, it was better than the truth.

She opened the door on the third landing and walked calmly out to the hotel hallway. It was empty. She fished her key card out and unlocked her door.

With a last glance around, she entered her room and locked it behind her. She sagged against her door and closed her eyes.

"Christ," she whispered. From the moment Kane had suggested she take pictures of him in the shower, she had been beset by images of him standing nude with water sluicing down over his magnificent body. Water droplets hitting, hanging suspended for a moment like a lover's touch before sliding down over those curves and hard planes.

After today, she knew him so much more than he'd understood. She'd seen him both physically and mentally through the lens of a camera and although most people wouldn't understand, a camera never lied. It had the ability to capture moments of truth.

One of those truths couldn't be denied. He was a magnificent male in his prime. What he'd taken as fear in her eyes had actually been desire. A need to do just what he'd suggested. She'd give damn near everything she owned if she could, right at that moment, take a camera into his bathroom and photograph him in the shower.

And what did that say about her?

"It says you're a healthy female who met up with someone who sparked your attraction. It is new for you. It's also a good sign," she said out loud. *Bull.*

After a long, cooling shower, Tania curled up in a tight ball, her hair wrapped up in a towel, the housecoat miles too big on her small frame, cell phone clutched in her hand.

Feeling guilty, almost dirty, she'd completed her shower in record time and called Jillian.

"You don't understand. I ran from him. The words I wanted to say wouldn't come out. My heart was pounding." Tania stared around the cold hotel room and wanted to cry. "I'm sure he thought I was terrified of him."

"And instead, you were terrified of your reaction to him." Jillian gave a delighted laugh and said, "You are going through something most women go through in their teenage years and honestly, even now when I have a new relationship, I'm exactly the same."

"But I don't have a relationship with him," Tania said in exasperation. "I just made a fool of myself. The last thing he's going to want is a relationship with me."

"So? Women make fools of themselves over men all the time and vice versa. Understand it's normal. It's natural. In fact, it's a damn good sign. Be as natural as you can be. You're attracted to him. It's going to feel like high school for a while, but you will handle it." Jillian sounded so positive and happy that it gave Tania hope.

"I hope you're right. I feel like he'll never talk to me again."

Laughter filled the phone line again. Everyone loved Jillian – especially men. If she said this was normal even for her after all the relationships she'd had…then maybe it was.

"He'll talk to you. That's the great thing about where you are and what you are doing. He can't avoid you. He's part of the seminar, too." Then she sobered up slightly. "Just make sure he's not some damn wife beater or alcoholic, will you? You need a nice, stable, caring man to be in your life. Not someone with huge problems of his own."

"Everyone has problems here," Tania said. "I don't know

which of his brings him here."

"Well, he's in therapy, so look around at the hotel guests and staff. Maybe there's a different man, one without the huge baggage a man in therapy might have."

At that, Tania laughed. "Really? So a man who's willing to step up to deal with his issues is a worse bet than some guy in the bar who won't even look at them?"

"No. And if the therapy was over and this guy had done what he'd needed to do, he'd probably be a great bet. In the meantime, remember everyone is part of the session for a reason." Jillian's voice deepened with worry. "Especially him."

"What? You don't even know him," Tania said in outrage. "Don't be so judgmental."

"I'm not trying to be, but you…you're an innocent in life. And someone is likely to take advantage of you."

Shivers rippled down Tania's spine. As long as it was Kane, she just might be okay with that.

"It's too early. You don't know this man. You need more than a one-night stand."

"Do I?" she whispered. "What if you're wrong there? It would allow me to test drive sex as to whether I can do it or not. Then if it doesn't—"

"If it doesn't work, you're going to be even more traumatized." Jillian's voice turned pleading. "Please, don't do this. Flirt a little, enjoy the sensation of feeling that kind of heat, revel in knowing that your body is responding…but do not jump into bed with him – at least not yet."

Tania hung up on her. Her hand trembled as she stared in shock at the closed phone. She'd never hung up on anyone before. She collapsed to the bed and let the tears run. After a few moments, when the sobs died down, she stood up and went to the bathroom to wash her face. She took a drink of water and stared at her teary face in the mirror.

"God, I hate when I do something wrong." Especially to Jillian. It wasn't her fault Tania was screwed up, but it was because of her that Tania was here trying to work through everything.

Resolutely, she returned to the bedroom and dialed her friend back.

"I'm sorry," she said before Jillian could speak. "I had no right to do that."

"Of course you did," Jillian sighed heavily. "I'm sorry for pushing you to the point you felt it was the only answer."

"I didn't want to hear what you were trying to say."

"Yeah, I got the message." Jillian's voice lifted from sadness to humor, making Tania smile.

"I just feel so…" she shrugged. "I don't know. I feel alive; different, confused but almost hot."

Now Jillian broke into her beautiful, lilting laugh. "You sound so normal. I'm so happy you called me. I hadn't expected this type of progress, but there's no doubt that's what I'm seeing." She added a smirk in her voice. "I guess I hadn't expected it to show this way."

"I had no expectations," Tania laughed. "Who could?"

"Just…be careful," Jillian dropped her voice. "Please. You're very special, and you've been hurt enough."

"True. And I'm not going to do anything stupid. At least I'm not trying to. If I get a chance to take this one step further…well, I don't know, but I honestly don't think I could go through with it and to have me run from him at that stage could hurt him – badly, depending on his issues." In fact, it was likely to devastate him. And he'd come here to heal, too. She didn't need to screw his world up more just because she was a mess.

"That's the thing about sexual attraction; what looks great at night time when the heat is coursing through your veins can look horrible in the morning. Worse because, in the cold light of day, we look in the mirror and hate ourselves, realizing we'd done something we wouldn't normally do. In the morning, our actions are hard to live with. But that mirror is one we have to look at every day."

There was such a serious tone in her voice, and Tania realized she didn't know all of her friend's dark secrets, either. Obviously, Jillian had some experience with the less-than-nice side of sexual attraction.

She didn't know what to say. "I'm sorry. I don't know because I've never been there, but I hate to think you have such memories."

"Sweetie, most single women who've lived the singles life have a few of them. Some are easier to forget than others. In your case, I don't think you'd be able to forget. It would just compound other memories you can't walk away from, either."

"Damn. That's probably very true." Tania walked to the window and looked out. "In which case, I can just enjoy the benefit of knowing the seminar is working, and I'll come home a better, more complete person."

"Yes, you are, and you will. And that's awesome!" Jillian sighed happily. "I'm so happy to hear the seminar is working. Now I have to run. Go eat and enjoy the rest of the seminar. If anything else comes up, call me." She rang off.

In a better frame of mind, Tania glanced at her watch and understood she was going to be late for dinner if she didn't move it. She wasn't even dressed yet. Ten minutes later, dressed in slacks and a light, cashmere sweater with a little makeup on to hide the crying session, and she was ready to go. She grabbed her purse, her hotel card, and walked out, damn near walking into Kane.

"Whoa. Easy there." He reached out and grabbed her arms to steady her. "I know its dinner time, but you don't have to rush. They will save you some."

Her barely-leashed hormones took one look at that smorgasbord of delight in front of her, and a second appetite surged to life.

KANE HELD TANIA slightly apart from him and studied her features. She'd regained her balance physically, but something appeared to have set her off emotionally. He stared into her blue eyes, watching them darken. Why? She wasn't struggling to get away from him, but her pupils were dilated and her body swayed closer.

His own body woke up. He dropped his hands and stepped back slightly, and he smiled down at her. "Hey, you okay?"

She visibly tried to pull herself together. "Yeah, I'm fine. Sorry." She gave a headshake. "I have to watch where I'm going. I came out of my room and you surprised me."

"I'm just hoping to get dinner before it's too late."

On cue, her stomach growled. She gasped, and then laughed. "I guess my stomach has the same concern."

He grinned, happy to see her calming down and relaxing a bit. She was tense, had been most of the time he'd known her, except when she had the camera in her hand. Then she became someone else.

He motioned for her to precede him. She did, somewhat. She walked a half step in front of him, not quite comfortable that he was behind her. He walked, watching as she walked half-twisted as if to keep an eye on him.

Weird.

He took several larger steps to walk beside her, and she stopped trying to look behind her while she walked.

He wondered if she'd been attacked from behind at some point. He hadn't noticed this behavior before, but then he wasn't sure, and he cast his mind back to try and remember if he'd ever been behind her. He had, but he'd been a ways behind, like earlier this afternoon when she raced back to the hotel, not on her heels like this. And that appeared to be the problem.

He filed the tidbit away for later. He'd seen enough victims in his life to recognize some of the signs, but Tania was different. There were some things she couldn't hide, like when they'd first met. He was used to his size raising eyebrows. He'd also experienced some uncomfortable shuffling away when he sat down, like on an airplane, where people expected him to take up more than his single seat.

But in her case, she'd had the same reaction to him whether he'd been standing or sitting. As she was tiny, he figured she just felt dwarfed.

He'd seen it before. Some women liked a big man because it made them feel small and protected, while other women felt overpowered.

She reached over and pushed the elevator button, and then stepped back to give him space.

It was starting to piss him off.

When the elevator arrived, he stepped in first and slouched against the back wall, crossing his arms across his chest. He wouldn't want her to think he was going attack her in here.

The small elevator moved swiftly, but not fast enough for him to miss the worried glances she shot his way. He stared at the ceiling, feeling the same old burn inside build as old anger issues came to the forefront. His mood went downhill quickly as past grievances swamped him.

Damn females. Why couldn't they just be honest? Instead, they did this dance back and forth, always sending a guy from one side to the other. Being liars and cheats naturally, he figured the chances of finding a straight-arrow female to be impossible. It wasn't in their DNA. They were naturally wily and were born to manipulate. Most used their beauty to blind the poor male they were currently with.

Tania was a prime example, sending out all the right signals then immediately changing those signals so he had no clue what was going on. She was attracted to him, no way he could have missed those signals, but to look at her now…Christ.

The door opened at the restaurant lobby level. She walked out and headed to the restaurant, with another group stepping between them. They must have come from the stairwell. He was hungry, but at this point he wasn't sure he could eat. He stepped out of the elevator, walked to the front door, and stepped outside. The sun was still high, but with the buildings around, there were long shadows deepening the sky.

"Kane?"

He stiffened. Jenna. Of course, she'd be the one to find him. He was in a perfect mood to give her hell, too. He turned and stared at her, his jaw clenching at the narrow assessing gaze she locked on him.

"Hey." He tried for casual and curious.

And understood when her all seeing, all knowing gaze narrowed even more that he'd failed. He sighed then straightened. "What's up?"

"How are you doing?" she asked calmly as she walked a

few steps closer. "I don't see you looking for dinner yet. Not hungry?"

He was hungry, but food wouldn't satisfy this appetite. Damn Tania. With a sigh, knowing the therapist would see what she'd see, he said, "I was just getting a little fed up with Little Miss Rabbit always backing away, staring behind her as if afraid I was ready to attack at any moment."

Jenna's eyebrow shot up. "I hadn't realized she felt so intimidated. She's been doing so well."

That made him feel like shit, and he was a fair guy. "She is."

The therapist studied him for another moment, her expression lightening with understanding. "Ah. So maybe you're the problem."

He glared at her. "I'm fine."

She smiled. "I'm glad to hear that." She linked arms with him and tugged him back toward the restaurant. "I haven't eaten. Come and join me."

He didn't bother resisting. He was here to get help and as she'd said, he was the problem.

And that just sucked.

Before he knew it, he was seated at a table and ordering dinner. And damn if Tania wasn't seated next to him.

Had Jenna arranged that on purpose? He shot her a questioning look.

She smiled, reached over, and patted his arm. "Enjoy. The food here is a delight."

Tania, from the other side, leaned forward and said, "It is indeed. I'm really enjoying the visit here. It's a lovely location for healing."

Jenna leaned in closer to talk to Tania as if he wasn't there. He leaned back so they could see each other while they spoke across him.

Then when the faintest whiff of Tania's perfume drifted across his face, that was when he recognized he really didn't want to be anywhere else.

CHAPTER 8

WHAT WAS KANE'S problem? Tania had hoped he had not noticed her flustered state as they came down. He'd seemed normal enough, yet when she'd come walking into the restaurant worrying about where she should sit – beside him or a long ways away – she found out he hadn't followed her in.

Talk about a letdown. She'd been staring at the damn entranceway watching for him since.

When he'd sat down beside her, she'd been delighted until she realized he'd sat at the last empty chair and then had seemed surprised to see her beside him.

So much for the hope that he might be attracted to her. He didn't even know she existed.

Determined to be friendly regardless, she pasted a smile on her face and kept it there. Robin was on the other side. Halfway through dinner, Robin caught her eye and motioned toward the washroom. Taking her cue, Tania excused herself and followed Robin to the ladies' room.

As soon as the door closed behind them, Robin exploded. "What is going on with you?"

Tania stared at her in shock. "Huh?"

"Your face has been a movie all through dinner. You sat down and looked happy, then looked around and your face fell. Jenna and Kane walk in and you light up. Then something odd happened and you looked like you'd taken a major hit. Now, it's as if you're trying to hide something or trying to avoid something…hell…I don't know…but it's like you're trying too hard to not be affected by whatever is bothering you."

With the outburst over, she leaned against the counter and dropped her head back. "Normally, I wouldn't say anything, but whatever is going on has to do with Kane, and damn it, girl, you are a guppy in a sea of sharks. And Kane could turn out to be the king of the Great White Sharks."

In a small voice, Tania said, "I was that obvious?"

"Yes, you were," Robin said in a short voice. "I know we're all here dealing with shit. And it's private shit. Hell, I don't want all my dirty laundry hanging out for everyone to see, but you're glowing like a kid right now."

Tania walked over so she could stare into the mirror. There was no glow now, only bruises. This day had been tough, and it looked like it wasn't over. She didn't know what to say; surely the red all over her face said enough. Robin turned to stare at her in the mirror.

She sighed, and in a much gentler voice, she said, "I'm sorry. I didn't mean to hurt you. But your erratic behavior is like a neon sign. It never does any good to let a man know you are too interested. Interested, yes, but that you have no resistance to the attraction – no."

"It's all so difficult. I've never felt anything like this. Hadn't ever expected to, and now… now, I have no idea how to handle it." She ran her fingers through her hair, wanting to grab on and pull it out. "Apparently I'm not doing a good job of it."

"Just relax. Be yourself. Don't try to impress him. Don't worry if he doesn't like something you say or do. All relationships are improved when the two people involved are honest, both with themselves and each other."

Robin studied her own features in the mirror. "Before this," she motioned to the ruined side of her face, "I had several really good relationships. Keeping a relationship going is an art...maybe that's where I fall down. But you have to get one to learn how to keep it. And you're sending off signals that would confuse the hell out of any guy."

Tania's mouth fell open. "Wait. You just said I was too eager."

"And too confused. He wasn't there the whole time, so he didn't see the gambit of emotions flashing across your face for the last hour. Just calm down. If it's meant to be, it's meant to be." She shrugged.

"And the shark and guppy comment?" Tania said drily. Inside, she just felt tired, like her first foray had been bad enough that she should go to her room and forget all about Kane.

"He's a big, sexy male, and he knows it. You are a tiny, sexy female, and you don't know it."

Tania smiled. "I can see that."

"Sharks have their purposes in the ecosystem, too. Maybe he's learning to be a relationship man... Look, all I'm saying is I wouldn't want you to jump into anything and get hurt." She walked to the door. "Now, let's go finish our meal."

With the second person in as many hours warning her to tread carefully, Tania realized they just might know what they were talking about. Subdued, she returned to her chair and finished her plate.

"Tania, are you ready for a session tonight?"

Unfortunately, Jenna's question appeared to fall into a moment of silence at the table.

Tania froze. She worked to keep her face calm, but inside, her mind screamed *hell no!* The last thing she wanted was a third woman warning her to back off. She'd gotten the message. She chewed slowly while she considered her answer. The therapist would analyze everything she said, a failing of the profession.

"I'm really tired tonight. How about in the morning?" she said quietly.

She felt the heat of Jenna's gaze as she cut up a piece of chicken and ate it. When she raised her gaze to look at the therapist, Jenna smiled. "Sure, sounds good. How about a breakfast meeting? 7-ish?"

"That's early, but sure…at least I'll be awake for tomorrow's class."

Jenna smiled. "Good. Until the morning then." With a smile at everyone, Jenna stood up and took her leave.

Almost instantly, a tension Tania hadn't been aware of before eased. The teacher left the room and the kids were now relaxing. She grinned.

"Hey, what are you smiling at?" Robin asked with a big smile. "You appear to be in a good mood."

"Yeah, I pushed that meeting off until the morning." Tania grinned. Maybe she shouldn't have, but she needed rest from the emotional overload, and a part of her wanted to see if Kane had plans for the evening and if they included her. As that was the wrong thing to be waiting for, she decided to go up to her room. Standing up, she excused herself. "I have homework to do."

Kane looked up at her. "Are you going to go through the pictures?"

She nodded. "Yes, to see if I can find any worth keeping."

"Do you need help?" he asked, half-straightening from his

chair.

"No." At the surprised look on his face, she gave a small laugh. "At least not at this stage. There are hundreds of shots, and I'm most likely to delete ninety percent of them. When the numbers get down to something reasonable, then I'll show you and you can go through the ones I think might work."

He grinned. "In other words, you don't want me to see the less-than-stellar pictures."

"So true." She waved goodbye to the others and headed up to her room. Once inside, she brought out her laptop and started downloading the pictures. She had no idea how many she'd taken; only that she'd gone madly click-happy. The file was huge. She walked to the side counter and made herself a cup of coffee. She could have stayed longer, but she was happy to have time alone, time to find her balance again. Having one's behavior pointed out took a bit of adjustment. At twenty-four, she wasn't a kid any longer, but apparently she still didn't know how to behave in public. She could put the blame for that squarely on Kane's shoulders.

Kane's beautiful shoulders.

If she had to do a photography class and would not be able to choose her own subject, Kane made a hell of a second choice.

Hell, who was she kidding, Kane *was* her first choice.

Finally, the file was downloaded. She sat down with her coffee, opened her image program, and quickly started sorting through the pictures. She did a quick go-through and deleted the ones that were obviously junk, then went back through the remaining hundred. She created a file titled "Project" and dropped several good images into that folder. There was one of Kane standing and staring at the sailboat. She loved the way the camera had caught the wistfulness in his eyes. She plowed through the next group and picked out a couple that caught his hard jaw as he stared at something off screen. She chose the images that spoke to her. They said something about Kane, the man. The camera loved him, making it that much harder to sort through the last thirty images in the file. When she was done, she turned her attention to the group of pictures she'd taken while he'd worked out.

That was when she understood how the camera not only loved Kane, but that his body was made for this. All the beautifully defined muscles, the ripples as they moved and shifted…she wished for the first time that she had a video camera. He was a man in motion. Such a connection. In one shot, his jaw clenched, and his eyes were so focused. There was one of his bicep, the muscle so smooth and shiny but hard and tense with the effort he was exerting.

She put one of her favorite photos into a different folder she named "Special". Kane had just finished the workout; he'd collapsed back down to the mat. In her mind, she remembered the heaving chest, the quivering look at the hard muscle, but it was the look of relief, the look of pride, and that tinge of complacency as he realized he'd done it. He'd managed to complete his physically punishing workout again. He hadn't let it beat him.

She knew it was a competition for him. A challenge to see if he was up to it or if he was going to wuss out. He would not appreciate her thoughts, she was sure, but he had such a sense of satisfaction around him that she could only cheer with him. As she went through the pictures from start to finish, it was as if she was there all over again. Seeing the pain, the effort he exerted, hearing the grunts and gasps as he struggled to make his body do what he wanted it to do.

His skin glowed in one particular picture. She considered

it, wondering at the light that hit and bounced off his skin. A sheen of sweat had appeared just before she'd taken the shot and as she studied the next couple of pictures, she understood that the reflection had added something else to the picture. Like a mirror of what he was doing to himself.

She loved this one. Setting it aside, she moved through several more, but they were more mundane, showing his actions but not the highs and lows, not the emotion or the effort. They were technically good, but flat. She set them into another folder she named "Kane".

She wouldn't be keeping them but as they were good shots, just not great shots, she'd let him see them and decide for himself.

There were still a few more. Another one had an interesting light as it hit Kane's back and the muscles gleaming in the shadows. Very inspiring.

She snorted. Who was she kidding? The man was damn sexy and maybe there was something wrong with her, but the sweaty, hardworking man apparently did it for her.

Who knew?

And wasn't that something? She savored the warmth. Screw that, savored the *heat* coursing through her body as she stared at the pictures of Kane. Salivating was a bit much, but she had to admit, she wanted a taste of him.

She'd never thought to have gotten this far. Now that she had, everyone was warning her away.

Would having an affair with Kane be wrong? No.

And as she stared down at him, reality once again crashed down on her. She could sit here and dream all she wanted; it was still a hell of a long ways from actually lying down with the man.

She buried her face in her hands. She was a mess.

Of course she was. She was here in a goddamned therapy session, wasn't she?

Wiping back the tears from the corner of her eyes, she finished sorting through the pictures. As she came back to the one that had set her off earlier, she copied it into a folder she named "Secret". She almost felt dirty doing it, but if there was only one thing she could take away from this week, it was these pictures of Kane. Although he hadn't said she could keep them after the project was done.

Sighing, she went to turn off her laptop when there was a casual knock on her door.

She stood up and walked to the door. "Who is it?" she asked. She hated peepholes and never used them to look outside. She'd seen too many movies showing horrors on the other side of the damn door.

"Kane."

Oh shit.

She straightened her shirt, brushed her hair back off her face, and opened the door. "Hey."

He smiled down at her. "Just came to see if you got through those photos. We're both in the project, remember? You don't have to do all the work."

She laughed. "No, I won't. I'm still not sure what this damn project is supposed to be or how it's going to help."

He started to step inside before he stopped and looked at her. "May I come in?"

TANIA TOOK A deep breath and stepped aside. She followed him into her room. Here was another first. She'd never had a man in her bedroom, and she'd never had a man this close in a very long time.

"I'd like to see the pictures you took."

She nodded and disconnected her laptop. "Fine. Do you want to go to the coffee shop and look at them?"

He tilted his head and motioned to the small table where the laptop rested. "I thought I could just look at them here. It won't take long, will it?"

Disconcerted, she plugged in her laptop in. She shook her head. "No, it shouldn't. I deleted the bulk of them." She bent down, found the folder, and opened it.

He pulled the desk chair back far enough to be able to sit down. He leaned forward slightly and clicked through the images in her program. He studied each one carefully, stopping longer at one or two then moving past several as if they weren't as visually impressive. She knew they weren't all good, but she had to have something to start with.

He came to the end and studied the last one, the picture where he'd completed his workout, the pain, the suffering, but also the gain he'd achieved on so many levels.

"You're very intuitive."

She started. That's the last thing she'd expected. "Pardon?"

He waved at the pictures. "In fact, I'd have to say you're very gifted."

He'd surprised her, too. "I'm good, but not *that* good."

He snorted. "You see more behind a lens than you give yourself credit for." He clicked back a couple of pictures. "While you were taking pictures, I couldn't think of what you'd possibly find interesting when I was repeating the same movements over and over again. But you weren't taking pictures of the movements, but of *me* as I went through them."

She stared at him. "So? What else was I to take pictures

of?"

He grinned. "That's what I was trying to figure out. You captured more of me in these images than I thought was there to see."

He stood up. "On top of it all, the play of light and dark is interesting."

"We're supposed to do a theme of some kind, a journey." She studied the thumbnail pictures lined up in neat rows on the folder and twisted her lips. "There's not much there to go on."

"No," he said in a deep voice. "But I suspect there's enough."

He walked to the door.

She trailed behind him. "Does that mean you understand the instructions Jenna gave us? About a theme?"

"It means that I think I'm beginning to." He looked down at her. "Get some sleep, Tinkerbelle. You're going to need it."

Then he was gone.

Chapter 9

THE NEXT MORNING dawned bright and early. Tania woke up with Kane on her mind, which was to be expected, although the dreams had bordered on erotic but in a fantasy way. Not realistic, and that was also to be expected. The man wasn't for her, and a relationship wasn't likely to happen, therefore her subconscious had kept it in fantasy. But she could still dream.

Throwing back the covers, she remembered her early morning meeting with Jenna, and damn if she wasn't going to be late. She threw on clothes and ran.

At the coffee shop, Jenna sat with a pot of tea at her side, an open notebook in front of her and a look of concentration on her face.

Tania almost hated to interrupt.

As if sensing her presence, Jenna lifted her head and caught sight of Tania. A smile broke across her face.

Tania admitted that a smile from her stunning professor was like being brushed by a ray of sunshine. Tania didn't know Jenna's story, but somehow she'd arrived at a beautiful place in her life, and it showed.

Tania took a seat at Jenna's table. "Sorry I'm late."

Jenna shrugged. "If being late meant you had a good night's sleep, then there's no loss. It's not as if I've been waiting long."

The waiter arrived then, giving Tania a chance to order coffee and something to eat. She had an appetite, she realized with surprise. She'd expected to be so overwrought this morning that food wouldn't sit well, but instead she felt fine. Great, in fact.

"You look well this morning," Jenna said, a look of pleased surprise on her face. "Obviously, this week isn't stressing you out too badly."

Tania gave her a quirky smile. "Actually, it is, but in ways I hadn't expected. I also hadn't expected to feel so upbeat this morning, but there you have it."

With that, the two women started a discussion of yesterday's homework. When done, Tania understood a discussion of Kane and the project would likely be next. That sent a tremor through her. She had so much to say, yet she wasn't ready to say anything.

"How did yesterday afternoon go?"

"It was good." Tania grinned. "I enjoyed having a camera in my hand again. Kane is a great subject," she said, warming to the topic. "Some of the pictures are really unique."

"Excellent." Jenna smiled as she poured herself a cup of tea. "What have you learned so far?"

"He's easy to photograph; the camera loves him." She went into a discussion about trying to capture the different looks she'd seen in his eyes, the control he had and the drive to keep working out even when his muscles trembled with the effort.

"He's quite a man," she added soberly. "I don't know why he's here, but he's been very easy to work with." She added thoughtfully, staring out the window, "Maybe too easy."

"What makes you say that?"

"I think he sees me as damaged and himself as whole."

Jenna paused in the act of lifting her teacup to her mouth. "Interesting."

"He is. It's like he's only here on sufferance, but he's willing to do this if it will help me. But it won't help him because he doesn't have stuff. No..." Tania stopped. "More as if he has stuff to deal with, but this workshop isn't likely to help him deal with it, so he'll help me out in order to get through the week."

Jenna's eyes twinkled. "Another interesting observation."

Tania grinned. "All I'm doing is observing Kane."

Jenna stayed suspiciously quiet on that comment. Breakfast was served then, and the topic went to more general topics. Before she'd realized it, Tania was once again seated at the round table in the seminar room, waiting for the other attendees to show up.

And then Kane walked in.

Her spine rippled with awareness. She knew Kane had just walked in, and yet she hadn't even seen the man yet. She couldn't help the big smile on her face. She was both happy and excited, loving the feelings that lit her nerve endings along with the awareness of what was. This was all good, just as Jillian had said. It was good to feel this way; it felt right. As if she was finally normal in some way.

"Mind if I sit here?" Kane said, standing beside her. She smiled up at him, "No problem. There might be room." In fact, the chairs were bunched on the other side of her, leaving an abnormally large space for him.

He winked at her then sat down. Her gaze widened. She straightened up, thankful Jenna appeared just then to start their day off.

By noon, Tania was tired and cranky. There was nothing like listening to others talk about progress in their lives to make her feel like she'd made none. Regardless of how much progress she'd managed to create, it didn't look like it was enough. They broke for lunch and would resume working on their projects right after. Instead of eating, Tania headed outside for some fresh air. One of the men had several positive, uplifting stories to tell. She'd cheered with him and had fallen silent with the remaining members of the class when Jenna had asked if anyone else had something they wanted to share.

Yes, she wanted to share her news. She wanted to scream it out loud to anyone who'd listen. Her body was reacting like a normally functioning woman. She'd been in lust for her first time, felt that keen edge of a sword blade of attraction across her soul. It was good stuff – great stuff.

But it wasn't exactly shareable news.

"Not hungry?"

Tania turned. Kane had followed her out. "I just wanted some fresh air."

"In that case, why don't you grab your camera and we'll carry on where we left off and grab a bite to eat later?"

She opened her shoulder bag to show him the contents. "Already got it."

"Perfect." He walked down the pathway, and Tania raced to catch up. "Where do you want to go?"

"Out," came the laconic reply.

"Yeah, well, you've accomplished that today."

"I have. What's the next goal then? Yesterday, we followed my day. Today, we'll follow your day."

"Ha, in that case, we'd be studying all day."

He winced. "Then we'll need to find a midpoint between us."

"It's beautiful outside. We could just walk."

"There's a nice little Chinese restaurant down the boulevard a bit. How about we walk to our lunch?"

Feeling like they were sneaking away on a private lunch, Tania quickly agreed. She stopped just short of calling it a date in her head even though she really wanted to.

"Of course, you'll need to keep clicking that damn camera."

"I can walk, talk, and take pictures."

"Wow, a modern woman." His voice was teasing.

With light-hearted banter setting the tone, she took several pictures as he walked, having him stop and stand a few times so she could capture him with specific backgrounds. By the time they'd reached the restaurant, they were both arguing comfortably and Tania realized something else. It was the first time she'd spent any time alone in a man's company, and they'd been talking like old friends.

It was comfortable. Nice.

She didn't want it to end.

"LUNCH WAS GOOD, but I think I ate too much." Tania bounced at his side. Given their size difference, she had to almost run to keep up. "You barely ate," he scoffed.

"Ha, just because I'm not the size of a small mountain doesn't mean I didn't eat a lot."

He rolled his eyes. "Like I haven't heard that before."

"Sorry, I'm not used to this type of kibitzing." Her lips twisted wryly. "I need more practice."

That's when it hit him. She wasn't used to anything male-related. Talking like this, taking pictures, having a meal with a man. He half-suspected she'd never been on a date in her life. What he'd taken for fear had likely been just nervousness of being alone around males in general. She'd relaxed now, comfortable in his company.

Good.

"So, now what?"

"I don't know. We're about twenty minutes from the hotel, but you haven't taken many pictures yet. This means we have more homework to do."

She grew quiet at his side as they walked.

"What are you thinking?"

"I got a lot of pictures when you were working out, but I didn't get a couple that I'd been trying for."

"So you want me to go work out again?" Fine with him. Being around her was sending his libido off the wall. A workout would chase some of it back down to normal levels. Exhaust him so he could sleep at night. For all that he'd slept, his dreams had been heavy with Tinkerbelle content, and not in an innocent way. There had been nothing childish about those dreams.

"I don't know how often you work out. Maybe you don't do it every day, in which case, I'll wait until tomorrow."

"Except we're not going to have many days left."

She winced. "In that case…"

"Right, then back to my room to get my gear on."

"I'll meet you in the fitness room."

He slid her a sideways glance and realized she was trying to avoid being in his room. Too bad. That was starting to be the number one place he wanted her to be.

Chapter 10

THE FITNESS ROOM was empty when Tania arrived. She'd been hoping it would be, not sure how she'd handle being watched as she photographed Kane working out.

She hadn't lied to him when she'd told him she'd missed a few images she'd hoped to have captured. Several of the images she'd kept were close but weren't good enough in her estimate. He gave so much of himself to his goals that she could do no less in her attempt to capture the same intensity of his expression.

She sat down and systematically went through the contents of her bag, mentally shifting through the options to take the best images. Being inside limited the experience – she'd love to have him swimming in a lake. See the water droplets run off his skin in the moonlight. This set of stills appeared to be all about light and dark. She paused, lifted her head, and considered the homework assignment. That could be the theme. It was certainly the essence showing through the images. When Kane walked into the room ten minutes later, she asked him.

"Light and dark?" he frowned as if considering it.

"Think of the images I showed you last night. And the way light plays on your skin, your muscles as they move. The reflections," she said encouragingly. "Can't you see it?"

"Fitness is more like it. I can see that as a theme."

She paused and slowly repacked her bag as she thought about it. He'd been joking, she'd been sure, but maybe it wasn't such a bad idea.

"I'm doing mostly legs today," he warned.

She stared at him then shrugged. "As that means nothing to me, I'll learn as you work."

And boy, did she learn.

He did a warm-up that had her aching with sympathy, and then he started doing lunges, squats, and a mess of other exercises she couldn't begin to understand. In an attempt to anticipate his muscles moving and bunching at the right time to catch with her camera, she bent, crouched, kneeled, and twisted in positions she couldn't normally get into to catch the right shots.

By the time he shifted to using a huge long bar with weights on either end, he'd settled into a comfortable rhythm and her body was starting to ache.

"How can you do this all the time?"

"I like it. I like to feel my body working at peak performance. It's a fine-tuned machine and like any machine, it needs to be worked out."

"I'm sore just from taking pictures," she muttered.

"Good. Helps you to remember you have muscles."

"Ha. I do yoga all the time."

"Good for you. I don't bend and twist well."

"Like this?" She put her camera down, stood in front of him, then bent forward from the waist while wrapping her right arm behind her to curl around her waist on the opposite side.

"See, now that's not normal." He shook his head but bent forward and tried to imitate her. His huge biceps didn't allow his arm to move well behind his back, and his palm could only go to his spine.

She grinned. "See those of us that can, do."

"Smart ass." Good-naturedly, he squatted to lift his bar.

She marveled at the cords running up and down his neck as he added more and more weights.

"How is this a leg workout?"

"It's now an all-over exercise, but the legs get a hell of a workout," he said when he could. "You've been taking pictures, which muscles are showing up the most?"

She waited until he lifted again and took a serious look. His quads looked like rippled granite, his arms almost the same. Without a shirt on as he'd taken that off some time ago, his six-pack popped out like crazy.

"It's so hard to say. All of you." She walked around behind him, loving the way his neck muscles worked and the shine that highlighted the hills and valleys of his body.

"Do you do these exercises all the time?"

"No. I have to work with what's here. Normally, I have someone who spots for me. So I'm doing only basic lifts here."

She nodded, preferring he didn't do anything that was dangerous. She might be able to lift the empty bar, but with all those discs on the end…she wouldn't be able to even roll it off him.

With his next set of lifts, the sweat started to pour. She watched as one bead rippled down his neck. Then another rolled off his spine.

Her camera went crazy.

And she knew she had to do something else.

She reached out and touched one on the side of his face.

A SECOND TINY drop of sweat rolled off his forehead to

bounce onto his shoulder. Tania stood transfixed. Why?

"What's wrong?" Kane asked. He grabbed his towel and wiped the rest of the sweat off his forehead. He'd been working up a hell of a sweat this time. It seemed worse today. After last night. After seeing the pictures, he couldn't really explain it. It had been such an intimate look into him – his life, his body. It didn't bother him like a pervert watching him might have done. Knowing Tania was getting turned on was a hell of a turn on for him, too.

"Nothing," she said, her voice husky.

He snorted. "Well, something obviously is. Spill."

Mutely, she shook her head. "No. I'm fine. Sorry."

With a disgusted sound, he grabbed the bar again. He needed to do an extra rep, and that pissed him off. But better another rep than forcing the issue between them. There were too many damn issues between them.

And none of them solvable.

He'd been working up a sweat for a bit now. It felt good setting his rhythm, working his body, pushing it to do what it was meant to do.

Then she did something that caught the breath in the back of his throat.

She reached out and scooped up a drop of sweat onto her finger.

His groin tightened.

And damn if she didn't lick her finger.

He slowly lifted his gaze from her finger to her eyes. Their gazes caught and held.

Talk about a come on. But in her eyes, there was only curiosity and shock, and as he stared, he could see…desire.

Chapter 11

Tania couldn't believe she'd just done that. And in front of him, no less. She might have gotten away with it if his back was turned to her or he was so busy as to not have noticed, but not this way. She swallowed hard.

God, she wanted him. There was no way to hide it now. He knew. He had to know. How could he not?

Fatalistically, she waited for him to speak.

"My room or yours?" he said, his voice deep, thick.

She closed her eyes and swallowed hard.

"Can't handle a direct approach?" he mocked, anger biting his tone.

Tears clogged her throat. Damn it. "You're probably right," she said in shame. She closed her eyes and shook her head. After a long, shaky breath, she said, "Sorry," her voice faint, barely above a whisper. "I can't."

She spun and ran to the exit. Outside the gym room, she ran up the stairs to the relative safety of her own hotel room. But there was no escaping the heat in her loins or the sweaty palms, and even worse, the images in her mind. She wanted what she couldn't have, needed what her body could never get, and it was making her crazy.

Shame coursed through her. Not for feeling desire, not for wanting a man, but for giving him the impression that he could have what he had good reason to expect at this point.

She hadn't been leading him on, but it might seem like it to him. He was a sexually active, healthy male. She was a damaged, broken female.

The two did not fit together. Regardless of the images in her mind telling her she was a liar, she knew it was true. He needed something healthy and whole. She needed…to let go of a dream.

Then someone knocked on her door.

KANE SLAMMED HIS fist into the wall.

Goddamn it. He felt like he'd just pulled off Tinkerbelle's wings.

And he hadn't meant to. She got to him. He wanted to be man enough for her to play with and not give a damn, but he wasn't sure he could.

He wanted her like he hadn't wanted a woman in a very long time.

And she might want him, and she might think she was ready for this, but she wasn't, as he'd just proven.

Goddamn it.

Kane didn't know what he was going to say to her. He'd barely had a chance to figure out what the hell was going on here. She wanted him and he wanted her. Didn't that make for an easy solution? Apparently not. Women always complicated the simplest things.

The door opened in front of him, which surprised him. He'd figured she'd ignore him. Make their next meeting uncomfortable, where she'd retreat into herself and keep their relationship on a more formal level. Instead, she gave him a small smile, but the look of dread in her eyes made him realize she'd been churning up inside about this.

"Can I come in?"

Her mouth opened, but no words came out. Sighing, he pushed the door open slightly and stepped inside, almost forcing her to back up or be touched. Because that was really the problem here, wasn't it? He'd been slow to get it. Everything they'd done had been without physical contact. She'd gone out of her way not to touch him while they were seated or standing; she walked around him to get to the same place in an effort to not accidentally touch him. He'd only recognized it down in the fitness room, because after days of doing this, he finally understood that she'd only touched him – or anyone – once.

When she'd reached for that drop of sweat.

And it had hit him. He figured he understood the problem. He hoped she'd tell him the truth, but he didn't want to make her more uncomfortable. She had a look of doom on her face now as she led the way back into a close copy of his own hotel room. He avoided staring at the large bed in front of them. His body was too wired. It would be happy to head straight into sexual playtime, and as he'd had a hell of a time reining that back, seeing the wide expanse of a bed like this wasn't helping.

She turned to face him.

"What did you want to say to me?"

Her tone was polite and cold as if she was waiting for a blow, her shoulders hunched and her hands stuffed into her jeans pocket. As if she could get through this. She could get through anything if she had to.

He sighed, his determination to get to the bottom of this draining down to his toes. Who could stay mad at Tinkerbelle? Someone had to be an asshole to want to kick the woman when she was already down. He just didn't want her down for the wrong reason. Knowing he was likely to say the wrong thing but feeling the need to say something, he started with, "Look, I get that there is some trauma in your past. It's probably why you're here, since we're all here for something." He stopped. Her face had gone blank. Talk about giving an answer without saying anything.

He wanted to reach out and hold her. Give her a hug. Enclose her in his arms and tell her it would all be okay.

But she'd already learned that a touch wasn't always nice. That hugs were often a constraint and that life wasn't going to be okay. It would never be okay again.

"I get that you've been hurt, likely physically and emotionally, but I've never hurt anyone...especially a woman." Her gaze flew up to his, shock the dominant expression.

He started again. "You don't have to tell me what's going on, but the mixed signals were getting very confusing. But I want you to know that I got it. I'm slow and obviously thick, but I do understand. I'm not here to push you into doing something you don't want to do or aren't comfortable doing…"

She shook her head. "Maybe you aren't, but…"

She stopped.

He waited.

She dropped her head and stared at the floor.

"Okay, well. Look, I'm a big boy. I can handle a little sexual tension, a session of raw sexuality that isn't going where I'd like it to go." Her eyes flipped up to stare at him, then dropped to the floor again.

"I'm not going to jump your bones because you gave me a come-on. I'm not a callow youth who doesn't know his own limits, and I'd never do something you don't want me to do." When she continued to stare at the floor, he turned and walked back to the door before he stopped and turned back to face her. "I just wanted to let you know that I don't hold anything against you. If you feel brave enough to take the next step in this…" he waved a hand. "Whatever this is…I might be interested."

At her continued silence, he added, "Only, you're going to have to make it clear, because I can't take your actions like I would another woman's. So if you are, then just be honest and say so."

And he turned back to the door.

When he heard the single word, he stopped, puzzled. He turned back to face her. "What did you say?"

She took a deep breath and raised her eyes from the carpet to stare directly at him. In a tone of voice that said taking her medicine was good for her even if she didn't want it, she only wanted the benefits of it, she repeated what she'd said. "So."

His mind worked, trying to interpret her answer. Again, women seemed to make everything too complicated. "So, what?" he asked cautiously.

"I'm saying so."

And then he got it. His eyes closed. "Meaning you are interested in taking this another step and are saying so?"

"Yes."

So maybe this was simple after all.

"How far do you want to go?" He didn't know what he was up against, but this was unlike any conversation he'd ever had with a woman. There was no romance, no soft words, and no seduction. There was heat and raw, dry passion that crackled between them, something he hadn't ever felt. Not like this. It almost hurt, and the need was so strong it clawed at him. If it was the same for her, they'd burn up the sheets if they ever got there.

And again, she surprised him with her honesty. "I want it all," she said, "but I don't know what I can take."

"Take?"

"I was raped a long time ago," she said candidly, staring up at him. "I haven't been held by a man since. I couldn't. Not even my father." She bowed her head. He could just imagine the pain for both her and her father. It was a big admission.

A man? Interesting turn. The rape only confirmed what he'd already suspected. He was damn sorry for it, but he couldn't do anything about it at this point. "What about a brother?" She shook her head. "A good friend?"

"No. I have no males in my life, just two sisters and mother. My father and I talk on the phone, but he doesn't live close now."

He had to wonder at a life completely devoid of touch from the opposite sex. He had close relationships with his sister, brother, and both his parents. They hugged, touched, held hands; there were few physical boundaries between them because their relationships were founded on trust and respect.

She hadn't had the benefit of any male in her life since she was raped. Somehow, that made it all so much worse. "I'm sorry."

She shrugged. "It's been a long time." Her gaze slid to the side. "You think it's all good and you've dealt with it, but then something triggers the emotions and you realize it's not something you ever get over, or ever forget. It's not a sickness you can get rid of, but it is something you can deal with on a day-to-day basis. Like managing an incurable disease, it hurts at the oddest moments."

"Like?"

She smiled sadly, "Like when I see a family with babies or

loving couples and I understand it's not for me. It's for people who have normal, natural lives. Not for those of us who are broken."

"You're in pieces, but you can pull the pieces together."

"But I'll never be whole."

"You can be better than you were," he said seriously. "You can be the new you."

Chapter 12

She couldn't believe they were having this conversation or that she'd had the guts to open up. Everyone – her friends, therapists, and family – had all said it would happen at one time, but why with Kane?

Except that if there was a chance in the immediate future for her to be intimate with a man, it would be with Kane. At least he now understood. She wasn't sure she did. What could he possibly want from her?

Except clearer signals, apparently.

He ran his fingers through his hair and stared at her, perplexed. She wanted to run her fingers through his hair, too, but he'd likely freak out.

"What?" He narrowed his gaze at her.

She dropped hers to the floor.

"Speak up. You have to be clear. I can't be helpful if you don't explain."

She laughed. "Ha. If you understood what I was thinking, you'd be running like a crazy man."

He tilted his head to one side. "Maybe not. Try me."

"No, it's stupid." She spun on her heels and walked so she could look out the window.

"Nothing is ever stupid. If you don't speak up, you will have missed an opportunity."

She glanced over at him. "It's just that I don't know what

your hair feels like." She turned away from him again. "See, I told you. It's stupid."

"You never touch me. You walk around me like I'm someone to avoid, as if my touch is repellent."

"No." She spun away from the window. "Not because of that, because...I don't know...I haven't touched a man, like I said. It's foreign and it's instinctive to *avoid* touching."

"But you want to touch?"

Tears filled her eyes, burning the back of her throat. They'd come on so hard and so fast, she hadn't been prepared.

"Oh no. No tears. That's not fair," he protested.

She tried to smile, but the waterworks kept getting in the way. "Sorry, I didn't mean to."

"Okay, so try this: just nod. Do you want to touch me?" He stood so big and so strong and so very capable of knocking her unconscious with a single blow, yet all she could think about was how much she wanted to touch him.

She nodded.

"See," he said in a very gentle voice. "That wasn't so hard."

"Was too," she muttered, but she smiled at him.

He walked over to a chair, flipped it around, and sat on it backwards, facing her. Sitting down, he was almost the same height she was. Then he dropped his head onto his arms resting on the back of the chair and said, "Go ahead."

"Why are you doing this?' she whispered. It was stupid. It was just a touch. But for her, it was a gift. A freedom she'd never had. And for him, this was what? An experiment? Wanting to help? Why was he here anyway? She hadn't seen or heard him do anything that explained why he'd needed to come to a workshop like this. Or was he not an attendee? Had he come at Jenna's request? No, not likely. He'd been at several of the evening lectures, so there was something going on in his psyche. The thing was, as much as she cared about that aspect, she didn't care right now because she wanted what he offered.

Accepting it was a whole different thing.

"Because I can. Now, step closer and put your hand on me." He laughed lightly. "I promise I've had a shower."

She winced. A shower obviously hadn't been an issue for her before.

"Here, I'll make it easy on you." And he held out his hand.

She stared at it. It was just a hand. She'd shaken a man's hand before, hadn't she? A doctor or a lawyer, a cop's hand? She couldn't remember, but she must have.

She reached out and placed her hand in his. His fingers gently closed around hers, caging hers in. It didn't scare her. She tugged her fingers back experimentally, and he let her go. She took a deep breath. "Well, that wasn't so bad."

He chuckled. "Glad to hear it. Next?"

She shook her head. "I don't know."

"My hair, you said?"

He tilted his head, and like a moth to a flame, she couldn't resist the lure. She reached out to touch the silky, black waves. Short but with a hint of curl around his ears, his hair felt…normal. She laughed. "I don't know why I thought it would be anything else, but it feels normal."

He peered up at her from his odd position. "I would hope so."

She slipped her fingers through the waves, letting the curls wrap around her fingers. "It feels like a woman's hair."

"We do share similarities between the two sexes," he mocked.

She smiled and continued to stroke her fingers through his hair. He shifted suddenly and she bolted backwards.

"Whoa, easy now. I was only changing my position a bit."

She took a deep, shaky breath. "You startled me."

"Yeah, I got that. But I'm not here to attack you. Remember that."

"Easy to remember on a mental level, but years of fear on a visceral level make it harder to control these reactions."

"That makes sense." He studied her for a moment. "If you want to continue this experiment…" and he waited for a response from her. She held her hand to her chest and gave a sharp nod. "…then I have a suggestion."

She stared at him and waited. "We'll go to my room so you can leave any time you want to, instead of worrying about how to get rid of me here, and I will lie down and you can touch me as you want to."

Her face flushed hot.

He cocked his head, a knowing look because of what had to be a chartreuse color on her face. "I wasn't really thinking you were ready for that kind of touching."

She shook her head frantically, but inside, her heart, mind, and hormones were screaming, "Yes!"

He stood up. "Come on. We don't have tons of time here, so let's do this."

Before she'd had time to process it, they were standing inside his room. He walked to the bed, pulled off his shirt, and dropped backwards on his bed. "Go for it."

THIS WAS GOING to kill him. What had possessed him to put himself through this torture? Tinkerbelle was so damn attractive, but she was a bambina in the world of sex. She wanted to experience all the good stuff but had only been dished piles of shit so far in life. He'd love to be able to help her do this, but at the same time, he could hear his brother's voice in the background. "Dude, what has she got to do with your healing? You have a purpose there this week, and it doesn't include Tinkerbelle."

Except maybe it did.

As he lay there calmly, relaxed, waiting for her to get up the nerve to touch him, he realized he didn't know what the answer was for himself, but he wasn't stuffed full of rage at the moment. So that was an improvement.

Then he felt it.

Tinkerbelle's gossamer wing – okay, so not likely, but it was as gentle as that. He felt his stomach muscles bunching under her gentle fingertips. She slid them across his ribs gently, following the grooves and bumps of his torso that she could reach from her side of the bed. He'd have suggested she straddle him, but that would have sent her screaming. Too bad. The thought of her riding him was just about perfect. She'd have to be on top. As scared as she was, it would be the only way, at least the first time.

Once his mind started down that path, there was no stopping it. If he didn't watch it, she'd end up with an eyeful and this whole experiment would take a horrible turn. He worked hard at tensing his thigh muscle to keep his erection from getting any bigger. Realizing she'd stilled made him peek under his closed lid. She was watching his thigh. She had no idea what he was doing or why, but in true form, she was fascinated by his muscles. He groaned lightly. "I'm not sure how this experiment is going, but maybe you could say something. I feel very exposed here."

"Sorry," she said almost absentmindedly. "Is that why you

are tightening and clenching your thigh?"

He debated answering her. How much trust could she take?

Then he decided that in a safe environment as she was in, maybe she needed to hear the truth.

"No," he said, and winced. "I'm trying to not let my sexual urges bring on a full erection. I doubt you're ready to see that. Or touch that…" he added humorously.

Silence, except for her heavy breathing. He opened his gaze to see her eyes locked on his face, as if scared to look anywhere else. Her breathing was shallow, not quite hyperventilating but close.

"It's okay. I'm fine. I am not about to lose control."

She swallowed again.

And the devil made him add, "But you could if you felt like it."

He didn't think her eyes could get any bigger, wider, and rounder, but damn it, they did. Immediately, he was sorry. "I'm just kidding. I'm feeling a little odd lying here like this, so my attempt at humor was just to ease my discomfort level."

She stepped back. "I'm sorry," she said instantly.

He didn't move, afraid she'd run. "Why?"

"You're uncomfortable." This time, she raised her puzzled gaze up at him. "I imagine it's demeaning. I'm sorry."

"It's not demeaning. You didn't ask. I offered. Big difference. Sorry my humor was off the mark. I'm fine. I'm just lying here. You've hardly touched me."

She took a step back, and he recognized the mood had been broken. "Okay, I'm going to sit up." She watched as he swung his legs around and sat on the edge of the bed. "Now, come closer. I want you to sit on my lap."

Her gaze shot up to meet his. "Yes, that's a normal request. You'll see lots of girls sitting on their guy's laps in a park, at a party, at any place and any time." He smiled engagingly. "It's a good experience." He opened his arms wide. "Just sit down."

She looked like she wanted to, but the fear and the uncertainty was keeping her at bay.

He opened his arms. "Come on, Tinkerbelle. Just sit down."

She winced. "I'm being an idiot, aren't I?"

"Yes," he said, delighted when a laugh was forced from her. She took a step and plunked her tiny butt on his left thigh. "Wow, don't you have any cushion on you?"

"Not much."

She bounced ever so slightly and then shook her head. "Damn rock. So not comfortable."

"Maybe, but look instead at what you've done," he pointed out quietly.

His breath was almost lifting her hair, she was so close. She turned to speak and realized they were almost eye level and her mouth was almost touching his. And she froze.

Then she did something that almost broke his heart.

She said in a small voice, barely above a whisper, "Can I touch you again? There's something I want to do."

His eyebrows shot up. He was curious but trying to stay calm enough to give her the courage she needed, so he nodded. "Absolutely."

Her eyes locked on his for a moment as if to make sure he was serious, then damn if she didn't lean in and place her lips against his in a Tinkerbelle of a kiss.

He was stunned. That this foray into touching could lead to something more intimate had obviously crossed his mind, but he hadn't expected it to. He hurt knowing what Tinkerbelle had been through, but like she said, it had been a long time ago. Maybe not so painful as it would have been if the attack had been recent, but still ready to ruin her life in so many ways. An insidious poison that attacked at odd times.

He had seen her come so far in such a short time, and he appreciated that a lot of what had been missing in her life was an opportunity to move forward. Somehow, he'd become that opportunity.

Had Jenna predicted this turn of events? Surely not.

And just what did he want to do with this new job role? The priority was for Tinkerbelle not to get hurt, and that meant what? Not physically hurt? Not emotionally hurt? Both?

Did he want to be her opportunity? His body tightened, and he groaned silently. Damn it. He was male. Of course he wanted to bed her. But there was no guarantee he'd be putting himself through anything but exquisite torture and no satisfaction, other than what he'd give himself at the end of the day.

But this wasn't about him, and it wasn't about getting something out of this. It was about Tinkerbelle.

He sat in the chair, his mind consumed with that brush of her lips on his, when she did it again.

He sighed and let his lips open.

She stilled.

"Nice," he murmured so as not to scare her.

He opened his eyes and watched hers get bigger, but inside, deep inside, was a hunger he knew well. A hunger for what she'd never had. A hunger for what she really wanted. A physical hunger for a simple, caring touch, a sexual hunger to explore her own needs and an emotional hunger to no longer be on the outside of a relationship.

A hunger for freedom from this huge issue in her life.

And damn if he didn't feel many of those same hungers, too.

Then she lowered her head and kissed him a third time.

Chapter 13

Tania knew she shouldn't be doing this. For her sake, she wanted to continue forever because it felt wonderful, but she knew this had to be difficult for him. He didn't even know her, and here she was, using his body, his maleness, as some kind of educational toy. And damn if he wasn't perfect for the job.

With a sad sigh, she pulled back. "I should stop."

He kept his eyes closed, but his lips quirked. "Why? You haven't even started yet."

"Not fair, I kissed you."

"Ha," he mocked. "That wasn't a kiss."

She stared at him, curiosity in her eyes. Her mouth opened then closed again. As if unable to keep the words back, she said, "What's a kiss then?"

He opened his eyes and asked, "Do you not know?"

She flushed but faced him bravely. "Only what I've seen in movies or read in books."

"Romance books," he teased.

Her cheeks warmed. "Maybe."

"They aren't exactly realistic."

"True. But I already had a hefty dose of realism in my life, thank you." She stood up and walked to the window.

"Come on, sweetheart. I'm working really hard to not touch you and scare you away, so please don't let the odd comment do the same thing."

She turned around to study him. "Do you want to touch me?"

His eyebrows shot up and he snorted. "Of course."

She shook her head. "There's no 'of course' about it."

"Come here."

She took a tentative step forward, but indecision warred inside. Then she took another; in for a penny, in for a pound, or whatever the old saying was. If she was going to get anywhere, she had to step over these barriers. She walked closer until she stood in front of him. Slowly, he closed his knees, caging her in front of him. Her heart raced and she stared down at the tiny prison and stepped back. And he let her.

She took a shaky breath. "You know I can't stand to be held prisoner, right? Held down..." Her gaze bored into his, making sure he understood. "That force, that kind of strength and restraint will send me running..."

He opened his arms. "Sweetheart, have I done anything to cross the line?"

She shook her head.

"And I won't."

"How do I know that? What if you get angry, or sexually aroused..." she left that last bit hanging as once again her cheeks fired up.

"Meaning you think I'm likely to get so aroused that I'll rape you?"

There. It was out in the open. "No, I don't *think* you'd do that, but my mind and my body have a disconnect when it comes to this issue."

"Understood." His voice leveled off as if he fought some internal issue. "What exactly are we looking at here?"

She swallowed. "Pardon?"

"No, we're dancing around here, but let's lay it on the line. I'm a straight kind of guy. Are you wanting to have sex?" His gaze pinned her in place, delving deeper into her mind until she felt his presence inside. So deep inside, she swore he was in her body already.

"What I want and what I can do are two different things."

"So let's start with what you want."

"I want it all. I want sex, to enjoy sex, to be able to please my partner during sex."

The words slipped out so fast – there was no holding back with this man. She didn't know how it happened, but she was starting to care for him, maybe because he was being so gentle with her.

"And now the 'what can you do' part," he said.

She waved her hand at him. "Only what we've been doing."

"Except that yesterday, this morning even, you would have said this wasn't something you could do because it hadn't happened yet. Now if we go a little further, it will put what you can do closer in line with what you want to do."

"A little further?" she swallowed hard. "Like how much further?"

HE DIDN'T KNOW if he was using the right tactic, but it seemed important for her to push her line back a little further. She'd come a huge distance already, and if he was to list all of the first steps she'd taken today, it would probably surprise her – possibly scare her. So far, she'd done all the touching; he'd just been a male form for her to test her gossamer wings on. He was so much more, but she wasn't ready to see it, and maybe he wasn't ready to offer it.

He had no problems initiating her into lovemaking. He'd rather that than straight sex, and whether she understood it or not, she couldn't go through this process without having some feelings for the person she'd shared the journey with.

Was she prepared for that? Or would her own emotional overload not allow her to recognize it for a long time? He admired what she was trying to do. Understood the need in so many ways. And could see himself caring for her – deeply. What a quagmire. If he did want to pursue this and she wasn't able to take these next steps, was he prepared to stick around when sex wasn't going to be part of the equation? At least, not for a long time? He was no fool. Nor was he a teenager. He'd been married. He had loved and been loved, but there was no doubt a healthy, happy sex life had enhanced their relationship. To think of one without a sexual element…well, if he was honest, he wasn't sure he could do it.

And that didn't make him feel good. He was a sexual male in his prime, but he was starting to wonder if he wasn't still an immature male emotionally. How did one mature in that way – if it wasn't through moments like this? Through strife and pain. Well, he'd had a lot of pain…had he grown from it, or had he become stuck in his anger, unwilling to move past it?

Damn Jenna after all.

Maybe he was exactly where he needed to be, helping Tania resolve her demons. In the very act of helping her deal with her demons, he just might find that his only existed because he'd been keeping them alive.

Because it was easier.

It was easier because then he wouldn't have to trust anyone again.

And therefore couldn't be hurt at the level his ex-wife had gutted him.

If he ever needed proof of courage and need to trust, he only had to look at Tania. She'd already made bigger steps than he had in a direction he couldn't imagine having to deal with. And he'd been sitting inside his petty corner, refusing to come out because of someone who was no longer in his life.

What the hell?

How and when had he given away his power – and to her, his ex-wife – of all people?

Then he looked at Tania. Sure, she'd had more years to get over her trauma than he'd had, but since it had been such a physical violation, she had so many other issues to deal with.

And look at how well she was stepping up to the plate.

How could he do any less?

Chapter 14

Tania could barely breathe, waiting for his answer. An answer she received in the form of a half-smile. "In the spirit of cooperation and experimentation, what would be the next step you'd like to take?"

She frowned, looked away, and then glanced back at him. She gave him a little smile. "You could kiss me."

He grinned. "My pleasure." He stood up until he towered over her. Her gaze widened in shock and she swallowed. "Uhm, that's not going to work."

His grin widened. In a sudden move, he flipped her so she was standing on the bed looking down at him. She shrieked.

Surprised at the suddenness of the movement, she reached out and put her hands on his shoulders for stability.

"This isn't going to work, either." She shook her head. "You're too tall."

Kane shook his head at her innocence. He sat down and patted his knee. "Then you'd better sit back down again."

She frowned, jumped off the bed, and sat down again.

At his smirk, she glared. "What's so funny?"

"You. You let me pick you up, turn you around, and you willingly grabbed onto me to stop yourself from falling. Now you're back sitting on my knee. See what you've become accustomed to so quickly?"

Her mind turned his comment upside and downside as

she realized he was correct. She hadn't flinched when he'd lifted her. She had shrieked instead, but it wasn't due to fear.

Not from him.

"I'm not scared of you," she said, wonder in her voice. "You're big enough to squash me flat without thinking about it, but you wouldn't. At least, not to me. At least not right now."

"Never." He slid his hand up her slender back – gently, soft, indomitable. When he reached her neck, he squeezed ever so slightly and nudged her head forward. "Kiss me."

"I thought you were going to kiss me instead."

Their eyes met, locked, and heat coursed through her. She wanted to kiss him – wanted his lips on hers, wanted to feel whatever he could make her feel. His mouth so close to her own, his breath mingled with hers when he whispered, "Kiss me."

His words washed over her as her eyes drifted closed and she leaned in, placing her lips on his.

Instantly, the hand behind her head gentled and his lips moved on hers, taking a taste of her like he hadn't before. He brushed his lips back and forth, his tongue sliding across her sensitized skin.

"Open for me."

The words filtered through the haze in her mind, tugging at her to understand them – but she didn't want to. She pressed her lips harder against his. He slipped his tongue out. Her mouth blossomed under his, taking, sharing, needing as much as he gave her. She followed his lead and gave back every bit of the pleasure he was giving her.

She lost track of time…of place…of purpose. There was only one thing in her world right now – Kane's mouth.

His tongue stroked, teased, and tasted. She sighed and

sagged against him.

He trailed kisses down the side of her cheek, to her ear, and down the nape of her neck. She shivered, shifting to give him better access. He could have anything he wanted as long as he kept this up. In the background, someone was moaning, a sound that excited her almost as much as Kane's seductive touch. Then she realized the moans were hers.

And then she recognized something else – her arms were wrapped around his neck and she no longer sat on his knee. Instead, she was curled sideways in his lap.

She shifted slightly to look up into his face as he lowered his head and dropped a soul-stealing kiss on her.

She melted.

"You are lethal," she whispered when she could.

"Not me, you. Us. Together. Soooo…good."

He lowered his head again.

And she met him halfway. In fact, she was dying to taste him. After a lifetime of doing without and living with the fear of never getting to experience this and having someone here with her, having someone who was willing to let her experiment and had the advantage of being seriously hot felt so very good – she was a dying woman lost in a cloud of sensuality.

She wished it could go on forever.

He pulled back slightly. She whimpered and tried to tug him back down toward her. When he didn't budge, she opened her eyes slowly, loving the look in his eyes, like he was enjoying himself with someone he cared about. Such an addictive look.

"Hey," she whispered. Not wanting to move, she rested her head against his shoulder.

"Hey, yourself." He dropped a kiss on her forehead. "How are you doing?"

"Better than okay. Good thing I didn't discover kissing when I was in high school – I'd never have shown up for class."

Laughter rumbled through his chest. "I had that exact same problem."

"Ha! I'm surprised anyone goes at all if they understand this is an option."

"Which is why mothers don't want their daughters to find out too early."

"And why guys can't get enough?" She grinned, her bones relaxed, her mind empty, just enjoying the moment. And she wished she could stay like this.

He wrapped his arms around her and hugged her close. She froze at the unexpected movement then relaxed.

"Okay?"

"Okay, but I think that might have been a hug. Not sure as I haven't experienced a lot of them in my life." And she hadn't in many years. Her mother and sisters weren't demonstrative, not cold, just not the touchy feely kind of people. She was now wondering if Kane was. She'd loved her father dearly, but she hadn't been able to be around him for a long time. The strain had destroyed her parents' marriage. He'd stayed close for a long time but had been transferred back East years ago. She'd told him to go. It was better this way, knowing he was hoping for more and she had no more to give…

She hadn't finished speaking when she was engulfed in another hug, but there was no fear.

He eased his arms back. "There, a hug. Although they are even better when standing up."

At his comment, her eyes popped open and she was already bouncing to her feet.

Laughing, he stood and wrapped his arms around her in a

gentle hug.

And they stayed like that for a long time.

Until Tania's phone went off.

KANE HATED WHEN technology intruded. Tania reached for her phone, saw she had a text, and gasped. "Oh, no. We're late for dinner."

"Really?" Kane reached for his own phone and whistled long and low. "Okay, I had no idea it was so late." In fact, hours appeared to have disappeared on them. "Let's go before we miss out entirely."

He walked toward the door only to realize she wasn't following. "Tania?"

"I'm coming. I just…" Tania sighed. "I just don't want them all to know."

"Know what?" He glanced at his watch, ushered her out the door, and locked it behind him. "We're supposed to be working on our project. So we worked a little late. No one is going to know anything unless you say so."

"I've never been any good at lying," she muttered.

"No need to lie. We haven't been doing anything wrong." He opened the stairway doors. "Act natural. No one is staring at us. No one cares. Remember that."

When she didn't answer, he turned to look behind him to make sure she was following. She was, but a worried look had taken over her features. "Okay."

He grinned. "If you walk in like that, it's going to look like we're guilty of something."

She smirked. "I guess we are, in a way."

At the next landing, he opened the door and stepped into the main floor where the restaurant was. "And in what way is that?"

"We didn't do our homework."

They walked into the restaurant laughing and smiling. The others noticed, but no one made a comment.

Just like he'd expected.

Chapter 15

Dinner was simple, fast, and silent, at least on Tania's part. She smiled brightly at everyone, and when her food arrived, she tucked into it with a ravenous hunger.

"You must have worked up an appetite." Robin poked fun at her as she finished her own pasta.

Tania nodded as she forked up another mouthful of salad to avoid having to answer. Before she was halfway done, several of the other members of the group were getting up and drifting away. Good.

She settled back to enjoy the rest of her meal. By the time she was done, the table had mostly emptied. She smiled and ordered coffee.

"Tania, how was your day?" Jenna shifted from her seat at the far end of the table to one across from Tania. Robin chose that moment to excuse herself, leaving Jenna and Tania essentially alone. Kane was finishing his meal on the opposite side of the table.

The coffee arrived just then, giving Tania a moment to collect her thoughts.

"So, was it a good day?"

"Absolutely." She sat back and rubbed her tummy. "That filled a hole." Forestalling any attempt on Jenna's part to get too personal, she asked, "What's on the schedule for tomorrow?"

Jenna smiled at the change in topic and launched into the plans for the middle of the seminar. Realizing she'd skated by, Tania devoted the next half hour to discussing the rest of the seminar. Jenna had lots of work for them. In fact, as Jenna handed over a few sheets, Tania realized they'd missed the handout she'd given out before the group had ordered dinner. It looked like there was homework tonight.

Damn. She'd been hoping to spend time with Kane. Speaking of which, she lifted her head from her papers and looked around the room, but there was no sign of him. She did not notice when he'd left, but she'd studiously kept her focus off him so as to not draw attention to their relationship.

She wondered if he had the homework. The thought of having an excuse to see him again tonight made her toes curl. She tried hard to keep a straight face. The last thing she wanted was for Jenna to pick up on the attraction. Then she caught Jenna's eye and recognized it was too damn late. Jenna already knew.

Lifting her cup to her lips, she drained her mug then pushed her chair back. "I'll say good night then, see if Robin wants to work on this together." With a quick smile at Jenna, she walked away.

And damned if she didn't feel Jenna's concerned gaze as she escaped.

She texted Robin out in the lobby and asked if she wanted to work on the homework together, only to find out that Robin had done hers.

Double damn. Stay alone in her room or go somewhere to do it? She chose the pub attached to the hotel. She could grab a beer, sit down at a table, and work her way through the information.

How hard could it be?

Ten minutes later, she was sitting at a window table watching the sun's rays march across the horizon. Vancouver was a beautiful city, and the university campus was even more stunning. Sipping her beer, she started on the homework.

And cringed. The homework was a worksheet on their yet-to-be-seriously-started project. There was a place to list the theme, objective, and process. The project sheet was starting to read like a damn lab report.

Crap. This was definitely an assignment to do together. She brightened. A great excuse to see him again.

Which brought her full circle. Should she be spending so much time with him? Was it a good idea? She knew falling for him probably wasn't, but it was a little too late for that.

The man was hot, kissed like a dream, and photographed even better.

Where could she go wrong with such a choice?

While she sat there grinning, someone stepped up beside her. "Hey lady, want some company?"

And before she had a chance to answer, a young male slid into the seat across from her at the table.

"No, thanks," she said politely. "I'm working."

"No, you're not." He snagged the paper from her hand and tossed it beside him. "You're too pretty to care about stuff like that. Why don't we go find a room and see if we can't find something more fun to do together?"

Tania hated drunks and aggressive males, and worse, she hated being in a position where she had to deal with them. She had over half a beer left. She glanced around the room, wondering if there was a spot up by the bar. At least there, the bartender was likely to chase off anyone bothering her. She hadn't made it through this many years of university without seeing her fair share of drunken guys. But the man sitting across from her wasn't drunk enough to be at the pass-out stage. He looked to be just in the rosy glow of a couple of beers. Not too bad yet, depending on what kind of drunk he was.

She gave him a firm "No, thanks," and stood up.

He stood up, too, and leaned forward. "What's the matter, beauty queen? Am I not good enough for you? Well, I got news for you. I'm better than you, you fucking bitch." By now, his voice had risen to the point of attracting attention. Just why did it never bring help?

Bitterness clogged her throat. She'd learned a long time ago that people preferred to stay out of things rather than get into trouble helping someone else.

"Look, I just want to have a beer in peace and do my homework."

"Ha. Homework. You're nothing but a stuck-up bitch that thinks you're better than everyone else. Another of the uni bitches who hand it out to everyone but the working man."

She glanced around to find some guys watching with big grins on their faces. A few frowned into their beers but were trying to ignore the scenario. A couple of women standing by the door got up and left, and that was about the only avenue left to her.

She picked up her glass, guzzled back the beer, placed it on the table, snatched up her homework, and turned to leave.

He grabbed her arm. Inside, her nerves knotted and her pulse started to race. She jerked her arm back. "Don't touch me."

"Don't touch you or what?" he sneered. "I've seen stuck-up bitches like you before. You're all prissy-white on the outside but you're just another fucking cunt looking for a man between your legs."

She could feel his words like small darts hitting her on some visceral level. She hated it when guys did this, used a few beers to loosen their mouths so they could say whatever the hell they wanted. She backed up and tried to navigate a way through the full room. She just wanted to get to her room safely and alone. So much for the quiet drink idea.

She'd almost reached the exit of the pub when she heard something behind her. She spun around, and instinct and training had her immediately shifting to a slight crouch to assess the danger.

And damn if it wasn't the same guy. He stumbled forward. Another guy shoved him into an empty seat. "Leave her alone."

"What the fuck." Arms flailing, the drunk managed to stand up and resume his way to the exit. "I just want to go home."

Tania slipped through the door into the hotel lobby and waited off to one side.

The drunk came out and stopped. He straightened and looked around. He wasn't as drunk as she'd hoped. He'd had the presence of mind to fake it with the other man.

Sitting in the lobby, she was relatively safe. Hotel security would help her if the man got out of line. Better a minor drunk than a full-scale attack. She wasn't twelve anymore walking home from school, innocent in the way of the world and men. The man made his way to the front door of the hotel, and she relaxed. He was leaving, so there was nothing to worry about after all. Except the incident had left a bad taste in her mouth. She wanted to rest in the security of her room, maybe have a bath, and get through her homework. And a decent night's sleep would be good.

She walked to the wall of elevators and pushed the button to bring one to the lobby.

When the door opened, several people stepped off. She stepped on.

Just as the door closed, another man raced in.

The drunk.

Tania stumbled to the front corner of the elevator. She'd already pressed the close door button and wished she could open it again. She pressed it again several times. She'd take the stairs over an altercation any day, but the drunk zeroed in on her.

He stared at her, anger growing deep in his murky gaze. "Bitch. Think you're too good for me."

His fingers flexed. Tania risked a quick glance at the light above the moving elevator. It was almost time to get off, but she had to get around him. If there were other guests waiting to get on, that would be helpful.

Just then, the floor dinged and the double doors opened. She raced out, but he grabbed her shirt as she made her escape and dragged her backwards. She spun around and jammed her elbow into his throat. He roared and released her.

She desperately wanted the safety of her room, but she didn't want him to know where she was staying.

"Goddamn it. Get the fuck back here." She was already racing down the hallway, only he was faster and caught her just outside her room. He grabbed her and slammed her up against the wall. She cried out but kept her head. She rammed her elbow into his gut, stomped on his instep, then turned and shoved both fists upward into his chin before she brought them both down on the back of his head as he doubled over. She spun around and bolted.

Into a mountain of spitting fury.

Kane.

KANE THOUGHT HE'D heard Tania's cry outside the door. He'd raced into the hallway in time to see Tinkerbelle slam, stomp, and then give a doozy of a double-fisted blow to some guy's nose.

Blood was spurting between the guy's fingers even as he swayed to stay on his feet.

Then Tinkerbelle slammed into him. He grabbed her by the waist and lifted her to his eye level. She kicked out wildly, crying out in panic until she realized who held her. She hung suspended in his arms, gasping for breath. Then groaned, closed her eyes, and sagged in place.

"Are you okay?" he asked.

She opened her eyes to stare at him, stunned.

He gave her a little shake. "Damn it, Tania, talk to me. Did this asshole hurt you?"

She gasped and shook her head. "No. No, he tried…I hit him. I think I hit him." She kept shaking her head, only now the shakes were working their way down her tiny frame.

He lowered her to the floor, shoved her behind him, and eyed the asshole standing in front of him.

Some of the alcoholic haze was leaving his eyes as pain replaced it. He had both hands clasped over his face. He looked at Kane, then at Tania, then back at Kane. "I think she broke my nose." He blinked at the two of them, and then said to Tania, "Why did you break my nose?"

Kane snorted. "You think I'm going to let you get away with blaming her? You're twice Tinkerbelle's size. Do you think you can attack a woman and get away with it?"

The drunk looked at him. "She attacked me," he said in a

nasal voice. "She broke my nose."

"I defended myself. You attacked me," Tania cried. "At the pub verbally, then when I didn't like your suggestion, in the elevator."

Kane's fists clenched. Tinkerbelle was tiny. She was always going to have to watch out for predators. At least she'd taken some self-defense training. The world was full of assholes like this one.

Hotel security came running up the stairs, then quickly surrounded the two men. "What's the problem here?"

Kane pointed at the drunk looking closer to collapsing now, but whether that was from the drinking or the blood loss, he didn't know. Or care. "This guy attacked a woman."

"Did not."

Kane was surprised that Tania didn't immediately pipe up with 'did, too', as that was what he'd have expected. But she stayed quiet.

"I was minding my own business," he squeaked out, "when Tinkerbelle attacked me."

The hotel security guys looked at him and sighed. "Tinkerbelle?"

The drunk nodded rapidly. "She broke my nose." One security guard led the drunk to the elevator. "Let's get that nose taken care of."

"She broke it. Tinkerbelle broke it."

"Right, buddy. Sure she did. And how much have you had to drink tonight?"

The second security guard spoke through a device on his shoulder strap, letting the others know what was going on and preparing for the drunk to be received on the main floor. He turned to Kane. "Sir, did you hit him?"

Kane snorted and gave a hard smirk. "Nah, do you think

I'd have broken his nose? I'd have cracked that asshole's head wide open if I had the chance. Still will if he comes back."

"And his story about Tinkerbelle?" The security guard shook his head as if to say he'd seen it all.

Kane laughed and stepped to one side. "Meet Tania, also known as Tinkerbelle."

Tania lifted her hand in a small finger wave. "Hi."

Chapter 16

TANIA HAD TRIED to brush off the incident as minor, but neither the hotel security nor Kane would allow her to.

"He's made trouble here before. We have to take an incident report and contact the police. If we don't, he'll just come back and do it again."

The security man looked at her. "Consider if he were to do that next time to a girl who didn't know any self-defense techniques."

She sat back because of course, that had been her twelve years ago. Her attack hadn't been his first offense, either. He'd told her at the time that he'd done this before, but he preferred children; they couldn't get their stories listened to anyhow.

The reminder hurt, plus it made her responsibilities clear. She had to do this for the next woman's sake.

With Kane at her side, they went down to the lobby and she made a statement before she repeated the process with the police. Talk about overkill, but the men were adamant.

When it was over, she was drained.

They'd been drinking coffee during the whole ordeal, and now she was so wired she wasn't sure she could sleep.

After the day she had, she just wanted to not dream.

Hours later, alone, Kane had left her at her doorway after making sure she was okay. With a gentle but distant kiss goodnight, she made her way to her bed.

The nightmares hit a couple of hours later. Tania woke in a cold sweat, whimpering in her sleep as she felt the rough hand over her mouth, the ripping of her clothing, the male body swamping her, overwhelming her, and the never-to-be-forgotten feeling of being raped.

She lay there dry-eyed for a long time. When the memories faded back slightly, she got up and filled a glass with water. She walked around her room sipping the cold drink. She pulled her nightdress away from her clammy skin, hating that after so long, the memories could still overwhelm her. Still ruin a good night's sleep, take this rational, balanced woman and turn her into a bag of nerves.

She understood that the drunkard's attack had precipitated the nightmares always lurking behind the scenes to destroy her calm. Even though she understood, it didn't change the fact that it still happened, that nothing she did stopped the nightmares for good.

It had been months, if not years, since her last really bad nightmare. She couldn't remember what had set those off. Exhausted, she sat back down on her bed and flopped backwards. She didn't know how to go back to sleep. She'd brought melatonin with her, but taking it often left her groggy in the morning. She sat up and ran through several yoga moves to release some of the tension, but that just brought up images of Kane. He'd been wonderfully protective, almost irritatingly so, demanding she file a report and deliciously sweet with his goodnight kiss. She wanted so much more.

And she was a mess with nothing but a broken shell to offer.

She'd come so far and yet not far enough.

Immediately, a protest jumped into her mind. She'd come

a hell of a long way. She'd fought off her attacker, survived to see him taken away, and so what if she had a nightmare or two? Surely that was normal. She might not be whole, but it didn't mean she was so far gone she couldn't heal. It was – she'd just proven it.

And she'd keep on proving it.

But her one chance to get through a sexual encounter was with Kane.

Even her wording made her wince. Who'd want anything to do with that? Lovemaking? Yes. Getting through a sexual encounter? Nasty.

She could almost hear Jenna saying the terminology was important. It showed she was still distancing herself from the personal element of lovemaking. A sexual encounter was cold, clinical, like a lab experiment. She almost laughed. Wouldn't Kane love that description?

And then she remembered those arms around her, his lips moving on hers, his tongue…there was nothing cold about Kane, nothing clinical about what they'd done that afternoon. She glanced at the clock. Okay, yesterday afternoon.

Even now, her body warmed at the thought of those hands of his. How gently he'd held her. How his strength had been so controlled. She couldn't imagine what it would take for a man like that to lose control. He'd be a force to contend with. He had problems with women. She'd heard it a couple of times in his voice, saw the look in his eyes when he watched couples walk by. He'd been hurt. How he'd managed the hurt was the problem. She wished he'd talked to her, but he didn't trust her. Maybe that was the problem. Trust. She didn't trust any man not to hurt her again physically, and maybe he didn't trust any woman to not hurt him emotionally. Someone in his life had ripped a hole in his body, creating so much damage he'd been forced into therapy to try and heal himself.

Maybe for his career. Another woman? To stop his brother from pushing? Who knew what was the driving force going on in there, but he was here. And he was dealing. She didn't know how this project was supposed to help him, but it was testing her.

She sighed and realized if she wasn't going to sleep, she might as well finish her homework.

Tucked in bed, she came back to the first question – the theme of their project. She'd considered light and dark, but it wasn't quite right. She wrestled with it for a few moments then moved on to the next question. This one was easier as it was about process. She got to work.

A half hour later and she was done mentally, but she hadn't gotten even halfway on the homework. But maybe she was ready to try to sleep.

Closing her light, she crawled into bed and relaxed.

Then it hit her. The theme. Was her idea right? Could it work? She thought about the images she'd taken. The look in Kane's eyes, the changes from one day to the next. She hadn't even downloaded today's images, and she needed to. It would tell her if she was on the right track.

The theme – skin.

KANE WOKE THE next morning and immediately got angry all over again. He'd been so proud of Tania and her moves and pissed off at the drunk. Even more so when he understood this wasn't an isolated incident; this guy was a hell of an ugly drunk, and research would likely show he was a controlled, angry man who, when under the influence of alcohol, found it much harder to control the rage that lived just under his skin.

And he felt empowered to let it out and be the angry man who lived inside. Kane wanted the guy stopped before he really hurt someone. That it could have been his Tinkerbelle last night scared him shitless.

That he considered Tinkerbelle his terrified him even more.

What the hell?

He didn't come here for that.

Sex was one thing...this was something else altogether. The trouble is, he didn't know what. She was...broken...to use her words. He had his own problems. The last thing he should be doing was hooking up with someone who wasn't whole. He winced. But he wasn't whole himself – who was he to expect someone not dealing with major trauma issues to be looking at him?

Then he wasn't looking for himself. It's the last thing he wanted.

But Tinkerbelle was...different.

But she was still female, so how different could she be?

Very, he knew. Her experiences had molded who she was. She didn't have the deviousness of other women he knew. But he could be wrong. He'd been horribly wrong at the time when it had counted, and he didn't want to go through that ever again.

He showered, dressed, and headed down to breakfast. He was early, but maybe he could check in with security to see what had happened last night. The drunk had been spouting off something about suing Tinkerbelle, but he hadn't been able to describe her nor name her correctly. Kane hoped in the cold light of day that the man had come to his senses. Kane would push for him to be charged with assault if he could, but that decision wasn't his to make and if it came down to

Tinkerbelle pressing charges, he figured she'd just want it all to go away.

He'd wanted to ask her about her rapist. Had he been found? Charged? Done his time and been released? But he figured she'd tell him if she wanted to. It didn't stop him from wanting the details, though. He could put a call out to a buddy if he wanted to bad enough. He could get the details, but it seemed underhanded prying into her life, a life he'd been allowed to see just one corner of. A good corner, but still just a corner.

He'd be the first to admit he wanted into every corner.

He couldn't find the security guards, so he left a message for them to contact him later. Then he headed into the restaurant for breakfast where he found Jenna waiting alone at the table.

"Kane." She smiled up at him. "I was hoping for a chance to see you alone. What on Earth happened last night?"

He winced. "It might be better if you asked Tania, but as it involved security and police, I can give you the short and dirty version."

He explained, watching her face drain of color. "She handled herself well." He grinned, pride in his voice. "Actually, she handled herself really well."

"Well." Jenna shook her head slowly, letting out a gust of air. "Poor Tania. What a difficult thing for any woman."

"True. But it was also a win for her. After all she's been through, she wasn't a victim this time. She was the victor."

Jenna studied his face. "She told you?"

He nodded and smiled up at the waitress who'd arrived with the coffee pot. After she'd left, he turned his attention back to Jenna. "Yes, she did."

"Interesting."

"In what way?" God, he hated how Jenna said that word so often. He hated feeling like there was more going on here than he understood. Of course, there was – there always was – but he didn't want it to be a constant irritation in the back of his mind.

He waited for Jenna to answer.

"I'm just surprised she told you about her history."

"We're working on this project together, isn't it normal for her to have shared something like that?"

Jenna's lips quirked.

Okay, so that came across as slightly defensive. Damn.

"It's intensely personal." Jenna studied him closely.

He frowned. He should have seen that coming. "And…"

"Nothing. I'm happy she was comfortable enough to share with you."

He frowned at her, saw the twinkling in her eyes, and understood she was poking at him to see what might come out. He smirked. "It's early, professor, but not so early that you're going to get anything out of me."

"Oh, so there is something to get, though, is there?"

He glared at her, and damn if her laughter didn't ripple free.

He sighed and lifted his coffee cup. No doubt about it, he had it bad.

Chapter 17

TANIA DRAGGED HERSELF into the restaurant, wishing she could just go back to bed. She had a headache, and her elbow hurt after defending herself last night.

The table was full. She caught Kane's gaze, and damn if her heart didn't speed up at the possibilities promised in his eyes. He'd turn any woman to mush. Oddly enough, not one of the other females at the table appeared to be bothered, but there were several others in the restaurant checking him out. His size alone attracted attention. That his voice was deep, dark, and promised midnight dreams helped a lot.

She sighed. Talk about being lovesick. Or was it lust struck? Stupid body. It could have stood up and sang hallelujah when she was high school. She'd have enjoyed spending time in the back seat of cars making out, especially if the guys kissed like Kane. Then again, how many guys could make her melt like he had?

Tired, she took the last empty seat and caught the waitress's eye, motioning desperately for coffee. It had been a long night, and getting through the morning meant she'd need some serious fortification. With that in mind, she ordered a big breakfast. She might be short and small, but her appetite was seriously large. Her breakfast, when it came, made her sigh with happiness.

"Whoa, isn't that a bit too much food for you?" asked

Robin, who was sitting across from her. Tania shrugged. "I'll let you know in twenty minutes."

"What did you do, work out all night?" Snide jokes started up. She ignored them all and plowed through her meal. When she laid her fork down, she was surprised to see she'd cleaned her plate.

She reached for the last piece of toast and polished it off, too.

When she raised her gaze, it was to see everyone staring at her. She raised an eyebrow in question. Kane asked in a gentle, humorous voice, "Would you like seconds?"

She smirked. "I'm good until lunch, thanks."

Jenna picked up the conversation from there, after which, they moved to the seminar room and got started on the homework.

"Tania, did you get a chance to do the homework?" Jenna asked.

"In the middle of the night when I couldn't sleep, I worked on it." She sighed. "But is it done? No."

"Sorry about all the trouble you had. I hope you're happy with the way the hotel dealt with the issue."

She nodded. "They were fine." She really didn't want to go into the whole mess again, but several people were looking at her oddly. She said, "Some drunk accosted me outside my room last night."

The women cried out. The men stayed silent.

After a quick explanation of what happened after that, she ended with, "As a result, I didn't get much sleep."

"I bet," Robin said with feeling. "Take it easy today."

"Sure. I'll be fine."

"Are you fine?" Jenna asked seriously. "Why don't we go for a walk outside and we'll talk?"

It was on the tip of her tongue to say she didn't need to, but the truth of the matter was her nightmares had returned with a vengeance. If she could figure out how to get her subconscious to let this all go, her nights would be much better. And talking about it just might be the answer.

"Sure." She stood up from the table and handed her homework to Kane. "I'll work on this when I get back."

He nodded. "I haven't even looked at it yet. Go. Enjoy your talk."

"Thanks." As she turned away, he added, "You look tired."

"I am. The nightmares were bad again last night." She walked outside with Jenna.

KANE WATCHED THE two women leave. One was small and normally walked with determination and focus, but today it looked like taking every step was hard work. Tall, stately Jenna strolled easily alongside Tania; they made a striking pair. He sat back down and looked at the homework sheets, but his mind returned to Tania's comment. Why hadn't he considered she'd have nightmares? Of course she would have them. That attack had to trigger bad memories, and when did those memories usually hit the hardest? During the dream state.

Damn.

He'd never even thought of it, so he'd gone to bed and slept like a baby while she'd barely gotten any rest. He could have helped her. He didn't know how, but he could have slept in the chair to watch over her. Then again, she might have found that even more disturbing. It's not like she'd ever slept with a man – innocently or not.

But he could have done something. Instead, he'd given

her a gentle kiss and pushed her into her room with orders to lock the door.

Then his eye caught the theme question on Tania's page and the one word she'd written beside it. Skin. What the hell did that mean?

CHAPTER 18

THE FRESH BREEZE blew Tania's hair across her face as they exited the hotel's front doors. It was a beautiful day; even the breeze was warm. It was also early enough that the morning sunshine was fresh and bright and missing the muggy heat promised for later in the day.

"What were the nightmares about?"

Tania gave a broken laugh. "The rape. It's the same as always, triggered, no doubt, by last night's attack."

"Were you hurt last night? How bad was the attack?"

"Not bad in some ways, but bad enough." Tania shrugged. How did one determine how bad something was? "I was scared, but he didn't physically hurt me. I hurt him. I broke his nose, apparently." The reminder put a smile back on her face.

"Good. He deserved it."

"The police hauled him away, but I don't know the final story."

"I hope he's gone and stays gone. You don't need that around."

"No. I need sleep at this point."

"Do you want to miss the morning session and go back to your room?"

As tempting as that thought was, she didn't want to miss any time with Kane or the seminar. She was here for a reason and wanted to get as much out of this as she could. "No. I'll stay. I would like to stop the nightmares, though."

"Then lead me through the details. Let's see if we can find out what your subconscious was working on."

It took several minutes to relay the details as she remembered them. "I don't think there was anything new in these ones, just the same old, same old."

"But not as potent? You didn't wake up screaming?"

"No, not at all." Tania recognized the truth with surprise. "It was uncomfortable and I woke up in a cold sweat, but it wasn't nearly as bad."

"Good. Great, actually. When you think about it, last night's attack might have been a gift in that it gave you a chance to see where your subconscious thoughts are at. And it looks like they are slowly getting better."

"That's one way to look at it." She hadn't mentioned any of the intimate time she'd spent with Kane. It felt odd, almost disloyal to mention him in context of her healing to Jenna. Still, he might have had an impact on that same subconscious. As she thought about the problem, she realized Jenna was correct.

She was healing.

KANE TRIED TO single out Tania yet again to ask her about the homework. He wasn't sure where the hell she was going with that theme. He just knew he didn't want this to be a sex project. There was no way he wanted their relationship documented, and although she was here to heal, he didn't want his participation anywhere on paper. As long as she understood then he was good, otherwise…he was done with this assignment. She'd been sitting at the far end of the room after coming back with Jenna. He was surprised at feeling miffed that she hadn't come up to sit beside him. He wanted her to. He'd waited for her, had even saved her a seat. They were partners, damn it.

And she'd sat at the back of the class by the door. A half hour later when he checked, it was to see her empty seat. He glanced around the room, but there was no sign of her.

He frowned at the table. Given how tired she was, what was the chance that she'd gone to lie down? He continued to check on her empty seat until they broke for lunch. Rather than follow the group into the restaurant, he strode upstairs to her room and knocked quietly.

She opened the door. Her face lit up when she saw him. "Hey." She covered her mouth with the back of her hand as she yawned. "I just woke up."

"Ah. I wondered." He couldn't help but notice the sexy, tousled look she wore. "I was checking to make sure you're okay and had no ill effects from last night."

She smiled and pushed her dark blonde hair off her face. "No ill effects. Nightmares kept me awake, but as they weren't as bad as they have been in the past, I'll take that as a good sign."

"Are you ready to eat again then?" he teased. "It's lunch break now."

Her gaze widened. "I was going to have a quick shower, but lunch would be good." She considered it. "Give me a couple of minutes to get dressed again, and I'll walk down with you."

"Perfect."

Then to his surprise, she opened her door wider to let him in.

"You might as well come in and wait."

Damn if he was going to turn that down.

Chapter 19

TANIA SURPRISED HERSELF by inviting him in. There had been no need. He could have stayed out in the hallway for those few minutes. She bustled about grabbing her clothes, throwing the bedding back into position. With an embarrassed smile, she disappeared into the bathroom.

"Remember to be quick," he said.

"Be right back out."

In the bathroom, she reminded herself: Small steps, small steps. Well, she'd certainly been taking lots of small steps. Inviting him in was yet another one. Realizing the time was wasting as she stared in the mirror with a silly grin on her face, she dressed quickly and washed her face.

She opened the door and said, "Ready."

"Good, let's go." He walked out and turned to wait for her to follow. She closed and locked her door and almost ran into Robin. "Hey, I was just coming to check up on you."

Tania smiled. "Thanks. Kane here dragged me out of my room to make sure I don't starve."

"Ha. After your huge breakfast, you shouldn't need to eat again for a week." Her gaze wandered from Kane to Tania and back again speculatively.

Tania refused to let the heat rising swamp her cheeks. She walked towards the stairs – no more elevators for her – and called back, "I'm always hungry." She laughed and ran down the first flight. She had turned around the railing to start down the second when Kane passed her. He jumped.

"Hey, that's cheating," she called after his retreating back. She figured from the laughter floating upward that he wasn't bothered about any imaginary rules. He waited for her at the bottom of the stairs.

"Besides, your legs are longer."

He snorted. "So what? Pick yours up a little faster and you'd have made it."

"I doubt it." They walked into the restaurant and grabbed a quick meal as the laughter and joking continued. She'd never experienced anything like this relationship between a man and a woman. She loved it.

The afternoon session sent them off to work on their project. She ran back to her room, snagged her camera, and raced back down. Kane waited outside the front door for her.

After the heavy emotions of last night and the sense of freedom this morning, today's photo shoot couldn't be anything less than amazing. Life was just about perfect. Okay…maybe it was Kane who was perfect.

She walked beside him and said, "Where to?"

"I'm still not at home and still can't renovate my bathroom or do my yard work, so that leaves the touristy side."

"Sounds good."

"And then as someone took up much of my yesterday, I didn't get my workout in, so I will need to go to the fitness room sometime today."

"Perfect," she said, beaming. It was perfect. There were still some shots she wanted of him pushing his body. And for all she knew, he had different moves, new ones that would give her even better shots.

She almost wanted to start there. Crinkling up her face,

she said, "We could start in the fitness room if you want."

He glanced at her sideways. "Don't you want to go for a walk first?"

"Sure," she said, "And afterwards, we can go to the gym."

He shook his head. "You're the only female I know who is happy to watch a guy work out."

"Maybe I'll do some yoga myself this time." She rolled her shoulders several times. "Last night left a little too much tension in the muscles."

"Sorry."

She shrugged. "All's well…and all that."

A comfortable silence ensued as they walked along.

Then, as if he'd been thinking about the issue for a while and the words were just rushing through him, he said, "Is it? Are you over last night, or did it just make it all worse?"

Surprised at his outburst, she said, "I think it's better. I didn't wake up screaming in the night like I would have if this had happened a few years ago. I woke up and was aware that I was safe, understanding it had been a bad dream. It took a while to get back to sleep, but there were other reasons as well."

"Like what?"

"You." She said it honestly, not knowing how else to be. "You've been very patient and understanding with me."

"And?" He motioned to a bench beside a huge flower garden. "Why do I sense a question behind that?"

"It's just I don't want you to feel obligated to do what you're doing."

"Obligated." He rolled the word around on his lips as if testing it, tasting to see what it meant or if there were any hidden meanings behind it. "I don't feel obligated. I'm sorry for what you went through and am happy to help."

She flinched.

"Not the right answer?"

"There is no right or wrong answer. I want to hear the truth."

"But you don't like the answer."

She leaned back on the bench. This big man, this mountain of a man, was twice her size with so much more strength than she could imagine herself having. Look at the way he'd lifted her up to his face last night. He hadn't even struggled, holding her there like a child.

And now, he was worried about having said the wrong thing. "You're a special man, you know."

He lifted an eyebrow. "What brought that on?"

She grinned. "You, trying to help but afraid of saying the wrong thing. I'm glad you are helping me. At the same time, I'd hate to think that this is all about the assignment."

He lifted his shoulders then dropped them. "What does any of this have to do with the assignment?"

And damn if she didn't believe his bewilderment was for real. "Nothing apparently." She laughed, the sound rolling freely across the garden. "I'm just letting doubts color my thinking."

"Look. I'm a real plain, basic man. I'm happy to help you deal with your stuff while we're here. After all, that's why we're here. Right?"

Damn. Okay, so it was about the assignment, the course, and her being a screw-up. Still, the dark growing pit in her stomach had hoped he'd wanted more. She understood he'd given her – and with any luck would continue to give her – a gift. If she left this place a few steps closer to being whole to pick up a relationship with another man – one who might care for her – then it was a huge gift. He'd already done so much, she couldn't put her emotional crap around his neck, too. She wanted him like she'd never wanted another man. She understood men could want a lot of women for a lot of reasons, and few of them were the emotional ones that she needed, but maybe that was okay, too.

It was up to her to keep the dreams in check and work on fixing her reality.

Dreams were fine and all, but the reality was…he wasn't in love with her.

And she damned well better remember that.

KANE FIGURED HE'D done or said something wrong as Tania was quiet all the way back to the hotel. He didn't know what he'd done; he just knew he'd done something. It had been the same with his wife. She would never explain and always left him feeling like he was in the doghouse.

In Tania's case, he wasn't sure what had happened, but it was like she'd flicked a switch. She had gone from being bubbly and happy to being more reserved, as if she was putting him at arm's length, pushing him away.

To hell with that.

He left her to change while he thought about a game plan to get her back to normal, and maybe back into his arms.

He slowed in the act of stripping off his t-shirt. Was that what he wanted? Hell yes. He wanted her in his arms, in his bed, in his life.

He sat down in shock. Was he really saying he wanted a relationship with her? Past the constraints of the seminar? Really? What if she never could get around to having a sexual relationship? Was he ready for that?

When it came to relationships, she'd be work.

He flinched. "But so am I."

Was she interested in him only as the man who could initiate her into a fulfilling sex life without intercourse if need be? He groaned. His mind filled with images of ways to introduce her to the pleasures of the body.

He wasn't the only man who could, but he was the man who wanted the job the most.

But how could he convince her they should continue to see each other after this seminar?

Then he realized what he'd said. "Idiot. You told her you were happy to help her out, not that you wanted to be there for her."

She'd have likely taken his response as being friendly and trying to get through the course, not him being interested in her for her sake.

"Smooth, Kane. Really smooth." Not.

And then there was another aspect to consider – was she interested in him as anything but experimental material? He hoped so. He didn't mind being used in this instance. After all, he'd agreed to it, but what if her interests were only self-serving? He couldn't really blame her...but neither would it make for a start of a relationship.

Then there were his own issues. Trust. Anger. Betrayal.

And none of them seemed important. He'd been feeding the pain to keep it alive to stop him from considering other relationships. Now that he'd found something more important, he could let the hurts ease down where they belonged – in the past.

Damn, he hated when Jenna was right.

Chapter 20

Tania gave herself a mental talking-to. The man was gorgeous but disinterested. She needed to take what he offered and let him off the hook. Let him return to his life as he wanted it. The attraction between them was probably just proximity and promise. That there was a man who didn't mind kissing her made her hormones go crazy. Just the promise of dealing with her problems, of finding a man capable of handling her problems, made her jump on board. It wasn't real. Her feelings needed to be acknowledged but not acted upon.

And didn't that sound like something she'd heard in a therapy session.

Damn Jenna and her shrink babble anyway.

At the fitness room, she decided to do some stretches herself. She had her camera and bag to continue working on their project, but at the same time she knew her body needed some work, too. She'd taken the week off and that wasn't good. Her daily routine always included twenty minutes of yoga, and she missed it.

Knowing Kane would get there when he was damn good and ready, she set about moving through her positions.

The door opened when she'd slipped into the third one. In the mirror, she could see Kane open his bag and chalk up his hands, and then he went to work. She tried to focus on her movements, but it was damn hard. The man's body was a powerhouse and a joy to watch. Add in her artistic eye and her fingers were itching to grab her camera.

Another ten minutes and she gave up. Hopping to her feet, she opened her bag and grabbed her camera. It took a moment to set up, then she turned and walked over to Kane. He had a distant, unfocused look on his face as he recovered from a set of sit-ups. Personally, she hated sit-ups, push-ups, and chin-ups. But then again, she wasn't into anything that made her sweat like she'd been in a sauna or made her hurt so bad she wanted to cry.

Kane, on the other hand, seemed to thrive on it.

She shook her head and shifted into her art.

When he switched up to arm curls, she shifted much closer to work. She began taking photos of the muscles as they tightened and released, the film of moisture that rose to the surface, the fine hairs that shifted and moved then became locked in the sweat.

"What can you possibly find interesting in all of this?" Kane asked, his voice laced with irritation.

She took a step back, studied his face, and saw the pain, the frustration, and the anger. It wasn't a good day for him, at least here in the gym. "Do you want me to stop?

He snorted. "I want to go home. This week has been a fucking waste of time."

Ouch. She didn't think he meant her specifically, but as he was here for his own problems, if he wasn't making progress, then he would be pissed. She would be, too, in his shoes. That she was making progress and he was angry spoke volumes about where they both were at this time. It saddened her. "I'm sorry. The seminar is almost over. You should be working on your issues and not helping me with mine."

He spun around from reaching for more weights. "I shouldn't even be here." He waved a hand around. "This isn't my thing. I hate being inactive. I like purpose in my life, action. Not..." he threw up his hands in frustration. "Not whatever this is."

"I understand." And she did, but it didn't help him any.

She took a deep breath and prepared to be blasted. "If there is something I can do to help you deal with your issues, then tell me. I'd be happy to give back."

He stiffened, then relaxed. "Tinkerbelle, you've already helped. But some things just have to work themselves out over time."

"True. But there are some things you just have to jump into and let go. I often wonder if time isn't a crutch more than anything. I look back on the years where I felt I couldn't do anything, wouldn't push my boundaries – and then I never progressed."

"In your case, you couldn't. Some things do take time. In my case..." and he stopped, an odd look coming over his features.

"In your case?"

He sat down on the bench and shook his head. "It's stupid."

"It's not stupid if it matters."

"That's the thing. You said earlier that we feed something to keep it alive. And in my case, that's exactly what happened. I've been feeding something to keep it alive, but it's dead. She's dead. Gone," he said starkly.

"Oh my. Did you lose your wife?"

She raced over to his side, her palm coming to rest on his cheek.

He shook his head, but his gaze was haggard. "No," he

said hoarsely. "She aborted my baby and didn't tell me until afterwards. She told me she killed my daughter because she wasn't ready to be a mother."

His tortured gaze rose to lock onto hers. "I've been so angry, but it was more because I was grieving. How could I be so lost, so devastated by the loss of a child not yet born? She killed her. Wouldn't even give her a chance at life."

Tania didn't know what to say. Such a horrible event, and for his wife to have made such a decision without him said a lot about the state of his marriage. A state he himself wouldn't have understood until it was too late.

Compassion welled up inside and she couldn't help herself; she wrapped her arms around him and held him close.

He stiffened, then let himself be held. His arms went around her, holding on to her as the revelations just kept coming. He said, his voice barely above a croak, "It's me I'm really mad at, for not seeing what she'd do. For not having taken better care to avoid a pregnancy in the first place. For making sure my daughter was safe." He parted his knees and pulled her down to his lap. "All this time, I hated her, but deep inside, I hated myself. All this time I told myself that women weren't to be trusted, and it was me I didn't trust."

"I'm sorry," she whispered. "I'm sorry for all three of you."

He stared down at her. "That's the truth, isn't it? There were three injured souls here."

"Yes, but she could have handled it very differently, and she didn't want to. For whatever reason, she wanted to hurt you."

He stared out, a distant look in his eyes. "She was so angry when she found out. Children were in her plans, but down the road, a long ways down the road when she was ready, when the timing was right. She was a big planner, and this blew her plans off course."

"The time is rarely right for a major life event," Tania said, remembering her own pain and shock from so many years ago. Her parents had divorced as a result of it, her mother's life irrevocably changed by her daughter's assault. "It doesn't matter. We have to deal with the hand Mother Nature deals us. It's the *how* that makes us *who* we are."

Kane stared down at her, surprise lighting the chocolate depths.

"When did you get so wise?"

"After years of therapy," she said in a dry tone and smiled. "It's a funny thing, but when you least expect it, a breakthrough does happen and you wonder at your past…a past of just a few moments earlier before you had the epiphany."

His lips kicked up into a smile. "How true."

He leaned back and took a deep breath. "I feel both good and…exhausted."

She patted his shoulder. "I know what you mean."

A glint slipped into his eyes. "Nap time?"

She stared into his deep gaze and then understood. Heat rolled through her, coloring her cheeks. She gasped then giggled. "Oh, Lord." Then she nodded. "Definitely nap time."

His grin turned lethal. He leaned forward, dropped a kiss on her cheek, and whispered in a deep voice, "Your room or mine?"

Instantly, she said in a voice gone hoarse, "Mine."

HOW HAD THEY gone from being distant and irritated to racing like school kids down the hallway? He hoped they didn't meet anyone; Tania needed this.

Hell, he did, too.

His emotions were too raw at the moment to be examined with any intensity, but there was just such a sense of relief sliding off his shoulders with every step he moved further away from the pain. It would never dim his loss but it would firmly be in the past, where it belonged.

If she could get to this same point...wow.

She'd come so far already. Now could she go all the way? He almost groaned as his groin tightened. He hated to think how far away they were from where he wanted to be.

They reached her room undisturbed, and she unlocked the door and they slipped inside. Laughing and giggling like kids, she locked the door and turned to face him.

He opened his arms and she ran into them. God, he loved that.

Damn if he wasn't falling in love with her.

Chapter 21

TANIA WOULD DO anything to feel what Kane had made her feel last time. Knowing they had hours ahead of them made her whimper in the back of her throat. Instinct told her to crawl up his frame and go after more.

Pulling back slightly, she gave him a light push toward the bed. "Lie down."

He flipped his shirt over his head and kicked off his shoes. Standing at the end of the bed, arms wide, he fell backwards.

"I'm all yours."

She froze. "Oh, I hope you're right."

He lifted an eyebrow. "I mean it. Be gentle with me, sweetheart."

She grinned and pounced. She grabbed his closest foot and ripped off his sock. He laughed as her hands tickled his feet. He tried to tug his foot away, but she hung on. Releasing the bare one, she fought to get the sock off his other foot.

When he could, he gasped out, "What is this, a sock-free zone?"

She smirked. "Absolutely."

"Good, then you'd better be sockless, too," he warned. "Or else I get to remove them."

"Ha." She quickly stripped off her own socks. "Now I am."

"Good, now how about the pants and shirt, too?"

"Yeah, I don't think so." She shook her head. "I'm not playing that game. You still have your shorts on."

And before she'd figured out what he was doing, Kane lay stretched out before her only wearing white knit boxers. She swallowed hard. He rested his head on his hands and grinned up at her. "Now what are you going to do?"

"Admire you," she said honestly. "You're truly gorgeous."

His gaze widened. As she glanced up to his face, she was startled to see a wash of red working up his neck. "Really? You're okay to lie here in front of me in only your underwear, completely unconcerned, but I give you a compliment and you're embarrassed?"

A sheepish grin washed over his face. "I'll say thank you, and we'll move on."

"On to what?"

"Whatever you want; whatever you're comfortable with trying."

She sighed happily and went to crawl on the bed beside him but stopped. She looked down at her capris. She really wanted some freedom to move. Her t-shirt was more camisole than shirt, but her pants were heavy cotton without any stretch. Taking a deep breath and moving fast, she stripped off her capris, laid them on the empty chair, and turned back to face Kane.

He watched her, a smile on his face. "Doing good, Tinkerbelle."

She grinned; she was doing good. As long as he understood that progress could stop at any time…

Awkwardly, she climbed onto the bed and stared down at his massive body. "You're so big," she whispered.

"Yeah, so are my dad and my brother."

"Really?" At his nod, she turned her attention back to his

feet. In a whimsical move, she slipped one leg down to line alongside his foot. His had to have been twice the length of hers and was at least twice as wide.

A laugh rumbled through him. "I guess calling you Tinkerbelle wasn't far off. You are seriously tiny."

She gave an indelicate snort. "I'd never had it pointed out in quite the same way before. I'd have considered myself on the small side, but not like this." She placed a hand on his thigh, feeling it tighten into granite under her gentle touch. "You're so different from me. Your skin is thick, rough; your muscles – powerhouses."

"We're meant to be that way."

She nodded thoughtfully, loving the way his thigh twitched under her fingers, almost playing a rhythm. She stroked down over his kneecap, marveling at the sheer width of the joint. Hers would fit completely inside his with room to spare. "It's hard to believe the massive build."

"It's required to hold this massive body up," he said, amused. "Your kneecaps would crumple under my weight."

She couldn't argue with his logic, her hands now both stroking, learning, and feeling the differences between them. Loving the differences between them. And even more – loving the freedom between them. She sighed. "I know it embarrasses you, but I have to tell you that the artist in me finds you to be a perfect model."

"Model for what?"

"Everything." She lowered her head and dropped a kiss on his thigh. The smooth muscle twitched, so she did it again and again. She laid her cheek down on his thigh, looked down the long expanse of leg, and realized his toes were wiggling. She grinned, shifting so she could see his face. He lay with his eyes closed, accepting, allowing…

"You're a gift, you know."

Startled, he popped his eyes open, "What?" He shook his head. "Hell no, I'm just a normal man."

"One who's willing to lie here like this? That makes you special."

She slid her hand up to the edge of his boxers and stroked along the elastic edge. He bit back a gasp and she smiled. Exploring further, she let her finger slide toward the bulge in the center and watched in awe as it grew beside her fingers. She glanced up at Kane to find him watching her carefully. Then she closed her hand around him. He groaned and arched his head back.

She released him. "I'm so sorry. I didn't mean to hurt you."

He gave a garbled laugh, grabbed her hand, and placed it back on his shaft, wrapping her fingers around him again. "You didn't hurt me."

She moved her fingers experimentally. "Are you sure?"

"I'm sure. It feels wonderful."

"You don't look like you're enjoying this."

This time, he managed a full laugh. "Really, so how does this feel?" He slid his hand over her thigh to caress her bottom, his long fingers cupping her cheek before searching for and locating the silky thong strap between her thighs.

She froze at the first touch of his fingers and moaned softly at the exquisite sensation of his rough finger over her delicate skin. She moved her hips, pushing her cheeks against his hand.

"See, it feels good, but an almost-painful good."

"Yes," she whispered. Emboldened, she squeezed gently, loving the strangled sound escaping from his lips. "Like that?"

"Just like that. And like this." Once again, he covered her

hand and moved it up and down the length of him.

She'd heard of hand jobs, had seen movies of women between the men's legs giving blow jobs. She understood the mechanics but hadn't understood the lure. Now, for the first time, she understood.

She slowly withdrew her hand, loving the way he lifted his hips to follow her. She dropped a kiss at the top elastic band. "I think you're wearing too many clothes."

"Then take them off, baby."

The way he said 'baby' brought up shivers of desire and had her reaching out, snagging the material and pulling it down over his hips. Her gaze caught on the thick organ lying nestled in dark curls. Then, as if knowing it was being observed, it rose up and waved.

She swallowed hard, her mind consumed with the evidence of something she hadn't considered until now. As she removed his boxers and threw them onto the floor, she realized she had to put a stop to this. She stood beside him, now lying nude on the bed, with full expectations of something good to come out of this, but…

"Kane, I hate to tell you this."

She stopped, and he rolled his head toward her. "What's the matter, Tania?"

She motioned to the huge erection that both fascinated and now alarmed her and said, "You aren't going to fit."

KANE GRINNED THEN laughed and finally, unable to contain his amusement, he howled. He snagged her arm and tugged her on top of him, then held her head firmly while looking deep into her eyes. He said, "Do you trust me?"

Immediately, she nodded.

"Right. So trust me a little further. I will fit."

She shot a dubious look at the lower end of the bed, but she was now lying on top of him and couldn't see his anatomy. Good thing. He'd been unable to get the image of being buried deep inside her tiny body since this started. He should have considered that this stage would cause some cold feet but would have bet that fear, not doubt that this would mechanically work, would have been what set her off.

This one he could work with.

He rolled over so they lay side by side and looked into her eyes. Seeing the cloudiness in their dark depths, he said, "Please."

After a long moment, she whispered, "I'm willing to try but you have to understand… I might not make it."

He nodded. He knew that already. He could be in for the most frustrating time of his life, but he'd survive it. If she was willing to give him a chance, he could do no less.

In a slow, easy motion, he rolled her over onto her back. "Good. I think that considering I'm completely nude, you should be, too.

Her gaze widened as her shirt was flipped over her head and…and holy crap. She didn't have a bra on, and the most perfect pair of small, round breasts lay before him. He feasted his eyes on her. "Tinkerbelle, you are gorgeous."

Pink tinged her cheeks.

"Thank you," she whispered. He studied the nervousness in her eyes. "It will be fine, Tania. I promise."

She relaxed slightly. "I hope so."

He lay down beside her and tugged her into his arms before he kissed her.

Her lips opened immediately, and she wrapped her arms tightly around him. He knew what it took for her to take this step. He was humbled by her trust and was determined to make it good for her.

He kissed her senseless, exploring her lips, feasting on her mouth, smoothing tantalizing kisses across her cheeks and chin before coming back to drown in her nectar again and again. His hand stroked across her belly and traced the line of her ribs before finally cupping her breasts.

She arched beneath him, crying out.

"Shh, it's okay." But she twisted beside him, her body ready even if her mind wasn't. He lowered his head and tugged first one nipple then the other into his mouth. Such beautiful breasts deserved his attention, and he wanted to savor the opportunity.

Tania shivered and twisted. She had no idea what was happening to her. When he slipped his fingers through the patch of curls, she cried out and squeezed her thighs shut. He coaxed her thighs apart and slid his fingers into the dampness.

"Oh God, Kane."

"I know. Take it easy, sweetheart. It's supposed to be like this."

She flipped her head from side to side. "How can this be good? The tension...I feel wound-up, tied up in knots."

He slipped one finger inside, and her hips arched as she cried out again. He worked a second finger inside, cursing at his own urgency. She was so damn tight. He dropped his forehead on her flat belly and took several deep breaths. He could do this.

He pulled his fingers out, then thrust them in and back out. Sliding lower down, he pulled her thighs wide enough apart to make a place for himself, and he tasted her.

She shrieked. Her hands burrowed into his hair. "Oh, God, what are you doing?"

He smiled and replaced his fingers with his tongue.

She exploded seconds later, crying out as she rained all over him. He lifted himself up, fitted himself to the heart of her, and slowly entered.

She twisted and turned, pinned in place by an indomitable force. He searched her features but there was no fear, no panic. But something had unsettled her.

Inexorably, he slid deeper and deeper.

"I can't. No more. You don't fit."

Then she said the words that broke his heart. "Please, stop."

He shuddered in place, denial screaming through him. He was desperate to plunge in and finish this, her cries be damned, but he knew he couldn't do it.

Sweat beads popped out on his forehead, and he lowered his head until it rested on hers.

Then he closed his eyes. His body gave another long shudder as he regained another measure of control.

She whimpered. "I'm sorry."

"Shhh. Don't be." He didn't want her to be sorry. She'd taken such a huge step already; saying the wrong thing now could set her way back.

"I am, though." She opened her tear-filled eyes, and he felt her 'sorry' like an arrow to his heart. She figured it was her. There was such defeat in her gaze. Shame. "I can't do this. I won't ever be able to do this."

She started to weep. If there was ever anything guaranteed to kill his ardor, it was that. But he'd be damned if he'd let this be the ending. She *could* do this, but she had to know she could, and in order for that to happen, she had to trust him.

"Tania, easy, sweetie."

She sniffled.

He shifted to the side, sliding his hands down to her hips, and snuggled her tightly against him. He'd be dammed if he withdrew completely.

"Is this better?" he murmured, dropping kisses on her cheek, her nose, and finally on her mouth.

She nodded, shifting her hips experimentally. "I'm sorry," she said again.

He smiled. "Don't be. Look at how far you've come."

She frowned, shifted again, and looked down at their fused bodies. "Are you still inside?"

"I am." *Just not very far, unfortunately.*

"But..." and her frown deepened as she tried to think it through. She wiggled a little more, and then grinned. "I can feel you in there."

"I should hope so," he said with feeling.

"So, you do fit?" she asked cautiously a moment later.

He laughed. "I said I would. It's just so new to you. And yes, I'm big and you're little, but we fit together just fine."

"Only you're not as big as you were before, right?"

And damn if she didn't tighten her inner muscles. His response was immediate. Her eyes widened and she shifted again, then again. He rolled over so she was lying on his chest and gently nudged her up.

She sat up and gasped.

He shuddered.

"Oh my." She shifted from side to side then tilted her hips forward and back. Her inexperienced exploration was going to kill him.

"That's...different."

"Ya think?" his voice came out gritty and deep. A ripple slipped down his body.

"Oh, you like that, don't you?" She leaned forward, her

hips lifting.

He groaned and grabbed her hips to stop her from lifting off completely. As she sat down again, he groaned, and she smiled, a sweetly enchanting female smile.

He knew he was in trouble. She lifted and lowered herself again and then repeated the motion. Each time, her movement settled her slightly lower and he went slightly deeper. *Oh, dear God.*

A deep sigh slid from his chest. "Yesss," he whispered. "Sooo good."

He opened his eyes to see her face tilted to the ceiling, head back, long hair drifting down her back. But it was the look of inner concentration on her face that caught and held his attention. She was beautiful at any time, but like this, riding after something she didn't understand but knowing she was on the right path, she rode faster and faster and…stopped as her body exploded. She cried out and came to a shuddering stop.

"No." He gripped her hips and drove upwards, once, twice, and a groan ripped out of his throat as he climaxed.

She collapsed down on top of him and closed her eyes.

"I did it," she whispered. "Finally."

And fell silent.

Chapter 22

TANIA WOKE UP hours later, alone.

She shifted to study the room and almost cried out at the unexpected achiness. How come she had to pay after something that felt so good? And froze.

Oh, dear God. They hadn't used birth control. With everything else going on, her mind had been worrying about so much already that she hadn't once considered the issue. She fell back, scared.

Her instinctive reaction was shock. Her mind was saying this was not the right time, and she flinched. Hadn't Kane's wife said something similar? No, they weren't in the same situation. She'd been married, in an obviously steady sexual relationship, and should have had some method of birth control that worked for them. And Kane had likely thought she'd had some protection, but he'd never asked...and God help her, she'd never even considered the issue once.

As she laid there, her fingers splayed over her belly, it was hard to be upset. She'd wanted children since forever. If it turned out she was pregnant, she couldn't do anything but see this as a gift. It was not how she had planned it, and it was not how she would have chosen for it to happen, but thinking of a tiny child growing inside her right now made her toes curl with joy.

What would Kane think?

After his wife's actions, she knew how he'd feel about it. He would take responsibility and be willing to step up, but that's not what she wanted. She didn't want a child between them to be a responsibility. She wanted such a thing to be a joy. Beautiful. Special. Wanted. Yet she knew she'd love this miracle child, if she was so lucky, enough for both of them.

Then reality returned. Her cycle was due to start in just a couple of days, so chances were good she wasn't pregnant. It had happened to other people – but she wasn't that lucky.

It would be better at this point if she weren't pregnant. *Liar.* She'd be delighted if it turned out she was. Still, there couldn't be any more of this without responsible birth control. She had no idea which way to go, or even if there would be another incident. The seminar would be over tomorrow. They had all day to work on the projects before presenting them to Jenna just before noon. The afternoon would be a summary of the course, and she and Kane would be the last to present their homework. Thank God. She hadn't finished or made it anywhere close to finishing the project.

She scrambled out of bed and grabbed her laptop. It was after dinner. In fact, it was almost bedtime. She opened her laptop to find a note tucked inside from Kane.

Instantly, she gave a happy sigh. He hadn't left without a goodbye.

"Hey sleepyhead. I'm going to get dinner and will bring back something for you. If you want to call me, here's my number. Otherwise, I'll be back soon."

Her heart melted. Not only had he not been gone long, but he'd thought of her enough to bring her something to eat.

Then they had to do their homework.

She turned on her laptop, grabbed her camera, and started downloading pictures.

There were hundreds. While waiting, she stepped into the shower but kept her hair up and out of the water. She didn't want to sleep with it wet, and if Kane was coming back, she really didn't want wet hair to dampen his ardor.

In the water, she slowly moved the sponge across her body, wondering why everything felt so different, alive. As if his touch, their lovemaking, had awakened millions of nerve endings she'd never known about.

Considering the physical differences, she had to stop and consider – how did she feel mentally? Emotionally? Spiritually?

Standing under the heavy force while hot water beat down on her skin, she smiled, letting the water wash over her. She felt…wonderful. Renewed. Her heart was exploding with happiness, joy, love, and yes… relief. She'd made love with Kane. Sure, she'd had a little freak out, but with his help, she'd pushed through to a surprise ending. She'd never thought it could be that good. Sure, she'd heard other girls giggling over their sexual encounters and sharing stories – something she couldn't ever imagine doing about Kane. He was too special, the stories too intimate, the emotions too overwhelming. No matter where she and Kane went as a couple, she'd always be grateful for what he'd done.

He didn't want her gratitude. She knew that instinctively, but he had it regardless – forever.

She didn't know when the first tears started. Once started, though, she couldn't hold back and they cascaded down her cheeks to blend with the hot water beating down on her face. Then she started to sob. She wrapped her arms around her chest and cried.

She couldn't even begin to voice the outpouring of emotion. But as if a huge scab had been ripped off – a premature scab, as if the wound underneath hadn't reached that point of healing – the pus buried deep inside poured out.

The hot water beat down on her body as she cried for the little girl she'd been back then, for the lost years of innocence and for the many years in between when she'd existed in only half a world. The years after where she'd tried hard to be normal but had been faking it all the way.

She hadn't known how badly damaged she'd been until now, how thin and fragile her psyche. Now, her deepest fears had been opened and the darkest poisons festering inside released.

Time passed. She didn't know how long she'd stood under the water. She hadn't been aware that she'd dropped to a crouch, rocking herself back and forth, until strong arms grabbed her.

She shrieked and flailed her arms.

"Easy, Tinkerbelle, it's just me." Kane's voice washed over her, and she collapsed, sobbing against his chest.

"Sorry," she whispered over and over again. The water was turned off, and she was bundled up in a towel and carried out to the bedroom.

"You have nothing to be sorry for." He held her so carefully, as if she'd break. She'd have laughed if she could have, because she was already broken.

Her sobs slowed and finally turned into a damp sniffling by the time he had her tucked in the bed, a second towel moving briskly over her hair.

When he finished, he picked up the hairbrush and brushed her hair in long, sure strokes. She tilted her head back and let him.

It felt so good. It brought up one more piece of poison to be examined and maybe, if she was lucky, released.

In a hoarse whisper, she said, "He broke my ribs, my collarbone, and a finger. He was so angry."

The brushing stopped. For a long moment, she thought he was going to leave, but then the gentle movement resumed. Barely leashed anger resounded in his voice as he said, "Why was he angry?"

"He wanted a child, like seven or eight. Instead, I was thirteen and already going through puberty."

KANE WANTED TO kill someone, a specific someone. He wanted to pulverize the asshole that had taken a beautiful child and broken her because he'd made assumptions based on her size. That the asshole was a child predator to begin with made him sick of his sex.

That Tania had been dealing with this for so long, without a break, without an end, said so much about the person she was inside.

"Is that why you were crying in the shower?"

She immediately shook her head. "I'm not sure what started the tears. But it's like an old injury was finally brought to light so I could release it. Sort of like a purging. I'm so tired." She yawned. "I feel empty. But at the same time, I feel renewed, as if now I can fill those empty places with something good."

She curled up on the bed and fell asleep – just like that.

Kane stared down at her, wondering again at the trust in him. She'd gone from shocked and lashing out at him in panic before she understood who was in the shower with her to instant acceptance, letting him look after her.

Now she slept with the innocence of a child.

But her admission, something she'd never told anyone –

yeah, her admission had ripped his heart out. So much pain and horrible memories being brought to the light of day and then released.

It was exhausting work. She needed to rest. He looked down at his soaking-wet clothing, the hairbrush in his hand. "What am I going to do?" Her dinner was sitting on the desk. He'd passed Jenna in the hallway and had given Tania's excuses for missing dinner. Jenna hadn't missed much in that sharp glance of hers, but after making sure Tania was indeed fine, she'd walked away. There would be a therapy session tomorrow. A good thing for Tania. She needed someone experienced to help her at this stage.

Did she still need him?

And what did he need?

Right now, he could use a conversation with Jenna. He pulled out his cell phone and called her. "Do you have time for coffee?" he asked, thankful she was here at the hotel and basically on-call for the attendees. Stuff came up and people needed to talk. It was the first time he'd done this, though.

"Yes," she said instantly. "Shall we go to the coffee shop, or do you want to meet elsewhere?"

"Coffee shop in five minutes." He closed the cell phone, grabbed his hotel key card, and left. With any luck, Tania would sleep until he got back.

Jenna was waiting for him.

He slid into the bench opposite her, ordered coffee, and waited silently for it to be delivered.

"I need help." There, cool and direct – his style. "For Tania."

Her gaze narrowed and her lips twitched. "In what way?"

"She's had a major breakthrough, like a traumatic type of breakthrough. I don't know what to do for her."

"Tell me."

He took a deep breath, then something in him made him stop. He winced. "She might not like me talking to you. It's personal."

"Then let me tell you, and you can nod or shake your head." Damned if Jenna didn't run through the list of their lovemaking, bonding, bringing up old memories, nightmares, and an outpouring sob-fest.

He nodded, nodded, and just kept nodding. "Damn, you do know."

She smiled gently, so much compassion and understanding in her gaze that he realized she knew so much because she'd lived it herself. Then another piece of the puzzle called 'Jenna' slipped into place. She helped others because she came from a place of having healed herself.

Feeling better, he said, "So, what do I do?"

"Be there for her." Jenna's response was instant and confident, but then she ruined it. "If you can."

And that allowed doubt to enter his mind. "I don't know," he said in a low voice. "This is deep stuff."

"And now it's not so deep. All hurts, once opened to the light of day, have the power to heal. When we keep them buried and hidden, they only fester."

"She's come a long way."

"She has." Jenna sipped her coffee calmly, waiting.

He sighed. "I don't know if I'm up for this."

She nodded. "Then you need to say goodbye to her, knowing that your part in her healing journey is over."

Her quick response saying he could leave pissed him off. "I didn't say I wanted to get *out* of this, I'm just not sure I can *do* this."

"Understood." She waited.

Damn, he hated that. He stared moodily out the window, the late sun sinking in the horizon, throwing gorgeous hues on the hills surrounding them. The campus was beautiful but like everything, there was a dark side to it.

"I want to know her whole story, but at the same time, the bits and pieces I do know make me so angry."

She sipped her coffee. He turned to look at her to see that she was studying his hand. He stared down at his big mitt and understood he wasn't clenching his fist, even though he was angry. At a level he hadn't seen in a long time, it wasn't physical anger. He was hurting. For her. He knew he could never right the wrong. He could only help her make the most of every day, but it was a big job. Maybe too big. "I don't think I can help her."

"You already have."

"So much more needs to be done."

"That's for her to do."

"And what do I do for her?" he cried. "It seems so little."

"What you are doing is so very much."

He stopped and stared at her. "How? What am I doing?"

"You're caring for her, standing by her, being there for her, supporting her as she walks this difficult journey. That's something she's never had."

Jenna smiled, a warm loving movement that fascinated him. "You are doing the best thing anyone can do for her – you are loving her."

That was when he recognized what his next step needed to be.

To go back and keep loving her; not to let her put distance between them, to throw up barriers, to keep herself inside and him on the outside. But to give them a chance – to see what they could be. He had more insecurities than he'd ever had about a relationship, but the rewards were exponential as well.

He didn't want to miss this chance.

He shook his head. "It's really that simple, isn't it?"

"It usually is, but what about your issues? How are you handling your problems while you've been helping her deal with hers?"

He smiled at the way-too-wise woman sitting across from him. "That's the thing, isn't it? While I was so focused on helping her, I stopped thinking about my own problems and when I turned around, my anger was gone. It had dissipated, no longer letting me hide from the real problem; my wife's betrayal, the guilt of not having been able to save my child, and the grief of losing my daughter."

She reached across the table and laid her hand gently on his. "Sounds like you've been through a lot yourself."

"And came out on the other side without really realizing what I'd done," he admitted. "I was so focused on Tania, I'd let go of my own problems."

"It's called healing. And it often happens when we're more concerned about helping someone else."

He lifted his cup, drained it, and put it down. "Thank you. I'm going back to Tania so she doesn't wake up alone. Maybe tomorrow you can check in and see how she's doing."

"I will," Jenna promised. Knowing she watched him but not caring, Kane stood up and headed back to where he really wanted to be.

At Tania's side.

It was only as he approached her doorway that he realized he didn't have the key card to get back inside her room.

He dropped his forehead on the door. Shit.

Chapter 23

Tania woke up with a sore throat, burning eyes, and a happy heart.

She'd take the nasty physical symptoms any day – as long as she got to keep the happy heart. She had no idea what time it was. All she'd done for the last day was a mix of emotional outburst – sleep – emotional outburst – collapse.

She sat up in bed and looked around. She was alone.

And damn if she wasn't starting to hate that.

Then again, he could only be expected to be there so long. And she needed to give him the freedom to leave. It was the last day of the seminar, and although she didn't give a damn about completing her homework and handing it over to Jenna, she did care about fulfilling her own commitment to her healing. Without her assignment, she'd never have gotten here – she might have in another way at another time, but the fact was, she was here.

And she was so grateful. Checking her laptop for the time, she found out it was six in the morning. She needed to get the homework done.

She needed to free Kane. Make him understand that she was grateful he'd been here, but if this wasn't where he wanted to be…then that was okay, too.

It wasn't, but she wasn't going to try to keep him on a hook. She'd gotten over worse, and coming into this seminar, she'd have been jumping for joy to think of making it this far.

Determined to end the seminar in a good frame of mind, she set about sorting the latest images. As she worked, the theme started to build more in her mind. She planned on printing the images on the hotel printer. She needed the images in black and white, but they had to tell the story properly.

She worked for a solid hour and felt like she was making progress as she found an image of Kane, relaxed, happy, and almost carefree. She'd taken it when they'd gone for a walk yesterday. He'd been giddy, almost running back to the hotel room. Excited. Natural.

A little later, she realized she was hungry and spied the restaurant bag on the desk. She hopped up to see what Kane had brought her last night. A couple sandwiches were nestled inside a takeout carton. Perfect. She made herself a cup of coffee and polished them both off. Apparently, lovemaking and healing had improved her appetite. She could just imagine the others' comments. At seven, she called down to the front desk and asked about printing the images, then she emailed them to the receptionist, who promised to print them and hole punch them for her.

Tania dressed and packed up her room. Since it was the end of the seminar, she'd elected to leave as soon it was over. She didn't know if other participants were staying another night, but she needed to get back to her normal world.

She'd be sorry to leave. It would hurt in a way. This place would always stay in her memories. A special place, a special time, and a special man.

Once she was ready to go, she decided to check out and leave her bags at the reception area. She could collect them at the end of the morning session. She needed to sort the printed pictures and put a few comments on a couple of them.

With a last look around, she stopped, grabbed her camera, and took several pictures to remember this room by before she took her leave.

Downstairs, she handed over her keys and luggage and accepted the pictures in return. Now, if she could find a way to tie the pages together – a small strip of leather would be perfect – but such a thing was highly unlikely.

"Do you need anything else?"

"Now that you mention it," she said, "Any chance you have a strip of leather of any kind hanging around?"

The woman's gaze widened. "I have a single shoelace that's been sitting in this drawer since forever, would that work?"

She opened her drawer and pulled out one long, single strand.

"Perfect." Borrowing scissors, Tania cut the strip into three equal pieces. Then with her pages and strips, she moved to a comfy seating arrangement in the lobby and went to work. First, she used the laces to tie the pages together in the three different punched holes. Then with the black marker, she wrote *"Skin"* on the title page. Then she added a couple more lines.

Next, she turned to the first image. On that page, she wrote *"The beginning..."*

After that, using the minimum number of words possible, she explained the steps that Kane had gone through to push himself to do what he needed to do to get the job done. Even though he hadn't seen the journey for what it was at the time, it had ended up being his journey and, through that, her journey. As one had healed, it had triggered healing in the other. They'd been perfect partners. On another page, she had a picture of Kane's hand held out toward her. She titled it *"The Gift – Acceptance."*

On the next page, she had an image of her hand she'd taken in her hotel room, outstretched as if to meet his hand. She titled that page *"Acceptance of the gift – another gift of acceptance."*

On the last page, she had a picture – the only one she really disliked as far as clarity went – but it was powerful in its message. The picture was of her hand being held in Kane's hand. Hers tiny and his huge, but hers cradled very gently by this powerful man.

She titled this last image *"A gift offered and a gift returned"*.

By the time she was done, she had to sniffle back tears. She flicked thorough the images again and felt like the theme *was* the title. In none of the images was there at any time a piece of clothing, not even a little bit of material to denote clothing existed. In fact, the images stripped Kane down to the basic man inside and out. No artifice. No hiding. No covering up. He was who he was, and it was showed here in all his natural splendor. As natural and as honest as the day he was born, he was wearing the only thing he couldn't remove – his skin.

KANE WOKE UP with a shock of feeling like he was in the wrong place. He bolted upright and threw off his covers. He was in his room. Memories flooded back. He'd taken the wrong hotel key when he went to meet Jenna.

Tania would have woken up alone.

And he'd lost the opportunity to wake her up gently, slowly, lovingly.

Now he realized it was morning, and although he hoped she might still be asleep, she could also have already headed down to the restaurant for breakfast. He dressed, packed, and leaving his stuff behind for the moment, raced down to her room. He knocked, but there was no answer. He knocked again. Then kicking himself again for having taken the wrong key last night, he went to check the restaurant. But he couldn't find her. He frowned. Walking over to the reception desk, he asked the receptionist if Tania had been by.

"She's checked out."

He froze. "Pardon?"

The woman gave him a bright smile. "She was up bright and early, handed back her key, and has officially checked out." She glanced behind her. "Oh, but her luggage is still here. She's part of the seminar, right? So she's likely headed in that direction."

Thanking her, Kane took off to search for Tania. If her luggage was still here, then she was, too. That was all that mattered. He'd find her somehow. Ten minutes later, he spotted Jenna exiting the elevator. "Jenna, have you seen Tania?" He quickly explained about her checking out but still being here and his not being able to find her.

"There are lots of little seating arrangements throughout the hotel. She could be in any one of those. She also might have gone for a walk."

He nodded and turned to look out the front door. She might be out there. He glanced at his watch. "We're starting in what, a half hour?"

"Less. I'm grabbing some tea and going over there now. We're starting early so I can get into the presentations."

He winced. "Right. The homework."

She laughed lightly. "I presume that's what she's doing

right now."

"Oh, most likely." And he'd forgotten all about it. "I'll catch up with you in class."

He did a quick search of the hotel. Not finding Tania, he decided he needed some coffee. He'd rather have something much stronger…

With cups of coffee in both hands, he headed to start the last day of the seminar. He couldn't even begin to explain to his brother what he'd gone through here. Trying to explain what he'd learned from the seminar would be tough because what he'd learned had come from Tania herself, and that wouldn't have happened except for that damn homework. Damned if Jenna hadn't planned that all along.

How could she have known? Had she known? No, surely not. She didn't have any psychic abilities that would allow her to see who would be the best fit with another. But she'd created a magical opportunity when she'd paired Kane with Tania. And he'd asked her to change it.

She'd refused. Thank God.

He walked into class to find Tania sitting beside Robin, both of them involved in an animated conversation. He almost didn't want to interrupt, but Robin spotted him first. She said something to Tania, who spun around. He caught the barest whisper of relief in her eyes, and she smiled up at him.

"Hey. Is one of those for me?"

"Yeah, I wasn't sure how long you'd sleep."

"I woke up early, ate the sandwiches you brought me last night, and then finished the homework."

"Yeah, about that homework." He'd always done his fair share on group projects, but right now he felt like he'd let her down. "I'm sorry I haven't contributed much."

She laughed. "You are so wrong. You contributed the most. Wait until you see it."

"Shouldn't I be adding something to it?" he asked, curious now. He'd seen her theme, and that had made him pause. He'd planned to clarify her thoughts on that subject but had completely forgotten about it with everything else going on. He presumed she hadn't put any images in the project that he'd not be happy about, but as only Jenna and the two of them were going to see it, he could live with it regardless.

"You can if you want to." She handed it over, but Jenna walked in just then and started to wrap up the seminar. She had several guest speakers in to talk with them about the healing journey as she took groups aside and went over their projects.

The morning passed quickly as the speakers were both witty and fun, and although they never made light of their own painful pasts, they showed how far they'd come. After seeing Tania's major growth, Kane had so much more appreciation for them. He'd barely had a chance to flick through the project Tania had put together, but he did read and tried to absorb what she'd done. The depth of what she'd captured astonished him.

The title amused him and confused him until he slowly recognized that there was only skin showing in each of the images. The deepest parts of him had been laid bare by her camera. He was alternately embarrassed and awed by her skill. He understood the captions but thought she might have given him more credit than he was due, but then he came to the last few pages and he stopped. Damn if his eyes weren't trying to burn with tears. He saw his hand outstretched and had no recollection of when she could have taken the image, then turned the page to see her hand unfurling, hesitantly, carefully, but still making the effort.

He turned the page to see the two of them holding hands and realized she hadn't created a homework project, but had instead created a work of art.

Only there was one thing missing.

He leaned over. "Do you still have that marker?"

She pulled it out and handed it over without saying anything. She watched him though, a question in her eyes. He smiled, and on the last page he added three words.

Jenna walked up behind them as he finished.

"Tania and Kane, it's your turn."

Chapter 24

Tania wanted to see what Kane had written, but there was no time. Jenna held her hand out for the project and Kane passed it over. She shot Kane a look and whispered, "What did you write?"

He gave her a small smile and said, "You'll have to wait and see."

She rolled her eyes at him. Nervous now that Jenna, with her eyes that saw too much, would read more into the project than Tania had intended, Tania took her seat. The three of them sat at a table where they could all look at the project. In the background, the speaker was going into another story as the group before them took their seats.

Tania wanted to go back to the others and skip this part, but it wasn't to be.

Jenna held it up and read the title. "Skin. What a powerful title." Then she started at the top of the title page and proceeded to read it out loud,

"Skin

A journey of healing

A journey for healers

A journey from the inside out."

"Isn't it, though," Kane said.

Jenna glanced up, her gaze going from one to the other, putting them both in the spotlight of her gaze that saw too much, and said, "Is there anything you want to say about the project before I take a look?"

Kane glanced over at Tania and raised an eyebrow.

Tania shook her head, suddenly tongue-tied and wishing she was anywhere but here.

Jenna smiled. "Then let's take a look."

She turned to the first image where Kane stood staring wistfully, yearning for something in the distance. Tania knew he was staring at a sailboat, but she'd cropped the image so only his face showed. Jenna turned the page, stopping to read the caption and study the images.

Only once while she worked her way through the pages did she say anything. She said, "You are truly gifted with your camera, Tania."

Tania wiggled, a bit uncomfortable with such a personal project being seen for the first time. It said a lot about Kane. She hoped he didn't mind, but it also said a lot about her. She knew that a part of her did mind. The rest of her said deal with it.

It was why she had come, to bring light to her darkest places. She'd done that big time.

After what she'd been through so far at the seminar, this was nothing.

She could do this.

She sighed. "Thank you. It's something I really enjoy doing."

Jenna moved from page to page, stopping to read and study the captions. At one point, she looked up to study the two of them, both so silent and still, and then continued her progress without saying a word. When she finally got to the page where Kane's hand was outstretched, Jenna smiled, and maybe it was Tania's imagination, but she thought Jenna's eyes were over-bright. When she got to Tania's hand tentatively held out, Tania knew she was correct.

Then she turned to the last page and sniffled, then sighed happily. She lifted her teary eyes first to Tania and then to Kane, and her smile warmed. "It's beautiful. Sincerely, heartwarmingly beautiful."

"Tania is responsible for the entire project. She took the pictures, put this collection together, and added the captions." Kane had to say honestly. He couldn't take credit for Tania's success. "I only added one piece to the project."

But Tania was shaking her head. "Not true. You were there every step of the way."

Jenna turned to Kane. "Which part did you add, Kane?"

He grinned sheepishly. "The last line."

Jenna looked down. Turning the last page over, her eyes watered again.

"What does it say?" Tania asked, curiosity getting the better of her. She wished he'd told her first.

Jenna looked from Kane to her. "You haven't read what he wrote down?"

Tania shook her head. She jumped up and ran around so she could see for herself. On the last page, in thick bold printing, Kane had added, "To Be Continued…"

She gasped and burst into tears.

Kane stood up and opened his arms.

She ran into them and sobbed as they closed securely around her.

This was what she'd always wanted. The only thing she could say she'd never had.

A man to love her – broken, mending, or healed; someone

who could love her for who she was, regardless of where she'd been or what she'd been through. And she'd finally found him.

Kane.

SCARS

by
Dale Mayer

Chapter 1

ROBIN CHILDERS WAITED at the side of the small conference room, her stomach in knots, her palms sweating. She did that a lot these days. Wait. Wait for the days to pass. Wait for the months to pass. Wait for time between her surgeries to pass.

To the next surgery she didn't want. Another surgery she had to have – or stay a freak that scared little children and caused horrified stares wherever she went.

Not the life she'd planned.

Not the life she'd imagined for herself.

Not the life she'd wanted.

But it was the life she was currently living. And that sucked.

Big time.

While watching the other participants enter, she had to acknowledge she wasn't alone in not liking her life.

Everyone appeared to be walking to death row. Here because of outside influences, because other people wanted them to attend. Or maybe here because they understood that they needed to be – yet hating the necessity that forced them to take this step. And yet they still came. Because they needed this.

Everyone was here for whatever magic their instructor psychologist / therapist, Professor Jenna Komak, had to offer.

In other words, they were all desperate.

To heal. To ditch the ugly in their lives. To find a way to live a 'normal' life – whatever that meant.

It was an odd thing to realize that she'd signed up for this on her own. Empowering. No one had pressured her to come. No one had paid the heavy fees for her. One brave morning, she'd determined that this was the next step in her journey, and she'd taken it.

She'd even managed to stay positive right up until it was time to leave for the workshop. Then reality hit her. Not only was she going to a seminar to help her deal with a painful issue, she was going to have to leave the university campus where she lived and travel to a hotel in downtown Vancouver. Be out in public. Deal with strangers.

At least at the university, people were used to seeing her. They stared, but less and less as they became accustomed to her face. Yet to do this workshop, she'd have to leave her hidey hole and journey out *there* – a place she'd hidden from as hard and as long as she could.

It had been easy to push the anxiety into a small hole in her stomach as she dreamed of the promise of finally getting the help she needed. That hope had kept her going. Now that she'd arrived, her gut in knots, her palms sweaty just from the thought of what she was doing. Doubts plagued her.

Damn. She was an idiot. A masochist. Maybe she needed her head examined after all. Something Jenna was sure to do. And that was pretty scary. Robin had issues. Duh.

Sure, everyone did. One of hers – the big one – she wore for the entire world to see. All other issues stemmed from there. Although if she were honest and more self-aware, she could probably find issues from her past at the root of this, too. But she had no plans to do that. She was here to deal with a specific issue. Not to try and deal with them all. There were too many. They hurt too much.

No. If she could deal with one issue, then she could return to a more normal life. The rest of her issues would have to wait until later. Much later.

It was her reaction – and other people's reactions to her face – that terrified her. And therein lay the problem.

She had to get over herself.

And that was a shitty deal.

Hating the inside shakiness threatening to take over the rest of her long frame, Robin turned to watch the other participants amble in to take their places. Her glance strayed past then caught on her friend Tania sitting silent at her side.

"Hey," Tania said, nervously.

She was just as nervous, maybe more so, but just as determined as Robin to move on in life. Only Tania's scars were inside. Hidden from the world. Private. She had the discretion to share on her time frame.

"Are you sure you're okay?" Robin asked her, studying her friend's face in concern.

Tania shrugged. "I'm fine."

Robin heard the tremor in Tania's voice, and then there was likely a matching one in hers.

The two of them were a mess.

Just then, Dr. Jenna Komak walked in.

And the class tension eased back. That woman exuded a presence. Calm. Capable. Caring.

She knew them all individually and they all knew her. Everyone here had attended evening classes with her and had been vetted and approved to take this special workshop. Most of them were students from the same university. But not all. They were a mix of men and women.

Yet there was a common denominator – they were all damaged.

SEAN WILSON SLOUCHED in the back of the room. Separate from the others. Like he'd always been. He still questioned his sister's request. By rights, if he was here, Paris should be as well. And she'd wanted to come but had been refused, with a gentle suggestion to wait for another session a few months down the road. Maybe she'd be ready then.

Disappointed, Paris had then asked Sean to apply and if he got accepted, to scope it out for her. See if it would help her. He'd expected to be rejected even faster than Paris had been, so Sean had applied. And been accepted.

Paris had been overjoyed for him. Sean had been terrified. It was so not what he wanted. He didn't want to listen to other people's problems. He didn't want to share his own. He'd done a lot already. Was studying psychology to help him understand more. But that was on his time frame. Not here. Not now. Not surrounded by strangers. Who would want this? But there was no backing out now. He wouldn't be able to. Not and still face his sister.

Now he was here in the hotel, stuck, and likely to be spending a week in very uncomfortable situations trying to be polite in the group therapy sessions that rubbed him the wrong way. He'd been in those before. They were not fun.

He had no wish to have this prof dig around in his head. Regardless of the prof's cool confidence in her ability to help everyone.

He barely stifled back a snort at that thought. Looking up, he realized several people were staring at him. So okay, he hadn't been as silent as he thought he'd been.

"What?" he asked the Goth-looking woman in front of him, giving her his bland face – willing her to say something.

The woman raised an eyebrow then smirked as if seeing something he hadn't expected her to see before turning away.

Damn right. He slouched back, stretched his long legs out in front of him and crossed his arms across his chest.

Sean had never backed down from a fight in his life. And had never apologized. He wasn't about to start now. Maybe he'd have saved himself a lot of pain if he'd learned that lesson as a child. Then again, he'd never been a fast learner. Besides, Paris was and it hadn't helped her any. She was the one that should be here. Damn. Why had Jenna thought Paris wasn't ready? And yet Jenna thought Sean was?

Although he hadn't come for help, or planned on being helped, there was room for it. His life was a mess of sleepless nights, bad nightmares during the few moments of shuteye he did get, followed by slow, dragging-his-ass days as he pulled himself through the daily requirements of being a human being on this planet.

Something he'd looked at cutting short a time or two. But not since becoming an adult.

And it was due to his sister that he hadn't completed the job. He might not be worth saving – but she was. She'd needed him to get *that* job done.

At least that's what he told himself. And none of it changed the fact that he was empty inside. Filled with pain and sorrow. He lived in the shadows. Alone. He looked normal to everyone else – calm as if he lived in the light.

Except there was no light in his soul. Just darkness.

And now he was in a seminar geared to drain some of that darkness away. But what if that darkness did disappear? And there was nothing left inside?

Chapter 2

Given that last night had been the introduction to the workshop, along with an overview of what would take place this week in general terms, Robin knew today would be a case of getting down to business.

Especially now. The morning break was already over. Now there was a sense of waiting. Expectation. She glanced over at Tania to see her gaze locked on Jenna's face. They'd all hear about the special project Jenna had designed for each of them. That could go either way. Robin preferred to work alone. Although it would be fine to work with Tania, as she already understood Robin's issues and she was one of the few who understood some of Tania's.

Jenna had a stack of papers in front of her on a clipboard. Notes of some kind. Jenna didn't waste any time welcoming the group back. As if understanding that Jenna had shifted gears, several people sat straight up.

Robin slid lower in her seat.

"All right. We're going to start with the assignment that you will each do during the week."

She listened as Jenna outlined a weeklong project everyone would have to complete during their stay here. As she heard the general details, Robin couldn't help but feel a huge sense of relief inside. She lowered her gaze in case Jenna caught a glimpse of that look in her eyes. If Jenna saw, she'd change Robin's assignment. No one was allowed to be too comfortable – not in a workshop like this.

Still, she couldn't help but wonder what possible project she'd be called to do. School was easy for her, so a report didn't worry her. The project would also help her get through the week. Something to focus on so she could ignore the others. If she had to, she could even present it to this class. After all, here they were all equals. And all broken.

"I understand there could be some resistance to the individual assignments."

A ripple worked its way around the small seminar room.

A knowing smile slipped across Jenna's beautiful face. "Given that, I suggest you remember why you are here. What you hope to get out of this week, and keep in mind that you all came to me and in everyone's case..." she stopped to look each participant in the eye then continued, "I have evaluated your situation and came up with what I believe is the best way forward for each of you." She smiled, her gaze whispering back across their faces. "So remember that when you hear what I have planned."

Robin sat back and swallowed. Hard. Oh Lord. She wanted this to be a simple, school report type of project, but her gut said she wouldn't be so lucky.

And she wasn't.

"We'll start with Sean," Jenna said. "Please come to the back of the room with me and I can go over your assignment." Jenna looked down at the document in her hand and nodded once. She glanced up and pinned Robin in place. "Robin, you too. You'll be working with Sean."

Ah hell. So much for working with Tania. Or for working alone. She glanced over at Sean. She'd recognized the look in his eye earlier. He didn't want anything to do with this workshop. She had no idea why he was here, but it wasn't to heal. But from the look of him, he needed to do that very badly.

SURPRISED TO HEAR his name called first, Sean stood up and shoved his chair back out of the way. The beautiful professor motioned to the back of the room, presumably to discuss his project. Here went nothing.

Why was he here again? Still, it was just a project. He was already here, so what the hell. At least he'd be able to report back to Paris. He wondered what the project was. As he started weaving through the tables and chairs to the back of the room, he heard Jenna call out a second name as his partner. Partner? These were individual assignments – weren't they? Had he missed something? He hoped so. Teamwork was something he did well at school, at work. In his personal life – not so much. Sure, this was a category altogether – but there was no doubt this was damn personal. He was a loner. And that was by choice.

As Robin walked past him, he remembered her from last night, where she'd spent the better part of the 'getting to know everyone' session sitting in a corner and making it plain she had no intention of getting to know anyone. He understood that. He felt the same way but so far this morning, her attitude hadn't improved. If anything, from that slight curl of her lip, she'd taken a turn for the worse. She had stunning black hair that hung down straight over one side of her face so it appeared that she could only see half her world. Her hair was black and her skin cream, and it reminded him of a black and white personality.

Too bad for her.

Well, he could deal with whatever. This was only for a week. He'd tolerated much worse for much longer.

How hard could this be?

Chapter 3

Needing her air of indifference to hide the inner turmoil, Robin sat down at the chair that Jenna indicated and crossed her legs. She waited. Sean sauntered over like he didn't give a damn. He probably didn't. With his attitude, Robin had no idea why he was here in the first place. He was odd. Tall and slim with wide shoulders and slim hips. He was built for gentlemen suits and wore jeans with more holes than material. It was that cocky "screw you" look on his face that she couldn't stop watching.

No one was that cynical naturally. Something bad had happened to him. It was the only reason for the aggressive front. And maybe he was afraid of it happening again. No, she studied the casual indifference as he flipped a long leg over the back of the chair to sit in the seat. No, it – whatever *it* was – would never happen to him again. That look on his face said he meant business. That curl of his lip – an almost dare you to try *it* again. That set of his shoulders almost waiting…he'd been hurt once, and he'd be damned if he'd allow that to happen again.

There'd be no repeats in Sean's life. No second chances. She doubted he knew what the word forgiveness meant. Yet he was here. At this workshop.

"Robin?"

Robin jerked, realizing that both Sean and Jenna were

staring at her as she'd stared blatantly at Sean. Color washed up her neck. Jenna's look was curious. Sean however, his look was purely aggressive. Shit. She straightened, plastered an apologetic smile on her face, and rushed to say, "I'm sorry. My mind was just caught on other things."

Out of the corner of her eye, she saw Sean's lips slide in a downward smirk. He didn't believe her. Knowing she'd be in for a very long week if they didn't get off on the right foot, she gave him a real smile and apologized sincerely.

His gaze narrowed in surprise.

She turned her gaze back onto Jenna's approving look and almost smiled again. Damn, she was going to turn into a real Girl Guide if she wasn't careful. Still, she hadn't meant to pry or be too inquisitive – not here. Everyone had secrets. And they were entitled to them.

Especially these people.

"It's fine. I don't mind if you look," he said mockingly.

The insinuation in his face had her back stiffening and her shoulders going straight. She turned to face him head on. "Good, then I'll look."

She returned his look with a mocking one of her own, her gaze sweeping him from head to foot. Then she gave him a tight smile, watching as one of his eyebrows shot straight up. So he wasn't used to people standing up for themselves. Especially women. Interesting. She filed that tidbit away.

"What do you see?" This time he seemed genuinely curious, not mocking.

She hesitated. She shouldn't tell him. He was an unknown quality to her. Violence lurked under the surface.

"Go ahead," he scoffed. "It's not like you know anything about me."

Still, Robin held back. She glanced over at Jenna to see

her watching the exchange, a tiny smile playing at the corner of Jenna's mouth. Damn. She wasn't going to step in and help.

Screw it. He'd asked, so he might as well know. "I see a man who's been so badly hurt he doesn't give a shit about anyone or anything – and especially not the world in general."

Silence.

He leaned forward and studied her face, what he could see of it. She glared at him defiantly.

"I thought the head doctor sat in the other chair." He snorted. "What are you, some kind of amateur hobbyist? You like to dig into people and see what makes them tick?"

"I like to watch people," she said, holding the defensive note tight inside. "And there are a lot of people out there to watch."

"Then watch *them*. Not me." After delivering that short terse message, he sat back and stared at Jenna.

At least the attitude was gone. She turned to face Jenna. "So what is the assignment?"

Jenna rifled through her papers but as far as Robin could see, it was more a ruse to give the two of them time to calm down. As if. Robin waited impatiently for Jenna to reorganize the papers then pick up the top one.

"A friend of mine coordinates special programs," Jenna said, peering over her paper at Robin as she added, "at a local hospital."

Robin stiffened. Nothing like bringing up hospitals to push her buttons. Then Jenna would know that. Forcing herself to relax, she tried to stem the panic that was churning in her gut. If just the word hospital could do that to her...

"BC Children's Hospital," Jenna said.

Robin gasped. No, not a children's hospital. Robin stared

at Jenna in shock. She didn't understand why her feet hadn't already taken her the hell away from this room and from this woman. She didn't dare plead with Jenna for a new project but damn it, she wanted to.

She couldn't do children.

Not today. Not tomorrow. Never.

"Andrea has agreed to have you and Sean spend some time there so you can complete this report."

Robin went numb inside. Everything shut down. She couldn't hear Jenna's words. She wouldn't hear them. But the response tumbled from her lips. "You do understand that you are subjecting these children to a horrific sight – right?"

Jenna smiled. "Am I?

She didn't dare look at Sean to gauge his reaction. Then again, he'd likely have no problem with this part.

It didn't matter. She couldn't do it. She couldn't do hospitals. She couldn't do children.

Shuddering, she stood up and stumbled against her chair. She half-registered that Sean had leapt to his feet to help her but she managed to avoid him. *Leave. Get away.* That was all she could think about. She had to escape.

She reeled backwards, then seeing a space between the chair and the wall, she took it, bolting for her freedom. For a world that didn't involve projects, hospitals…or children.

SEAN TURNED BACK to look at Jenna. "Well, aren't you going to go after her?"

Jenna smiled in that calm, serene way of hers. "No, I'll wait for her to come back."

"Come back?" He twisted around to look at the way Robin had raced out then turned back to glare at Jenna. "Why the hell would she?"

"Because it's what she wants." She lowered her head to read the documents in front of her.

Frustrated, Sean didn't know what to do. He glanced around at the others but outside of the casual glance his way, no one appeared to have noticed Robin's outburst.

"Why don't I do the project on my own? You can come up with a different one for her." Hell, he could do that easily. He didn't necessarily like children, but he didn't hate them. Not wanting to do something was not the same as being incapable.

All of a sudden he realized he was standing awkwardly in front of Jenna, trying to figure out what just happened. While he could empathize with Robin for Jenna pushing her buttons, she knew there'd be lots of that happening this week. She should have been prepared for it.

If anyone could prepare for sudden silent sabotage of one's deepest fears...

Then again, he had to trust in Jenna. She'd had incredible results with her program. If she could help Robin – good. He didn't trust anyone – particularly when it came to his head or heart.

And as long as Jenna stayed out of his head, she could do what she needed to do to help Robin. Because Robin obviously needed her. Although he'd suggest using something a lot less violent than the two-by-four Jenna had already hit her with.

The noise level in the room continued and somehow...the other participants managed to ignore what was happening in this corner...or were doing a good imitation of it. Likely it was a case of self-preservation as they'd be here themselves soon. He glanced around and caught a couple of people looking up, only to drop their gaze when he caught them staring at him, but he got that reaction a lot from people.

He stared down at his feet and considered his own actions. It seemed he'd acted out of character himself. He'd jumped to his feet to help Robin when he'd seen her distress, his hand out to her. He'd instinctively tried to go after her. Even now, he could barely stifle the urge.

And how did that work? Normally he wouldn't have given a shit. He didn't get involved in people's lives. He hated drama. Except in the case of his sister.

For her, he'd do anything.

But Robin wasn't his sister. She didn't look or sound or act like her. So why the hell had he reacted? Or was it because Robin hurt like Paris hurt?

"Sean? Why don't you sit down?"

He turned back to stare at his empty chair and then at Jenna. He really was standing there like a dolt in the middle of the room. He relaxed his hand, realizing for the first time that he'd been standing with clenched fists.

Shit.

Catching her concerned glance, he said, "I'm fine." And threw himself into the chair to wait. If Jenna could sit there calmly, then so could he. He slumped lower in his chair, leaned his head back and closed his eyes.

This place was making him crazy already.

"I'm sorry."

Robin's soft voice hit him hard, the hurt in her tone making his stomach cramp. Her simple apology hit him harder. She said it easily, the words flowing off her lips. He had so little practice he doubted he could have done so well in these awkward circumstances.

He opened his eyes and rolled his head sideways to see Robin standing in front of him and Jenna – much as he had a moment ago with her hands clenched into fists. He stared at the long fingers, seeing the white-knuckled grip, and saw his sister in her yet again. That was so Paris. Take a hit, run away long enough to collect herself, then come back and face the music – or more often than not – take another hit. It both pissed him off and made him admire her. Something he didn't want. He didn't want to feel anything for anyone. Especially not others as screwed up as these people were.

Damn, he needed a shrink. And groaned. Look where the hell he was. He turned to watch Jenna.

Jenna smiled up at her gently. "That's fine. I'm glad you're feeling better. I only need another moment to finish the instructions."

Robin sat down on the edge of her chair and listened quietly.

He gave Robin full points for demeanor. She appeared locked down but was holding on. He couldn't have been so calm. A few moments later, he wasn't calm at all.

Shocked, he listened to the rest of Jenna's final instructions. "What are you talking about? I'm not going to sketch these kids."

Hearing a strangled sound from beside him, he glanced over at Robin, remembering her earlier words to Jenna. Why would the kids be scared? What the hell was going on here? He hated knowing there were undercurrents he didn't understand. He was only here for his sister's sake. Hell, she was the one that should be here. Paris loved kids. She'd do fine with this project.

Him not so much. Good thing he didn't give a damn. As his glance slid across Robin's face, he thought he caught a glimpse of something, but he'd just missed it. His eyes drifted past then hit reverse.

And locked on Robin's face. Was that a tear? Not that he could see much of her with hair covering most of her face. What the hell was going on here? His gaze switched from Jenna's, which was full of compassion, to Robin's, whose head was down as she stared at her feet. Her lower lip trembled, too.

Ah shit.

There were a lot of things in life he could handle and there were a lot he couldn't. A lady's tears topped that last list.

"Sean, you don't have to," Jenna paused before adding smoothly, "In fact, I want you to sketch Robin with the kids."

Robin groaned softly as if in pain.

Hating this, Sean glared at the woman who had the ability to get under his skin like no other. She saw things... private, personal things... "How did you even know that I draw?"

Jenna's lips slowly tilted into a full-blown smile that made his stomach roll. What was she up to? "You were doodling in the evening lectures – something to keep you occupied while your sister attended," she added the last bit with wry humor. "And those doodles were good. Not only that, but you are a seriously gifted artist."

"Really?" He threw up his hands. "So what if I doodle? That's it. I don't do portraits." After a moment, he added, "And I certainly don't do pretty."

Now her smile deepened with understanding and empathy. He couldn't look. He shifted his gaze in Robin's direction. Her eyes were downcast, her hands clasped on her knees as if not even hearing the conversation.

Sean waited in uncomfortable silence. Damn it. "Look," he said, exasperated and starting to feel cornered, a situation guaranteed to get his back up. He hated being forced into doing anything. "Just give us the assignment and we'll take it from there."

This time, Jenna laughed. "You already have it."

He stared at her, his mind trying to grasp what it was obviously missing. "What? Just draw pictures of Robin and the kids? That's it."

"No, that's not it. You need to find a theme that fits Robin. I want you to study her and see the theme that runs through everything she does. Everything she is. And that's what you draw. Not Robin and the kids. The theme of Robin."

She stood up, and Sean realized he wasn't going to be able to ask much more. "Wait," he said, "Why did you pair me up with Robin?"

And Jenna's smile brightened. "Thank you for asking that," she said. "As part of your assignment, at the very end, you will answer that question for me."

"Ah hell," he muttered. Served him right for opening his mouth. He should have known better. After all, his mouth had gotten him into a lot of trouble as a child.

But like any other stubborn, knot-headed male, he'd grown more defiant, angrier, and the cycle had just repeated.

Robin didn't seem to be too affected by the conversation. She still seemed completely frozen in place.

"I'll leave you to think about this for a few moments while I go and discuss another group's projects with them." And she stood up and walked back to the rest of the participants, calling out two other people's names. When Sean turned back to Robin, it was to find her walking out the door to the main lobby. Alone.

Chapter 4

Robin walked into the dining room and took a seat in the corner at the far end, her back to the wall. The one place where she felt safe. From here, she could watch everyone else. Damn, there was Sean. She didn't want to have lunch with him. In fact, she wanted as little to do with him as possible. He disturbed her on so many levels.

Not only because he'd seen her little emotional breakdown, but because of his sudden jump to help and his standing between her and Jenna. He might not realize how that looked, but Robin knew. Jenna would also know exactly what it meant. She doubted Sean had any idea there was a white knight lurking inside that cold, derisive exterior.

He might have his mile-high defenses between him and the real world, but it appeared to be a little thin when he came in contact with girls in trouble.

Sean walked over and sat down across from her.

Because he was okay to leave his back exposed to the others and had just enough self-confidence to not give a damn, irritation flared.

"There are other places to sit," she muttered, not capable of being abrasive and cold.

"There are. But as we need to discuss some of the issues about this project," he motioned for the waitress to come over before turning back to her. "I figured this would be a good time to get a few things settled."

She stared at him. "Like what?

"Bus or car?"

"Bus."

Instant and honest. She hated travelling in cars. Not since her accident. She took the bus everywhere.

"Okay, maybe I should have said truck or bus."

She stopped and frowned at him. "Truck?"

"I have a heavy duty Dodge Ram."

She watched the water droplet on the side of her water glass slide down the side. She touched it with her fingertip and ran the wetness across the glass. She sighed. "Still a bus."

"Fine. But you might want to consider that it will mean being in each other's company for longer, and it'll be harder to get to the hospital on a daily basis."

She stiffened and turned her gaze to look outside the window. "Why the hospital?" she murmured.

"I wasn't exactly thrilled to be going there myself, but as it's Jenna's project and we came here trusting in her…"

Robin shot him a scornful look. "Like you give a shit. Why are you here anyway? It's not like you want to be helped. And if you're not doing this for yourself, why are you here?" Her mind spun on the possibilities. She couldn't help testing a couple of them. "Unless you're being forced to attend? Or attending to help someone else?"

He stared at her. "Why the hell would I sit through this garbage and do this stupid report for someone else?"

There wasn't much redeeming about that tone of voice, but there was something…something in his eyes that said she was on the right track. "Because you want to help someone. You're a fraud, you know?"

He leaned forward, his fists clenched. "If you were a man,

I'd…"

She leaned forward, glaring at him nose to nose and said, "What? Punch me out? Is that how you solve everything? Physical violence?"

An odd look came over his face. He took a shaky breath and sat back. He stared out the window at the people walking by. Just then, the waitress came and asked for their order. Robin ordered a cheeseburger and a salad. Sean, without even looking at the menu, ordered a burger and fries.

"That's what I mean. You want to wreak violence, but only a small part of you does. I have no doubt," she rushed to say at the glint coming into his eyes, "that given an opportunity to beat down on someone, you'd dive right in. But they'd have to deserve it."

And damn if he didn't stare back at her like she'd just lost her head. "What the hell are you talking about?" He shook his head. "You know nothing about me."

She smiled. "I know more than you think."

SHE BETTER NOT. Brooding, he sat across from one of the biggest mixed-up females he'd met in a long time. Of course he'd also seen more of her than he had anyone else in a long time. She'd had a breakdown at the thought of the children's hospital, ran away, came back, then chose a seat at the furthest corner in the restaurant to watch everyone like a hawk. She might be studying him, and damn, she seemed to be doing a good job of understanding him too, but she didn't *know* him.

If she really knew him, she'd have run screaming out the door already.

Like everyone else had.

He wasn't the most popular guy. That was okay. He had

his sister. Paris was softer, gentler than he was. She'd taken the path of least resistance and had suffered more for it then. He'd taken the full frontal aggressive route, but he was suffering more now.

At least that's what Paris said he was doing. He thought it was all psychobabble. Still, he loved her. She loved him. They had each other, and there'd never been anyone else in their lives for more than a night or two. Neither had a partner in any real sense of the word – only each other. Through the tough times, that had been enough.

Except Paris wanted more in her life. Children. A husband. To be loved in every sense of the word. Sean wasn't sure that she could ever have such a thing. And he knew he couldn't. So it was not something he'd ever brought into his psyche as a wish or a want. Why yearn for what he couldn't have? But Paris did, and by God, he'd do what he could to see her get it.

One of them deserved to know what happiness was.

"What is it?"

The voice penetrated the black cloud in his mind. He started, realizing he'd been glaring out the window. With considerable effort, he pulled himself out of the place he always ended up in – regardless of his best efforts to not go there.

Moodily, he played with the fork on the table. Pivoting it over end to end. He didn't know what to say.

"Never mind. It's obvious that the subject is painful."

He raised his gaze to stare at her, marveling that her hairstyle completely hid the one half of her face. Why? Was she blind in that one eye to the extent that it didn't bother her to only see with half her normal vision?

"It's not painful," he said abruptly. Then frowned. Why

the hell had he said that?

"Well, it can't be pleasant. You looked like you wanted to kill someone."

He smiled darkly, remembering his thoughts. "Can't. That's already been done."

She raised her eyebrows and narrowed her gaze at him.

Let her think he was a killer. Let her think the worst of him. That would keep her away.

"Well, if that's the case, you didn't kill them."

Damn. Was she for real? "Who are you, Pollyanna?"

It was her turn to frown. "I don't know the reference."

He waved his hand. "Really? Loosely, it means you have a positive-look-only-on-the-bright-side-of-life attitude."

"I don't," she protested. "I'm nothing like that."

"So you decided I haven't killed anyone? Are you nuts? I'm perfectly capable of killing."

"Oh, absolutely." She grinned. "But only in the right circumstances."

He stopped in the act of picking up his coffee cup, stared, then shook his head. "You aren't making any sense." Trust him to get paired with a lightweight in the brain department.

"You are capable, but you haven't done it yet. That's probably part of the anger. You wanted to be able to do something like that, but you couldn't…"

Just as he was about to lash out at her again, she added, "…someone beat you to it."

Holy crap. She was dangerous. How the hell had she figured that out? And what was he going to do about it?

Just as he was about to open his mouth and Lord only knew what was about to pour forth – because he had no idea – the waitress arrived and placed full steaming plates down. He had a massive amount of fries in front of him. On cue, his stomach grumbled. The waitress was rattling off something about enjoying their meal, but he was already reaching for one long particularly good-looking fry on his plate – when it was snatched out from under him.

Astonished, he could only follow its trail where it disappeared into Robin's mouth.

She caught his look and grinned. Then she laughed and laughed.

When she could, she said, "Sorry, that fry had my name on it." She giggled again. "And the look on your face was so worth it."

Stunned, but at her huge face-splitting smile that completely transformed her features, he picked up another fry and studied her. When she'd laughed, her hair had moved slightly. Now that she was eating, the hair was brushed out of her way with a quick movement of her hand. And he realized that the hair was more than a style. It was a front. Behind which hid scars. And from what he could see, they were long and ugly.

Hence the comment about what Jenna might be subjecting the children to.

He ate slowly, thinking about all the things her and Jenna had said…and not said, and realized that this was likely one of the core issues why Robin was here. The one side of her face was stunning with pure white skin and huge green eyes that could cloud with emotion or twinkle with laughter. Her hairstyle was dramatic and eye-catching. But she kept to herself and avoided letting anyone see the other side of her face. And now he understood why.

What impact it was going to have, he didn't know. But as they had a lot of work to get done, maybe honesty was the best policy.

Deciding to be upfront, he asked, "What happened to

your face? House fire or car accident?"

She stilled, then choked on her food. She swallowed hard, her gaze flickering in his direction then back at her burger. He kept his gaze steady, figuring he already knew the answer.

Finally, she reached for the glass of water and took a long drink. Her voice was cool and controlled as she said, "Why?"

"Considering what we have ahead of us, I'd appreciate knowing how your face became scarred."

She stared at him, belligerent but direct. God, he loved that about her. She never seemed to back down. Maybe it would get irritating if she turned out to be one of those women who needed to pick fights to clear the air or one who just liked to cause trouble – create a little drama. Yet it was refreshing to see someone with enough backbone to stand up to him.

"I'll tell you if you tell me how you got your scars."

Ouch. He hadn't seen that one coming. He settled back slightly. "What scars?"

She used her fork to point at the open collar of his shirt, then moved it to the side of his neck by his ear before it finally dropped to his hand. Scarred areas visible to the eye of anyone looking. He'd given up trying to hide the scars a long time ago. They were small and not unsightly. The biggest scars were inside. Of course it was a different story once he took his shirt off. But that rarely happened in daylight and as he wasn't physically self-conscious – who gave a damn?

But she was right. They both had scars. If he wanted answers, then she had the right to ask for answers as well. His usual lie well-prepared, he opened his mouth and out came the truth instead. "I was abused as a child."

His own gaze widened in shock as the truth came out. A truth he never shared. Jenna knew. Paris knew of course.

She'd been there. But that was it. Except for the odd doctor and social worker or case worker. People without faces. Where he was a number only. A statistic to help fill in the dots on their data graphs.

Her eyes widened first in shock then softened in sympathy.

That part he didn't like. He said brusquely, "Your turn."

"It was a car accident." She winced. "My father was driving my mother, brother, and me to a special event. I'm the only one that survived."

And damn if she didn't chip away at another stone on the defensive wall he'd built to keep others out. A wall he'd never been in danger of having any breach before.

But this woman...she had weapons he had no defenses against.

One of them was her forthright honesty.

Chapter 5

ROBIN PLOWED THROUGH her cheeseburger, her mind screaming with things she wanted to say. Only her mouth was focused on getting the food down. She had wondered when she'd seen the small scars. If he'd been abused like he said, chances were there were many more scars under his clothing. Ones he could hide. She couldn't.

She wished they didn't have to go to the children's hospital. Her stomach twisted at the thought. Not to mention she had to get there somehow first.

Given the scale of her accident, she rarely shared the details. There was no point. It was hard enough to deal with people's reaction to her face – and the rest of her body, but if they knew the rest – yeah, that was more than she could handle. At least most of the people in the hospital either knew already or didn't bother asking many questions. They'd seen and heard it all before. She had no idea how they could handle all the sad cases day in and day out, but they did, and for that she was grateful. They'd made her time in the hospital that much easier. Not easy, mind you. There was nothing easy about this process.

"Are you having reconstructive surgery done?

A simple and calm question.

She responded in kind. "I've had many. There are many more to go." She shrugged. Might as well tell him the truth.

"I've had enough. Of always being in the hospital. Of trying to deal with the pain and the drugs. Of slowly recovering. The cycle just never ends."

He nodded. "So you've put them on the back burner for now."

"It sounds simple, doesn't it?" She quirked her lips, staring down at her plate, not seeing the half-demolished food. "But it's not. No one understood when I said enough."

"No one else is going through what you are going through, so how could they? At the most, people can empathize – they can't understand unless they've been there."

God, he was scary. He understood. And by his own words, he'd been there. She assessed the small scars and then studied the broad shoulders. He'd likely had a few surgeries himself.

"The shrink stuff is hard, too," she muttered.

"Actually," his voice deepened, "I think the shrinks are the worst." His gaze wandered over her face, studying the side she carefully kept hidden from the world. "I could deal with the physical pain as I healed, but the emotional pain, the healing of the mind – now that part was torture."

And he went back to eating his fries.

She understood so much of what he'd just said and yet he said it so casually. He'd admitted so much freely. It made her question her assumptions about him. She didn't think he'd open up easily, yet he'd admitted so much so fast.

Maybe they had more in common that she'd first thought.

Her cell phone dinged. She checked the incoming text then winced. "Jenna says the person we're to meet is available after 1pm today."

Sean, his own phone in his hand, said, "Good."

She glanced over at him in surprise. "What's good about it?"

"The faster we do this, the faster it's over."

She couldn't argue with that.

"Back to the earlier question – my truck or the bus? I understand why the bus given your history, but the truck would be more private and faster. We'd be there in less than fifteen minutes."

He waited, seemingly unconcerned about her answer. She wanted to take the damn bus. "Truck."

And found satisfaction in the flicker of surprise in his eyes. He didn't know her as well as he thought. Then again, as she stared at her hand starting to shake with nerves, maybe she didn't know herself either.

HE WONDERED WHAT her impulse would cost her. Would she actually get in his truck? He knew driving was riskier, but in his truck, she was as safe as anything other than fate could keep her. It wasn't new but it was big and solid.

He paid the lunch bill, aware that she hadn't even noticed, now all balled up inside at the idea of sitting in a vehicle again. Then again, this is what these types of sessions were all about. He could help her do this.

He was good at helping out. It kept the focus off him.

Grasping her arm above the elbow, he led her out to the vehicle, not giving her time to back out. If he let her go to her hotel room and change or even collect something to bring with them, she'd changed her mind. Better to drag her forward and have her face this.

She moved like a robot beside him. Perfect.

He clicked the remote lock and unlocked the passenger

door. He led her straight there, opened the truck door, and half-lifted her in. Without wasting any movement, he reached across and snapped her seatbelt in place and snugged it up tight. Then he shut the door and walked around to his side.

She never said a word.

Neither did she move a muscle.

He hopped in, buckled up, and started up the engine. To ease the silence, he turned on the radio, then after a careful look around, he pulled the truck out of the hotel parking lot. A good driver already, he drove extra careful today.

Once he was back out on the main street, which was a short straight run up to the hospital, he glanced over at her. That she was still sitting and hadn't tried to bolt said a lot about where she was at in life right now. His gaze landed on her white-knuckled grip on the seatbelt strap. Or not.

"You're doing great. We're almost there."

She made a small, almost indiscernible sound.

"Another couple of minutes more," he said quietly. Sure enough, he could almost see the huge building from the road. He pulled ahead and made the turn to bring him into the back lot of the hospital. He heard Robin let out a heavy raspy breath.

"How did you know where to go?" she asked her, her voice subdued.

"I've lived in Vancouver all my life." He winced. "And it's the only children's hospital here."

There was a long silence as she digested his words. "I'm sorry."

"Don't be. You didn't do it, and it was a long time ago."

"It might have been a long time ago, but that doesn't mean I have to like the cruelty."

He pulled into a parking space and turned off the engine.

It was only as he opened his door to exit that he realized that she was referring to his childhood. "I…" he said, slamming the truck door and coming around to help her out, "don't either."

Together, a truce of some kind settling inside, they walked into the building he'd spent way too much time in as a child and a young teen. If he wasn't receiving care, Paris was. She'd suffered so much more than he had. He'd been hurt, but she'd been victimized in the worst of ways over and over again. He'd been unable to stop it and when he had finally had the chance, like Robin had guessed, someone else had done the job for him.

Maybe that was a good thing. He didn't think once he'd started stabbing the bastard that he'd have been able to quit until the old man was nothing but hunks of raw meat.

He had to wonder what his life would have been like if the rage that had consumed him that day hadn't spent itself. There'd been one cop whom he'd swung at, the bloodthirst and rage still burning bright, who'd let him hit it out, kick and punch and fight until he couldn't fight any more, and the cop never once laid a hand on him in retaliation. Only as a way to restrain him so he didn't get hurt himself. When he'd finally crumpled to the ground, a mess of bleeding raw emotion, the cop had said that he now needed to help his sister.

From that moment on, he'd been there for her like he hadn't been able to be there for her before.

He thought of that cop a lot but hadn't seen the man since. What did it take to be someone who could see the need in a child to pound someone to the ground and take the blows while not hitting back? To come from a place of such deep understanding that he allowed himself to be the target for as long as that child had needed? Did that cop know he'd saved Sean's soul that day, even as Paris had saved his life earlier?

Since that day, Sean had never had the anger return to the same extent. Whenever it did rise up now, it was lighter, softer, and less intense. He knew that one day that rage would no longer be there. He could see that now. The cop must have seen it then.

For that, Sean would always be grateful.

He glanced over at Robin and wondered how she'd vented.

Had she vented?

Or was she, like Paris, walking around, the raw wound open and still oozing day in and day out without ever having a way to heal?

He couldn't think of anything worse.

At least he'd managed to punch and kick out at the world at the damage that had been inflicted on him and his beloved sister. His hard-won healing had started from that point forward.

Chapter 6

THE TRUCK RIDE was over. She'd actually ridden in a vehicle again – and survived. She wanted to laugh and jump and cry all at the same time. Only she was afraid it would end in tears – hysterical ones at that. It was stupid to feel so overwhelmed. She'd call the venture a success but as it would not have happened without Sean putting her in, buckling her up, and locking her down to keep her there, it was hardly *her* success. She'd been white-knuckled the whole time. She glanced down at the nail indents in the palm of her hands. At least she hadn't cut the skin.

The sun shone high above, a bright beautiful sky signaling that she was alive and life was good. Privately, she admitted, now that the trip was over, it hadn't been that bad.

Now if she could get through the next hour or so.

As if afraid that she'd bolt, Sean hooked her arm into his and led the way through the imposing double-door entrance of the huge building ahead of them.

Inside the hospital, Robin tugged back on Sean's arm to stop and look around. And take some deep breaths. Just the noise, the smell…memories hurtled back into her mind, bringing back the same panic she'd experienced before her last surgery. And memories from even before that. Tears collected at the corner of her eyes.

She couldn't do this.

She didn't want to do this.

She *had* to do this. Oh God. She closed her eyes and worked on regaining her sense of balance. It was either that or take off back to Sean's truck. She shuddered. And then what? Get back in the vehicle and wait for him to do his thing here?

So scared she could hardly move, a sound slowly penetrated. Off to the left, someone wept quietly. Low deep sobs. Female sobs. Sobs that seared into Robin's heart. She'd heard enough of those. From patients she couldn't help. From the families of those she couldn't help. From herself.

Hospitals seemed to thrive on pain. Sure, many patients walked out in better shape than they walked in, but so many never walked out. These places were both lifesavers and the worst kind of hell for some. She wasn't sure which side of that divide she stood on right now. She hadn't been able to handle it the last few times she'd been in one.

Sean tugged on her hand, bringing her attention back to her surroundings. She glanced over at him, seeing the concerned frown on his face. She shrugged, struggling for control, and said, "I'm fine."

"You don't look it."

"I just want to look around." She didn't dare tell him that this was hard for her. Hell, it wasn't like he didn't get it. She'd been standing there like an idiot for the last five minutes. Obviously something was wrong with her. Did Sean understand what she'd gone through in a different hospital? Alone?

Even if he did, he didn't know about her connection to *this* hospital. She'd sworn to never go back into a hospital for all the reasons she was experiencing right now. The panic. The inability to breathe. She might have panic attacks in her life now, but she swore they'd started while she'd been in the hospital.

She was a mess, and a lot of that was triggered by being in here.

At another hard tug on her hand, she squared her shoulders obstinately, needing another moment to try and see her surroundings rationally.

The reception was oriented to younger children, with the sitting area decorated with bright animal pictures painted on the wall. The large waiting area was mostly a playroom for the younger kids. There was so much here, but was geared to the kids and not the parents whose lives were torn by the events that brought them here.

Sean tugged at her again, nudging her toward the elevators on the left side. With a last glance at the full playroom, she followed him. Tough day already for her. She'd taken a trip inside a truck and was even now standing inside a hospital. Hard to believe.

But she'd managed so far. Now to get through the next hour…then do it all over again in reverse. She was afraid she'd lose her lunch as her stomach started to heave. Instead, her gut locked down. Her chest squeezed tight. She couldn't breathe.

"Are you okay?" Sean gave her arm a slight shake.

After swallowing hard, she shot him a look as her world stabilized. She was here with him, for a report. Not for a trip down memory lane. Thankfully, she had something to focus on. She gave herself a shake and straightened her shoulders. "I'm fine."

"You should be," he said in a serious tone. "You've already beat back several demons."

That surprised her. She shrugged dismissively. "Doesn't feel like I came out the winner."

"That's because the day isn't over." And he grinned.

The kindness and light in that grin shocked her. Warmed

her. It almost felt like a hug.

Just then, the elevator doors opened and she was saved from having to answer. They stepped out. Sean automatically turned right and she followed. She had the name of the person that Jenna had said would be waiting for them but didn't have a clue where to find this person.

Sean appeared to. He walked through a series of doors and led her into a different world. As if he understood where these doors were actually going to take them. A world he recognized.

One of chaos. One of noise. One of children.

As if a whistle had been blown, the children realized they had company.

Silence fell. The kids stared at Sean, and then shifted to Robin.

She gasped. Her insides locked down and fear pulsed through her. *She could not do this.* She dropped her gaze to the floor, grateful her hair covered her face.

And she shut down.

IN AN INSTANT, silence switched to chaos.

Sean stared at the craziness going on in the large room. After giving him and Robin both a long assessing look, the kids returned to doing what they'd been doing originally. Playing. There were multiple couches, tables and even a couple of beds on both sides of the room. At this end, some children were lying quietly watching the others. In the middle and at the far end, there was chaos as children played video games and....

Some kind of party must be going on. He didn't remember any laughter or screaming for joy when he'd been here as a patient. And he'd been here lots. Not long enough to get to know anyone. But often enough for the staff to get to know him. Then again, he'd never been in a common room like this one.

He couldn't help that shrinking sensation with his emotions before they rolled free in a totally inappropriate way. At least, inappropriate for here. He couldn't rant and rave over the things done in the past anymore. He'd dealt with it all as much as he could – at the time and ever since. But every once in a while something – someone – got to him.

Like this group of kids. When this was over, he was going to hit the bar tonight. Not that he could drink himself into oblivion. He never did. That required a level of trust of the fellow man that he didn't have. But a few to take the edge off – maybe. No. Definitely.

"Hello?" A tall woman in a nurse's matched set strode toward them, a spring to her step and a bounce to her ponytail. Her smile – it was breathtaking.

Sean took a deep breath and raised his voice slightly to be heard over the din. "Hello. We're looking for Andrea Schulenburg."

"And you found her." The woman tapped her name tag, bringing Sean's attention to the name and position she held but before he could read it, she'd already turned and called back to two kids who appeared to be trying to have a sword fight with plastic knives.

A grin tugged at his mouth. He did love the resilience of kids. He had no idea why any of them were here but there were kids in bandages, wheelchairs, and casts. Some appeared to be missing limbs and still recovering from surgery, and still others were prone and hooked up to multiple tubes. Some of those kids lay unaffected; others smiled wistfully at the other kid's antics. The nurse called out. "Mark and Brian, no bouncing on the beds, please."

The boys jumped up and landed on their butts one final time before putting the plastic knives away. Interesting that she'd complained about the jumping but not the swordplay. While he'd been a patient here, he didn't remember being allowed either. Then again, it probably depended on the group of kids that were patients at any one time, group dynamics being what they were.

"I presume you are Sean Wilson and Robin Childers."

Sean nodded, seeing Robin not acknowledging the question in any way, her head down. Her fists clenched and released in a pattern he knew all too well. He tried to cover for her, saying pleasantly, "Yes. Thanks so much for letting us come."

"The kids are happy to have some excitement to brighten up their day." She smiled up at them. "Sean, I understand you are doing an artistic study. Do you have some kind of plan for what you want to happen here? A theme that I can help organize the children for?"

Sean looked at Robin sideways, a little lost on that theme aspect. If she had anything to contribute? She'd gone so still.

As in frozen.

Crap. His protective instincts rose to the surface and he shifted slightly, deliberately placing himself in front of Robin. He wished he could do this report alone. Robin might *need* to do it, but he wasn't seeing any sign that she was *ready* to.

Andrea stared at him, waiting. Right, she'd asked something about the theme. Sean didn't know what to say. Hell, he had no idea himself. He shrugged. "I don't have a theme in mind yet. I'll be doing some sketches of the kids. So I just need a place to sit and work."

And a place for Robin to hide. She'd be of no use today. Not that he had any idea what she was supposed to do here anyway. It would have been good to know her issues with children were so traumatic. He had some issues too, but more than that, he wanted to keep his inner child at a distance. That child caused a ruckus when he was free.

Staying detached from these kids would be harder. If he could focus on the artwork, he could avoid getting hooked on the kids. He hoped.

"Just a table? Do you need the kids quiet?" she asked, doubt coloring her voice even as her eyes darted from one child to another.

"Ha." He laughed, gesturing at the room behind her. "That doesn't look possible."

A bright grin transformed her face again. "No, at least not for long."

"Motion," Sean said. "They are all in motion. That could make my job difficult."

Andrea laughed. "They are kids. As soon as they heal enough to be able to move, they are constantly in motion." Her smile slipped. "Many are in between treatments. This is an escape for them. A release. Until the next time. And it's just as important as their surgeries."

"Sleep hard and play hard." Sean watched the kids shift to yet another game. In a way, he was glad he'd seen this. He was here now as an adult. He could look back on the memories and keep them in their rightful place. This scene completely eclipsed his memories of the pain...and the shame. And that was a good thing. The sketches were going to be fun and lively. Just like the subjects.

Trying to pull himself out of the weird mood that had suddenly set in and yes, to compensate for Robin's odd behavior, he turned to look around and saw a small table off the side by the window. A couple of chairs were there on the opposite side. He pointed to it. "How about over there?"

"Actually, I was just about to ask if that would work." Andrea was already walking over and moving chairs about so there were two on one side and one on the other. "This should give you a decent amount of light, and you can see the kids from here."

Grabbing Robin's arm, he led her over. Once there, Sean dropped his bag on the table. It made a louder thunk than he was expecting.

Robin jumped. She stared from the bag to him and back at the bag as if just now seeing it for the first time. He frowned. What the hell? She was acting really out of it. And it didn't look like she'd be pulling herself together anytime soon. He was afraid she'd explode, she was wound up so tight.

In a sudden move, she grabbed a chair, pulled it back, and sat down. He watched her as she watched the kids surreptitiously. She was acting both fascinated and repelled… yet…there was a hint of loneliness, sadness. He turned to watch the same two boys who'd been sword playing and were now arguing, and he could almost understand.

He didn't have any good memories of childhood, but he understood what had been the best thing – Paris. Having his twin there meant he'd never been alone. They'd fought and played from instant to instant. In all things, the one lesson he'd learned as a child was to enjoy the moment. It was always over too soon.

Chapter 7

THE SMELL...
Robin kept a smile pinned to her face. The children wouldn't notice if it was real or not. They'd be too busy studying every aspect of her and making a decision based on nebulous things like instinct. Hopefully they'd ignore her. She needed them to. As she needed to ignore them. It was the only way she could survive the next hour. Just the sound of their play made the bile rise up the back of her throat. They'd see her any moment now. Damn. She'd turned her back on them, but they were kids.

They'd come closer any second now.

She swallowed hard, her mind racing for things she could say when they came. She didn't want to be mean to any of them – they were obviously going through stuff of their own, but no one here seemed to understand how much more trauma they'd go through if they saw her face.

She'd seen it firsthand. She knew how the kids would react. The adults had a hard time with her too... but it was the children she was trying to save. Damn Jenna. How could she do this to them? They were sweet, innocent little kids. They didn't need more monster faces to wake them up in the middle of the night. No child deserved that.

Lost inside, she was oblivious to what Sean was doing. A shudder slipped down her spine. What if she just left? She could sit out in the main lobby and wait. Though that wouldn't be fair to Sean. Except that she'd have to deal with kids there, too. Maybe if she could keep her face hidden and stay silent, they wouldn't realize she was here.

It would be best for everyone.

Andrea had disappeared somewhere – likely back to the far end where the kids were. Good. One less person here to make her feel uncomfortable. Immediately she kicked herself. God, how selfish. This wasn't about her. She was trying to save them.

"Robin?"

She glanced up enough to see Sean out of her one eye. He was frowning at her. Of course he was. She wasn't exactly contributing.

"Are you okay?"

For some reason, that pissed her off. Of course she wasn't okay. But she was here and that might not count very high in his book, but it did in hers. She could have bolted. Was still considering it, but as long as she remained, she'd count this as a good day. She just had to get through this.

"I'm fine," she said brusquely, against her best efforts to sound normal.

His eyebrow lifted and his lips twitched. "Right. I believe that." He dropped his head and lifted his pencil to the paper and drew the first line.

There was no hesitation in his movements. Not where he'd start or what he'd start with. His pencil hit the paper and moved swiftly in sharp strong lines.

She almost hated him for that confidence. That control. He didn't have to feel bad here. She didn't know what Jenna thought this project would do for her or Sean, but she knew Sean wasn't planning on taking it seriously. She wished she felt the same way. She could use a bit of attitude in her life.

She also could use a bit of healing. No, there was no point in fooling herself. She needed a lot more than a little. Realizing this was where she was going to be for the next hour, she closed her eyes and tried to disappear. Until a child's voice interrupted her.

"Hi."

"Hi," Sean said. "What's your name?"

"Jonathon, but you can call me Jon." The bright tone didn't hide the wobbly frailness of the boy's voice.

Robin froze, her heart hiccupping at the boy's name. She didn't want to open her eyes and look, but she couldn't help herself. Her brother's name had been Jonathon.

Peeking through her lashes, she studied Jon. The little boy appeared to be about eight years old, tight black curls covering his head. His face showed some damage, the reconstruction already in progress. He didn't look anything like her brother – thank heavens. That made it easier to gaze upon him. He stood beside Sean, his attention completely absorbed in Sean's movements. At least he'd ignored her. And maybe if she kept her eyes closed, he'd continue to do so.

"Hey, cool," the boy said in awe.

Sean laughed. "What's cool?"

Robin had to open her eyes to see. The little boy was pointing at Sean's picture. From her angle, she couldn't see what he was drawing, it all looked like random black lines. Not to the little boy apparently.

"You're an artist."

"Nah, it's just a hobby."

Robin heard something in his voice that made her look over to study his face. He was resistant to the idea of being an artist for some reason. She'd never seen anything he'd created, but she had to admit that the more he resisted, the more curious she got.

"Are you going to draw us?" He pointed to the nurse. "Andy said you were."

Sean nodded. "Along with Robin here."

Jon looked back at Robin, who dropped her lashes, then over to Sean then back again. "Are we going to see her face?"

Sean looked over at him. "You can't see it?"

"Sure. But I meant the part that she keeps hidden."

"Ask her."

"Nah." He leaned closer and dropped his voice, adding, "She doesn't look friendly." He backed away, shot one final look at Robin, and dashed back to the others.

Robin's gaze followed the child. The room appeared to be males only. Jon grabbed a small plastic car and vroomed it across the floor, completely at ease.

Boys. Thinking of that, she turned to check out what Sean was doing. And found his hand moving like wildfire across a large sketchbook. And she meant like wildfire. She wouldn't be surprised if smoke rose up from the paper. The look of concentration on his face was fascinating.

He was competent, focused…passionate.

She wished she knew what she was supposed to be doing for this project. Sean was supposed to sketching pictures of her *with* the kids. That meant she was supposed to be *with* the kids. Not sitting like a statue at his side. She got that. But how? Better she just stay in the shadows and let him do his thing.

Lord knew that's what she wanted to do – but it hardly seemed fair.

Not that fairness was high on her list of concerns at the moment.

SCARS

SEAN WATCHED HIS hand shift across the paper. As if controlled by another's hand. He couldn't be doing this. Or rather, he'd not sketched in this manner before. Then he really hadn't done much sketching, period. He'd joked to himself about giving Jenna stick figures. He'd done some nice stuff before, but not much of it, and he didn't have the time now to do a good job on all of them either. Not in a week. He had no idea how long it would take to complete this report because he didn't have a good grasp of just what he was supposed to be doing. It had been a long time since he'd actually completed any artwork. He was rusty.

He flexed his fingers, seeing the oversized knuckles, the slightly uneven shape. His knuckles were stiff, the fingers aching. He'd never thought to hold a pencil like this again. His father hated to see him with a sketchbook and pencil. The punishments had been severe. Memories flooded his psyche. His father, going into rage, grabbing his hands followed by that horrible crisp snapping sound... Broken pencils...broken fingers...broken dreams.

Easing his gaze from the image in front of him, he looked up and glanced down the room, catching Jon's sharp features, his quirky grin, his guileless eyes. His hand never hesitated.

If he was superstitious, he'd have tossed the paper away or better yet, burned it. But he'd started the picture consciously. He remembered making that decision to start on the right-hand side of the page center but slightly lower. He just didn't remember much else. That was because he'd been busy watching Robin.

Emotions swamped him, and his hand slowed. He shaded the shadow side of Jon's face, added a rough patch to his elbow. Thickened a wrinkle on his shirt.

His mind turned over what he'd seen. What he'd felt. What he'd witnessed. And they'd only been here for an hour…

Chapter 8

Robin tried to stay in the same place and watch the children. Tried but failed. Inside it was as if a scab she'd placed over her painful memories had been ripped off before the wound had a chance to heal. Memories of families. Memories of her brother. Of laughter. Of pain. Of being normal. Of never going to be normal again.

If she let it, the pain would cripple her. Send her back to a dangerous time if she wasn't careful. She'd had no family to hold her to reassure her that all would be well. No familiar face smiling lovingly at her. No loving voices telling her she'd be okay. She had always woken up alone, reliving the loss of her family each and every time.

She rubbed her eyes at the reality of her situation. She was alone. Right now, surrounded by children as she was, she'd never felt more lonely.

"It doesn't make any sense," she whispered.

There was a sudden stillness beside her. She glanced over at Sean, realizing he'd heard her. And his hand had stopped.

Hence the odd silence. The odd scratching sound had been going on in the background. A low level grating noise she'd barely noticed...until it stopped.

She wanted to look at his pictures, but for the same reason she didn't want to see any of it. She was scared he was sketching something she wasn't. But she was more scared that he'd see more than she wanted him to see and sketch exactly what she was.

A coward.

"Can we leave yet," she said in a harsh whisper.

Sean looked at her then cast a quick glance around the room before dropping his gaze to the page. "I'm almost finished."

She nodded but kept her eyes averted. How long had they been here? How long were they supposed to stay? She had no idea what arrangements Jenna had made.

"Okay. We're good." Sean stood up. The sound of his chair being pushed back pulled her out of her reverie. She stood up quickly, almost knocking her chair over. She hated her awkwardness. Hated the return of that instinct to run. That need to get the hell away.

Then as if a herd of elephants were rushing toward her, she realized several kids had raced toward them.

A fine tremor rippled through her. A faint film rose on her skin. And her breath caught in the back of her throat. She needed to get out of here.

Now.

SEAN WATCHED ROBIN escape from the room ahead of the kids. Again. It seemed like her normal defense when a situation became untenable. And apparently a group of kids was untenable. He packed up his pencils and tossed the bag over his shoulder as he was suddenly surrounded by the group of boys. "Goodbye guys."

"Bye," came a chorus from around him.

"Can we see the picture?"

He laughed. "I'll show you on our next visit."

"K."

"Are you coming back tomorrow?"

"Yes." That last question came from Jon. Sean grinned and waved at him. "See you tomorrow."

And he walked out. He had no idea where Robin had gone, but there were few places she could go. As it was, he found her waiting by the elevators, leaning against the wall with her eyes closed.

"Ready?"

She nodded but didn't look at him.

Silently, they moved downstairs and out to the parking lot. She got in with no trouble, almost uncaring, as if she was bothered by something much bigger.

He had no idea what. Or why. And was running short on empathy at this point. They'd both faced a few demons today. He couldn't believe the drawings he'd been working on. He was on a high. She was on a low.

Somewhere there had to be a meeting ground. Surely.

Instinctively, he stared down at his fingers and flexed them. Maybe the long break from sketching had actually helped his skill level improve.

He started the engine and drove back to the hotel. He checked the time. It was after 4pm already. They'd ended up being at the hospital for three hours. It had seemed to be half that time. A quick glance at Robin's clenched fists and he realized that for her, it had likely seemed twice as long as it had been.

Just minutes from the vibrant core of Vancouver city and only a few blocks from the hotel, he said, "Feel better?"

She never answered. He looked over to see her staring straight ahead, her face blank.

"Robin?"

No answer.

He really didn't know how if he should push or not. He was working on it but hated to get involved. Given a chance, he avoided people. Avoided attachments. He was a loner by choice.

So what the hell had happened to him that he was even caring enough to ask?

He pulled into the parking lot and turned off the engine. He turned to Robin, who still sat motionless. "Look, today must have been tough on you. I don't know what happened to scare you back inside yourself, but obviously something did. If you don't want to talk to me – fine. Then talk to Jenna at least. Talk to someone."

Slowly, she turned her head and stared at him. He winced at the bruised look on her face, the moisture glistening in the corner of her eye, and had a powerful want to know what had caused it.

And she had a powerful need to say it. To give voice to that agony inside, to admit it existed. To give it life that she couldn't.

His gut twisted. But not for him.

He'd been there before. Figured to never return but watching her…God, it brought up all of his own shit. Ha. Determinedly, he squashed that back down deep into his psyche.

So many people gave into their fear. And when fear took over, they lost the ability to fight. Then it was over before it started.

Something Robin appeared to have done.

He'd used anger to solve his problems. Not any better than Robin's method, but preferable as it empowered him. It was, however, difficult to control. Giving into the anger blinded him. And if he got in too deep, the rage made him incapable of rational reason – something he had to be mindful of. Still, anger had gotten him through the worst times of his life.

That it was just a front for the real problems didn't matter. This system worked for him.

Robin didn't appear to have an angry bone in her.

Forgiveness was the only way forward for both of them.

Robin might manage it in her lifetime.

In his…fuck that.

"Let's get you inside. Maybe a hot shower before dinner will help."

He hopped out and walked around the truck. He opened her door and nudged her forward. Silently, they moved through the hotel until Robin stepped into her room and locked the door. Standing outside, Sean heard the snick of the lock. Good. He walked toward his room, his cell phone already in his hand. Once inside, he called Jenna.

Chapter 9

ROBIN WAITED UNTIL she heard Sean's footsteps head back down the hallway. She collapsed backwards on her bed.

"Damn it."

She wanted to quit. Just walk away and count this as a bad deal. One she couldn't deal with. She'd tried and it didn't work. So she'd walk away. Try again another day. Another year maybe. Because that's how long it would be before she tried something like this again.

There was a knock on the door.

She ignored it.

The knock came again. "Robin? It's Jenna."

She groaned. She didn't need this. She wasn't ready. Everything was too raw. Too vulnerable.

"Robin, I'm not going to go away."

"Damn it."

She got up off the bed and walked to the door. She unlocked it and opened it to face her. "I'm tired."

"And stressed, and you've had a shock."

Jenna's voice was gentle. Caring.

Tears filled her eyes. She shook her head and backed into her room. Jenna followed. Robin sat down on the edge of her bed. She brushed away the tears. Jenna sat down beside her. Close but not touching. Robin desperately wanted a hug but knew it would be her undoing. "Tell me what happened."

"Nothing happened," she cried. "I sat there for hours in complete silence locked away in fear." She threw up her hands in defeat.

"Of the children?"

"I don't know. First the truck ride...maybe that started it." She tried to sort it out in her head, but it was still so dead inside. Unclear. Like walking through a fog. Or a land mine. She could never quite forget that Jenna would be analyzing everything she said. She gave a broken laugh. Then again, that's what she'd come here for.

"The hospital was the next button. The smell...it got to me immediately and after that, it got worse. I felt as if I walked through quicksand, going deeper and deeper with every step." She closed her eyes, hating the trip back through her miserable day. "I shut down before I got into the ward."

"So you went in afraid and expecting the worst."

Robin lifted her head to gaze at Jenna. "How could I not? You know the last time kids saw my face, they ran screaming from me."

Jenna smiled gently. "And did it happen today?"

A broken laugh escaped. "I didn't let it. I never let anyone see me." She shook her head in an exaggerated movement, highlighting the hairstyle across her face. "I kept my back to everyone, said nothing, and was the basic living statue you'd see on any street corner." She frowned at Jenna, finally understanding. "So no, it didn't."

"So then it was different than last time."

"Not really," Robin defended herself. "It was just as bad."

"Was it though?" Jenna was gently persistent. "Not really. You weren't laughed at. The children didn't mock you. They didn't run from you in terror."

"But I still hated it," Robin cried. "And it could have happened."

"Sure, but you hated it *because* you were expecting a disaster. Waiting for it to happen."

Robin swallowed and tried to stare back defiantly and couldn't quite make it. It took several tries then finally she managed to clear her dry throat. "You don't know what it was like...the fear choking me to the point where I can't see or hear or feel anything."

"I do understand." Jenna reached out a hand and gently rubbed her shoulder. "The thing is, you went there. On your own."

"And failed," she said bitterly. "Miserably."

"Oh no! Not at all," Jenna exclaimed. "Don't ever think that."

Robin threw herself backwards on the bed. "Are you kidding? That's the only thing you could call this. It was terrible. Publicly visible in body, but definitely concealing my face and hiding out, completely terrorized, inside."

"What did the kids do?"

"Nothing," she cried. "They did nothing."

"Nothing? As in they didn't speak to you? They crowded about Sean or they took off and did their own thing?"

Robin closed her eyes and tried to remember exactly what had happened. "They stayed down at their end, then I turned my back on them and didn't see anything else. After a while, a little boy walked over to see what Sean was doing. He was a big enough shock. I couldn't look at the others after him, so I have no idea if they were looking at me." She shrugged. "But everyone does."

"And if everyone does, why wear your hair like that? Why not pull it back so they can see? Then they will see and finally stop trying to look."

"Not likely." Robin ran her hands over her face. "That's not the way it works. They look but because they can't get close enough to really see enough, and because it's not polite to stare, they constantly try to get a clearer look. It's like always being under watchful eyes. As if they're waiting for me to give them all a chance to see just how bad the damage is."

"If it's just children, then let them. They will be honest. They will exclaim and ooh and aah, maybe cry out a little, and they will get over it."

"I'm sure they will – eventually. But in the meantime, they will scream and have night terrors. I can't be responsible for that!" She shuddered and swiped at the tears dripping down her cheeks. "I couldn't sleep for months after those kids ran screaming from me."

"But that was then. This is now," Jenna said firmly. "Your face has progressed from that time, and you're a different person."

"No," Robin replied. "I'm not. I'm still a monster."

SEAN SAT IN the dining room and brooded. No one came close. Good thing. He had no idea what he was supposed to do about Robin. He hoped he'd done the right thing by calling Jenna. That's what she was here for. That's what they were all here for. By rights he should be rejoicing that Robin had a breakthrough…or something. He just hoped it didn't break Robin.

In a black mood, he ordered a beer and sat quietly in the corner and drank. He should have food, but he wasn't hungry. He felt like he should have done more. But she wouldn't talk to him, so what more could he do? That's why he didn't like people clogging up his life. They were complications he didn't want.

And he wouldn't have let Robin get under his skin if it wasn't for the constant reminders about Paris. He'd have known how to help his sister. Robin was a stranger. Less of one now than she had been earlier, but still a stranger in many ways. Or rather, he felt he understood her more because of Paris, but she'd consider *him* a stranger. And that was a different story.

A plate of roast beef and veggies arrived in front of him. He looked up at the waitress in surprise. "I didn't order this."

"Jenna ordered it for you," she said with a smile. "I'll bring your salad in a moment."

Surprised, he watched her stop by another table and take their order. The smells wafting up from his plate smelled great. He was hungry. The food would go a long ways to help fill him up. The emotional pit wouldn't be so easy to fill, but at least he finally admitted that maybe the pit needed filling.

He took his first bite and smiled as Jenna sat down at the seat opposite him. "Thanks for dinner."

"Thanks for the heads up on Robin."

That took some of his appetite away. He stared down at his meal and asked in a low voice, "How is she?"

"Better now. Recuperating."

"She should eat," he said, forking up a bite. "It's been a long day."

"True. She might come down."

He studied the prof's beautiful face then shook his head. "You don't believe that."

"Well, I hope she does, but if she doesn't feel like being around other people, she can always order room service."

"True." He pondered that. "It would be better if she came

down."

Jenna's head tilted in acknowledgement. "That doesn't mean she can do more today." With a gentle smile, Jenna stood up and left.

He watched her slim figure sway between the other tables on her way out. He'd love to know her story. She was one attractive woman. And very empathetic. He didn't think that came easily. In fact, he highly suspected she'd gone through her own hell and had somehow come out the other side clean and intact, ready to help others.

Speaking of others…he pulled out his phone to text his sister when it buzzed in his hand. Paris. Of course, being twins, things like that happened all the time.

How is it?

He raised his eyebrows at that simplified phrase. Of course she meant the workshop. But what could he tell her? He texted back. *Fine.*

Such a simple answer, but what else was he supposed to say? That someone around him had a major breakdown and the process so painful and disturbing he wished he hadn't seen it? At the same time, he knew things were changing. Inside. Outside. He couldn't explain it, but the solid center he'd been standing on was…gone.

That it might be a good thing didn't change the discomfort of it.

The next text from his sister said, *Are you learning anything? How do you think the workshop would be for me?*

And that made him wince.

She'd likely do very well here. He didn't know why Jenna had suggested another session down the road would be more helpful, but he had to admit he didn't know how Paris would handle stressors like Robin had today.

Paris usually went all out or all in. There were no half measures for her. And although strong and caring, she was so very afraid inside.

He was hesitant as to what to tell her. How did he explain that for some, it was painful to be here? For others, like him, it was painful to watch others go through their stuff. And have his own issues flare. It was easy to stomp those issues back down deep inside for the moment, but it could get harder to keep a lid on them if the chain reaction of events speeds up.

He ordered another beer and stared out of the window, only just now realizing he'd picked the same corner of the dining room that Robin had earlier. He sat in the far corner, his back to the wall where he could watch the world go by. Like Robin had watched the world go by.

What was he going to do about her? A connection had formed between them, whether she was aware of it or not. Should he go and see her tonight or did he leave her alone and see how she was in the morning? He had no idea if the project was off…and a part of him would be relieved, yet another part would feel disappointed. He'd caught a glimpse of something he wanted for himself.

To free his inner artist.

He'd sketched like a demon today. He hadn't expected that. He had seen something in those kids' faces that had tore at his heart yet he'd managed to capture much of their uniqueness on paper – at least of Jon. He didn't need someone else to tell him the images were good, he knew they were. He could see it. He'd been waiting to see Robin's reaction to his drawings, but as she'd locked herself up inside, he doubted she'd even seen them.

He put down his beer bottle and went to stand up when he saw her.

Robin. Dressed in black, her skin whiter than usual, with shadows under her eyes and her shoulders straight. She was facing the world. She'd taken a hit, ran away, and was now back again. Interested, he sat down and waited to see what she'd do. This had been her pattern all day. He'd wondered where she'd learned to take the hit and still get back up – or was that a natural characteristic? It was something Paris had never learned. She'd taken the hit and stayed down out of striking distance.

Whereas for him, he'd taken the hit, but it had been a matter of pride to not go down. And if his legs were knocked out from under him, he'd jumped back up.

Robin strode into the room with a casual controlled air. But the furtive glances at the other occupants said much to her state of mind. The controlled mantle was in place, but it was thin. Too thin. He waited for her to see him. She was heading straight for him. Or for her spot.

She looked up, saw him, and her steps faltered.

He smiled at her. "Glad to see you're feeling better."

She made a small motion with her hand. "A nap helped."

No doubt it would, but he highly doubted that she'd had one.

"Do you want this spot?" He stood up and motioned to his seat.

Her lips quirked. "Thanks, but I'll be fine on this side." And she slid into the seat across from him.

Chapter 10

Robin studied Sean's face, noting the relief in his eyes. Had he been worried about her? To that extent? Surely not. He didn't know her. Then again, he'd been with her at the hospital. Seen her reaction.

She turned her gaze to look out the window. It was overcast and growing darker by the minute. Vancouver was known for its wet gray skies. Still, the summer had been good to them and the plants did need a regular amount of rain, so it was hard to complain. Besides, it suited her mood perfectly.

So why that compulsion to come down to the restaurant? She could have stayed safely hidden away in her room.

Lost as she was, she barely registered the voices beside her. She pulled herself back to hear Sean asking for a menu for her. She shook her head. "I'm not hungry."

He overruled her. "Bring her a bowl of soup and a salad please."

She stared at him in bemusement. Normally she'd have been pissed. Today, that required too much energy. "That's going to get you into trouble, you know."

He raised his beer bottle and took a healthy swig, but he kept his eyes on her.

"What is?" he asked when he could.

"Being a protector."

His eyebrows shot up. She wondered if he had any idea

how often he reacted like that. Or if it was only with her.

"I'm hardly a protector."

"Except that's exactly what you are. You kept everyone away at the hospital," she gave him a crooked smile. "Brought me home even though I was barely functioning, and then when I was safely in my room, you contacted Jenna to let her know I was in trouble."

He put the bottle on the table a little harder than necessary. "I only did what anyone would do."

"Really?"

The waitress returned just then to set a full bowl of some kind of cream soup in front of her and salad to the side.

Robin nodded toward the light meal in front of her. "Most people would not order me a meal."

"Well, someone did the same for me tonight, so I'm just passing it on."

But those eyes of his were watchful. Assessing.

"I'm fine you know." At least she was better than she had been. "It was a tough day, but I'm feeling more in control."

His gaze narrowed slightly but didn't ease back. It was as if he was probing to the very depths of her. She couldn't tear her gaze away. Somehow the tenor of the glance shifted from probing and distant to heating up, a shortening of that gaze so they were almost connected. It was…intimate.

She tried to pull her gaze away and couldn't. He held her completely in his power.

And yet instead of being nervous or uncertain, she felt…comforted and so very aware of him.

"Definitely a protector," she whispered, her insides tightening with a slow heat. Did he feel it? She searched his eyes, looking for an answering awareness in his gaze.

Instead, he lowered his gaze, effectively breaking the contact.

And left her feeling bereft. Shuddering from the shock to her system, she picked up her spoon and tasted her soup. Clam chowder. Delighted, she ate until there wasn't a drop left. Feeling replete and still with a salad to round out the edges, she sat back with a happy smile.

"Thank you," she said sincerely. "That was delicious."

"Apparently." He motioned to the well-cleaned out dish. "You look like you could eat a second one."

"No," she laughed, "I'll be lucky if I can eat the salad."

"Well, go for it." He slumped back with a half smile on his face. She eyed him carefully then shrugged and lifted the first forkful of the greens. She barely held back a moan. "Even this tastes wonderful. I don't know what happened but my taste buds seem amplified."

"Maybe it's all that emotional stuff."

"Stuff?" She grinned as she popped another bite in, then mumbled, "Maybe."

It took only a few minutes to polish the salad off as well. When it was done, she stared down at her empty plate almost in dismay. "Regardless of the reason, I'm grateful. I haven't enjoyed a meal so much in a long time."

"Good. Now a good night's sleep and you'll be ready to face tomorrow."

She wrinkled her face at him. "You just had to remind me, didn't you?"

His lips twitched. "As we have a long week ahead, it helps to keep everything clear."

She nodded. "Probably. That doesn't make it easier to deal with." Neither did it help her stomach digest a wonderful meal that was starting to lose its astonishing taste. Her stomach started to sour. But the truth was the truth. "And considering that, I think I'll head to my room and try and get some rest before I have to face that mess all over again."

She stood up. He stood up with her. "I'll walk you back up. I'm going to my room also."

"It's early. There's probably some evening session happening here with Jenna." Not that she planned on going. She'd had as much shake up as she could handle for one day. She caught the shift in his features. She stopped to study him. "You have no intention of going, do you?"

At the slight shake of his head, she had to ask, "Why are you even here? It's not to learn – that's obvious."

He nudged her gently out of the way as several people tried to walk past. Then he led her toward the bank of elevators. The same group from the restaurant was also getting on, so there was neither room to maneuver nor any privacy to speak. At the fourth floor, they got out and he walked her down to her door. There he stopped, took the card from her hand, and unlocked it. He pushed it open and motioned for her to enter.

"How did you know my room number? Earlier I mean, when you brought me back here from the hospital." It just hit her. She hadn't told him. So how had he known?

"My room is next door."

HE WATCHED CONFUSED interest whisper across her face. She stepped back to glance down the hallway as if looking for his room. He pointed to the door slightly down from hers.

She nodded, gave him a quick smile, and closed the door in his face. He heard the snick of the lock.

As a message, it was pretty clear. He walked to his room and entered. Tossing his key on the dresser, he pulled out his cell phone and called his sister.

"Hey, I'm so happy to hear from you," Paris said. "Now spill. How's it going?"

He brought her up to date, minimizing Robin's afternoon.

"She'll feel better tomorrow," she said. "It's hard at the time but afterwards it's such a better place to be in."

"As long as she can do this day after day. We have to go several more times."

"Well, I hope she can for your sake. You need to work on your own issues."

"What issues?" he scoffed. "I don't have any." At least none he planned to work on here.

"How about your inability to let anyone close?"

"What inability?" He frowned. "I don't know what you're talking about."

"Yes, you do," she said sadly. "You don't trust anyone. You *won't* trust anyone."

He pulled his shirt off and tossed it over the chair. His shoulder ached from clutching the pencil today. Not that his shoulder needed a reason to scream. That was the weakest part of his body. Once an abuser knew your weakness, he had control over you. He looked at the mass of scar tissue that completely deformed the joint. And saw his father's bloodshot eyes, that grotesque look of hatred in his eyes, and that unholy light of joy as he dug his thumbs hard into the damaged joint…and jerked the ball free…again…

"Sean, you there?"

Shaking as the memories sent a shard of pain down his shoulder and chest, sweat breaking out across his forehead, Sean cleared his throat and said, "Yeah, well. Maybe I'm just always meant to be alone."

"No," his sister cried. "You aren't. None of us are meant to journey this way."

"How do you know?" he asked in a serious tone. Holding the phone tucked between his neck and shoulder, he closed his eyes, the painful memories receding, and let his fingers massage deep into the knots, loosening the tightness of his injured joint.

While the pain eased, he considered the work he'd done today. The sketching had been intense. More than he'd thought. He'd never felt so gripped in the middle of drawing like that before.

Had never thought to experience such passion for his art.

He finished his call to Paris and hung up the phone. There was a pool in the hotel. He should go and do a few laps then sink into the hot tub. The heat would do wonders for his sore muscles. That and a good night's sleep and his arm would be as good as new for tomorrow.

He checked the time. It was after 8pm. Would the pool be still open? He needed to find out. His physical health was one thing he couldn't afford to let go. It only took a couple of minutes to change. He grabbed the spare towel in the bathroom, his key card, and walked out.

There were a couple of people doing laps in the pool and several more in the hot tub. Well, maybe the hot tub would be cleared by the time he finished his laps. He dropped his towel and dove into an empty lane. Doing the front crawl, he could feel his shoulder pull and pinch with every lift. He knew this routine and settled in for a long swim. He lost track of his laps, instead going by the fatigue level in his body.

When he figured he'd done enough, he pulled himself out of the water and sat at the edge for a long moment, giving his trembling muscles a moment to calm down. He took a deep breath and stood up, realizing just how tired he was. He'd overdone the swimming tonight. Instead of being strong and refreshed by morning, he was likely to be tired and sore. Not smart.

The pool had emptied and even the hot tub was down to just one person.

He slowly walked over. He was tired now, his arm sore and throbbing. At the hot tub, he dropped into the water and sank until only his head was above. And let the heat work its magic. He closed his eyes and rested.

Afterwards, he'd blame his fatigue for not noticing the odd silence. When he did finally realize the atmosphere around him was pregnant with something unusual, he sat up on the bench under the water to look around.

The shocked gasp had him turning his head. And he gazed directly into Robin's horrified face.

While she stared at his damaged shoulder, he couldn't help but stare at her damaged face.

Chapter 11

Robin had seen one person swimming when she'd entered the pool area. But after realizing that the hot tub was empty, she'd made the decision to stay. She really wanted to soak. Her insides felt wrung out. Her muscles were achy, and the injured side of her face throbbed from clenching her jaw. The stress was killing her, even now that it had slid down to manageable levels. She could have tried to go to sleep, but just the thought had sent her nerves tightening. She was afraid the nightmares would return.

After lowering herself into the warm water and feeling her muscles soften and relax, she knew she'd done the right thing. She sank completely under the water, letting the heat soak into the muscles and skin of her face and head. Alone, she could relax and not worry about prying eyes.

Until Sean had arrived.

Why him?

Why now?

But as always, there was no answer. She could only stare at him in shock. Dear God. She'd seen the small scars on his hand, his fingers, his neck. The tiny portion that showed under his shirt.

There was no way she could have guessed at the rest.

No one could have.

His right shoulder was shiny and rippled with the mixed

of damaged and healed tissue trying to live peacefully together. There had to be some injury to the actual joint from the grotesque look of the pitted muscles. Her heart softened, ached. Damn. What he must have gone through…

Her gaze wandered his wide chest, seeing the small burn-like scars, cuts that had been too big or too deep to heal without proper care. So many of them. She knew his back was likely worse.

"I'm so sorry," she whispered.

He jerked slightly, then sat up and glared at her, giving her a clearer view of his chest.

And she knew.

"You said you were abused as a child." She shook her head. "That's a lie." There was no other way to say it. But she tried. In fact, the words spurted out on their volition. "You look like you were tortured on a daily basis for years."

"Apparently," he said carelessly, the tone of his voice mocking. Distant. And she understood.

She couldn't help it – tears burned the back of her eyes. She blinked them back furiously, then realizing that wasn't going to be enough, she dipped her hands in the water and gently bathed her face, trying to hold her emotions back. It was the last thing he'd want. *That* she understood. Sympathy was one thing. Pity – quite another.

When she could, she straightened and looked over at him again. He'd leaned his head back and closed his eyes, letting the bubbles come up to cover the rest of him. It didn't matter. She'd seen enough of his body to know he must have had a horrible childhood. And he'd survived. Thrived even. But now she understood the mocking cynical edge to his voice, that glare in his eyes, that hidden sense of having seen the worst people could offer. That power of no longer giving a damn.

Feeling the pain welling up again, she sank below the water, reveling as the warmth closed over her face. Soothing her stinging eyes.

When she surfaced again, she settled back down against the back of the hot tub and wondered at him being able to go to the children's hospital so easily. She snuck another glance over at him. Lord, she ached as she looked at him. And she thought she had it bad.

Talk about a reality check.

HE HATED THE shocked look on her face. He thought he was immune to seeing that. Especially on a woman. Hence keeping relationships at a distance. He'd had enough one-night stands to know he needed to cover up in the morning before the women saw the details in daylight. Most weren't likely to care as it was always dark and they'd been there for their own needs. There'd been no emotion involved. But he'd seen enough revulsion on some faces to keep that sense of distance.

Screw them all.

As he lay there relaxed, letting his body soak up the warmth, he let his mind dwell on what he'd seen of her face. Compared to his shoulder, he didn't think it was bad. Still, for a woman, it was a part of her body that was so very visible. The scars, the twist to the corner of her eye, the sunken cheek where the muscle underneath had been damaged would be hard to hide.

He could see work had been done. And more was needed. He didn't know if she was in between surgeries or they'd done what they could. At least for now. She hadn't clarified that point.

The look of his shoulder was nothing. It was functional and that's what mattered. He no longer cared what anyone thought. At least he tried not to. In the summer, at the beach, he covered up for other people's sake. To avoid making them uncomfortable. To avoid the inevitable questions.

Especially for Paris. The sight of his back, his body, never failed to bring tears to her eyes.

He'd do anything to avoid hurting her.

He opened his eyes to study Robin, watching as her face broke through the water, her hair streaming behind her. From his position, he could see the hairline behind her cheek was further back, her ear disfigured, and the cheekbone covered with bright shiny skin. She was still healing.

He could only imagine the trauma Robin had already gone through.

His gaze wandered downward to the pink angry streak down her neck and realized as he studied her shoulders – she was likely as badly scarred as he was. She wore a modest one-piece bathing suit. It couldn't begin to cover her injuries. He doubted she went swimming in public. It said much about her day that she was here at all.

He didn't give a damn about his scars.

And she likely cared too much.

He'd been like this since forever. And knew that it was the price of survival. Besides, what was the alternative? He suspected from the look of the scar tissue on her face that this was a fairly recent development in her life. "Have you ever been married? Engaged?"

Oh shit. Where the hell had that had come from? He sank a little lower in the water. Not that he could go much deeper and still breathe. "You don't have to answer that. It just popped out."

"No," she said, "I've never been married or engaged. Came close a time or two, but it didn't work out."

"Ah," he muttered. Christ, he sounded like a dolt. He should just shut the hell up. He didn't do small talk. Or relationships.

"Not an issue," she murmured quietly. "I haven't had time for relationships since the accident."

Ah, this was the first time she'd mentioned that. Dare he ask? But curiosity got the better of him. "How long ago was the accident?"

"Almost six years now," she said absentmindedly.

At least her voice said it wasn't an issue any longer. Likely she'd had a normal childhood, happy and stable, before her world blew apart. Yeah, life was like that. "That must have been tough."

"Yep. But not as bad as a lifetime of abuse. I was happy and settled and thought I was heading forward in life. Had a long term relationship with dreams of that whole house, white picket fence and the perfect two kids."

"And what happened?"

There was silence, then she sighed heavily. "I found out that the perfect dream requires two perfect people, not one that is badly damaged."

The sadness in her voice got to him. There were layers of emotion in her tone. Old and new. He could understand that the dream might need to be changed. But it didn't have to be discarded completely.

Chapter 12

ROBIN SETTLED BACK into the water. Waves of depression washed through her.

Just the reminder of all those long evenings talking and planning out her future – her imaginary future with boyfriends and girlfriends over the years. How sad. She missed those hopes and dreams the most. It didn't need to be as bad as it felt to her – she knew that.

At least, she'd been told that many times. However, to know she was supposed to feel something other than what she did made her feel worse. Like how wrong was that? Just because people said something was right didn't make it true. Only she wanted them to be right. She wanted to be able to look forward and see sunshine and roses. A life full of laughter and love. Where children didn't run from her and men didn't cringe when they saw her.

But dreaming a dream didn't make it a reality.

"Thoughts?"

She gave a broken laugh. "Not worth repeating."

"Ah. Stuck in that self-pity mode, huh?"

She froze. How dare he? She opened her eyes and glared at him. "What do you know?" she said bitterly. The words were flying out before she had a chance to hold them back. Damn. Because he of course did know. Just in a different way. Groaning, she closed her eyes and sank back, muttering,

"Sorry."

"Why? Because you think it's not fair to lash out when you're hurting? It's not, but haven't you heard that life isn't fair?"

Damn him for being so reasonable. She wanted to *really* lash out. She wanted to hit him – have him be a target that she could pour her anger and frustration out on. But what good would it do other than be a temporary release of the emotional stress building inside? Besides, he'd already learned life wasn't fair. She had no business feeling sorry for her lot in life when his had been so much worse. She'd been loved while young, had grown up in a nurturing environment, her every need cared for.

And him…she wondered if he had any good memories or if it was all one black pit of pain and despair. His situation made her angry on so many levels. That it stopped her from feeling justified in her own anger and pain was just one of the less nice ones. She hated being petty and selfish. Sure, she had it rough, but as she'd seen today, some of those kids at the hospital had it rough, too. Some people never survived the horrors of their lives. Then there were people like Sean who'd survived – but at what cost?

"There's nothing I can say…" Sean said. "That someone else hasn't already said,"

She opened her eyes and stared. "You are right there."

"So I won't. It's normal to feel angry, depressed even, but from what I have seen of you – you are anything but normal."

That she hadn't expected. Nor did it please her to hear it. After all like he'd said – the little bit of her that he'd seen…wasn't much. And not enough to judge her. Good or bad. "You know nothing."

"And you're going to make sure that I don't know any

more, right? Use anger to keep others away. Keep your pride intact, thinking what the hell, it's all you have left anyways, might as well use it, right?"

She swallowed the hard truths, her mind locking onto his angry comment. Had he done that? Was she doing that? Was pride all she had left? True, pride that kept her head high in situations where she'd rather run away, but it wasn't pride that had kept her hiding away at home, too scared to deal with more of the public than she had to. Where had her pride been then? In hiding with the rest of her.

"Ha," she said defiantly, "You don't know me."

She watched his lip curl, feeling her anger blaze inside. She clenched her fists. As soon as she realized what she'd done, she shoved them under the foaming water, a shudder working its way down her thin frame. She had to regain control. She'd leave, but she didn't know that she had enough spine to walk out of the water. It had been hard enough coming here as it were. She only managed it as she knew the hot tub had been empty.

It had been that philosophy that had gotten her through most public meetings. People were curious, sometimes sympathetic, but they weren't part of her life. She whispered under her breath, "Everyone is just grateful that they don't look like me."

"Isn't that too cynical of an attitude for someone your age?"

She opened her eyes to see Sean staring at her. It wasn't disapproval she was seeing in his eyes, but they were dark with something. And she realized he'd heard her. Heat flushed over her cheeks. "Sorry, I didn't mean to say that."

"You did, you just didn't mean to have me hear your rambling. Besides, I think you give people too much credit.

They aren't thinking about any of that stuff. They just want to do whatever is required for their moral compass to feel comfortable and still be able to get up the next morning and look at themselves in the mirror."

She had to admit, he likely had a better take on humanity than she did. It made her feel oddly more comfortable. As if he really did understand what her life was like.

She wafted her hands around in front of her, her fingers slipping through the foam and bubbles as she contemplated people and humanity.

"How many more surgeries are there to be done?" he asked.

One side of her mouth instinctively twisted downward. "None."

"Meaning there is nothing more the doctors can do for you, or that you won't go for any more surgeries regardless of what the doctors feel they can do?"

The gentle curiosity in his voice threw her off balance. She never had a chance to get to know him because he always showed her a different side of his personality. She knew he didn't like her as a woman – not even a casual one-night stand, but there was something in his demeanor that had been caring. Maybe as one would for a hurt animal. Maybe it was nothing special for her. "I'm done with surgeries."

"Ah." A wealth of understanding laced his voice. She glared at him.

He leaned back and closed his eyes, as if happy to sleep while she was now angry and bitter.

"What? Am I not allowed to say enough?"

"Of course," he said equitably. "After all, why look normal? You can stay angry and bitter this way."

Shocked, she cried out, "That's not fair."

"Life isn't fair, sweetheart, I keep telling you that."

"Then get your own body fixed up. Surely there is something they can do about your shoulder."

"Nope. This is fixed."

She stared at the puckered skin. "It doesn't look it."

"Yeah, but I did the rounds of surgery and this is what I am left with. And you know something – I am okay with that."

She frowned. Surely he couldn't be as blasé about that. Then again, it was his shoulder, and it could be hidden most of the time from prying eyes.

"Doesn't it affect your love life?" She hated the need to know, the curiosity not something she was entirely comfortable with. Had he had the same horrified reaction from women as she'd had from men? That he was comfortable with his body even though he was as disfigured as she was didn't help. In fact, it just added to her off-centeredness.

"Nope. Don't have one to begin with, and if you meant my sex life, then you should have said so, and the answer is still no. The women who I have sex with don't care."

Damn if that didn't leave her stunned, her mind flooding with dozens more questions. He separated love from sex. Whereas she hadn't had sex with anyone she didn't love. Had he loved anyone? Or did he call sex, love? Love was a pathway she didn't expect to go down again. Not after being hurt the last time. She'd carefully wrapped up her bruised heart and packed it away in ice. Like so much of her life.

"What about you? How is the scarring affecting your sex life?"

Really? He'd asked that? Then again, why not? She had. "My boyfriend and I had been together for two years before my accident. He told me afterwards that there was no way he could have sex with me again. Not even as a mercy fuck."

The crude words left her mouth in a vitriol of pain. She stilled. Oh my God. She hadn't said that, had she? What was it about this man that could set her emotions and her tongue off like that?

She'd never shared Tom's parting words with anyone. Not even to her therapist.

How could she? Tom had been serious. With those few words, he'd broken her heart and driven her self-confidence into a pit deep inside, never to see the light again. After that, she'd iced over her heart to avoid being hurt again.

Until Sean. Why him? Unless it was because he was safe. After this week, she wouldn't have to see him again. Or because he was as broken as she was.

Wincing, she waited for Sean's response, but there was only the effervescence of the water popping gently between them.

"A mercy fuck?' he asked in a delicate voice, humor bouncing from letter to letter.

Closing her eyes, she groaned again, grateful that he couldn't hear her above the bubbles. "That's what he called it."

She stared down at the foam bouncing against her chest, wishing she'd kept her big mouth shut. Then that appeared to be part of this week. Being someone she normally wasn't. Awkward. Scared. Always putting her foot into her mouth and leaving it there. She despaired of the rest of the week given the way it had started. She already wanted to go home. Hide away again. So she wasn't put into these situations. She wanted to go back where she was comfortable. Normal.

Sure, she'd be alone, but that was the reality of her life. This being out in public was like wearing a second skin – one that didn't fit well. She wanted to keep tugging it into place.

And trying to keep her mind focused on the things going on this week wasn't working to avoid the burning sensation on the back of her eyelids. Sean's burning gaze.

After a few moments, the air relaxed slightly and dropped that expectant air. She relaxed back.

"Can't say that I've ever had a mercy fuck."

He said it in such a wondering tone that it caught her funny bone. And against all odds, a surprised giggle escaped. She gasped and opened her eyes to see his big grin.

She couldn't help it. She beamed back and said, "As I turned him down, neither have I."

His belly laugh rolled out free and clean, making her realize that Tom's issues had been just that – his issues. She didn't need to make them hers. And she hadn't realized how his comment had burned. How she'd frozen up on the inside. And how much sharing his comment had freed her.

"Good for you. You are worth so much more than that."

She shook her head and opened her mouth.

"Stop. No more self-degrading comments. You are beautiful. And your beauty is only becoming more obvious as each surgery lets you shine a little brighter."

"And if I chose to not have more surgeries?"

"Then you'll stay just as beautiful as you are now," he said comfortably. He leaned back, dropping his head to the edge of the hot tub. Then added, "You have to go beneath the skin and see the layer underneath."

She pondered that wisdom from another person as scarred as he was. Hard to understand coming from someone with that hard edge he carried around himself like a shield. How could he spout all this stuff and be as messed up as he was?

"If that's true, why are you so touchy about your looks?"

He laughed and barked out, "Because everyone out there is like you – they judge by the covering. I don't want people like that in my life. So I let them see the harder edges so that they won't want anything to do with the inside me."

"Or it's a shield that you use to make sure no one can actually see the real you inside."

"Or that..." he said carelessly. And fell silent.

Somehow she knew that this topic was over. He'd done a lot of work and had made some profound insights. This is who he was.

He was comfortable with himself. As for the rest of the world? He didn't give a damn.

IF THERE WAS ever a guy who deserved punching, Robin's ex was it. A mercy fuck? It boggled the mind and Sean found himself getting pissed all over again. He couldn't help but wonder how much of Robin's issues were caused by his fellow men. Probably too damn many of them.

Then again, all of his had been. His father had been a right bastard. Sean had no memory of the love of his mother, who'd taken off when Paris and he were young, leaving them with their father.

He'd learned. Not fast and not easily. Still, he'd not have survived without his sister. Their bond was strong as they'd been forced to depend on each other for survival.

Something Robin hadn't had. She'd gone from having a loving family who'd always been there for her to being completely alone in an instant. Everything since she'd had to do herself, for herself, by herself.

He couldn't imagine how tough that would have been. How wearying. What happened when she hit a wall and crumpled in defeat? Could she get up and keep going without someone there to help her? Or was that why she struggled for as long as she could then slowly gave up and had gone inside?

Since he'd been an older teen, he'd been fascinated with the psychology of people. Why they did things and what it would take for them to change that behavior. He didn't like many of them, but their behavior fascinated him. He had high hopes for his future once he graduated but had no clue what area he wanted to work in. Maybe profiling. He wouldn't mind helping to put bastards like his father behind bars.

Paris had laughed and said that him taking a psychology course made perfect sense. He was trying to figure out their father.

She was only partly correct. He'd figured out their father. He even understood his mother, she'd been a victim too. But what he was trying to figure out was himself – so he didn't end up like his father.

Deep stuff. He wasn't sure how much progress he'd made. But watching, hearing Robin's struggles made him realize that although the details were different, their journeys were similar.

Not that she'd appreciate hearing that.

Any more than she could handle being told that she was beautiful. She was. In fact, the newly awoken artist in him wanted to grab a pencil right now. It was almost time to go back to their rooms. He had an idea for the report now. He wasn't sure he had the skill to pull it off, but for the first time, he really wanted to try.

His father had tried to separate Sean from his art. He hadn't completely succeeded. But neither had Sean been able to do much since. It had taken Jenna to bring that spark back to life. Who'd have thought?

Chapter 13

ROBIN WOKE THE next morning groggy and tired. Talk about a shitty night. When she needed a sound sleep, life had given her a crappy wake up every hour on the hour, only to finally fall into a deeply disturbed sleep at 5am. Like what a joke. She needed her defenses strong today. Of course, this way she'd have little resistance against the world and maybe that would be a good thing – it could shake things up.

Things she wasn't ready to shake up.

She winced. And said out loud, "That's why you're here, idiot." And that couldn't happen while her defenses were strong. This way sometimes, things would slip under her weakened guard and prick her where she needed it most.

A horrible thought. God, she'd be glad when this week was over.

She rubbed her eyes and lay still contemplating the day ahead. She had to go back and see the kids.

It had to get easier. Her chest constricted in dread. They were just kids for Christ's sake. These kids were traumatized enough. And was she supposed to let them see her as she really was and face their horror? Was that the lesson Jenna wanted her to learn? Cause that just sucked big time. She'd already faced that reaction. Look what little good that had done – she'd run away as far as she could to get away. Then had been unable to get out. She was out now. Because of this seminar.

The last thing she wanted was to go back into hiding again.

Yet there was already a thin steel rod of stress running through her. She could feel the slight vibration, that inner shakiness that said her stress levels were rising. She wanted to be able to let the kids see her as she really was, but she couldn't. Not really. And there was no way she'd be able to smile at them as if everything were okay. Nothing was okay. And coming here had just magnified that. Especially after meeting Jon. Just hearing his name hurt.

Jonathon. She missed him so much.

So many buttons pushed already this week, and it was early in the week…

She was going to be a different person by the end of the week. It remained to be seen if that was a good thing or not.

There was a knock on the door. She frowned but threw back her covers, and just dressed in her cami and underwear, she approached the door. "Hello?"

"It's me," Sean said from the other side.

She instinctively opened the door wide enough to peer around the edge. "What's up?"

She studied him, still blinking the sleep out of her eyes. *He* looked great. Like he'd had a dozen hours of sleep. She envied him.

"Breakfast. It's late." He motioned down the hallway. "I wanted to make sure you were up."

"Just." She yawned. "How late is it?"

"Almost 8:45am."

Damn.

"I'll be ready in five." And she slammed the door.

Turning around, she stared bleary-eyed at the room and the tossed up bedding then galvanized into action. She dressed quickly, tossed the bedding back into place with a few quick movements, and rushed out the door. There wasn't even time to eat. And that was also no good. She walked into the seminar late enough that Jenna was already talking to the class. There was only one place left. Beside Sean.

Crap. She slipped into place, hoping to ignore this man who disturbed her too much. He reached over and placed a takeout cup of coffee and a still-warm muffin in front of her.

Oh happy sigh. She might want a break from him, but there was no doubt that a man who would go out of his way to make sure you were awake in time to start the day and then think far enough ahead to make sure you had a hot coffee and a bite to eat was a definite keeper. And the ice around her heart melted a little bit more.

Three hours later, she'd settled into place. Coffee, lectures, a couple of group sessions, and she was feeling more normal. More centered. Nothing had pushed her buttons. It was all good.

She was looking forward to catching up with Tania over lunch. See how her week was going. She'd watched her with the big muscleman Kane a few times and had been worried for her. They'd managed to catch a few private moments to talk so far but that was all. That Tania was still functioning and managing to be relatively calm and normal said a lot about her state of mind. And her progress. Although maybe nothing in her world had blown up – yet.

And just like that, all the thoughts, worries, that sense of increasing dread that she'd worked so hard at keeping under lock and key came flooding back into her mind. She didn't want to go back to the hospital. Didn't want to see those kids. Didn't want to go back out in the world. This hotel was not home, but it was as safe a territory as she could claim here.

In an hour – maybe two – she'd have to leave. And she didn't want to. Didn't dare to. She had no way to know what would happen. But she knew all kinds of horrible things could.

She walked into the dining room when her cell phone went off. She pulled out her phone and stared down at the text message. No, not possible. Everything inside of her revolted.

Sean spoke just then, startling her. "Are you ready? We'll pick up something on the way if you're hungry."

Blindly, she looked around the dining room slowly filling up, her gaze landing on Tania a few tables in front of her. How could she get out of this? Push it back at least another hour. *She wasn't ready*, her mind screamed.

Sean reached out and snagged her arm gently. "Let's go."

And she went.

SEAN HAD READ his text, looked up to locate Robin, and found her frozen in place with her phone in her hand. It was the look of blind panic in her eyes that had gotten to him. She'd been chipper and happy all morning. Too chipper and too happy. He'd watched her interact with the others, getting into the swing of the morning lectures and the smaller group projects. He doubted anyone else had noticed the overloud voice, the over-enthusiastic agreements. The too bright smile. But he had. And he hadn't been able to keep his gaze off of her.

Now she looked to be on the verge of an all-out panic attack. That couldn't happen. He'd never get her to the hospital if she did that.

"What kind of food do you fancy?"

Her voice wooden, she replied, "I couldn't eat a thing."

"I could." His stomach took that opportunity to growl at him. "In fact, I'm going to need to." He kept his hand on her arm and dragged her gently out the front door. As she had her purse with her and as the day was warm, he figured that maybe he could nudge her straight out to his truck. He didn't know what he'd do about food, but it looked like takeout was on the menu. Not that eating and driving was a good idea.

The earlier he got Robin to the hospital, the earlier they could leave. She obviously didn't like this shift in their schedule. He was a roll-with-the punches-kind-of-guy. Paris needed a little more warning.

Like Robin.

He got her outside before she'd realized it. He was glad he'd stashed his art stuff inside the truck already this morning. If he'd had to go and get it now, he'd have a much harder time with her. He also needed food before he started another marathon art session. It was only as he led her to the truck that she baulked. And he remembered how she felt about driving.

Was nothing easy?

"You did fine yesterday. Sure, every time is a new time, but you've got this. In the scale of all the other things you've got to deal with, this one is easy. So let's just do it."

He opened the truck and helped her up onto the seat. He had her buckled in and the door shut before she had a chance to protest. He hopped into the driver's side and made short work of getting the truck out onto the main road.

There was a drive-through sandwich place up ahead. He pulled in and ordered two large subs for the two of them. Realizing it was useless to ask her preferences given her frozen features, he also ordered two bottles of water to go with the meal.

After accepting the food and paying, he did a drive around the block so he could get back onto the road heading in the direction they needed to go.

He checked the dashboard clock. They were going to be a little early. That meant eating in the parking lot.

So be it.

The drive took longer today with the heavy lunch hour traffic. He pulled the truck into the hospital parking lot, found a spot close to where they'd parked yesterday, and shut off the engine. He opened up the bag of food and pulled out a sandwich. He handed it to her. "Eat."

She stared at him and frowned. "I'm not hungry."

"Yes, you are. And your stomach needs this. All that stress and tension is eating away at you from the inside. Give it real food to work on and save the lining of your stomach."

She accepted the sandwich and rested it on her lap. He handed her the bottle of water. Then he pulled out his lunch, opened the wrapping, and took a big bite.

Food. He closed his eyes and let his stomach catch up with the message as he methodically ate his sandwich. He'd missed too many meals in his life to be interested in missing any more.

Chapter 14

Robin stared down at the paper-wrapped sandwich then over at Sean. He ate with gusto. Enjoying this moment. This meal. This bite. It didn't take much to realize he was a large appetite kind of guy. He did make the sandwich sound good. She slowly unwrapped hers and peered at the filling. Looked like layers of mixed meat and lots of veggies. Her kind of sandwich. Tempted, she picked it up and took a tentative bite. The aroma of salami and tomato with a hint of mustard caught her nose at the same time as her taste buds sat up and paid attention. It was good. Actually, it was really good.

She didn't realize it but within minutes, she was well into her big sub. She looked sideways and caught Sean staring at her with a big grin on his face. She scowled at him. "What are you looking at?"

"You. Glad to see you're enjoying it."

She glanced down, realized she was almost done, and said, "I am. Thanks."

"No problem." He unscrewed the bottle of water and drained it mostly dry.

She watched one eyebrow rise as he kept pouring down the liquid. She thought she drank a lot of water, but he had her beat in that department.

Afterwards, she finished her sandwich, crumpled up the

wrapper, and popped it back into the bag. She opened her bottle, took a drink, and said, "Okay, let's do this."

She opened her truck door and hopped out while he was still absorbing her words. She didn't wait to see if he followed or not. She heard the truck door open and slam shut followed by long strides hitting the pavement until he was beside her. But he never said a word.

Good. She was taking advantage of a momentary surge of courage to get into the building. With any luck, she'd make it into the damn ward too.

But it wasn't to be. As soon as the elevator doors closed in her face, she could feel her stomach knot up. She swallowed hard. Then again. Under her breath, she repeated, "I can do this. I can do this, I can do this."

"And you can," Sean said quietly at her side. "Easily."

That was when she realized he'd heard her. "I wish I believed you."

He laughed.

She refused to let him get to her. She got that this was easy for him. That he did understand what this trip was doing to her. However, there was nothing funny about it. And *that* was something he should have gotten.

The heavy metal doors slid open. She tensed up inside. Taking a deep breath, she walked forward.

"Have you got some kind of plan of action as to how to handle this today?" Sean asked quietly at her side.

She shot him a sharp look. "Survive."

"How about asking something really small of yourself that would make it an improvement on yesterday?"

She tried to focus on his words. "Like what?"

"Maybe sit facing forward so that the kids can check you out in a different way."

"What good would that do?" She could do it easily enough, but she wasn't sure it would make any difference.

"It's something."

She shrugged. As far as that went, it was a pretty damn small something. Yet her mind caught on the concept. Was there a small step she could take? Regardless of how small, it would be a step in the right direction. Progress was progress…no matter how small.

In the distance, she heard shrieks of laughter covering up the din of quieter screams. The kids.

She stopped in the middle of the hallway. *She couldn't do this.* She went to turn around when she was suddenly jerked off to the one side. She glared at Sean.

"I'm fine."

"Right. That's why you're standing in the way. Come on." He gave her arm a gentle jerk and shifted her in the direction of the kids' ward. "We can get through this."

He walked a half step in front of her, making her feel like she was being dragged. Probably how it looked to everyone else, too. She hated this ball of fear in her stomach that was sinking lower and lower.

Hated that she felt this way. She understood the phrase 'giving away her power' but hadn't really recognized a situation where she'd done just that.

But this was as close as she could imagine it being.

The double doors were in front of them. Sean stopped, gave her a hard look, and said, "Now buck up. We're here. Don't go in there looking like a victim."

Her head snapped back. She glowered at him. "What if that's how I feel?"

"Tough. Deal with it." He surprised her with the harshness of his tone. "I don't care about how you feel right now.

You don't give those kids any more reason to worry than they already have." He reached up and snagged her chin, lifting it to glare into her eyes. "Consider that these visits maybe aren't just about you. Maybe they are for the kids. So give a little – don't just take."

He dropped her chin and strode through the door, his big portfolio banging against the door. She stood in shock and listened to the kids screaming his name. Where had his anger come from? Maybe she had deserved it, but it didn't explain the source.

Then again, she hadn't considered if these visits were causing him stress, too. Jenna had to have a reason for both of them coming here. He was right. She'd been so focused on her problems she hadn't considered the impact of their visits on the kids or the impact on him. Ugh.

Stumbling in the changing landscape of her reality once again, she followed behind him, watching his interaction with the boys. Sure enough when they saw her, they quieted slightly and stepped back a little. Giving her space. And she realized that they weren't so much afraid of her face – they couldn't see it after all – they were more afraid because she was sending out scary vibes.

She was scaring the kids just by her own fear and the walls she'd put up to keep them away.

Talking about seeing a different perspective. She slowly made her way over to the table where Sean was setting up his work. The same little boy, Jon, stood watching at the side of the table. As she approached, he held his ground. Her heart ached. He was so young. And was going through something traumatic from the thin look to him. He was mobile, with crutches, but his hair was too thin and his eyes too big. She'd promised herself she wouldn't focus on any one child –

especially not any one boy – in order to try and keep her sanity. She hadn't expected that one particular boy would focus on her.

Jon's gaze had locked on her face. Watching every move she made. He'd said she was scary yesterday. Maybe she could take one step forward. Not for her sake, for his.

"Hi," she said.

Jon's gaze widened. His gamine grin lit up his face, temporarily pushing the abnormally white skin and heavy black circles under his eyes away. "Hi."

She was disarmed. With a sigh, she sat down on the same chair as she had last time and faced him. Just like Sean had suggested.

SEAN WATCHED ROBIN'S actions from the corner of his eye. He hadn't wanted to be so hard on her, but she'd needed something to snap her out of her mood.

He'd seen some people, namely Paris, frozen by her emotions, but had assumed she was the odd case. Robin was proving that theory to be wrong. He smiled down at the kids who clamored around him, "Give me a moment to unpack, then you can all see the drawing. I did a bit more on it. Maybe if it all goes well today, there will be a couple of other pictures for you to look at soon."

He smiled as several jumped up and raced to the far side of the room as if understanding that he couldn't work if they bugged him.

A couple of the boys stayed behind, quietly watchful as he opened up his portfolio and took out his sketchbook and pencils. He was looking forward to sketching today. The picture had been sitting on the back of his mind, his fingers itching to work on it. In fact, after getting back to his room from the pool, he'd done a bit of work on it. He hadn't planned to, but there'd been something about the little boy that had needed something more. He'd spent only a half hour on it, but the way the boy's eyes look had gone from good to right was perfect. And that was important.

There'd been something in that little boy's gaze. And it hadn't let Sean go until he caught just that look. It bothered him that the space for Robin was blank. He was supposed to be drawing Robin.

Not the boys and Robin, but Robin and the boys. At the moment, he looked to be getting an F on this report.

And he didn't care one bit. He stared around at the kids' faces as he opened the pages to the right place and watched the several heads crowd closer. These kids could use whatever was available to make their day brighter.

He'd been one of them at one time. He understood. More so as these kids likely had family. Friends. Someone who cared for them. He'd watched from the outside. Hurt on the inside. Alone, he'd taken refuge in defiance. Pride. Aggression. It had made it easier to think of the world as one he had to battle. One where he needed to strike out first before he was struck himself.

He sorted through the pencils on the table and turned to a clean page. He started with long lean lightning strokes, trying to capture the sense of the kids staring at them. Their gazes moved with the long strokes of black, as if willing the image to show up clear enough for them to identify what it was. To guess what he was drawing. Then one boy shouted, "Hey, that's Mark."

A little boy leaned forward. "No way, that doesn't look anything like me."

Sean smiled quietly and let his hand add a little shading, thickening the line around the ear, adding a few tufts of hair.

Mark said, "Hey, it is me. That's so cool."

"Do me. Can you draw me too?" asked Jon, his voice weak, his body frail compared to the two robust boys he stood with. Sean glanced up, caught the wistful look in the boy's eyes, and his heart ached a little. No wonder this little guy affected Robin so deeply. "Sure," he said, "I'll give it a try."

He shifted to a different corner of the page and with a softer stroke, he quickly sketched in several curls a small upturned nose, freckles, and the long scrawny neck. It was the look in this boy's eyes Sean wanted to capture. The lost, not-expecting-life-to-get-any-better look, yet shining in from the back was something that made his heart warm…the glint of hope.

These kids needed all the hope they could get.

Chapter 15

"**W**OW." JON STARED at his picture. "That's awesome."

As if emboldened by Sean's picture, he turned and studied Robin. He took a deep breath and asked, "Why does your hair cover most of your face?"

Robin stared back at him. Why did his voice have to sound so much like her brother? His features were mobile with curiosity and childlike honesty. Given that, she told him the truth. "The one side of my face is badly scarred. My hair hides the scars."

His gaze locked on her face, studying the long fall of hair. She could almost see the wheels of his mind turning, figuring out, trying to imagine the damage and really wanting to ask her to show him, but not quite comfortable to take that step. Good thing. She was a long ways away from taking that step herself.

Hoping to stop him from gathering up the courage, she turned her attention to Sean. He was busy sketching. She marveled at the surety of his strokes, the absolute knowledge that his hand needed to place those marks where they needed to go.

Fascinating. She didn't have an artistic bone in her body. It was mesmerizing to watch it unfold in front of her. Sean had collected an assortment of observers from Jon to a little redhead boy with crutches to a set of twins wearing a series of leg braces. She had no idea what was going on with them, but they had a stoic look on their faces as if this wasn't anything new. And given the odd bend to their spines and legs, she suspected they'd had several corrective surgeries already with many more to come. It hurt her to realize what they were going through and likely not understanding how long and arduous the road ahead was going to be. Maybe that was a good thing.

"Daniel and David, give the man some room to work." A different nurse than they'd met last time walked toward them. She had a smile on her face but she was older, more reserved. She appeared to be okay with their presence, but she wasn't exactly rushing toward them enthusiastically.

She caught the woman's eyes, saw her gaze narrow speculatively, and Robin dropped her gaze to the floors. Adapting to the children was one thing. Adapting to curious adults was something else altogether.

But…she'd be damned if she'd keep hiding. She shoved a steel rod down her spine, straightened up, and stared back at the nurse. In the face of her own assertiveness, the nurse shifted her gaze away from Robin's face. Damn right.

Instead, the nurse nudged the twins back out of the way, not that they'd been in the way, and moved them toward the other end of the room. Robin let her gaze follow them, noting the fatigue in their arms, the droop to their shoulders by the time they made their way to their beds.

"Will you show me your face?"

Out of the blue, she felt like she'd been sideswiped by Jon's question.

Sean spoke up before she had a chance to answer. "It's not polite to ask something like that, Jon. If she wanted people to see it, she'd wear her hair differently so as not to hide it."

"I know...but..."

Sean, his voice firm, said, "No. Not right now. She'll let you see it only when she's ready."

"Scars are cool," Jon said.

"Some scars *are* cool. Some scars are tough."

Jon, his attention caught by the odd tone of Sean's voice, stared at him speculatively. "Do you have scars?"

"Sure." As if knowing what was coming, Robin watched Sean lift his hand off the paper and hold it out for Jon to see the shiny white marks along the back of his hand, the abnormally crooked fingers and thick knuckles.

"Neat." Jon studied them carefully. "Those don't look bad."

"Not now they don't. At the time, they were pretty ugly."

"What happened?" piped up Jon, his gaze never leaving Sean's hand.

"It's a long story. But the short version is one should never play with chicken wire."

Robin caught her breath. What could he have been doing with chicken wire to get marks like that? Or had he only said that to give Jon an answer he'd understand?

She glanced up to find Sean watching her, laughter in his eyes, inviting her to join in.

It was impossible to ignore it. She smiled back.

"You look like you're doing much better today."

She wrinkled up her nose at him. "The sky hasn't fallen down. The building hasn't collapsed. The children haven't run screaming..." She managed to swallow the word *yet*. "So far, so good."

SEAN STUDIED HER for a long moment, then he picked up his

pencil and turned his attention back to the image he was creating. "Well, I'm proud of you."

She gave a half laugh. "Why, because I haven't bolted yet?"

"Actually – yes. That is a good sign. You also spoke to Jon. Who knows, maybe in a day or two you'll be comfortable enough to interact more with them."

"Maybe with Jon." She glanced around and realized thankfully that Jon had gone over to play with his friends. "It's easy to remember his name."

Sean, shading the shirt of one child, paused. There'd been a wash of emotion caught up in her voice.

"That accident that caused such damage to my face..."

He looked at her, saw the wet eyes, and waited.

"My baby brother was killed in that car accident. There was fifteen years between us. He'd have been close to Jon's age at the time he died. His name was also Jonathon."

"Ah hell." He put the pencil down and reached out to squeeze her shoulders gently. "I'm sorry, Robin. Did Jenna know?"

Robin flashed him a teary look and nodded.

"Of course she did."

Damn Jenna anyway. As if Robin didn't have enough to get over. An asshole boyfriend, multiple surgeries that took so much out of her she didn't care to have even one more. She'd travelled this road alone plus carried the survivor's guilt of being the only one left alive.

He dropped his hand and checked his watch. They'd been here an hour already. He wasn't going to have any pictures if he didn't get back to it. "I'm so sorry,"

She gave a brief nod but her head was still down and only her sniffles could be heard. She'd gone back inside.

Where no one else could go.

And that was starting to piss him off.

"Hey you," he said, his voice sharp, telling. "Stay out here. No more hiding."

"I wasn't trying to hide." She shrugged and the words burst out. "Why does he do this to me? He doesn't even look like Jonathon, but...there's something about him..."

"Sorry about that, but we have another hour and then it's time to go." He motioned to the kids around the room. "The reason we're here early is they have something else going on this afternoon. So this is almost over. Stay present."

"I am," she snapped, "I thought I was doing a fine job of it, too."

He grinned. "Much better." And it was. He'd rather have a female snapping at him than crying any time.

He watched approvingly as she straightened up and with her one good eye glared at him. "Wait. Don't move. Just stay like that."

Ignoring her snort, he flipped to a clean page and started sketching. She shifted slightly. He snapped out, "Don't move. No slumping. Stay straight and glare at me."

"That last part won't be hard," she said, aggravation in her tone, the set of her shoulders. "But I'm not a model. I can't just freeze in place."

"Try," he urged. "There's just something about the way you were sitting. It caught my eye."

His arm and hand moved at a desperate pace, trying to catch that elusive bit of imagery that he'd seen for a fraction of a moment.

There. Just as suddenly as he'd started, he stopped.

And stared.

"Let me see." Robin leaned forward to look and gasped. "Oh my!"

Chapter 16

Robin stared at the simple rendition of her sitting with her head slightly to the side and her nose upturned slightly. He'd captured her profile in what appeared to be just a few strokes. A few extra thin lines appeared to add shading. It was stunningly simple. Incredibly dramatic.

From the corner of her eye, she watched a slight tremor shake his hand that held the pencil. She let her gaze roam up his arm to where the edge of his t-shirt stopped. The t-shirt that hid the incredible damage to his shoulder. He might be a great artist, but he had physical difficulties in actually drawing.

No. She stopped considering it. He could draw, but not for long. If he drew on a regular basis, then the muscles would slowly build in strength and endurance. She hurt thinking about the ache he had to be experiencing. She sat back, her arm massaging her own shoulder. "It's very good. You're very good."

His lips quirked. "Thank you."

Yet his tone was dismissive. "No, I mean it." She reached out as if to touch her image but held back from making contact. "You really are talented." She looked up to study his face, noting the self-mockery. "You don't believe it, do you?"

He shrugged. "Sometimes I seem to be able to make something decent. Often I can't. I gave up out of sheer frustration. A lack of control is often the death of an artist, and sometimes," he shrugged and lowered his voice. "Sometimes my arm gives out completely."

She nodded. It was as she had suspected. "Still, it's something that you could strengthen and improve on."

His lips quirked. He tossed the pencil down. "If I cared enough."

"How could you not?" she exclaimed. "This," she wafted her hand toward the image, "is a gift."

"A common gift," he said, derision in his tone. "Many people draw."

"Not like you do." There was no way he could be lumped in with all the other artists in the world. He'd managed to capture the very essence of her – not just her, but the emotions coursing through her. The frozenness to her face, her smile on lockdown at all times. And the look in her eyes…that glare, but also what he'd pulled out from behind it.

She sat back studying that one aspect, then said in quiet tones, "You're very perceptive."

Silence.

"In what way?"

She made a strangled sound, took a deep breath, and said, "The fear in her eyes."

"Whose eyes?" he asked calmly.

Robin closed her eyes. After a long moment, she admitted, "*My* eyes."

He smiled at her gently.

"Am I really that obvious?" She turned to stare at him, almost hating him at that moment. "Is that what the kids see?"

He shook his head immediately. "No. Not at all."

"So what…you're just more perceptive than most people?" She glared at him, hating the anger coursing through her. And hating him for seeing that, too. Damn him. She got up and walked out of the ward.

SEAN WATCHED HER stride toward the double doors. Her pattern was still in effect. Run away to regain control then return when she could. He stared down at his picture, then turned to a clean page and with the last image he had of her in his mind, he quickly sketched her in the middle of her strategic retreat.

He didn't know why he felt the compulsion. She fascinated him. He'd seen compassion in her eyes when she looked at the kids, he'd seen pain in there too, but she'd managed to hold it back. Managed to keep that lid screwed down tight. It might be a glass lid that allowed others to see in and her to see out, but it was damn thick and secured in place.

What would happen if that glass broke?

The need to be normal drove her. Sent her to this workshop. Forced her to the hospital. No. He thought about that for a moment. She wanted to function normally. Only she'd never be normal.

She was too unique for that. Too special. Besides being normal was overrated.

Sensing sudden movement, he turned to see Robin already in her seat. His mind stopped for a second. She'd left, hadn't she? He blinked, trying to sort out what just happened.

She glared at him. Well, at least that was the same.

"I never left," she said by way of an explanation. "I kept remembering your damn words."

He lifted his left eyebrow, not understanding.

"My pattern. You said I always run away then come back." Moodily, she stared around the room and the kids that likely hadn't noticed her even leaving. "I got to the door, even went so far as to push it open, and realized I was doing it again. You were right about my behavior pattern. And as doing the same thing over and over again keeps bringing me the same result over and over again, I have to change it. I want a new future. That means I need a new pattern."

"Or no pattern. All patterns eventually become a habit and a crutch." He should have kept his mouth shut. But instead of being upset or thinking he was being patronizing, she gave a gurgled laugh. "Well, there's no shortage of crutches here!"

Chapter 17

ROBIN SETTLED BACK, thinking about her old life – before this week. She wondered just how bad it would have gotten. Would she ever have left or found a way to make her living without having to leave her home? She knew that there was a name for people who couldn't leave their homes, but she was damned if she could remember what it was. She hadn't been that bad, but how long before she'd slid all the way down?

"Thoughts?"

She winced. "I was actually thinking of how close I was to becoming one of those housebound people."

"Ha. You're a long ways off from ending up like that." He grinned, his pencil working on the paper. "You are here. You are working on your problems. You're getting stronger all the time."

"And you, what are your problems?" She sat back, watching the mixed emotions slide across his face. Irritation. Sadness. Denial. "Why exactly are you here? Or you aren't going to tell me?"

"There's nothing to tell."

"Well, you don't appear to be learning anything about yourself. Or being taxed emotionally in any way." She frowned at the lack of expression on his face.

"What kind of reaction should I be showing?" He sat forward, one eyebrow raised. "Tears? Sobs? Crying out in frustration or pain?"

"No, of course not." She stopped, confused. Just what had she expected? Maybe awkward silences? Going off on his own. Walking out in a temper.

"Truthfully…?" She shrugged. "I'm not sure."

"Well if and when it ever happens," his grin lit up the room, "then we'll both know."

She watched the look on his face. The humor masking the forced calm. The neutrality. The cold anger. And she knew a little more. "No, you wouldn't cause a scene. You'd get your back up and stare down anyone who'd dare hurt you. You'd never run away." She smiled gently. "You'd make sure they paid though. One way or another."

His eyebrows shot up. "You make me sound like an arrogant assassin bent on revenge."

"The image almost fits." She couldn't hold back the grin. "You're definitely assassin material."

He choked back a laugh. "Really?"

"Really."

Just then a commotion stirred up behind them. Robin turned at the foreign voice. "Excuse me, but we need to ask you to leave now."

"Oh right." Sean jumped to his feet. "Time ran away from us."

"Sorry," Robin said, standing up as well.

As she walked to the door, she heard a little voice behind her. "Are you leaving?"

She paused, her heart aching. Please don't let it be Jon. She was afraid to look into his face. See the lost look. The loneliness. She wanted to walk away. To pretend she hadn't heard him. Instead, her feet turned on their own will.

Jon stood in front of her. There was a thin detached look plastered on his face. She took a step back and smiled at him. Or at least she tried to smile. It wasn't successful. His features didn't change. There was still that faint hope, that desperation, that needing *something* from her. Something she didn't have to give.

"We have to go now." She leaned closer. "You have something else happening this afternoon."

Those fathomless eyes stared at her. Did he understand?

Sean tugged her arm. "Come on, we need to leave."

She looked at him pleadingly. He caught her gaze, and then turned to look at Jon. "Hey buddy. We'll be back tomorrow. Okay?"

The little boy stared up at him, that gaze not shifting. Then he nodded once.

SEAN LED ROBIN downstairs via the elevator and back outside, right into the pouring rain and across the parking lot to his truck. Just when he wondered if she was going to be okay, she separated and walked over to the passenger side of the truck and got in on her own. Progress. He watched while she buckled up and then locked her door. Good. She was much better today. Both about riding in a vehicle and about being here at the hospital. Maybe a couple more days would be enough for her to show real progress on the other issues. Although that little boy Jon was likely to be the end of her.

He reminded her of her little brother, had facial scarring similar to her own, and was in the middle of multiple surgeries. She could relate to him on a level Sean couldn't. But she refused to. She couldn't because she was stuck in her own pain. Her own mirrors.

She could do a lot for Jon.

Jon could do a lot for her.

But they both had to be able to meet somewhere in the middle for any of that to happen.

"What do you think happened to him?"

He didn't pretend to not know who she was talking about. "I don't know. Maybe you should ask him."

As soon as the words were out of his mouth, he wished he could bring them back. One rule he'd learned in hospital was to not ask too many questions. Some of the stories were easy, but many were tragic. It might help the child to share, but it didn't help those listening. Many had stories that hurt. And more often than not, it didn't take a newcomer long to realize there was always someone worse off than you.

"No, that would put him on the spot."

"Like asking you puts you on the spot?"

Silence.

He risked a glance her way. She was staring out the window, her face turned away from him. But there was that cold frozen profile again. Her face would be so mobile when she was with her friends or in the workshops. But with him, he was treated to the cold visage and lack of emotion.

"Why are you always so quiet around me?"

She turned to look at him. "I'm not."

"Sure you are. You spend more time being silent around me than you do talking to me."

She shrugged. "Up to now, you've been with me when I've gone through some difficult times."

Really? He snickered. "Nothing you've been through has been difficult. On the scale of what could have happened to you, this is all minor. It's time to get over you."

He hadn't meant to let that spew, but it was the truth and

therefore he didn't wish to retract the words and neither would he apologize. Paris had gone through so much worse than Robin and she'd never complained. He knew they were different people, and he thanked God he'd seen this moment today because it highlighted their differences in a big way.

Robin had the surgeries available. So many people didn't. She had a rough go of it. But there was a time to end that self-pity, too. So what if her face was disfigured? So what if she was sick of hospitals? Life was like that. Sure she'd lost her brother and the rest of her family and that just sucked. But this was too much "poor me" stuff. He wanted her to buck up and get over this mess.

"Wow."

He never said a word; he pulled the truck to a stop at the red light and glared out the window. "You live the life of the entitled," he snapped, "You have so much and all you can do is focus on the things you don't have."

"You mean like most people do."

"Maybe they do, but that doesn't mean they should."

"And what makes you so sure about what I should do?" she asked, but at least there was heat in her voice, anger in her tone.

"Good. Get mad. Feel something. Anything is better than always shutting down. That makes you…"

"A victim. Yes, I know," she said, her voice calmer but still strident. "But you don't need to speak to me that way; I do it enough for both of us."

"And there's that damn self-pity again. Whatever else is burning a hole in your gut, get it out and get over it. This is a slow painful death. And over what?"

He glared at her, his own temper building to the point he was likely to say more than he should. He'd probably already had. He revved the truck engine and hit the gas too hard, spinning the tires slightly on the wet pavement as the truck lurched forward. He watched her grab for her arm rest. And that just made him angry.

"You don't know what pain is. You don't know what rejection is." He snorted. "And for all your losses, you still haven't learned to roll with the punches."

She snarled in outrage, "What, so because I wasn't abused all my life, I don't have the right to feel my own anguish? I don't have the right to be upset because your life was so much worse than mine was? Is this a fucking contest?" Her voice rose to a high pitch at the end.

"Hell no." He half laughed. "If it were, you'd have lost a long time ago."

"That doesn't mean I'm not allowed to feel what I feel."

"Of course you can feel it. But feeling it and wallowing in it is not the same thing."

There was only silence for the rest of the trip. When they reached the hotel, she hopped out of the truck, slammed the door close, and ran inside ahead of him. He didn't know if that was to avoid him or to get out of the rain. That question was answered as she raced ahead to the wall of elevators. He followed close enough to see her step into the elevator, the door closing in his face.

He took the stairs three at a time, a dozen words boiling upwards. He came out onto the floor to see her walking to her room. No, not walking – running. She made it to her door, fumbled in her purse for her card, and finally managed to find it. She opened her door just in front of him, entering just as he reached her. She turned, saw him, and jumped back.

"What, did you come to gloat?" she said, tears spilling down her cheeks.

"No," he said, hating the pain he'd caused. She'd needed to hear the words, but he wished he hadn't been the one to say them. He took a deep breath and broke his own long-time rule. "I came to apologize."

Chapter 18

APOLOGIZE? SHE WANTED to rip his head off. But his words broke the dam and instead of yelling at him, the tears flowed faster. He gave a muffled curse and suddenly she was tugged into his arms. She didn't want this. Not from him. But instead of pulling back, she was blubbering all over him. Worse yet, his comfort was working.

Damn.

She let the hot tears slow before finally stepping back to look up at him. "Sorry," she said, trying to speak in a normal voice and knew she'd failed when he snatched her back against his chest. A few straggling tears leaked. She sniffed a couple of times and tried to raise her hand to wipe her eyes, but her arms were pinned against his chest. A strong, whipcord-lean chest. Nice. She sighed. God, she was a mess. She should be slapping him silly for holding her like this, but all she could think about was that lean muscle beneath her hands...just waiting for her touch. Not that that was likely to happen. Too bad. She loved sex. Adored the sense of intimacy, of being part of a special twosome.

God, she missed that. And now that her libido had awakened...

She tugged her hand free and swiped at her cheeks. She must look a mess. "Excuse me," she muttered. His arms dropped away, letting her step back. She escaped into the bathroom. There, she stared at her ravaged face in the mirror. And damn if her tears didn't start to pour all over again. Still sniffling, she turned on the water and washed her face, hoping the cold water would help the puffy redness. She delayed as long as she could. What were the chances that he had left her alone?

If she'd read him right, none at all.

She didn't know where his harsh words came from, but he'd been right. Maybe not right to say such things to her, but he'd been right to have thought them. And she'd needed to hear them. As if the hospital visits weren't enough to remind her that her life could be so much worse.

When had it all become too much? She studied the left side of her face. When had she stopped planning for a better future? When had she really given up on the idea of finding love again? After the accident? Recently or somewhere in that long uphill climb in between.

Drained and thinking she'd somehow lost her way, she opened the door to find him still standing where she'd left him. She stopped just out of arm's reach. "Thank you."

He raised his eyebrows. "For being mean? For making you cry?" His voice hard and full of self-recrimination.

"No," she said gently, "For the reminder that life could be so much worse." She shrugged. "You were right. I was wallowing. It's an easy thing to do." She twisted her lips in a half smile. "As much as I don't like what you said, I needed to hear it."

She walked to the still open door and opened it wider. "You can leave now. I'm not going to do anything stupid." She was trying to give him a way out. He made no move to take it.

"Then as I said those truths, maybe you'll also listen when

I say *this* truth. You're a very beautiful woman."

She made a strangled sound, her hand already moving in a dismissive gesture when he reached out and caught her hand. "Stop. I've spoken the truth in all ways. Now listen."

She stilled. Her gaze locked on his face. Why would he say such a thing? As she searched his features, she realized another truth. He believed what he was saying. He was obviously blind but from his perspective, he believed she was beautiful.

Something inside loosened, warmed. She realized yet another bit of her icy shield around her heart had thawed again.

She sighed. And shook her head. "You need glasses."

"No, I don't." He smiled gently. "I can see you're working on your issues. That you are stuck on your exterior appearance. That you can't see the brave, valiant woman that I see. I'm sorry for that. Because if you could, you'd realize that you'd already accomplished so much this week, and it's not half over."

There was such a mix of emotions inside that she felt heavy, fatigued to the point of not being able to walk any further. Good thing she was already in her room. She slipped around him to sit on her bed. There was nothing intimate about the setting. Not like there could have been with having a man in her bedroom.

She rubbed her hand on her temple. "I'm trying to deal with my issues and failing miserably. I'm trying not to get hung up on my appearance, but that's a bit too big a step for me right now. All I see is the breakdown of who I am. The utter worthlessness inside. There are so many people worse off. I have nothing to complain about. See, you were right."

"Look, I'm sorry. I was harsh and cold. I knew you needed to be smacked out of your self-pity, but I don't want you to take it so far that you can't see how well you're doing."

"I'm not doing well at all." She lay back on her bed. She just wanted to curl up into a ball and have the world go away. "Are you sure you're not a shrink?"

He laughed and sat down beside her. "No way."

But there was a tone to his voice. She looked over at him. "What?"

There was a slight hesitation, then he said, "Nothing."

It was her turn to frown at him. "What, so you can poke and prod at others but not share anything yourself?"

But the moment was gone. He shrugged and with a lopsided grin said, "Those that can…"

She reached out and slugged him.

SEAN LAUGHED. HE reached out and tugged her forward into his arms and gave her a hug. A real hug. A gentle, non-threatening, hey-I'm-here-for-you type of hug. And was inexorably grateful when she didn't pull away. He'd been harsh on her. But it had worked and wonder of wonders, she appeared to have forgiven him.

"Let's go for dinner. Food will help settle the nerves."

She pulled back slightly. Her face was still punchy, but the smile was back in her eyes. "Thanks."

"Stop. Don't thank me. You are helping me as much as I'm helping you."

"Now if only I believed that." She studied his face carefully. "And the only way I could is if you'd explain."

He opened his mouth to push her off again and was surprised to hear the truth slide out. "I came for my sister's sake."

Robin tilted her head, her gaze narrowed thoughtfully. "Explain."

"Can we do this over a meal? I'm starved."

"As long as you do so." She grinned. "Although how you could be after that huge lunch, I don't know. Let's go."

They headed down to the restaurant and instinctively headed to the corner. Sean let her take her seat while he sat across from her. They barely had a chance to sit before the waitress was there with menus.

"I don't need a menu," he said and proceeded to order the house burger with fries. He waited as Robin smiled brightly up at waitress and said, "Make that two."

Damn, he liked that. A girl who could eat. And never whined about watching her weight or complaining about being on a diet. He'd seen Robin in a swimsuit and damn, but she was built. Nicely rounded yet slim and long lean limbs. Just the way he liked them.

After that, the waitress delivered water then coffee. By the time she'd left them alone, Sean realized Robin was itching for answers.

She leaned forward. "Well?"

He grinned. "Let me explain." And he proceeded to tell her about Paris trying to get into the workshop but being told to wait and asking him to attend for her.

Robin leaned back and stared at him. She slowly replaced the cup of coffee she'd been holding. "Wow. That's a wonderfully weird thing to do."

That startled a laugh out of him. "I guess it's odd but as she asked..." He shrugged. "I love her. She's trying to heal, and if there is anything I can do to help her succeed in that direction, I'm willing to do it," he said simply.

He studied her glistening eyes in confusion. "Why are you crying now?"

She sniffled several times but smiled though the tears. "It's a wonderful thing to do. I'm glad you care so much about her."

"She's had a tough life." He shrugged self-consciously, feeling exposed. He wasn't used to sharing his personal life. And never his personal feelings. Still, he owed Paris a debt he could never repay. "She was there for me all those years. There's not a lot I wouldn't do for her."

"I can't imagine what your childhood must have been like."

"We had no childhood," he said shortly, hating the sharp edge of anger rising up inside. The pain. The betrayal. No child should have to deal with what he and his sister had dealt with. No one person should – child or adult. Just as suddenly as it came, the anger sank back down.

"No, I imagine not." Robin took a sip of her coffee. "What does your sister do?"

"She's a nurse and works with children."

That brought Robin's eyebrows up. "Like where we were today?"

"Sort of, but not quite." He shook his head. "She works in the maternity ward."

"Good for her. I'm not sure I could do that job."

"She's a gentle soul." He smiled. "And she loves babies."

"Sounds like she should have a dozen of her own."

"That won't ever happen." He couldn't help it. His voice hardened as the memories piled into his brain and plugged up his thinking. Paris's abuse had been different than his but just as violent. Just as insidious and just as permanent.

Robin gasped in sympathy. "I'm so sorry for her. It's one thing to not be able to have children if that's not something you particularly cared to do, but if it is…" She winced then added, "I can't imagine anything worse."

Sean nodded. "She struggles with it sometimes. She loves to see the happy mothers, the beloved children. Every once in a while it's tough on her. Particularly when she has mothers in having their third and fourth and not wanting to be having the child. Stuck by circumstances or timing or just not caring enough to do something about not getting pregnant. And all she can do is help the woman through the process. Sometimes they are very voluble about their dislike of the whole process and in particular the child."

"Oh no." Robin shook her head. "It's a terrible thing in today's world to think of such a problem. Every child deserves to have a loving home and adoring parents. At least one parent."

"I feel the same way," Sean said. "Then again, I don't plan to have any kids, so it's not a big deal for me."

He stared out the window, feeling the intensity of Robin's gaze heat up. There was no way to explain that he was afraid he had more of his father in him that he suspected. That he'd rather kill himself than hurt a child like he'd been hurt. That he'd never want to be the kind of father like his own and that genetically it was all too possible. The pain had to stop somewhere, and he'd chosen to make sure it stopped with him.

"Maybe Paris will be able to adopt a half dozen, and then you'll have lots of nieces and nephews to practice your parenting skills on," Robin said lightly.

"No practice required. But I do think I'd enjoy being an uncle."

At that moment their food arrived, breaking the conversation at a great place. Sean tucked in.

Chapter 19

Robin's shoulders and back were knotted again. She rotated her shoulders and winced. Between the stress and fears, she'd locked her muscles, and they'd retaliated by staying locked. She was going to have to go to the pool and hot tub again. She'd left Sean outside in the hallway. He'd looked as if he wanted to say something to her. Do something. Invite her somewhere. She'd needed to be alone.

Only now that she was alone…she didn't want to be.

She'd checked her emails and studied her notes for tomorrow, thinking to get ahead on the assignments, only to find her mind unable to focus.

Now she had to wonder if her real wish to go to the pool had more to do with the possibility that Sean might go there as well. Or he could be sitting in the bar. She tossed that suggestion aside. She didn't think he was a drinker. Not a heavy one anyway. That would mean it was all right to lose control. She highly suspected control was important to him.

He'd held her with that same careful control. She couldn't believe how much she missed being held by a man. One who cared? Sean didn't care about her more than what they were to each other through this course… but she was starting to realize she wanted him to. Would he want to stay in touch after this week was over? She pondered that question while she got changed into her bathing suit. She had no idea where in the lower mainland he lived. She thought everyone in the workshop attended UBC, but she hadn't seen anything to indicate that Sean was a student.

He also wasn't here for himself.

She had mixed feelings about that. It was like he wasn't supposed to be here. Wasn't *trying* to heal like the rest of them. She'd have tacked on that he wasn't as broken as the others in the workshop, but she was realizing that in many ways, he was likely worse. Those in the workshop were at least admitting that they had problems and were willing to work on them. Not only willing but eager. Sean, by contrast, hadn't acknowledged he had a problem. At least not to her.

Although he'd been very good with the children. And how he could be, she didn't know. Given what he'd shared about his childhood, she had to wonder at the scars. He had many outside, but there were just as many on the inside.

How could there not be?

Still, he was remarkably normal.

Because of his sister.

There'd been love and support between them. A bond she imagined had been forged in hell. A bond that had kept them alive. Kept them sane. They'd both survived and thrived as well as they could, but they'd also hit that point where they couldn't do much more on their own. They needed help. Paris knew it. She'd been looking to come to the workshop. Robin could only imagine her disappointment.

From what little Sean had shared about her, Robin felt a kinship. She'd love to meet her. She couldn't remember ever seeing her at the evening sessions. Then again, she hadn't seen Sean there either. Although lately Robin had been missing more classes as it became harder to force herself out of her home. That tiny space had become an all-too-comfortable jail cell.

Crap. Unsettled and determined to stay in the progressive path, she snagged her housecoat off the bathroom hook and let herself out of the hotel room. She took the stairs to the pool deck and quickly stashed her belongings in a cubicle. There were several people in the pool and the hot tub appeared full. That was fine. She needed to work her poor muscles. Physio had helped all those years, but she needed to keep up the exercises. Something she often forgot.

Walking to the end of an empty lane, she curled her toes and dove in. The water was refreshing and cool. She struck out strongly and lost herself in the rhythmic pull of the muscles.

The car accident had left her with more than obvious scarring. The damage to her right leg, hip, and shoulder were likely to bother her most of her life. She'd taken the impact directly. She'd been leaning over her young brother when the collision happened and her hip had taken the worse of it, but the force had thrown her forward and sideways. It was the shards of glass and the multiple shattered bones and lacerations that had done the most obvious damage.

She remembered lying in the vehicle hearing the rescuers talk about the deceased in the accident. She'd thought they'd been talking about her. It hadn't been until she'd woken up in the hospital and found out that everyone else had died except for her.

It sucked to be the only survivor.

SEAN WATCHED AS Robin strode up to the edge of the pool in her typical straightforward attitude. She gripped the edge of the pool with her toes, her long muscles flexing, and she dove off in perfect form. She'd had lessons somewhere along the line. Lucky girl. He rarely thought of all that he'd missed out on in his childhood, but the differences between those normal families and his showed up at the oddest times. Like now.

She was a stunner even with the tight skin and the shiny look to her face. He could just imagine how far she'd come if the accident had been as bad as he suspected. Her shoulder had been injured and he doubted she was aware of it, but she walked with a limp when she was tired. In the morning, no one would notice. By the end of the day, she slowed down and it became more pronounced.

He thought of a bad accident with her in the back seat getting hit – if the impact had been on her side of the vehicle, it would explain the limp on her right side. He imagined her hips and possibly her ribs had taken the brunt of the hit. He winced just thinking about it. One minute you're talking and laughing and then smash…you were hit broadside and there was no more laughter in your world.

He knew she felt guilty. That she'd lost her younger brother had to be tough, but to lose *all* her family at the same time…wow. Considering everything, she'd been a trooper at the hospital. Not that he was ready to tell her that. He hoped she was ready to let her hair down – or rather put her hair up so she'd be who she really was to those kids. He doubted any of them would run screaming from her.

Between the kids in that ward, there were some major injuries and a lot of reconstructive surgery going on. They were – in the words of boys everywhere – 'awesome' looking injuries. He grinned, remembering the few times some of the other school kids had seen his injuries. They'd been jealous. It had made it easier to live through the experience. He and Paris used to play a game trying to determine the length of time for their bruises to change color. Sometimes they never had a chance to know because fresh ones were laid on top of the old.

He looked back down the empty lane where he'd been doing laps. He'd wanted to ask Robin to come up to the pool area with him but had sensed her refusal. He was used to that. Now he'd ended up here with her anyway. Sounded good to him. He just had to maneuver the two of them alone together again.

Long and lean and strong on the inside. She might not agree with that assessment, but then again, she didn't see herself the way he did.

He did another lap and felt his shoulder struggle to pull its weight. He'd been at it for long enough. Every day it seemed to get better, but if he dared miss a day or two, it was as if all progress was lost and he was back to the beginning. He used the pools at the university a lot. He wondered why he hadn't seen more of Robin.

With both of them being on campus, their paths had to cross sometimes...

UBC was a huge campus, almost a city in itself, with so many paths and buildings and different routes to travel that there was no need for two people to meet if they didn't want to, but as they both attended Jenna's evening lectures...

It was too bad they hadn't met before – several times even. If they had, they'd be much further along this path right now. And he had no doubt where that path was going. Except he felt different about her. He didn't want the same thing. Hell, that was a lie...he did want the same thing...he just wanted more. So much more. Paris would be delighted. He wasn't so sure. He hated this uncomfortable feeling. This sense of always looking to see where she was. What she was doing. Always thinking about her. Worrying...

Christ. This sucked. He was a long ways away from taking her into his arms and loving her the way he wanted to make love to her. Those scars she was so worried about were meaningless to him.

In all ways.

Now if only he had the chance to prove it to her.

Chapter 20

Robin stopped when she couldn't lift her arm for one more stroke. Maybe that had knocked her libido back down to reasonable levels again. She was hot, but it was from exertion and not sexual tension. She hoped. She didn't want to see Sean and put it to the test.

Breathing deep, she pulled herself up to sit on the edge of the pool until her breathing calmed down. She lifted her arms and wiped the water from her eyes. Normally she swam with goggles, but she'd forgotten hers at home in the fear and excitement of packing for the workshop. Swimming goggles had hardly been a priority. Blinking several times, she turned to look around. The pool had emptied and there were a couple of people left in the hot tub. It looked too damn far away to bother. But her body throbbed with pain.

And the hot water would help. She brushed her hair forward to hide her face before clambering to her feet. It was only as she stood swaying in place that she realized how tired she really was. By the time she made her way to the hot tub, she was ready to collapse. And damn, that hot water was going to suck the last of her energy away. Getting back to her hotel room was going to be a bitch.

She stood at the edge of the hot tub contemplating her options.

"Robin? Are you okay?"

Sean. She glanced down at him. Of course he'd be here. Why couldn't it be Tania? She'd barely seen her friend thus far at the conference.

She gave Sean a wan smile. "I'm okay. I think I just overdid the swimming part. Now I'm afraid the hot water will finish me and I won't be able to get back to my room."

He stood and reached up to gently grasp her elbow and helped her into the hot water. "The water will help the sore muscles, and I'll help you get to bed."

She almost laughed at his wording. Before her accident, she'd have teased him about the double entendre. In this case, it was likely accidental. Too bad. She wished he would help her to bed – his bed.

Groaning at the warmth as she sank into the water, she closed her eyes and dropped her head back on the edge. "This feels so good," she murmured.

"Yeah, it does."

Because they weren't alone, he sat down beside her. Keeping her voice low, she asked, "How's the arm after today's session?"

He opened and flexed his right hand a couple of times. "Better."

She snorted. "Not likely."

"What?" He grinned. "You think you know me now?"

"Oh, I know you." She smirked. "The good and the bad."

There was a stilted silence. She rolled her head in his direction and smiled at him. "What? Did I say something wrong?"

He shook his head. "I was just thinking how few people really know me. Paris is the only one."

"And now me."

There was a tiny sound followed by something that

sounded like *I wish*. But he'd spoken so low she wasn't sure. Going on instinct and hating to think of him so alone, she reached over and covered his hand with hers.

Immediately, under cover of the foamy bubbles, he closed his fingers over hers.

Her heart thumped and she smiled on the inside. She leaned her head back and for the first time all day, she just relaxed. The heat soaked deep into her muscles, letting the damaged and recovering tissue ease back their tightness, which in turn helped them to relax.

A few minutes later, she groaned softly. "This was the right decision."

"Definitely."

There was a teasing note to his voice. She grinned and opened her eyes to see they were alone in the hot tub. She twisted to search the rest of the large room and found to her surprise that the big room was completely empty.

"Wow, where did everyone go?" She settled back into the water and let her body float upward in the water. She loved doing this, but normally the hot tubs were too full of other people. She let go of Sean's hand and stretched out completely. "Hope you don't mind," she said with a laugh.

"Go for it."

She leaned her head back and floated, letting the water bubble up around her. God, it felt good. "Too bad it's not big enough for two of us to do this."

The next thing she knew, Sean had stretched out on the surface of the water, gently bumping up beside her. She laughed.

The world, for all the troubles of the last few days, seemed ideal right now.

"This is perfect," she said, her eyes drifting close but her smile still firmly in place. "I'm really glad I came tonight."

"Almost perfect," he said, "but there is one place I'd like to see you in even more."

Her eyes flew open, her head rolling slightly to face him. "Oh, where's that?"

She was gently turned and then shifted so she was upright, the water churning around her waist. While she was still adjusting to her change in position, he tugged her into his arms and said, "Right here."

And he lowered his head and kissed her.

AS FAR AS impulsive actions went, it was one of the best he'd taken in a long time.

The cool chill of her lips hid a banked heat that he couldn't get enough of. He wondered if he ever would. She had the sweetest, softest lips. He coaxed them to open for him. Her response was tentative at first, then she seemed to get over the shock and she became downright enthusiastic. And that was all he needed. His hands slid down her wet back to cup her rounded buttocks and pulled her tight against him. She wiggled closer.

He groaned.

She moaned.

He crushed his lips against hers before a heavy shudder wracked his frame. He eased back and slipped his tongue inside to duel with hers. Regardless of her initial response, she was there with him all the way now.

And damn him for starting this in a public place.

He wished they were standing in her bedroom where he could take this further. Take her to bed like he wanted to. A thought never far from his mind lately. Foolish. He wasn't here for this. He hadn't come looking for this.

Neither was he going to turn this down.

He was a healthy male. She was a dynamite sexy woman who'd lost her self-confidence. If nothing else, he could help her with that. She was still that same person – only now she was so much more.

She needed to remember that.

To learn that deep inside.

To take it in and own it.

He hadn't learned his lessons easily. Three days ago, he'd have told anyone that he hadn't learned any lessons. That he'd had no lessons to learn. In his arrogance. In his disdain of his fellow man. In his need to stay separate and detached from everyone around him, so as to not get hurt.

Then Robin happened. She'd shown him just how far he'd come – and just how far he had yet to go. He had no experience with long-term relationships. The last thing he wanted from her was a one-night stand. That left him uncertain, nervous as to how to proceed. Before, he hadn't cared if things worked out with a woman. Now he didn't want to screw up.

On that note, he pulled back and tugged Robin against his chest, her head tucked under his chin.

He held her close. He held her against his heart.

Just where she belonged.

Chapter 21

Robin shook so hard she needed to lean against him for support. For a first kiss, that was unbelievable. Talk about mind blowing. And all she could think about was another one. Heat fired through her at the thought. God, if she had this type of response to his kiss, what would making love be like? She whimpered then caught her breath, hoping he hadn't heard her. But he dropped a tender kiss on her forehead, then another on her temple. She tilted her head back, giving him better access if he wanted it.

He lowered his head and dropped a gentle kiss on her lips.

"We're going to need to take this up somewhere private or be prepared to be interrupted here."

She stiffened, jerked back, and hurriedly looked around. "Dear God, are we alone?"

A warm deep laugh rumbled up from his chest. "We are. At the moment."

"Jesus." She sank back into the water and dropped her face in, letting the foam rush up and over her features. She couldn't believe she'd forgotten where she was. She sat up, brushing her hair back off her face. She didn't know what to do – how to proceed. She took a deep breath. "I think I'll go up to my room."

He helped her out of the hot water before walking ahead of her to pick up her robe and wrap it around her. "Come on.

I'll help you back up."

"What about your robe? Did you not have one?"

He laughed. "I didn't bring one. I just came down in my shorts and..." He stopped and looked around the space. "And...my t-shirt." He walked over several feet and picked up a green shirt she hadn't noticed until now lying on the tiles. As she watched, he tugged it over his head then turned to her and held out his hand. "Come on."

It felt momentous. A turning point.

It also felt...right.

HE ESCORTED HER, damp footsteps tracking behind them on the hotel carpet, to the back elevators. Within minutes they'd reached their floor. He led her to her room and waited for her to pull her card out of her robe's pocket and unlock the door.

So far, she'd said nothing. Had given no sign of her intentions.

His stomach knotted. He wanted her with him tonight. And tomorrow. God, he had it bad. And he hadn't had any warning. He hadn't seen it coming. It had blindsided him. From one moment to the next.

No, that wasn't quite true. She'd crept up on him slowly, gaining a little more inroad to his heart every hour, every day. What the hell did that make him? Besides a fool. All of it pissed him off. The uncertainty. Not knowing his next step. What to say. How to act.

With the door pushed open, Robin stepped inside and turned to face him.

His frustration waned. Expectation rose. He wanted to close his eyes – therefore he stared right at her. And waited for her say something.

Sex was straightforward. He didn't know how to handle relationships. No idea how to start one. He'd never had to. Or even to understand if they had the start of one. God, he hoped so. He didn't think he could trust himself to make these types of decisions if he was wrong this time.

He couldn't be wrong. *This* couldn't be wrong. It felt too right.

She smiled, reached up, and kissed him gently. "Thank you."

"Ask me in." The words blurted out of his mouth with all the subtlety of a green teenager.

"Do you think it's wise?"

"Ask me in," he repeated, hating the tiny plea that entered his voice, hoping she didn't hear it. When she studied him…and never said a word, he couldn't bear it and he added one thing – one thing he'd thought to never say in this situation. "Please."

Chapter 22

Oh Lord. She'd been all set to refuse him – her mind at odds with her jumping jack hormones. Then he'd said please…and that final layer of frost around her heart started a downward slide.

She pushed the door open wider.

His gaze widened. He glanced from the door to her, and when she didn't move, his eyebrow rose and his lips quirked. "Is that an invitation or only half an invitation?"

She gave him a slow easy smile. "I guess it doesn't matter – both say yes."

He entered and closed the door behind him. The shadows fell across his cheekbones, his forehead giving him a fallen angel look. She hadn't turned a light on, and now she was glad. The darkness was a blessing. It hid so much. And showed much more.

Snick went the lock. He turned to face her, his gaze heavy lidded, his eyes almost black with emotion, and opened his arms.

He was even now giving her a choice.

She didn't want one. She needed this. She was grateful that he didn't appear to be put off by her disfigurement. She had no trouble with his scars either. She'd suspected sex with Sean would be a wild ride. And damn it, she wanted to strap in and enjoy.

And yet she hesitated.

It had all gone by so fast. She barely knew Sean. No, her mind rejected that. Sean no longer qualified as a stranger. She might not know all the details about his life, but she knew the person that stood before her – probably as well as she had any man. Then again, she'd have sworn that her boyfriend, Tom, could never have said the things he'd said.

Comparing Sean to Tom was wrong. They were nothing alike. Sean was the antithesis of Tom. Sean was…complicated. Yet he had an honor system and a code. They might be difficult to live by, but she'd take that over superficial any day.

She smiled up at him.

He opened his mouth, and in a gentle tone, asked, "Second thoughts?"

"No," she said. "I was just thinking how much I prefer deep, dark, and broody to shallow and superficial."

His eyebrows shot up and he stared at her, his head tilted slightly to the side. He was confused. Good. It would serve him right. He'd kept her off balance more than she cared to admit. Before he could formulate the question that was working through his psyche, she stepped into his arms.

She reached up and tugged his head down and kissed him.

As his arms closed around her, more comforting than lover-like, and his lips were warm but not hot, she quirked her own lips slightly. He was still giving her a chance to back away.

She pulled back slightly and dropped her robe to the floor. Now she stood in her wet bathing suit. She stepped back one more step, deeper into the shadows. She slipped the straps off her shoulders and lowered the clinging material to her waist. She watched him as he watched her.

There was no way he could see the details, but she knew

what the shadows would highlight.

When he gasped slightly, a flush rising slightly across his cheeks, she grinned inside. Good. In a hard tug, she had the bathing suit pooling on the floor. She gave the material a kick and sent it flying across the room and stood before him. Nude. Scarred. Ready.

"Second thoughts?" she asked, repeating his earlier words, motioning to his modest attire. "And just so it's a non-issue. I'm on the pill to regulate my cycle." She wrinkled up her nose at him. "The drugs from the surgeries messed things up big time."

He galvanized into action so fast she laughed. But her laughter was choked off a few seconds later as she was picked up, swung into a wide circle, then tossed on the big bed.

And he came down on top of her.

"You are amazing," Sean said, before he covered her mouth with his.

As long as he thought so, she'd let him live the dream a little longer. Even join him in it for a little while. At least as long as she was in his arms.

Then she couldn't think as his kisses turned her insides to mush. Still damp from their wet bathing suits, their bodies steamed as legs tangled with legs and hands caressed and stroked what each could reach as they both gave and took in equal measures.

She realized dimly, somewhere in the back of her mind, that he was good at this. Like he was seriously good at this. He was so caring, attentive, appreciative. He made her feel special. How sexy was that?

She realized, as his lips teased a hot blazing trail of kisses downward to one breast, a breast with some scar tissue marring the perfect flesh, that she was the richer one in this situation. She'd loved and had been loved. She knew what it was like to wake up beside someone you cared about in the morning. To feel blessed they were in your life.

She could show him some of that.

Except he was frying her circuits, making it so she couldn't think. He took her nipple deep into his mouth and suckled. She reared up, gasping with joy and frustration. God, she wanted him. Like now. Like hot and ready and inside her now.

"Sean," she cried out, twisting beneath him.

"Easy, sweetheart, take it easy."

"No," she cried out, her hands tugging on him. "Not easy. Now."

When he refused to slide up higher, she shifted downward and rolled him over. He laughed and flipped onto his back, tugging her over and with him.

"Patience," he murmured, pulling her down to his mouth and kissing her with one of his heavy, drugging kisses that she craved.

"No patience," she gasped against his lips when she could. "Next time. We'll take it slow and easy then."

She planted a knee on either side of his hips, slipped down his body until she felt him, rigid, hard, hot at her center. She sat up and lowered herself slowly, oh so slowly, until he was seated deep inside. Watching his eyes cloud with passion was a turn on like no other.

Sean groaned, his eyes slowly closing, his fingers clenching her hips, holding her in place as he ground his pelvis upwards.

She shuddered, already so close to the edge.

"Jesus, you'll be the death of me," he whispered in a husky voice.

"Not yet, but soon," she murmured, her eyes closed. She

started to ride. Initially she set a slow languid pace, reveling in the sense of fullness, the perfect fit of the two of them, the hard leanness of his body, but Sean urged her on, faster and faster. She leaned forward to brace her hands on his chest, holding her rhythm. Sean held her hips back from going too high.

She cried out, "Sean..."

"I'm here," he whispered. "'Faster...

"I can't..." She tried to go faster, but her urgency and drive sent her rhythm off. Frustrated, he did a quick flip, startling a cry out of her, as their positions reversed. He lifted her leg over his arm and plunged deep.

She shrieked, her back arching as tiny explosions started deep inside. Then she came apart.

With a heavy guttural groan, he followed her.

SEAN ROLLED TO the side, completely wiped. He groaned lightly and tugged her into his arms. "I'm wasted. You completely wore me out."

She sniggered, the cheeky sound bringing a smile to his face.

"If you're worn out that easily, you'll be comatose by morning."

He shouted with laughter and kissed her again. She responded with all the enthusiasm as she had the first time. God, he loved that about her. The honesty of her reaction. The responsiveness of her passion. The clarity of her need. He needed that.

He needed her.

He was starting to think he'd need her forever.

Shuddering with the emotions swamping him, he pulled

back to stare down at her. And realized he'd not taken the time to look at her. To *really* look at her. The room was dark. And he wanted to see her in the light.

The shadows earlier had hid her beauty.

He reached for the lamp switch.

"Don't." Her voice was harsh, clear. She cleared her throat. "Please."

He let his arm drop, not sure what to say yet hating that she didn't want him to see her like this. And not sure what to do about it.

He tugged her into his arms, his cheek against hers, and just held her.

After a long moment, he pulled back slightly and looked her straight in the eyes. He watched her gaze widen with worry. He smiled reassuringly. "It's all right. If you don't want a light, that's okay."

She searched his gaze and he let her see the acceptance in his eyes. The acceptance in his heart. He understood. More than most.

"Thank you," she whispered.

"You're welcome." He dropped a kiss on her nose. Then her cheeks. He pushed her hair back so he could look at the scarred side of her face closer. He hadn't done that yet. Hadn't had a chance to. He hadn't wanted to push. Now it wasn't pushing. It was time for rejoicing. Well, maybe not. She wasn't there yet. But he could help her take one more step toward it.

He kissed the spot where the tight skin pulled the corner of her mouth up and back. Bright pink skin, no longer angry, but quite normal looking – *if* it would ever become normal. It may not. He was fine with that. She was beautiful to him. Beautiful inside and out.

Somehow he had to make her see that. He grasped her

face and held it firmly so she couldn't pull away while he kissed every inch of the shiny skin. Worshipped the misshapen skin and the rough edges where the scars joined the smooth healthy skin. She wouldn't need much more to make this all perfect looking, but he did understand how imperfect something in progress looked. He had been there. Was still there.

Yet his scars didn't appear to bother her.

So he needed to make sure she knew that her scars didn't bother him.

He followed the line of her neck down to her shoulder blades where there were more scars. More spots where her skin was marred from its creamy perfection. But not taking away from it. In fact, as he pulled back to stare at the pink skin, it added to it. She was beautiful.

And she misunderstood his actions. She slapped her hand across her shoulder, hiding. "Don't look," she whispered. "Turn away."

"Never," he whispered and showed her how much he cared about her. How much he adored her. How much he worshipped her. Her perfect body. How all the spots she hated only added to her beauty. To her uniqueness. She was stunning in her passion.

They had hours ahead of them. He planned to make sure she knew that by morning. That she knew he adored her. Every inch of her.

He smiled as he looked down at her and whispered under his breath, "But I'm up for the job."

She looked up at him, a puzzled frown on her face. "What did you say?"

"How about I show you instead…"

And he lowered his head.

CHAPTER 23

MORNING BROKE SLOW and hazy for Robin. Within minutes, she realized something else. She wasn't alone.

Memories flooded in. Last night. Sean – all night. Oh God.

What a night. Considering she'd gotten no sleep, she had no right to feel as rested as she did. She felt energized. Invigorated. As if she had a whole new day in front of her. She reached up and rubbed her face with both hands.

And stilled. Her hand gently stroked the scars on her face. Maybe not a *new* day. Still, it was a different day. Different from yesterday at least. That she'd take.

She looked over to see Sean stretched out dead to the world in the center of the bed. Her back was tucked up against him. She smiled. She might feel on top of the world, but he looked dead to the world. She wanted to giggle and shout for joy but held back. He needed what little rest he could find. She'd just slip out and grab a shower. Then wake him up.

It was early yet. They had a little time before going down for breakfast. Thank heavens, she thought as she stared into the bathroom mirror. She was going to need every bit of that time to make herself presentable.

She stepped into the shower and let the hot water sluice down over her body. She wanted to keep his scent on her, but they'd made love so many times, she was afraid that it would be obvious to anyone who walked past her. This night had been special. Important. And she didn't want to share it with anyone.

She wanted to keep it between just her and him.

They hadn't spoken of love. Of tomorrow. Of togetherness. In fact, they'd barely spoken at all.

The water splashed into her face and she laughed, loving it. The spray both stung and soothed at the same time. She stood, face forward, grinning like a madman.

And realized time was running down the drain along with the water while she'd been standing there like a fool. She finished, then turned off the water and toweled dry.

She brushed her hair into her normal style, covering her face. She stared her face for a long moment, wondering if it was time to change but realized that she wasn't ready for that much change.

Gathering up her towel, she walked back into the bedroom and quietly got dressed. When she was done, she sat down on the side of the bed, stared at the masculine feast in front of her with regret, and woke him. "Sean?"

His eyes flew open and he stared at her. And heat kindled deep inside. "Good morning," he said in a gruff voice. He tugged her down to sprawl across his chest and gave her a deep morning-after kiss.

She was flustered by the time she managed to pull back. "It's late. We don't have time for any more of that."

"Ha." He gave her a lazy grin. "We could miss the workshop. Spend the day in bed."

"Oh boy," she muttered half under her breath, unbearably torn. Memories of the night swamped her body with remembered heat. She wanted that again. And again.

"As tempting as that is, I do need to complete the workshop." She smiled regretfully down into those languid eyes and sighed. "I really want to stay here but..."

"But you want to go the workshop more." He tugged her back down, kissed her hard, and then set her back in place. "Right then. I need to shower and find some clothes." He looked around, gathered up his clothes, and snatched up her robe, a question in his eyes. When she nodded, he put it on and slipped out of her hotel room. She followed him to the doorway and watched as he slipped inside his room. The door closed quietly behind him.

He hadn't said a word about how long he'd be, so she wasn't sure what she should do. Wait for him? Go into his room and wait for him? Or head down to the restaurant and wait for him there?

She should have asked. Oh well, it was too late now, he was likely already in the shower and wouldn't hear her knock. She headed back inside and packed up her notes for the morning session and cleaned up her bathing suit still sitting on the floor. She hung it up, a silly grin on her face. Would she ever see it again and not smile from the memory?

After hooking her housekeeping tag on her door, she walked down to the elevators and clicked the button. She'd wait for him down at the restaurant. As the elevator doors opened, she walked out into a small crowd. It was a popular hotel. There looked to be a large group checking out, even though it was still early. She slipped around them and came face to face with Jenna.

Jenna's face beamed. "Hi Robin, you're looking particularly bright today."

Robin managed a sheepish grin in spite of the heat washing up her neck. "Thank you. It's amazing what a good night's sleep will do for you."

"I'm glad to hear that. If your sleep is improving, that means you are healing on some level."

That made sense. She was healing. She could thank Sean for that.

Not wanting to share the details of the healing process with Jenna, Robin walked past with a murmur, "I need to get some breakfast."

Jenna nodded, a pleased smile on her face. "You don't have much time, but you can grab something to go."

Lord, she hoped they weren't that late. She checked the clock on the restaurant wall as she entered. Ugh. It was after 8:30. She really didn't have much time. And Sean had even less. She took a seat up at the front and ordered toast to eat now and several muffins to go. She gulped down a cup of coffee drenched in cream and ordered two more to go. After scoffing down her toast and wondering at her appetite, she gathered up her purchases and carried them over to the seminar room. It was already full. Tania was sitting in some kind of cold truce with Kane. The workshop was half over – at least she thought it was, she'd lost track of time. Was it Wednesday or Thursday today?

After a quick glance around, she realized Sean still wasn't there. She took a seat where there were two empty spots and sat down. She immediately went to work on the first muffin. Lord, she was still hungry. If Sean didn't get here soon, she was going to eat his two as well.

Just then, the chair beside her was pulled out and Sean sat down.

He reached for a coffee, assessed the muffin situation, and grabbed up two for himself.

She kept her head down in case her smirk alerted the others to the change in their relationship. She didn't care. Her body glowed and her heart sang. She had no illusions that this was a relationship. By his own admittance, he didn't know what one was. But she was grateful for what they did have. She hadn't felt this alive in months.

Quite possibly years.

AFTER A LATE arrival for the seminar and a crazy busy morning working on Jenna's assignments, before Sean realized it, they were breaking for lunch. He rose from his chair when Jenna called them over.

"Sorry you two, but this afternoon at the hospital is out," Jenna said. "You'll need to work on your project here at the hotel. It's possible you might be able to go later this evening, otherwise it will have to be tomorrow morning. I'm hoping that after two days there you have enough to get some serious effort done on the project just in case your time is shortened even more."

She turned to walk away when Sean stopped her. "Why? What's going on?"

"One of the kids has taken a turn for the worst. The other kids are having a tough day."

"Maybe we should go today especially for that reason," Sean said. He was afraid he knew which boy had taken a bad turn. Figured that Robin, from the frozen look on her face, had jumped to the same conclusion, too. She shuddered. A visible shake of her shoulders that must have gone straight to her toes. Shit. She didn't need this. Hell, neither did he. He'd had high hopes for more private time. At Jenna's initial words, he'd wanted to shout for joy. Now he knew that a private afternoon in bed with Robin wasn't going to be.

"No. The department head has requested that not happen. The children want their privacy while they deal with their emotions." She studied Robin's features even as Sean studied Jenna's.

"It's Jon, isn't it?"

Jenna's face became a polite mask. "Who?"

"A little boy that looked so very much like my brother."

Jenna's face became a mask of concern. "I'm sorry if that is the case. He's still alive though, so we have to hope."

"I want to go see him."

"No." Sean and Jenna both shouted.

Robin squared her shoulders. "Yes. I need to. Don't you see? I've associated him with my brother. I couldn't help it. There were so many similarities. Now that he's in trouble, I want to be able to do what I couldn't do before."

Jenna walked closer, her hands reaching out to grasp Robin's. "You don't know this boy. You aren't family. You can't go in and see him."

Robin's eyes glistened. Sean felt his heart sink.

"I have to go say goodbye," Robin whispered. "I have to."

She broke free of Jenna's hands and turned, running from the room.

"Damn it." Sean glared at Jenna. "See what happens when you meddle in other people's lives?"

She gave him a sad smile. "It's what I do. Before there can be healing, one must let go of the blockages. In this case, Robin has never fully grieved for her family. She can't go forward until she finally lets go of the past."

Sean knew she was right but hated hearing it. He didn't want Robin to suffer, and she was going to do plenty of that before this day was over.

He started after Robin.

"Sean." Jenna called out.

He turned but didn't walk closer. "What?"

"What are you going to do?" she asked, her gaze a pool of compassion. She might meddle in other people's lives, but she didn't do it lightly. Every time one of her students hurt, Sean realized Jenna did, too.

He said quietly, "Talk her out of it, or take her there myself."

She stilled, her gaze intent. "Why?"

He looked to see if she was serious. Realizing she was, he shook his head and said, "Because that's what friends do."

And he walked away, wondering at her last question. Then made a startling realization. He had no idea what friends did.

Because he'd never had one before.

Chapter 24

ROBIN SAT ON the edge of her bed, her mind in turmoil. She hadn't realized how much her life was on hold because she'd never had a chance to say goodbye. She'd grieved for her parents from the moment she'd understood what had happened. It had been hard, so hard, she hadn't been able to deal with the loss of her brother at the same time. It was as if she'd compartmentalized the losses. Her parents in one and her brother in the other.

Now the last compartment had been opened. Because of Jon. The two were mixed up inside her head. Her heart. She'd never had a chance to say goodbye to Jonathon. Somehow that mattered. The shrinks would call it closure.

In theory she hadn't had the same opportunity with her parents either, but having grieved for them already, it felt like the process was complete in some way. Not so with Jonathon.

That was just stupid. How could the death of another little boy help heal the loss of the first? It couldn't. It just made two wrongs. Not one right. She flopped back on the bed, her mind dimly aware that housekeeping had come...and gone. The pungent smell of a heavy night of lovemaking was...missing. She wanted to cry. She wanted something to hang onto from last night. Something to remind herself it had been real.

Cause this was reality now. Last night was one bit of fantasy she'd hold close forever. But there was no way she'd be having a relationship with Sean. She wasn't his kind. He wasn't her kind. She didn't know what her kind was anymore, but she wasn't into one-night stands. Given that she'd done just that, he could be forgiven for thinking she was. Maybe there were people who met once a week. Met every Tuesday for servicing. His and hers kind of servicing. God, what a horrid thought.

As she lay there, a pounding on the door slowly penetrated the fog in her mind. She didn't want to see anyone. Didn't want to speak with anyone. Her mind filled in the next line automatically. Didn't want to care for anybody.

It all hurt. And she was tired of being hurt.

She froze as another truth popped into her mind. It wasn't so much that she was tired of the pain of the surgeries, but that she was tired of being hurt. Of being the one that hurt. If she didn't have more surgeries, she couldn't be hurt anymore. She wouldn't wake up in pain, live in agony for days, weeks of recovery ahead of her.

Except an innocent child had run still screaming from her – so she'd been hurt anyways. Confused, not knowing how to move forward, she'd gone inside and stayed there. She was a mess.

The truths coming at her so hard and so fast were chilling. She didn't know when the tears started. Didn't know when the door opened or when strong arms lifted her, turned her, and enclosed her against a warm hard chest.

Sean. Somehow he'd gotten into her room. She couldn't be angry. How could she be when he was all she wanted right here and now? To be held. To be loved, even if just for a moment, so that she could curl up and know someone else was there to share the burden. Even if only for a little while.

But he needed to know the truth. She really wasn't worth saving. She was small. Selfish. Weak.

In a broken voice, between the sobs, she told him. About needing to say goodbye. About needing the pain to stop. About needing to fix this now, while she could. If she could. And about not being worthy of his care...but she needed it anyways. She hoped he could stand to be with her a little longer because she didn't think she could do this alone. She didn't want to put herself to the test and fail...one more time.

She put her arms against his chest and pushed back so she could look into his face, but she could barely see as her tears flowed like a waterfall down her face. "I'm sorry," she sobbed. "So sorry."

"For what?" he whispered. "For being on this planet in the journey called life as the animal identified as a human?"

She choked, giggled, then sobbed some more.

"You can never *be* perfect. You *are* perfect. You can never be whole, you *are* whole. You can never be better than you are at this moment." He smiled so tenderly more tears welled up. "You are the best you can be right now."

She shook her head, her hair flying wildly about her head, only to end up clinging to her face. "I've done nothing. Don't you understand? I should be over this. I should have completed the surgeries by now and all this," she waved her arm at her face, "Would be over and done with. I'd look normal. Or at least as normal as I can be."

"So you can do that next week. Get back to the business of doctors and hospitals."

"Next week? Maybe." She threw up her hands. "But only if I can say goodbye this week."

There was a gentle pause.

Then he asked slowly, "What do you need to do to say

goodbye?"

"I have to go to the hospital," she said painfully.

"I hate to say this, but you can't be allowed to confuse the boys – Jon is not your brother."

"No," she whispered sadly, "But you have to understand, it was *that* hospital...my brother Jonathon died there. I was in a separate hospital. I never got a chance to see him again." She stared around the room blind to her surroundings. "He died alone."

She took several shaky breaths. "The last memory I have is when we were hit. My mother screaming. My father yelling, and my brother, my baby brother, never saying a word. He just lay in a crumpled heap of broken bone and torn flesh."

"I was injured and trying to get free. Trying to get to him when the fire started. The rescue crews were trying to free us, and the flames kept growing bigger."

She stopped, her voice trembling, unable to form a word. She burrowed deeper into his chest. "I need to go to the hospital. Even if I can't see him. I need to walk the hallways. See where my brother had been. See where he'd died and if I can, say goodbye."

"How would it help to walk the hallways of the hospital that's full of children, especially since the one you want to see isn't there?"

She smiled through her tears. "I don't know that it will, but I have to try."

He stared at her intently. And he nodded.

"Let's go then."

After that, they moved quickly. After all, who knew if they'd be allowed to see Jon and if they were, how long he actually still had.

"THANK YOU."

He stood up, wrapped an arm around her shoulder, and led her gently to the door. "Let's go. We don't have much time."

"We might not even be allowed to see him." He knew that. She'd already mentioned it once. It was as if she needed to go over everything again to reassure herself that she was doing the right thing.

He stayed silent and walked outside the hotel parking lot. He helped her into his truck and started up the engine. For someone who'd promised to never enter another hospital – especially this particular children's hospital – he was there a lot. He drove the now well-accustomed route to the hospital and parked in the visitor parking lot.

It was early afternoon now. Time they'd have normally been in the ward. They'd only been there twice, but he'd figure the third time would have been the charm for Robin. Now he realized she wasn't likely to get that third time. That was too bad.

Robin had the potential to beat a mess of issues with these kids. Jenna had been right there.

That didn't mean he liked her methodology. It had been harsh. Cruel. And incredibly terrifying for Robin. It didn't matter if she had signed up for this workshop, she hadn't known what she was signing up for.

He led the way through the hallways. It wasn't visiting hours yet, but one could get away with all kinds of things if one walked with purpose. He stopped outside the ward where they'd been for the last two days and turned back to look at Robin.

She held back. "We shouldn't disturb them."

"So what do you want to do?"

She turned back the way they'd come. "I want to find Jon."

Just then, the doors opened behind them and Andrea walked out. "Oh dear, did you not get my message?"

Sean nodded. "We did. We're so sorry to hear about him. It's Jon, isn't it?" At Andrea's nod, Sean glanced over at Robin and asked, "Is there anything we can do for him?" He nodded to the room behind them, "For them?"

Andrea shook her head. "No. At this point, we don't have an update on his condition. The kids are pretty upset. They just want some downtime."

"Is that the right thing for them?" Robin asked. "Isn't a distraction a better idea?"

"What do you suggest?" Andrea eyed Robin curiously. "Or are you just asking a general question?"

"Both in a way." Robin murmured. "I guess I won't be able to see Jon, will I?"

She shook her head. "No, he's in the ICU. No one is allowed in but immediate family."

"Does he have any?" Robin asked.

The nurse pursed her lips. "I don't actually know. Most people have someone."

Sean and Robin shared a look. "Not in our cases, we didn't," Sean said quietly. "We both understand what Jon and," he tilted his head toward the ward, "the others are going through."

Her gaze sharpened. "I hadn't known."

"No one does," Robin said. "Not really."

"Well, you might be able to stand outside Jon's room and see him, but you won't be allowed in." She turned back to the ward, and said, "As far as these guys go, I'll see how the mood is if you want to check in with me after that."

Sean smiled. Nice. "Thanks, we'll do that." He slipped an arm around Robin's shoulders and turned in the direction of the ICU unit. With any luck, she'd be able to at least see Jon from the hallway.

They walked quietly toward the ICU, Robin ever silent at his side. It took ten minutes to get where they needed to be.

With every step, the air around Robin seemed to deepen, darken.

"Are you okay?" he asked.

Chapter 25

"I'M FINE," SHE whispered. "It just feels so…" She shrugged. "…odd to be here." Like it was wrong for Jon to be here.

"So do what you need to do and let's leave. We don't need to go back to the ward if you don't want to. Andrea will understand."

Robin nodded. "We'll see."

She hoped she was together enough to want to go and see the boys, but as she'd been dragging herself, kicking and screaming, to that same room the last two days…

They came into the super silence of the Intensive Care Unit.

"I wonder where he is," Robin asked, hating to look into the rooms without knowing who was on the other side. Out of the corner of her eyes, she saw movement. A mother sat down beside a bed to her left. Robin smiled. At least that person had someone who loved them.

They walked to the end where Robin stopped outside a room. She caught a glimpse of a small figure lost in the huge bed. That was Jon. She knew it. Felt it. Her instincts were screaming at her to run. That she wouldn't like what she found. That she should leave before she got too close to the issue and got hurt – again.

Run, her mind screamed. *Save yourself from more hurt*,

run.

She refused to let her feet follow those comments.

No more running for her.

She planned on staying right where she was.

For better or for worse.

She walked over to the window to see Jon's small fine-boned features looking slack and hollow-eyed. He slept, which was the best thing for him. She hated to see him lying there so alone. From outside, she had to assume it was a majorly bad turn. She could only stand and stare, her heart breaking. Was this what her brother had looked like before he'd died? Had he been all alone like Jon? The thought almost brought her to her knees.

Instantly, Sean wrapped his arm around her shoulders. "Hey, take it easy."

"He looks so lost. So alone."

"We don't know that. He's getting the best care he can get. We just have to hope." He stared into the window. "I wonder what happened."

A nurse stepped up beside him and said in a quiet voice. "There were complications from what should have been a simple surgery."

Robin gasped, her hand going to her own face. The nurse nodded. "We do our best, but sometimes, through no one's fault, things go wrong."

Robin understood the inherent truth of that statement, all the while hating the unfairness of the situation. "Is he dying?" she asked in a small voice.

"There's a chance he'll pull out of this. If he makes it through the night, he'll have a much better chance."

She hoped he made it. There was little enough she could do but whisper her prayers with all the heartfelt emotion she could put behind it. Something she hadn't had a chance to do for her brother. She wasn't religious, having been raised without, but figured there had to be someone out there to help.

She closed her eyes and bowed her head, letting a gentle prayer ripple through her thoughts. When she opened her eyes, she turned to the nurse and said, "Is there any chance I can stand beside him for moment?"

The nurse shook her head. "It's not allowed. Neither will he know that you are there."

"Just for a moment," she pleaded.

There was enough hesitation in the nurse's gaze that she pressed home the advantage. "Please, I promise I won't touch him."

Sean stepped forward. "You can go in and wait with her."

Sighing, the nurse turned and led the way over to Jon's bed. "You get five minutes. You can touch his hand but nothing else."

Robin, nervous but excited, followed. When she realized Sean wasn't following, she turned to look back at him.

He smiled reassuringly. "Go. I'll wait right here.

She gave him a brilliant smile and followed the nurse to Jon's side.

SEAN FOLLOWED ROBIN'S progress to Jon's bedside. She reached out to stroke the small hand. Then she bowed her head. He could see her lips moving. He wished he could hear what she was saying. As he watched, she talked to Jon, smiled, and maybe even laughed a little. He was amazed. What was she saying? He turned to gauge the nurse's reaction. At the softening of her features and the gentle smile on her face, he took that to mean that whatever Robin was saying was coming from heart.

And that girl had a big heart.

Watching her warmed his lonely heart. He'd never met anyone like her. Had never thought to either. Such women were for other men. Whole men.

Men who had a heart left to care.

He'd never realized he was one of them – until now.

Chapter 26

ROBIN WALKED OUT of Jon's room, tears in the corner of her eyes but with a smile on her face. As soon as she saw Sean, she ran to him. His arms closed lovingly around her. She nestled in close, waiting for her heart and emotions to calm down. When she could, she pulled back slightly and looked up at him. "Thanks for being here."

He dropped a kiss on the tip of her nose. "Always."

She smiled, "Now if only you meant that." She deliberately stepped out of his arms and turned to the hallway. "I'd like to go see the boys now."

His gaze narrowed. "Are you sure?"

"Yeah, I promised Jon I would." At his startled look, she added, "I don't know why..." She shrugged. "But it seemed like the right thing to say at the time."

Once there, he turned in the direction of the common room, tucked her arm into his, and led the way.

At the ward, Andrea met them at the doorway. She smiled and said, "Just for a few minutes."

The two walked a dozen feet inside and stopped. The kids turned to face them, a mixture of hope and fear on their faces. Robin smiled. "I just visited Jon. He's holding his own right now."

Andrea gasped.

The kids ran closer. "Is he getting better?" the first one

asked.

"I can't say that for sure. I can tell you that he's sleeping and the doctors are hopeful." At her words, several of the kids seemed to relax. She didn't want to give them the wrong impression, but everything she'd said so far had been the truth.

The closest boy approached. "Hi. I'm Brian."

She stiffened. It was one thing to deal with necessities. It was another when this became close and personal. Dealing with children on a one-on-one basis could get very personal. Closing her eyes briefly, and then opening them, Robin took a deep breath and whispered. "Hi Brian."

"What's wrong with your face?" he asked bluntly, in the way of children. At least they were honest. Then he added, "It looks something like Jon's. Are you dying, too?"

"No, I'm not dying," she responded lightly, knowing that the slightest negativity could send the boys into a wave of depression again. She tried to brighten her smile. "I was in an accident."

"I was in an accident, too," he said after a moment. He indicated his missing leg.

She studied his stump. He was on crutches and doing fine. "Looks like you're motoring around just fine."

He shrugged. "I'd rather have my leg back. But I'm getting a new super fast – like superhero fast – fake one. It's got weird curves in it." And he waved his arms in the air, sketching the image. She had to laugh. "So you're going to be a superhero now?"

"Nah. But maybe I'll be close." He brightened at the thought and hobbled back several paces. Several other boys joined him until a large group stood around staring at her. They were going to ask more questions. She could sense them gearing up.

Andrea stepped closer and murmured, "Are you okay?"

Robin nodded. "Sure."

She knew what the kids wanted. She couldn't hide anymore. Maybe never could. And maybe it would help them to see her as a separate person. Not related to Jon. And if they saw that she was fine and had survived all her surgeries, maybe they'd have a little more hope for Jon, too.

"Do you want to see my face?" Robin asked, proud of the calm in her voice. Better to get this over with. It would stall the questions that made them all look ready to burst.

"Yes!"

Just as she went to lift her hair back, Brian turned back to the other kids and said, "If you want to see her face, come here."

"Oh dear," Andrea said beside Robin.

She should have expected such a response. Brian seemed like a rambunctious kid and like many boys, he had a ghoulish appetite. Well, she could do that.

"Ha," she said with a real smile. "It's not even Halloween yet, maybe you guys are too scared to see."

That brought a half dozen running over.

"Now you did it," Sean said, laughing. "Nothing like showing boys something that might tweak their ghoulish senses."

"I figured better to get it over with." When all the kids were around them and she could see a few dealing with visible scars of their own, she said, "I was in a car accident many years ago. It was really bad. I'm the only one that survived."

"Did you lose your family?"

The soft voice spoke up from the left and Robin saw a little boy she hadn't noticed before. Maybe it was because he blended into the chair so well. And had curled into a tiny ball. A protective ball. There was no visible injury, but there was no one in the room that couldn't hear the pain in his voice.

"Actually," Robin took a deep breath. "I did. I lost them all."

There were horrified and yet avid gasps from the kids.

She kept her eyes locked on the little boy now facing them. "It was really hard at the time, but now it is much easier."

The boy shrank back slightly. "I don't want it to get better," he whispered and closed his eyes.

Robin studied his tiny form and thought back to the initial days of holding on to the memories of her brother, her mother, and her father close to her. Especially when the bright memories faded, the exact words she used to remember in her mind – slipping. Then she'd hung on even harder – feeling disloyal somehow. Afraid she'd lose everything if she lost the last of them. They were her life. And now they were gone. If she couldn't keep them with her, she'd be alone.

It had taken several more months for her to realize – she was alone regardless.

"Hey, can I move your hair back?" One particularly persistent little boy asked. He had red hair standing straight up and freckles completely covering his face. Except for the long raw scar wrapped around his jaw. Swollen yet healing, it made his jaw oversized.

"I'll do it," she said. She leaned forward and said, "Ready?"

"Yes," they shouted.

She slipped a hand upward and under the long dark hair and pulled it back, leaving her face completely visible.

"Oooh."

"Wow."

"Gross."

As each of the kids ran through their favorite expressions, she couldn't help but laugh. "And now you know."

"It's not bad. Why do you try to hide it?"

"Because some people made hurtful comments, so I started hiding it." She shrugged. "Maybe I shouldn't have, but there it is."

Brian grinned. "If I had a face like that, I'd enter into a zombie movie and see if I could get a part."

She felt Sean's start of surprise at the comment. And realized he was still behind her. She dropped the hair and slid her comfort zone back into place. She turned back to the boys. "Now you guys tell me what happened to you."

Most of the kids jumped in with their war stories of accidents, surgeries, and all manner of things that could go wrong with the human body. The kids relished it. It was a chance to go over their experiences with someone who understood. Someone – an adult – who had been there.

It was a chance to be listened to. Survivor stories and a chance for their story to be the worst. The hardest. The most graphic in detail. She didn't know when she somehow ended up being one of them. When one young boy, she thought his name was Jack, mentioned the waking up in the morning with stitches and staples across his belly, she felt her insides knot.

"It's a horrible feeling, isn't it?" she said, wincing. "When you look down for that first time and you have long metal shiny things holding your insides together. That if you move the wrong way, breathe too heavy, all your guts are going to fall out."

The boys lit up at that, and the details of their experiences grew and the goriness increased. She sat back and relaxed.

She'd forgotten just how accepting and non-judgmental kids really were. They didn't care if her face was scarred – they just wanted all the bloody details of how she'd gotten that way.

At least these boys did.

SEAN HAD A pencil in hand and several pieces of paper scavenged from Andrea. He'd felt the need like nothing else had felt so right in a long time. He wanted to put Robin down on paper. Preserve this part of her – in case he never saw it again. He didn't know if it was last night, Jon, the boys, a combination of all the issues, but she was looser, friendlier. Relaxed. Open. She was...special.

His hand shook with intensity as he tried to capture that look on her face. The exuberance. The liveliness. The real Robin. Or what he imagined the old Robin from before the accident was like.

He loved that the boys had taken to her. Even regaling each other with the war stories of their experiences. She'd fit right in today. The last two day's behavior was gone – as if it never existed.

Healing was like that.

He wanted to laugh and shout with joy. But he couldn't. He didn't want to draw her attention to her change in behavior. Nor take her attention away from the boys. Not when she was doing such a great job at being herself.

Of course they'd loved her face. He'd seen their mouths twist in Os and their eyes cringe in awe and...respect.

She wore her war wounds as they did. She was older. She was an adult.

But she was one of them.

Chapter 27

Andrea said in a loud voice, "Okay boys, Robin and Sean have to leave. They were only here for a short visit today."

"Awww. Really?" several the boys cried out.

"We'll be back," Sean said. "Tomorrow. We'll be back for one more visit tomorrow."

"Okay."

Robin walked out backwards, waving and crying out to the boys, "Bye."

As they walked toward the elevators, she laughed and raced down the stairs, only stopping when she reached the bottom and needed to catch her breath. Sean, grinning at her side, said, "What brought that on?"

As she opened the door to the main floor, she said "I just felt an outburst of energy. Needed to move. Needed to run."

"Okay then, now that you have so much energy, what do you want to do?" Sean led the way to the exit and out to the parking lot.

"Do you know a decent restaurant around here? I'm starved."

He laughed. "I know a mean Chinese restaurant a few blocks over."

"A mean Chinese would be perfect."

He made a couple of right turns and then a left and suddenly turned into a parking lot and parked. The change was so sudden she couldn't believe that they were already here.

But she was game. And suddenly so hungry she couldn't stand it. Inside, the place was just gathering a small crowd for the dinner rush. They took a seat in the back of the large room. They were brought menus almost immediately and the waitress never had a chance to leave as they ordered immediately.

When the waitress finally left, Robin sat back with a fat smile, loving the sense of accomplishment. The sense of freedom. She'd overcome several hurdles today. She'd manage to show her scars and instead of running away from her screaming, the boys had been enthralled. She'd had the floor and they'd been a willing audience. After the emotional time with Jon, she'd been overwhelmed. Heartache had ruled. But then she realized that she had something she could do for the boys, help them feel better about Jon. She hadn't had a plan of action, but it had all happened naturally.

She was good with that.

The food arrived and she fell on it with a vengeance. Lord, it felt good to have a hot meal.

SEAN WATCHED HER eat with enjoyment. She inhaled her food. It was good to see. So was the progress she'd made. Unbelievable progress. He could only imagine where she'd be by the end of the week.

He studied her covertly. She was so focused. So appreciative. Stopping to savor the tastes in her mouth. And God, her mouth. At the tightening in his groin, he tried to focus on something else but once the floodgates had opened, memories from last night rushed through his body.

A shudder ran though him. God, he wanted her. Right here and now.

He closed his eyes and struggled for control.

"What's the matter, aren't you enjoying it?" she said in between bites. "It's good. I'm really enjoying it."

"I can tell," he said in a gritty voice and quickly polished off his plate. The sooner they left, the sooner he could get her into his bed. It was all he could think about.

She was – his mind came up blank for a moment – a butterfly, newly released from her chrysalis.

Ready to fly.

He was so glad he'd been here to see it.

As he drove back to the hotel through the heavy Vancouver traffic, he realized with a sinking feeling that she didn't need him anymore.

That she could finish this on her own.

And he'd never been more afraid. To be alone.

CHAPTER 28

THE AIR IN the truck chilled the closer they got to the hotel. She didn't really understand what was happening until they pulled into the hotel lot. She was exhausted but also seriously revved. She needed to unwind somehow. She hopped out of the truck, waited for him, then headed for her bedroom.

"Now what?" Sean asked in a cooler tone of voice than she was used to hearing. "Pool? Rest? Pub?"

Something was up. She stopped and looked at him. With a wide grin, she said, "I was thinking more along the lines of bed."

And watched as his gaze lit up and his grin turned devilish. "A girl after my own heart."

With a giggle she took off, leading the way to her bedroom, Sean fast on her heels.

She rolled over the next morning and grinned. Sean was sprawled on his tummy, taking up most of the room. He was a serious bed hog. He looked like he hadn't moved after collapsing in the middle of the night. It had been a night of heated sex like she hadn't known possible. Even now, her body ached all over. And she'd loved every minute of it.

She knew their time here was coming to an end, but as she stared at her hot sleeping lover, she wondered if he would be interested in trying out that whole relationship thing he said he didn't do.

Technically, two nights together was no longer a one-night stand. She knew she wanted to keep seeing him. They were dynamite in bed, and he was the only male that didn't seem to be put off by her scars. Then she hadn't given many a chance to see them.

In reality, he'd been there for her in ways she hadn't really understood. Hadn't thought such a thing was possible. She'd been wrong. As he'd shown her. She leaned over and kissed his cheek. He shifted slightly under her gentle touch. A wave of love swept over her. He'd been the catalyst for her healing this week. She wasn't done, but she was well on her way. And she had him to thank. And Jenna.

Speaking of which, she glanced over at the clock and realized she was supposed to start the morning with a one-on-one session with her. And she was going to be late. She dashed to the bathroom and her shower to get started for the day.

Even rushing, she was still late for her meeting. She stepped into the small room that Jenna had taken for business during the workshop, a take-out coffee in her hand, a big grin on her face. "Good morning. Sorry I'm late."

Jenna looked up and smiled. Her gaze seemed to see into Robin's very soul. And her smile deepened. "Looks like you had another good night."

"Well, I didn't get much sleep, but it was a great night." Robin laughed and took her seat.

"Sounds like you and Sean are getting along well."

Robin nodded. "Honestly, it's not what I expected. *He's* not what I expected, but I'm delighted with what I've learned about him."

"Good." Jenna clasped her hands together on the desk and leaned forward slightly. "So tell me what you've learned."

That made Robin pause. Was Jenna asking what she'd learned about Sean or about herself? She wanted to ask but didn't want to go in the direction of Sean unless necessary. It seemed too personal and almost against Sean to talk about him. "This week has been tough in many ways. There's no doubt that much of my issues stem from the loss of my brother." She went on to explain the need for closure, how being able to see Jon last night had helped and how difficult going back to see the other boys afterwards had been – and how rewarding.

After she finally fell silent, there was a warm caring energy in the room.

Jenna sat back, a proud smile on her face. "That sounds like you've made wonderful strides this week."

"I have." Robin couldn't stop grinning. "And I have you and Sean to thank for that."

Immediately Jenna shook her head. "You did all the work. I provide the circumstances for the change, but you had to walk the walk."

"And I did, and I feel wonderful for having done so." She stood up. "I guess we have workshop stuff to do this morning before our last visit to the kids."

"That's right." Jenna stood up. "I'll be doing one-on-one sessions with everyone this morning, so today is really a chance to go over the report and fix anything that needs more work as well as see what other things are needed to round it out."

At the reminder of the report, Robin froze. "That's something I don't know how to help with. I have no idea what Sean has been doing on it, if anything."

"Well, it's required first thing tomorrow morning, so you have today to figure it out." Jenna's voice was firm, her face beaming as if to say 'you can do this.'

The only thing was, Robin knew she hadn't contributed anything. She hadn't even given Sean time to sketch her. And his arm hurt when he worked too long. She frowned as she wandered into the seminar. They should have gone to the hot tub last night. Let his muscles relax. She'd been letting him take care of her, but he hadn't been taking care of himself. And she, so broken up about everything going on in her psyche, had let him.

Damn. Now she felt guilty.

Inside the workshop, groups were working on their project. There was no sign of Sean. She glanced around, looking for Tania, but she wasn't here either. Out of sorts and wondering what she should do, she sat down to wait.

A half hour later, there was still no Sean. She gathered up her stuff and returned to her room. He must be still asleep. As she unlocked her door and walked back inside, she realized he wasn't asleep. Or in the shower. He was gone.

She let the door close and stood there, staring at the rumpled bed.

Maybe she should have said something to him? Woken him up? Texted him? She pulled her cell phone out of her pocket on the off chance she'd gotten a text from him, but there was none.

Making a quick decision, she walked back out, headed to his door, and knocked.

There was no answer.

SEAN SAT IN the far end of the coffee shop – the opposite end of where he always sat with Robin. He wanted to be alone. To think. To work. To deal with his own crap. He'd already texted Paris several times, but it was hard to express what he was feeling. Then his cell phone battery had died, putting an end to the conversation. He'd forgotten to place it on his charger last night. Damn. That was something he rarely forgot.

Still, it was a good way to get out of the conversation. He wasn't used to sharing. Didn't quite know how to do it. Wasn't sure it was a good thing to be doing. He'd always kept things locked up inside. He understood the psychobabble of letting it all go, he was taking psychology classes after all, not that he'd shared that fact with many people.

He had to admit he'd learned a lot about himself while here this week. And about others. That absolute need to heal. To move on with their lives. Everyone here came from a different place on the healing scale – if there was such a thing, and everyone was approaching the problem differently. He had to wonder if Jenna was psychic with the way she'd been pairing up couples. Was that a good thing? Or was she off the marker on everyone – including him and Robin? No. In that respect, she'd been right on the money.

He brooded as he stroked and shaded his latest picture. He'd somehow amassed a large collection of sketches of Robin. He wasn't sure how or where or when, but there were some where she was a tiny image in the corner and then others where she was larger but faded. He didn't remember doing many of them, but he must have done. And he'd done four new ones already this morning.

Robin had become the biggest subject of his life. And the only one he wanted to draw. Stupid. Crazy. Paris had said so in her last text. She was probably right. He'd been called crazy more than once. His father used to call him that before slugging him across the head. Or more accurately, he'd say,

"Crazy bastard."

Then beat him again. Maybe he was crazy, but it had been his way of surviving. And it had worked. But once again, he had to wonder if his mental state was something he could trust. He'd never been so lacking in certainty before. He desperately wanted a relationship with Robin. But not even he could stretch ripping up the bed sheets for some of the hottest nights of sex in his memory as a relationship.

That was a physical need. There'd been no emotional involvement in it. Except the sex had been so incredible, and he knew it was from the emotions coursing through him.

But he wasn't so sure about her.

And that was the part he was troubled about.

The last thing he wanted was for Robin to advance to a whole new world – and leave him behind. Sure, he hadn't come here for himself. And he knew this was the place for Paris. No doubt about it. But now that he could see what was available in terms of progress and healing, he wanted some of it for himself.

Just like he wanted something from the new and improved Robin – to have a place in her future.

He turned the page and started working on the next picture.

If nothing else, he'd have these images to keep his memory of her alive long after this workshop had ended.

Chapter 29

ROBIN FOUND HERSELF alone at lunchtime, too. She was worried about where Sean might be. Was he okay? It was almost time to leave for the hospital. She didn't know what to do. She wanted to see the kids today. Wanted to get the benefit of her last day here. She was feeling better about herself than she had in a long time. Now if only she knew what was going on with Sean? They had one more night. She was selfish enough to want it. Every last minute of it.

And she had no idea if he even cared enough to push his one-night stand rule into three nights. Had she pushed him too far already?

God, she hoped not. She dove into her meal when it arrived. The burger and fries reminded her of Sean. It was only as she finished and hopped to her feet to get ready for the hospital when she saw Sean busy working on the back corner of the room. As she walked closer, she realized that he was working on their project. She stopped and winced.

A huge load had been placed on his shoulders. She'd had to do nothing on that report. How unfair was that? She was a complete failure in the artistic department. That just made her feel worse. As she approached, maybe because she approached, he slammed his sketchbook closed and packed away his stuff. He stood up as she arrived at his table.

He stopped and stared at her, a shocked look on his face.

She frowned. "What?"

Sean frowned, looked down at his shoes briefly, then gave a half-hearted shrug. "Glad to see you. I was wondering how to track you down."

"Ah," she pulled her cell phone out of her pocket. "Cell phone." She waved it at him. "I've sent a half dozen messages, but you haven't answered any."

With a sheepish grin, he admitted, "I forgot to charge my phone last night so my phone is dead."

"Ah shit." She laughed. "I thought you were mad at me for some reason."

His eyebrows lifted. "Of course not. Why would I be mad at you?"

When he said it in such a commonsense voice, she realized that she'd been foolish. "Sorry. I wasn't thinking straight." She motioned to his sketchbook and portfolio case. "I was feeling guilty as I hadn't been able to help you."

He smiled, closed the zipper, and said, "No help required."

He pushed his chair under the table and said, "Are you ready to go to the hospital?"

She nodded. And followed him out to the parking lot.

At the hospital, they both walked the now familiar path to the children's ward. She wanted to stop in and see Jon but decided not to in case he'd taken a turn for the worse as she wouldn't be able to hide it from the kids. They could stop by afterwards. At the door, she took a deep breath and pushed it open. And walked inside.

"Robin"

"Sean."

"Hey, they're here. I told you they'd come again." Brian led the pack that was hobbling, wheeling, and limping toward them.

Robin had to admit as far as welcomes went, this one was great. She also had several things in her hands that she'd picked up this morning. Thankfully, Vancouver was a main center and almost anything could be bought right around the corner. In this case, the big mall under the city had provided a fortune in games. She'd asked Andrea what they could bring for the kids, and that had been her suggestion. Not having kids, Robin had no idea of the cost involved in buying video games. Like seriously...

The gifts were also from the both of them. She had no intention of asking Sean to pay. Not only had he had no say in what she was doing, but he was the only one doing the report that was also from her. Not to mention all the meals he'd fed her at the beginning of the week.

"What's in those bags?" Brian asked.

She laughed. "Something for you guys, but I'll show you later."

The little tiny boy sat up and looked at her. "You aren't hiding your face today."

Silence. Everyone stopped to study her new hairstyle. And she realized she'd completely forgotten about it. But it explained Sean's shock when he'd seen her earlier. She'd pulled her hair back on both sides and French-braided it down the back. The disfigured side of her face could be clearly seen.

It had felt like the right thing to do. She used to wear it that way all the time. It felt natural to do so again.

She pulled up her chair, realizing that Sean was setting up at the table like he usually did. She smiled at the little boy. "I guess I don't want to hide away anymore."

That was greeted with silence.

"It's not that bad," said the boy.

"Thank you. I'm glad you think so." And she realized that if she didn't care about who saw her face, maybe others wouldn't care either. She'd shrugged. "Besides, it's only until the next surgery…" She grinned. "Then I'll have different scars!"

The kids laughed. "Will you come back and show us?"

"Maybe I will at that. I don't have a date yet," she said, "but hopefully it will be soon."

She'd actually gone as far as calling her doctor's office and leaving a message. If she was ready to move forward, then she was ready to move all the way forward. She felt so much better, so much lighter since making that call, as if another unfinished part of her had settled into place, too.

The visit with the kids went by too fast. Before she knew it, it was time to open up the bags of gifts and hand over the new games. As the shrieks of laugher and excitement filled the air. Sean, his stuff packed up, stepped closer and murmured, "That was a great idea."

She smiled. "I wanted to make sure our parting was good for both of us."

With the kids screaming goodbyes into their ears, the two walked back out of the hospital. She looked over at Sean, who'd been so silent during the whole visit, and said, "Hey, you okay?"

He glanced over at her. "I'm fine."

She wasn't sure she believed him, but there was little she could do to get him to open up. He'd tell her if he wanted to, and only when he was ready.

VIDEO GAMES AS gifts. A great idea, and one he'd never have thought of. Gifts were not a big part of his world. He tried to remember for Paris's sake as she'd missed so many, but it never occurred to him for anyone else. It said a lot about Robin's upbringing that she understood the appropriate times and gifts.

Trust her big heart.

"Do you want to go see Jon?"

A bright smile broke across her face. "Yes please."

Except the ICU unit was awash with people. There were different nurses on, and Jon was being attended to by several doctors.

Sean watched the worry tug on Robin's features as they stood out of the way. He waited. This had to be tough, but she'd had a chance to see Jon last night and that had been a gift. No one ever said the gift would be offered twice.

He reached over and hooked her arm to his. She cast one long look at Jon's room then resolutely turned away. He was proud of her. She'd made a lot of changes. This was yet another one.

"Let's go," she whispered.

CHAPTER 30

THEY WALKED INTO the hotel to find Jenna waiting for them. "Robin, I need to speak with you."

Surprised, her stomach sinking at the tone of Jenna's voice, Robin walked off to the side of the hallway. "I'm sorry to tell you this, but Jon, after a better prognosis this morning, has taken another turn for the worse. He's likely only got hours to live."

Robin gasped, tears welling up in to her eyes. "Oh no, I'd so hoped."

Jenna smiled, her own eyes misty. "We all did. Life is precious and it's so hard when it's taken away from us early. It's so much worse when it's a child. I'm telling you as you seemed to be so attached to him. If you still need to say goodbye..." Her voice trailed off.

Robin didn't know what to say. She'd said goodbye last night. She wouldn't be able to see him now either, especially if he was worse. As they'd just seen.

"I'm going to go to my room," she whispered. "I need some time alone." Frozen and sad, although she'd known it was a distinct possibility, she'd so hoped for a better prognosis. But why would her wishing something change anything? It hadn't helped her parents. Her brother had still died. Now Jon. Still, she had to keep hoping.

Had Sean followed her up the stairs? She was so lost in the

fog of pain and grief. She understood grief. She'd lived with it so much already. People died every day. All the time and in the most horrible of ways. She sat for a long time on the single chair by the window and stared out. What could she do? Nothing. Jon's time might end tonight, so what did she want to do? Just sit here in sadness and grief, or find a way to remember him?

She didn't want to be alone tonight. She wanted to rejoice in life. No, she wanted to celebrate Jon's life. Jonathon's life. That he'd lived and died so young was tragic, but she couldn't help it. The only thing she could do was celebrate both boys' lives. She just wished she knew how.

After washing her face, she knocked on Sean's door. He opened it, concern darkening those beautiful blue eyes. "Hey."

"Hi. Are you okay?"

She shook her head, tears forming in the corner of her eyes. "I will be, but right now I'm still..." She shrugged.

He opened his arms and she walked into them. This was what she needed. To be held. To be loved. To know that she wasn't alone. "I feel so bad for him."

"And yet it's not over. He might still pull through."

She nodded, her head rubbing up and down against his shirt. "I know that. I'm trying to stay positive."

"Do you want to go see him?"

"I don't know."

Her cell phone went off. It was Andrea.

"Robin? Apparently Jon is awake and asking for you. I hate to even call, in case this isn't something you want to do. He's not doing well."

"Oh no, Andrea," Robin said immediately. "I'll," she looked over at Sean, who was nodding, and corrected herself, "we'll be there as soon as we can."

"I'm sure he'll be happy to see you."

Without talking, Sean shrugged into his jacket and grabbed his keys.

They were at the hospital in twenty minutes. It was visiting hours this time. They walked through to the ICU and saw the same nurse they'd seen last night.

Her face lit up at the sight of them. "I'm so happy to see you. He was asking about you earlier."

Robin said in a low voice, "I understand that he's not doing well?"

"No, but the doctors are trying a new drug," she held her hands out, "I'm scared to jinx it but…" She took a deep breath and smiled. "They are cautiously optimistic. Again, he has to make it through the night. He needs strength to fight this off."

Robin walked to the doorway and looked back the nurse, who nodded. Emboldened, she walked into the small unit and sat down on the edge of Jon's bed.

He was asleep. "Jon, I'm here."

And damn it if his eyes didn't open. He tried to smile.

"You don't have to talk," Robin said. "I know you're feeling yucky."

His eyes drifted close. Then they popped open. "Did you feel this bad after your last surgery?"

She had. But it had been emotional. Psychological. Not physical. She thought about how to answer. "Not the same, but I did feel really bad."

Jon's lips curved into a tiny smile. "Good," he whispered. "I'm glad it gets better."

The words caught in her throat. "It does. You have to fight off the bad stuff and keep focused on the day when you're going to feel better."

"Do you think I'll get better?" he asked hopefully, but his gaze was dark, fearful.

"Absolutely," She remembered from her own surgeries, how important it was to stay positive. To have hope. "You have to believe it yourself. Think of good things. Happy things. Think about having ice cream with Cheerios." His eyes twinkled. "Or about kitty cats and puppy dogs."

"I love puppies," he whispered. "I always wanted one."

"Then think about the day you'll have a puppy in your arms. And think about the day you get to look into the mirror and see your face whole and great-looking. And the day you look back at your life and say it was all worthwhile."

"I can do that." Now a real smile peeped out. "I *really* want a puppy."

"And maybe when you get past this, you can have one."

They spoke for a few more minutes while he told her about the neighbor's dog that was a golden lab. As it was the first she'd heard about the neighbor or his home life at all, she stayed quiet and let him talk. After a few moments, another woman walked in. "Oh hi. Are you Robin?"

Robin nodded. She looked down at Jon and realized he'd fallen asleep.

"Thank you for coming. I know how important it was for him." She introduced herself as Cindy, Jon's mother.

Relieved to know that Jon wasn't alone, she said, "He's a wonderful little boy." Then she told her about wanting a puppy.

Cindy tried to smile, but it was interrupted by the flow of tears. "Now if we could just get him through this, I'd be happy to get him a puppy."

Sean led Robin away as Cindy sat down at Jon's bedside. The last image Robin had was of her picking up Jon's hand

and talking to him, much as Robin had.

She was sad when they walked back out of the hospital. In a soft teary voice, she said, "I'm glad he was awake."

"Hopefully he'll pull through this."

She nodded and stared up at the sky. It was overcast and dark gray. A storm moving in. "Do you want to go anywhere else or just back to the hotel?"

"To the hotel, please."

He nodded, wrapped an arm around her shoulder, and led her back to the truck.

Back at the hotel, they walked up to the elevators together. In the hallway, he stopped and looked at her. "Do you want to be alone?"

She heard the cautious note in his voice. He wanted to do the right thing. She didn't want anything to do with that.

She did not want to be alone.

"No," she whispered. "I don't. I want to forget everything negative and sad in life. I want to rejoice and celebrate life." In truth, she didn't want to be alone ever again.

He moved her toward his bedroom. "In that case," he said, a crooked smile on his face as he unlocked the door. "I think I might be able to help."

She searched his gaze, wishing he'd say something. Something to take her off this cliff of uncertainty. She'd already been blessed with the time they'd had together, but she wanted more. She'd take what she could get right now — especially if that was all there was going to be. She didn't dare do or say anything to ruin this moment. She might not get another one. "Do you think you're up to it?"

He grinned before he took her hand that rested on his chest and slid it down to the growing bulge in his pants. "I think I am. But maybe you need to make sure."

And with that, he closed the hotel door and led her to his bed.

THE NEXT MORNING, Sean was grateful to be the first one awake. Finally. He dressed quickly and slipped out to go to the coffee shop and picked up several mugs to bring back to her. When he returned, she was still asleep. He put the mugs down and kissed her awake.

She groaned.

He smiled. He could so get used to this. She opened her eyes, saw him, and smiled, a slow languid smile that set his loins to pulsing with heat again. "Unless you want to be late this morning when we have to present the report, I suggest you don't look at me that way."

"What way?" she asked, her eyes warming.

"That way, witch." He straightened and walked over to bring her the mug of coffee. "See, I've been busy already."

She propped herself up against the headboard. "I'm glad to see that." She took a sip. "Must be all that experience."

He laughed. "I don't have any of that, remember."

She smiled and took another sip.

"Besides, by my count, this is our third night together. So that's either three one-night stands in a row, which doesn't make sense," she said lightly. "Or we're in what you'd call a relationship."

He grinned. "That was my take, too."

"Except you said you didn't do those." Those intense green eyes stared at him. Was that uncertainty in her gaze? Surely not.

"I said I didn't do those." He reached over and kissed her – hard. "Now I do." He ripped back the blankets. "And we're late. It's almost nine."

Her gaze widened. "Really? Wow, we are late."

Sean headed to the shower, wishing he could drag her in there with him, but they had no time. Drying off, he walked into the bedroom to hear her saying goodbye on her phone. "Who was that?"

"That was the hospital," she said with a brilliant smile. "Jon not only made it through the night, he's apparently doing much better this morning."

"Wow. That's great."

She bounced out of bed. "It's fantastic news." She snagged his robe off the back door, "I've got to get dressed. Do you want to wait for me or…"

"I'll be knocking on your door in ten. Then we'll need to run down to the workshop. We have to pack up and check out by noon, too."

She winced. "Crap. I'd forgotten. Okay. I'm gone."

And she bolted to her room.

Chapter 31

They were late. They raced into the seminar room, looking like guilty children. She was sure everyone would know. But no one said anything or even looked at them sideways. They took their seats just as Jenna saw them.

She smiled, nodded, then opened up with, "Reports are due today. I'll be addressing the teams in the back corner. When I call your name, bring your report and your partner and we'll go over them. You know the order that you fall into with one change. Robin and Sean will be last, after Tania and Kane."

The first pair stood up. And the morning started. Nerves abounded. Robin had no idea what Sean had done. She'd done her daily homework, she wasn't sure if he had, but she'd contributed nothing to the report. She wanted to say something to him about it, but he was so calm. Laid back. She envied him.

The morning passed quickly as they listened to the speakers brought in for the occasion.

Out of the blue, Jenna called out, "Tania and Kane, your turn."

Robin heard Tania's intake of breath. She turned to see her friend already standing up. The tank-like-Kane dwarfed her as they walked to the back. She wondered how their week had gone. She couldn't wait to catch up with Tania next week.

It would be quite the conversation. As they weren't first, she turned to Sean and asked, "I know it's late, but is there anything I can do to help with the report?"

He smiled and said, "You already have."

"Ha. Have not."

"Have too."

She rolled her eyes and paid attention to the speakers who were visiting for the morning session while everyone gave the reports. At one point, she heard something from the back and turned around to find Tania throwing her arms around Kane, tears in her eyes.

Robin could barely hold her own back. Boy, was she looking forward to catching up with Tania.

Then it was their turn.

"Robin and Sean, please bring your report."

They both stood up. She took a deep breath. "Here we go."

At the back, there were two seats for them. They sat down, Robin now feeling horribly nervous. She'd had nothing to do with this. She didn't feel like she should be here at all.

"Sean, it's over to you."

He opened his sketchbook but held it in such a way that they still couldn't see the pages. He started speaking. "I was going to title this project Scars. After all, that's been a major part of Robin's journey, mine too. But then I realized I wanted to emphasize the positive and not the negative, so I changed it from Scars to Chrysalis."

Robin held back a strangled sound then. As he looked at her, she realized that she hadn't quite kept it back. She schooled her features and waited for him to continue.

He laid down the book and she saw the first picture was a small sketch of her, her face small and faded on the page.

There were just a few lines, but the clarity was incredible. On the same page, there were a few kids, but they were distant and unfocused on the edge of the paper. At the top of the page was a battered up caterpillar but so faint as to be a watermark.

He turned the page.

And again at the top of the page was a caterpillar, slow, swollen and heavily scarred as if it'd had a difficult life.

There her face was in greater clarity, more detailed, and so were the group of kids. She watched in awe as he moved them through several images of her and the boys, her face mostly down or hidden by her hair, and with each picture there was more detail, more clarity of her features. As if she was walking through a fog, and with each step she took her features came more into focus. In each instance, the caterpillar stayed a pale narrative of the story. So clear that even a child could understand.

Her hands clasped together as she realized how he'd taken the child aspect and run with it.

On every page, Sean narrated her journey, her self-discovery, her progress. And damn if that caterpillar watermark didn't tell the same story. At one point, it was hidden, tucked away in its cocoon. Hidden in its home...as she'd hidden in her home. The cocoon hung from a desolate branch alone and unloved...but by the very nature of the animal, Robin knew it was changing on the inside.

She listened, dazed, as he spoke of admiring her, respecting the size of the bridge she'd crossed.

He came to the second last page and was quiet for a long moment. Finally he said, "This is why I changed the name from Scars to Chrysalis."

Robin twisted around slightly so she could get a better view of the image. And gasped in shock. Her face looked like a photograph instead of a sketch and then touched up with Photoshop. She had a beautiful smile on her face, her injured side was there, but the damage somehow didn't seem to mar her features. The woman in the picture...she – glowed.

And the cocoon – the bottom had blown apart, letting the butterfly escape. And how beautiful it was. Gossamer wings, a delicate body with the hint of grace and power in its form.

Her hand to her face, she brushed the tears away. And whispered, "Oh my God, Sean, she's beautiful." She shook her head. "Both of them are."

Sean took her hand in his and said, "No, *she* isn't – no *they* aren't – *you* are beautiful." He reached up to tilt her chin and deliberately kissed her on her damaged cheek. "They are both you. And both of you are beautiful."

"How can you be so blind?" she marveled, studying the picture. And then she got it. "I thought there was a fog blocking the woman's features. But it isn't," she said excitedly. "The viewer is being led step-by-step into seeing the woman on the inside." She gazed at him, marveling at his genius. "To see the woman under the fog, under the layers."

"Or to see the woman under the...?" And he waited.

"Scars."

"I'm not blind. You are – were. Now..." He tapped the image. "Now you can see what I've seen every day. This woman emerging from behind her own self-imposed fog." He gave her a slow melting smile, and she knew she was lost forever. This man had seen her for who she truly was. And had been strong enough, brave enough to help her on her journey to see it, too.

Jenna said, from behind them. "Robin, what did you learn about Sean?"

Robin laughed, but she gazed into Sean's eyes as she

spoke. "That he's a fraud. That he's been hiding in the darkness just waiting for a chance to step into the light." She shook her head and motioned toward the sketchpad. "And boy, when he stepped into the light, it was a spotlight."

She thought she'd drown in the love shining from his eyes.

"Sean?" Jenna asked. "Remember the question I asked you to answer as part of the assignment?"

Sean smiled, his gaze locked on Robin. "Turn the page."

Robin, curious, broke her gaze to watch.

The last page showed an image so powerful, so simple, with just a couple of strokes that surely it was impossible to show so much detail of the two of them. Sean held Robin in his arms, holding her as if he'd never let her go.

And there was the butterfly again, her wings fully extended, ready to take off and fly for the first time. And just above her, in darker lines, giving a more masculine defined look, was a powerful butterfly, hovering off to one side…waiting for her to take off so he could fly with her.

A sob escaped. There was a title and subtitle above the image, but Robin could barely read it for the tears coursing down her cheeks. It said,

Why Robin?
Because she's perfect…for me

Robin burst into tears and threw her arms around him.
He wrapped her up tight against his heart.
Just where she wanted to be.

Scales

(Of Justice)

by
Dale Mayer

Chapter 1

Paris Wilson sat with her back to the wall and waited as the room slowly filled up for the first morning seminar. They'd all briefly met the night before but the real workshop started today. Set in downtown Vancouver, at a posh but business-style hotel, she couldn't help but feel this Inner Healing workshop could be the answer to so many problems. It had better be, especially after pleading with her professor that she was ready for this. It was a special workshop for university students under Professor Jenna Komak. And Jenna alone made the decision as to who would be allowed to attend.

Now Paris was here and couldn't wait to get started. She had picked a perfect spot to watch the other attendees but only be seen by a few of them as they looked around. Those she could ignore.

She'd ignore everyone if she could. They were a distraction. There was a reason she was here and she was anxious to get started. Several reasons actually. When her brother, Sean, had attended the same workshop earlier this summer, he'd fallen in love with a special woman he'd met there. Robin was stunning inside and out.

Paris was seriously happy for Sean. She'd always known he'd find someone someday – even if he hadn't believed it. Not only because he was her brother, but because he was a great man and a terrific human being.

He deserved to be happy. And that made all the difference in the world.

Brushing back her black hair, Paris knew that any of these other attendees could potentially impact her life in a similar way. In wonder, she studied the few people taking seats at the very front. She'd never been able to do that. Being front and center. It put too much attention on her. Considering how eager she was to get moving on this, she should probably consider the risks. Even though her hopes were high for the workshop, she knew she was asking a lot. She was eager. Too eager. She didn't have rose-colored glasses with which to view the world, but she had her brother's experience as a standard.

Dropping her gaze to her hands, her fingers picked away at the skin from the base of the nails. Ugly. Damaged. Falling to pieces. Gee funny, her outside matched her inside.

At that, she almost gave an audible snort but held it back at the last moment. It wouldn't do to attract attention in this setting. She settled back and watched as several men took their seats. The only men she knew well had been her father and her brother. Both of them were so much alike and so opposite in all the ways that counted. Other males she met seemed to be a mix of the two. Maybe that was good. Maybe not.

She'd been interested in a few men she'd met through work, but knew they wouldn't want her. What was to want? She was an okay size as in shorter than Sean but just a hair taller than his partner Robin. Even though she ate like a horse, she was slim, bordering on gaunt. Her brother said she was too nervy to keep any weight on. Whatever.

She had to admit to being a little on the driven Type A side, but she had a reason. After missing out on so much in life, she couldn't help but want to do more. Be more.

Then there was the mixed-up part of her that knew she

could never be enough. Never be good enough. She hadn't ever been *that* good. And that perception impacted her actions every day.

It was stupid. She was an adult now. Surely her childhood shouldn't be doing this to her anymore.

Except, whispered that gentle voice inside, *you weren't a child when it finally stopped. You were a teenager. So very vulnerable to the actions, opinions of those around you. Very impressionable at an age where you'd already been beaten into the ground. Knew there was no one out there that would save you. Already understood that the original fairy tales had the right of it, they were grim, heart-wrenching stories. Nothing like the pretty pink stories she heard other kids talk about with teddy bears and rainbows and unicorns even.*

Paris knew the bogeyman was real. And she knew that there was one inside of every single person – including herself.

"Is anyone sitting here?"

The deep dark voice shook her to the core. Surprised at the swarthy young man standing beside her, she stared uncomprehendingly at him. She glanced at the direction he pointed and realized she'd been sitting in one chair and taking up a second chair with her legs, subconsciously giving people no choice but to stay away. Jenna, their professor, would have a heyday with her body language.

Paris dropped her legs and muttered, "No, it's free."

Nodding, he sat down, turning his back to her.

She studied him covertly. As broad as Sean was lean, he was solid looking. Farmer stock. Big hands and forearms but not the muscle-bound body builder type. Nice actually.

And there was a faint smell, not cologne, subtler than that. Aftershave or even shaving soap. With his dark coloring, she imagined he had to shave a couple of times a day. He turned and gave her a bland look.

She flushed. Damn it, he'd caught her studying him.

Back in school, she had learned that if she went into class afraid, the teacher would pick on her to do a question on the board. She always got picked. However, if she walked in and couldn't have cared less about it, she never got picked. *How come she couldn't apply that same trick to the world at large?* Paris wondered.

The instructor walked in at that moment. The air magically twisted, becoming lighter, airy. The underlying nervousness quickly dissipated.

Paris was here for the same thing everyone else was here for. To heal.

They all needed to move past issues that stopped them from leading the fulfilling lives they all wanted. They all wanted to move forward.

Simple. Not.

Jenna had achieved phenomenal results with her earlier seminars, but at what point did her special touch run a little thin? Paris knew if the magic was going to run out, it would run out with her. She hadn't learned the trick of making her life happen easily. Nor of making it through life unscathed like so many people she knew. Neither did she expect much more than what she had.

But she wished…dreamed…fantasized of so much more.

Especially babies.

And there were just some things that no matter how much wishing one did, it wasn't going to happen.

Still, the alternative would have been worse. She was here, and she was strong and healthy and alive. She was good with that. There were alternative dreams she could dream.

She smiled.

And damn if her neighbor didn't turn and looked at her suspiciously.

It was her turn to give him a bland stare.

He cocked one eyebrow, a glint of amusement in his gaze before he shifted back in his chair and turned his attention to the front of the room.

Only she caught sight of a muscle in his jaw twitching in a steady pulsating manner.

Squeezing her eyes shut, she tried to focus on Jenna's words. That's why she was here. Her eyes popped open. Yet at the same time her neighbor, in the chair next to her, was starting to drive her nuts. She wanted to slap a hand over that muscle and make it stop.

Just part of her stress management techniques she had to work on. Fix what she could fix and ignore what she couldn't. So how was she doing on that second half? Lousy.

Jenna held up a stack of folders. "Good morning, everyone."

A murmured response rippled through the room.

"I'm glad to see you've all settled in, we'll work first on getting you divvied up into pairs and then hand out the assignments. Until I call your name, remember I mentioned homework last night? Well this..." She held up a stack of papers to the groans of those around her, "Won't be homework if you get it all done now."

And with that, she dropped the stack at the front desk and said, "Take one and pass them around."

Paris watched as the stack moved from one person to the other. She'd be last. Maybe that was okay too.

Jenna called two people's names and moved the couple to the back of the room where three chairs sat in a cozy arrangement in the corner. Paris kept half an eye on their reactions but as there were lots of smiles and nods, she figured the first couple wasn't unhappy with their assignment. A few moments later, the couple returned and Jenna called out two more names and asked the attendees to join her at the back.

Somewhere in there, the assignment sheet arrived on the table in front of Paris. She picked it up and sighed. This one was a sheet on dreams. Your dreams. Dreams you gave up on. Dreams you couldn't give up on. And the last one got to Paris – list the innermost secret dream you were too afraid to let yourself dream.

She stared at that question and wished she had an answer.

"For those of you working on the homework sheet," Jenna said. "Please add one question to the bottom of the sheet."

There were long, heavy sighs from those around her.

Paris looked at Jenna, waiting, wondering where she was going with this.

"Write down the biggest regret in your life and how the event impacted your dreams."

Shit.

Paris's hard-won calm disintegrated. That question required no thought.

She already had the answer. She lived with it daily.

She wished she'd never killed her father.

WHAT WAS PARIS'S problem? Cool name. If he'd read the top of worksheet correctly.

But the woman...her expression was that of a deer frozen in the spotlight. He stared at her, seeing the glassy eyes and the stark-white pallor.

Like what the hell?

Trying to sneak a glance at her paper again, he realized

she was filling out the question that Jenna had just added. All he could see was something ending with *her father.*

Figures. Every messed-up girl seemed to have daddy issues. While he turned back to his paper, he kept an eye on her. When she started to rub out the words written on her paper — words written in pen — he knew she wasn't all there.

The questions in front of him were beyond his understanding, but he had to ponder the concept. He wasn't about dreams. He was all about goals. Dreams were nebulous. Airy and light. Weightless. Euphemism for useless. He was a planner. A-one-foot-in-front-of-the-other-and-walk toward a specific end point kind of person. Not for the joy of the walk but because he was going to get somewhere specific. He was all about specifics. That he was here in this damn class said he was doing one of the steps that he needed to do to get on with his life.

Another check box was being marked off. Good. Therapy wasn't his thing, especially not his own. At least not now. No, he couldn't really say for sure why he was here except because of Jenna herself. He'd heard about Jenna's classes and had even attended several of her evening lectures. But he didn't *need* her class and he'd told her so. That's when she'd smiled that really witchy smile, her eyes glowing with laughter, and she'd challenged him to attend. To show that he'd taken care of *his* stuff. That there wasn't anything else she could show him.

"Hell," he'd said with a snicker, "of course I *could* do it, but I don't need to. I wouldn't pay good money for something like this."

With a laugh, she replied, "If you think you're immune, then write up a paper on it. If it's any good, I'll help you get it published. If you find out you're not immune, we'll revisit the subject of the report at the end."

Now that appealed to his sense of purpose. His portfolio was missing published articles – particularly in peer-reviewed journals. Even if having a shrink's name on his paper didn't help in getting a paper published, it was on his bucket list. And damn it, that bucket list was important.

So he'd accepted the challenge. And here he was.

So no, he hadn't been tricked into attending, but…it almost felt like it. Or maybe it was that he felt played…and had taken the bait. And that now he was where she wanted him to be.

But why?

To observe? To write his insights? There was lots of fodder here. Some of these people needed serious help.

He shook his head and scratched the word dreams out and replaced it with the word goals. When he was done, he realized the odd sound beside him was the sound of paper ripping. He snuck a glance over at Paris to see her trying to rip out the answer she'd tried to rub out first. Apparently, she was seriously determined to not let anyone see that answer. As he studied her, he realized that she'd actually ripped off the strip of paper and had rolled it up into a tiny ball.

Fascinated, he watched her struggle to find a place to hide the tiny item. He couldn't take his eyes off it. What the hell had she written that she wanted erased so badly?

His gaze swung back to the paper. She'd left the other answers intact. Just a long strip missing out of the bottom half. As if sensing his bewilderment, she lifted her gaze to his face. Her cheeks flared with bright colors as their eyes met, and she slammed her hand over the same hand that held the tiny ball of paper. The ball flew from her fingers, bounced on the table, and rolled toward him.

It was inevitable. The curious behavior he witnessed had him itching to know what she was trying to hide; what was written on the crumpled ball on the floor in front of him. Just as he reached for the paper ball, she snatched it up, their fingers brushing briefly as he watched the trail of her fingers to her mouth.

She popped the tiny globe into her mouth…and damn if she didn't swallow it.

Chapter 2

Paris shuddered with embarrassment. Oh God. Oh Lord. Please say she hadn't just done that.

She'd been so panicked when she'd seen him first glance at her paper. The answer she had written. An answer she'd never intended to share. There'd never been any consideration that someone else would read it. Of course Jenna. But then she already knew.

The thought of anyone else knowing…she struggled to control her breathing. Closing her eyes, she took one deep breath, then a second one. It was impossible to have a panic attack here, she didn't dare. She hadn't had one in a long time…

A shadow fell across her face. A heavy hand landed on her shoulder. "Are you okay?" asked a deep rolling male voice.

Opening her eyes in a flash, she knew before she saw that it was him.

Her gaze widened and she swallowed. Finally, she managed to nod and whisper, "Yes, thank you."

Hard eyes stared down at her, studying her. As though he was looking into the very heart of her. Quickly, her eyes slammed closed before he could see too much.

See the guilty stain on her soul. Sense the vast emptiness inside.

"Hey, take it easy."

The fingers on her shoulders squeezed gently. The warmth of his touch pulsed through her and she took another breath.

"Okay," she said, nodding as she opened her eyes and gave him a lopsided grin. "Believe it or not, I'm trying to."

"Try harder." That tone said *do it*. No excuses. And something about it worked. She straightened up, gave him a small nod of thanks, and glanced down at her paper. The paper was destroyed, ripped to shreds. "Wow, I really didn't like that question."

Her neighbor barked with laughter.

"Or you liked it so well, you had to taste it," he teased.

Without any malice or jeering in his tone, she took no offense. "A hang-up from my childhood," she admitted.

"Good thing the rest of the questions are fine then," he said, startling a laugh out of her.

"Paris and Weaver."

They both turned to face Jenna standing beside them.

"Sorry," Paris rushed to say, "I wasn't paying attention."

Jenna's sharp eyes landed on Paris's face. Her mouth opened as if to say something but she held back. Then she switched her gaze to Weaver and gave him a small nod.

And it was that nod that Paris really wanted to understand.

Because it was a small satisfied nod, as if she was happy with a decision he'd made. And what decision that was, Paris couldn't begin to fathom. Still, Jenna's arrival was enough to help Paris rebalance and get back on track.

Then Jenna's gaze widened as she stared at something on the table. Paris groaned silently. Her damn worksheet. Shoulders slumped, she opened her mouth to explain when Jenna said, "If you two could come to the back with me now, please."

And she turned and walked away.

Paris was confused for a moment, but she got up, reached for her paper, and realized it was gone.

As she spun around searching for it, she saw Weaver, and what a different name that was, hold out a small square of paper.

Stretching her hand out to accept it, she suddenly realized it was her worksheet now folded so the rips didn't show – into a perfect little star.

She laughed. "Thanks."

"No problem." He motioned behind her. "Let's go. Jenna is waiting."

HE WAITED FOR her to stumble to her feet and race to the back of the room. To get away from him? Or to get to Jenna faster? If so, she was the only one. All the other attendees had dragged their feet.

In his mind, he was taking notes on her character. While doing his masters in psychology, he'd learned, seen many interesting people, and heard fascinating cases. All of the bits and pieces of various personalities that made them the whole of who they were. Through these cases, he began to understand how events in life disintegrated the calm exterior of some and shattered the interior of others. Coping skills were as wide and varied as the people and the catastrophic event in their lives were.

Though he'd studied cases, attended cases as an observer, and had read widely, he'd yet to touch the tip of what made people tick. Jenna had a special touch. Partly why he'd attended so many lectures. To try and understand how she'd achieved the results she had from her workshops.

He wasn't sure what he was going to do with his degree. Something useful he hoped. But he couldn't do what Jenna did, and neither could he work in the hospitals where so many people needed help. He wasn't at the point of helping others yet.

Maybe down the road that could be an option but, he knew how quickly his own buttons could get pushed. Even after years of working on his own crap. There was a buffer layer between the buttons and reality, but somehow being at the hospital, working with patients, and dealing with major psychological issues made that cushion thin like nothing else. He always felt exposed when he was there. As if he wore a sign that made it clear he was exactly the same as they were. That they shouldn't look to him for help.

It crossed his mind that most people finishing their degrees felt ineffective in facing the world, afraid the world might expect them to have answers now that the initial stages of schooling were complete.

That's one thing he did know – he was short on answers.

"Weaver?"

Startled, he looked over at Jenna, who was waiting for him. When she motioned to the seat beside him, he realized he'd stopped beside the two women and had stood lost in thought while they waited for him to sit.

What an idiot. With an apologetic smile, he sat.

"Now that you are both here..." she waited and gave Weaver a brief smile, "I wanted to go over the project you'll both take part in." He started. No, that hadn't been part of the deal. Already having agreed to write, a paper, he didn't want to have to take part in the week-long activity. How was he going to find time to do both?

Yeah, he wasn't. So Paris could do the project while he did his paper. Sounded fair to him, but somehow he didn't think it would be that easy.

"Normally I assign a specific challenge to a two-person team…" She broke off and shuffled papers on her desk. "In your case, Paris, you have specific issues that you need to resolve, and I may have a way forward for you. In Weaver's case, he's dealing with the opposite side of the same coin, in a more minor way."

Weaver looked at Jenna then switched to see an odd expression whisper across Paris's face.

Cautiously, Weaver asked, "And what coin is that, exactly?"

A knowing smile in her gaze startled him as much as her answer. She said, "Justice."

Chapter 3

JUSTICE?

Paris couldn't stop the shaking that threatened to overtake her body. Was there ever a word that scared her more? The police had cleared her, she had not been charged. In fact, she'd been praised for her quick actions, her quick thinking. For saving her brother. But somehow inside she knew she was going to pay for what she'd done. It was a dark shadow that hung over her – all the time. Waiting for someone to know a miscarriage of justice had been done and finally take her into custody.

The thoughts, the fears, overtook everything. It was almost more than she could bear. No amount of reassurance from the police, social workers, or any of the numerous therapists she'd gone to removed the fear – she knew the truth. She was guilty.

One day the specter in her life – Justice – was going to prevail.

And then there was Constable Barry Delaney. His words – his warning. Something she'd never forget.

"Justice is easy," Weaver said, snapping her back to the present as he quoted. "There are no two sides to that coin. Black is black and white is white. Right and wrong are easy to sort out."

Paris glanced over at him, still shaken by the conversation.

Could he really be so naïve? Was anything in life that cut and dried?

"You're spouting lecture notes of our esteemed Professor Marshal Henniker, I presume," Jenna said with a laugh.

"You don't believe him," Weaver challenged, a glint in his eye.

"I know Henniker actively incites debates in his lectures, but he doesn't believe it either. However, as a teaching tool, it is effective in gaining student participation."

"I can imagine," Paris muttered under her breath. At the sharp look from Weaver, she pinched her lips together and stared back.

"You don't believe in Justice?" he asked mockingly.

"Of course," she said smoothly. "However, there are definite shades of gray in that argument."

He gave a half snort. "Whatever."

Jenna grinned. "So now you two can work out your project." She stood.

"Wait, what?" Paris asked. "What project? You haven't said anything about what we're supposed to do." The panicky part of her that was screaming for detailed instructions was something she hated. Steps to follow, so she wouldn't stray off the path or wander aimlessly and get nothing done. It wasn't that she needed to be micromanaged, but she did need to know what was required of her.

The thought of not knowing made her sick to her stomach. Things needed to be laid out in front of her. Expectations clearly defined. So she didn't do it wrong. So she didn't end up in trouble.

So she didn't fail.

"You'll figure it out," Jenna said cheerfully.

"No, wait," Paris said, a hint of panic in her voice. "We

don't know anything about what the project is supposed to accomplish. Why do we need to do a project in the first place?" she asked in what she hoped was a reasonable tone. Inside, her stomach twisted. There needed to be more direction, more to work with here. Didn't Jenna see that?

Jenna sat down again, studying Paris's face intently.

Paris flinched. Damn it.

"You're here to heal. You're here to grow past an issue that is impeding your growth. You're here to leave it behind and move forward as the strong, capable, caring woman you truly are." Then she smiled that beautiful smile that was like a radiant hug and added, "So a project where you actively work on this issue is the best way forward. It doesn't have to be about Justice, but it should be related."

And she got up, turned, and added, "Oh, and there is no right or wrong way to do this. In other words, you can't fail." With another beautiful smile, she left.

Paris watched her leave before glancing around the room. Everyone had someone. They were all talking in pairs, discussing their projects, their plans.

She was lost. Adrift, when she needed an anchor.

Weaver shifted in his chair until he was directly in front of her view, effectively blocking out the others. "So what would you like to do?"

Her gaze widened. How had she forgotten she wasn't alone? Weaver was her partner for this project. Instantly she felt better. "I have no idea."

"About justice. And it's to help you grow past your issues."

"My issues?" For some reason, that superior tone of voice maybe, his comment made her back bristle. "What about *your* issues?"

He opened his mouth, then thought better of it and slumped back into his chair.

"Yeah, I thought so." She glared at him.

"She said we were on opposite sides of the coin and we supposedly both have some work to do in that area, so really given what little she said, we need to find a way back to the middle instead of being on one side or the other," he said thoughtfully. "Not that it's an easy thing to do. How about how Justice has transformed our lives?"

Instead of answering him, she studied his face as he pondered the issue. Why was he here? Everyone in Jenna's classes were the same as she was, in need and broken in some way. Weaver looked out of place. Like he should be the lecturer, not the attendee. As if he had nothing to get over. Nothing to gain from being here. Except everyone did.

Even him.

She smiled. He just didn't know it yet.

WHAT WAS HER problem? Weaver tried to watch unobtrusively as Paris's lips twitched. As if she knew something he didn't. He narrowed his gaze at her.

As she looked around and then glanced back at him, he stood and watched her. Everything about her made her appear lost. Well, he for one was damn hungry. They'd been last or second to last in terms of getting their assignment and as assignments went, it was a complete dud. He should know, he'd just completed years of them. "Let's have lunch and discuss our options."

"Options?" she asked cautiously.

He wanted to smile but wasn't sure what her caution stemmed from and didn't want her to think he was making fun of her. Stepping aside, he motioned her to go ahead of him out of the lecture room. The other participants were collecting their belongings and starting to meander in the direction of the doorway. If they got to the restaurant first, he'd have a decent chance of being served faster.

"Options for the project."

"Oh." And damn if her footsteps didn't slow. With a gentle hand at her lower back, he nudged her forward slightly. "Let's grab a table while we still can. The group is coming behind us."

His steady touch propelled her forward to the hallway. He'd intended to remove his hand from her long lean back as soon as they were moving in the right direction, but something held his hand where it was, gently stroking the long lean muscles on the side of her spine. He desperately wanted to stretch out his fingers and explore the long ribs so tantalizingly close or drift around and see if his eyesight was as good as he thought it was at measuring her tiny waist. She had a yoga body and appeared muscled and fit. On one hand he yearned to know more about her, but at the same time knew her story would tug at his heartstrings and was better left alone.

He didn't do heartstrings.

He'd seen so much pain, death, and anguish, he knew he was better off alone, at least for now.

That way his buttons couldn't get pushed.

He also knew Jenna would have fun with him on her shrink couch. Sure, he'd come a long way, but that didn't mean there wasn't room for him to still travel down that road back to normal.

Yet, he'd come far enough to feel comfortable in his own skin. And comfortable enough that he didn't want to change that state again. Change hurt.

The frailty of the human condition was something he understood well.

And he didn't want to crash and burn. Rebuilding was hard. It took a long time. He had a lot of respect for those working on their own issues. But he'd made it to a point of not having to do more. It was possible to stop here at this stage if he wanted to. He'd done enough. He was good now.

Resetting his attention on Paris, he noticed her wispy long hair and super clean nails with the ragged edges. Her fingernails had ragged edges. He wondered at the familiarity he now recognized, the general look to her. Then he knew. It shouldn't have taken him so long. After all, he'd met many of them.

"You're a nurse."

She spun. "What?" Her voice squeaked out just the one shocked word.

His eyebrows shot up. Interesting response.

"I'm sorry; I didn't mean to get personal. It just occurred to me that you look like a nurse."

Her eyes darkened as she stared at him, taking a step back. They'd been hazel, but damn if they didn't look green now. She muttered something under her breath and turned away, almost racing toward the restaurant now.

Skittish, like a colt, he thought to himself, content to follow at a slower pace, wondering at the woman in front of him. She was an enigma.

And he was fascinated.

Chapter 4

WHAT THE HELL was wrong with her? Weaver was just another man. She worked with dozens of them. Most were decent, hardworking, take-their-paychecks-home-to-the-family kind of guys. There were a few players. Nurses were notorious for getting hit upon. It had been a joke in college with the engineers. As if they were a natural pairing. The guys had certainly believed it. As nurses had been generally pretty, compassionate, and nice people, they'd always been popular. If you knew one nurse and invited her to a party, then everyone hoped she'd bring her fellow students.

Paris got along with all the men at work, but she never got involved with any. She loved her job and would never do anything to jeopardize it. Her focus at work was babies. Mothers and babies. But mostly babies. Even being here for the week was pulling at her, making her worried about the patients she'd left behind. She trusted her coworkers; they were a brilliant team of specialists and cared about the patients as much as she did.

But nothing compared to the joy of the babies themselves. She adored them and wanted a half dozen but knew realistically two or three were more reasonable. Even if she couldn't have them herself. There were many babies out there needing someone to love them. And love was something she had in abundance. When the time was right, she would adopt.

Right now, though, she wasn't ready.

That was partly why she was here.

To become ready. To deal with her failures. Her belief she didn't deserve more. To deal with her lacks. Come to terms with the things in her life she could never have. Never experience. Adjust to her situation. To the injustice of it.

And damn, that brought her back around to Jenna and her words. Something she had said about her and Weaver being on the opposite sides of Justice. How did that work? In her head, Paris knew right and wrong was a gray area. It depended entirely on the situation. She had to believe that or else she would have turned herself in. And of course that was the problem – she couldn't believe that theory one hundred percent – but she wanted to. She was always looking over her shoulder, afraid that a mistake had been made in the system and the police were coming after her now. She wanted to be free of that fear.

"How about over there?"

Pulled back to the present, Paris glanced over at the window seat that Weaver had pointed out. "That's fine," she muttered. It was actually better than fine – it looked cozy, intimate in a way. This immediately brought to mind the heat of Weaver's hand on her back earlier as he'd guided her here. She shoved the thought deep inside and focused on her surroundings. The hotel restaurant was busy and didn't look to be horribly expensive. It also catered to downtown businesses and should offer a decent selection of food.

Not that she was very hungry.

He led the way and took the seat furthest away. She slipped into the closest one.

With a lift of a hand, the waitress came over immediately. As soon as she arrived, he ordered a double burger, fries, and coffee. When the waitress turned to Paris, she shrugged. "I don't even know what you have here."

The waitress rattled off the daily special and snagged a menu off a neighboring table. Except when she reached for the menu, the waitress mentioned fish and chips. Paris dropped the menu and said, "I'll have that, thanks."

After deciding on one or two pieces, and coleslaw and the fries, the waitress grabbed the menu. "I'll be back in a few minutes with coffee," she said, then hurried away.

"Have you eaten here before?" Paris asked. "You seemed to know what to order."

"I had breakfast here."

"Oh." That explained it. Paris hadn't slept well and had missed breakfast. She'd slipped into the lecture room with a take-out coffee and nothing else. At least she hadn't had a sugary cookie with it. But she'd been tempted.

Fish and chips weren't the healthiest of choices either, but she was really hungry and stressed and the afternoon was likely to be worse.

"So how do you see this report working?" she asked. "I'm used to being given a few more parameters than this."

"Partly why Jenna didn't give them to us." He shrugged. "She also knows I'm in grad school, and we often have to come up with a thesis statement and write a report about it."

Paris sat in quiet contemplation for a moment. "And what are you envisioning with this report then?" And how the hell was it going to help her? She dropped her gaze to the table, her finger aimlessly tracing the diagonal pattern in the tabletop.

"If you tell me why you're so stuck on the one side of justice or how it has helped or hindered your transformation, then I'll tell you mine. Our journey from here could be the report."

Paris sat back against the vinyl bench seat and stared. "And what if that journey is beyond us to make?"

"The journey is the issue, not the end result. As long as we make the attempt, then that is the report."

Holding back a sneer, she replied, "You don't seem to feel you have any traveling to do on that pathway."

He studied her, a surprised look in his gaze. "What makes you say that?"

"Your complete detachment at the concept. It doesn't make you afraid or worried in any way at the thought of doing something like this."

Instead of answering, he shifted his cutlery around in front of him.

And she watched, understanding she'd hit a nerve. "We all have something to learn," she said gently. "Even when we don't think we do."

Lifting his head, his eyes shone. "I'm not saying I don't have anything to learn. I'm just not sure I have anything to learn in this area…"

"Ah. Interesting."

The waitress arrived, cutting off further speech. Paris watched as he attacked his plate of food with more enthusiasm than necessary. It said much about his state of mind. She smiled and lifted a fry. "See, you do have much to learn in this area."

He froze, his burger mid air, his gaze dark, defensive. "What I might have to learn doesn't mean I'm ready or able or indeed willing to do so here."

"Ditto."

There was a moment of silence as he chewed and swallowed his food. "So tell me what you think about Justice. And then tell me what you'd like your stance to be."

How about the fact that she hated the topic? That she hated the concept of there being two sides to the issue. Since when was anything so clear-cut, so black and white. Figures that Jenna would pick up on it. Anything that made Paris feel so strongly was something to explore when it came to therapy. She stared out the window, wondering what to answer.

"I am not sure I have a stance on it, actually. I think the circumstances often determine my view."

"Explain."

She shrugged. "I'm not pro-abortion, but if the mother was raped, I could easily understand her not wanting the child."

"Except it's not the child's fault, and it has the right to life."

"Exactly what I mean." Now they were getting somewhere. "There are a lot of debates and understanding required for either side. Gray areas."

He frowned and continued to eat. "Or do you have a specific stance, but on a specific issue."

Stopping suddenly, she could feel the flags of heat burn through her cheeks. "Maybe. And maybe not," she snapped. "What about you? What are you so decided on that Jenna thinks you need to learn something different?"

He laughed. "Jenna doesn't know anything about me." Then he shut up.

"Did you attend her lectures? Her evening classes?" At his nod, she asked, "Have a special meeting with her about this seminar?"

He nodded again.

A smile spread across her face and she sat back. "Then regardless of what you think she might or might not know about you, I can tell you she understands more than you think."

Did he see that? She looked for a glimmer of understanding, but when there was only a hooded glance her way, she wasn't sure she'd gotten through to him. And that damn tiny knowing smile that played at the corner of his lips. What was with that?

"You think I'm wrong, don't you?"

"Not at all." He shook his head. "But my situation is different from yours, so my discussion with Jenna would have been slightly different than yours would have been."

Paris held back her smile. She understood. He thought he was different. Thought he didn't have the same problems the other participants had. Well, she didn't have that problem, but her brother sure had. At least until he'd been through one of these seminars.

Weaver, she suspected, would be the same.

"What are you doing at the university?"

He dropped his gaze to the table then hesitated, as if undecided as to what to say. Fair enough, she thought as she absentmindedly took another fry and bit off half of it.

"I'm completing my masters in psychology."

Oh shit. That couldn't be good. Then he really did it.

"Jenna was one of my Profs last year," he said calmly. "I'm going to write a report on her workshop. She says if it's any good, she'll help me get it published."

Paris dropped the rest of her french fry on her plate. Shocked, she said, "You mean this workshop is a school assignment? I'm supposed to be part of some damn study so you can get a professional checkmark?" Now that was too much. Blinking back the sudden moisture in the corner of her eyes, she got up from her chair and walked unsteadily out of the restaurant. Out of the hotel. Too bad she couldn't walk out of the damn workshop.

HE SHOULDN'T HAVE told her. He'd made a monumental mistake. Why? He knew better. But she'd gotten too close. He'd gotten defensive. Not wanting to believe her. He gazed out the window, deep in thought. The one time he needed to keep his big mouth shut. He cursed under his breath. Of course he knew better. This was a report. A study. One never told the subjects when they were involved, if they needed to give natural responses. Once they had the information of belonging to a study group, they acted differently from a different set of parameters.

Still, she might *not* be in his report. He hadn't figured out how to target the report yet. And he'd never use names.

Given the little bit he'd seen of Paris, he didn't think she knew what a parameter was. She appeared to be a ball of insecurity masquerading as something with poise and confidence and failing entirely. Like a five-year-old girl using mommy's makeup and parading through the house trying to look grown up. Instead, she looked exactly like a little girl who was trying too hard.

Paris was definitely trying too hard.

Still, he'd done something horribly wrong. As he stared out the window, oblivious to the scene on the outside of the glass, he realized there was no help for it. The next step was to go to Jenna and confess.

Crap.

He hated being in the wrong. Hated apologizing. It always made him feel lousy. Something he never quite got over.

He learned from a young age that being wrong meant a

good beating. Even now, he had to talk to the adult side of his nature and explain that getting your ass kicked for being wrong was a long time ago. This is what life is all about now. Deal with it.

Chapter 5

"I WANT A new partner," Paris said baldly from the open doorway. If she hadn't been staring at Jenna so closely, she might have missed seeing the slight headshake before it firmed up.

Jenna lifted her head and gave Paris the sweetest smile.

"No." Paris entered the room and plunked down on a chair beside her. "No excuses or platitudes about why this pairing is a good idea or anything else. I am no one's assignment," she cried out, her voice rising. Then anger bloomed. "And no way am I going into a damn report about my experiences this week."

A cloud briefly dimmed the joy in Jenna's face. "I'm not surprised you feel that way," she said gently. "I would too."

That made Paris pause. "Then why me?" she asked, her hands curling into fists. "Why would you pair him up with me?"

"Because he needs you," Jenna said, compassion and understanding in her voice. "And you need him."

"No way." Paris shook her head, her long black hair flying everywhere. "I need understanding and tolerance. Patience. Someone to show me the way. To help me take the steps I need to take." She glared at Jenna. "I don't need someone who considers himself my superior in all ways. Who thinks he can analyze what makes me tick. Who thinks he knows what's best for me."

As Jenna opened her mouth to answer, Paris rolled right over her. "The only person who can know that, the only one who understands my life to that depth to make those types of answers, is me."

She stood. "I won't have it. I won't be in his damn report."

And she hurried to the door.

"What if I told you," Jenna called after her, "that writing that report was his lesson?"

Paris hit the brakes at the doorway. "What do you mean?"

"Everyone is here to learn. Everyone here has some major roadblock in their life that they need to move past. How they move past is just as important as making sure that they do get past it. Weaver needs to write this all down. He needs to put it into orderly form. It's all about control. Detaching from his own world, that he might understand how other people are learning to help themselves."

"And what will that give him? Except boost his satisfaction of being better than everyone?" Paris asked in a hard voice. "It makes it very hard to like him, you know."

Jenna smiled a breathtaking smile, as if she'd come to some major realization.

"Of course it does. So why do you think he does it?"

"So no one will like him," Paris joked. Then as Jenna nodded slowly, she walked across the floor to stand in front of her. "He doesn't think he's likable, right?"

That smile rose brighter.

"He figures no one will love him anyway, doesn't he?" And Paris understood. "So he's going to push them away before he gets pushed away."

She collapsed on her chair. "Damn."

SCALES (OF JUSTICE)

HE WAS FILLED with regrets. *What are you going to do about it, idiot? Apologize? Tell Jenna you won't do the report as you've messed this up already. And just what is she likely to say?* Weaver pondered the issue as he paid the bill and wandered out to the lobby. She'd smile and tell him to fix it.

How the hell could he do that?

Really, all he wanted was to get this report published. In a way, he needed the credits. They could be damn hard to get. He wanted to move forward into his field and help people. He understood he might not be ready, but no one said he had to go full bore into this. A little at a time – at a rate he could handle. That worked.

So what if he lost a little skin scraping close to his issues or gained another scar or two? More scars would just add to the many he already had. But then, Paris had scars of her own, he'd seen some of them. And even he could feel the open wound he'd caused.

"So apologize," he said out loud. "That's the place to start."

Glancing down at his watch, he realized he had a little time before the afternoon lecture started. Good. He could get a start and write down his impressions. The things he'd picked up already. And there were a lot.

The seminar room was empty when he arrived. He took his seat and opened his laptop to take a look at the report he'd set up but hadn't done much with yet. Now he let his mind go and let his fingers fly on the keyboard as he wrote down a description of Paris. It was her that interested him.

Confused, valiant, emotional. Damaged. Obviously hurt, but tired of hurting. There is strength in her, but she has never been strong enough to deal with the core hurt. She's alive, but a part of her is dead.

He stopped and read what he'd written. Wow. So much for analytical. This was literally emotional, the impressions from his gut. Though there was no way to verify if he was right or wrong, his mind and heart said he was on track. Paris was an eager beaver desperate to get over something and get on with the next stage of her life, and that concept both terrified and excited her. Failure was not an option, yet he suspected it was quite likely the outcome. Not that he'd wished that for her, but she was a mass of confusion even for herself.

Then there was the damn project. How did that work if there were no outlines to follow? No theme to grab onto. No guidelines. He highly suspected it was Jenna's way of making them think. But that didn't mean Paris would get the outcome she hoped for. The outcome she needed from it.

So what could he do to help it become reality?

He owed her after all. And he wanted her to be okay with this report.

So he'd need her to be okay with him.

Only he'd done a damn shitty job so far.

The next step would be to figure out what project to do and let her do it. So now what would transform her from being an unwilling participant to a willing one?

A slow smile crossed his face as he picked up the paper he'd been using for doodles and folded it once then twice. His smile widened. He finally understood one thing – the theme of the project. This was all about transformation.

CHAPTER 6

Tuesday

THE NEXT MORNING, Paris took her seat beside Weaver, giving him the briefest of glances. He was waiting for her. Before she could say anything, he said in an apologetic tone, "I'm sorry. I didn't mean to upset you."

Then he placed a small folded bird on her desk. She was charmed at the delicate wings and precise features of the tiny bird. In order to create something so beautiful and fragile, there had to be something soft under that hard exterior of his. The gift wasn't enough to forgive him, but it helped to break the awkwardness of their first meeting since the fight.

"It's okay. I'm still not happy about it, but I understand."

"You do?" he asked, startled.

Nodding, she explained. "I do. I don't want to be in any report, but I understand that you need to write one."

He kept his head down as if in deep thought, as if her answer was what he wanted to hear but maybe just not quite the right way. Well, too damn bad. She understood his machinations more than he did apparently. He'd been studying other people so much, Weaver had forgotten to look closer to home.

Paris, on the other hand, had started with herself and had gone on from there. Already she had learned a lot, but there was more. She felt it. Who knew what she'd learn as she moved into studying other people? She'd come willing to learn but damn, this project business had shaken her.

And that upset her too.

Still, the desperation to get what healing she could kept her here. Even if that meant working with someone who wasn't ready to heal.

"What about our project?" she muttered. "I'd feel better if I knew what direction we were supposed to take."

"I was thinking about a report on transformation."

As he spoke, he pointed to the origami bird. "We both need to learn to grow. To change. Theoretically, to transform. From the old to the new. Whether by understanding how our stance on any issue, justice included, can be muted to something else or by looking past another person's point of view or something else entirely unrelated."

"True," she said slowly. "But that is a word. Transformation. What would we do the report about?"

"About how we have transformed ourselves so far and where we want to go. Maybe put it into stages. One, being where we've been. Two, being where we are. And three, being where we have to go."

Warming to his concept, she listened as he fleshed it out further. "Use Justice as the vehicle."

"Sounds good, but honestly that's just self-analysis. Hardly the scope of what Jenna wants out of us." Paris knew that a project like this could be difficult, but she'd expected something different. Something more public. In public. Dealing with people. At least Sean and Robin's had been. She'd heard about Kane and Tania's project from Robin, but not the details. They'd only had to go into the public for Tania to take pictures. So maybe that was internal too. She didn't know.

"Maybe that would be okay." She shrugged. "Let's ask Jenna about it."

"Why?"

"Because I don't want to do anything wrong or waste time going off in one direction that we're just going to have to redo it."

"And I don't want to ask because if we do, we're opening ourselves up to it being wrong," he countered. "Whereas if we leave it and do the project the best we can, it won't be wrong. It will be our interpretation of the project."

"You don't like being wrong," she said with a wry smile. "So you ignore the process and decide you're right from your perspective."

"And you're scared of being wrong so you go and ask over every little stage to make sure you aren't."

That was dead on. She sat back, surprised. "Wow, this could be tough working with you."

"And you," he came back with immediately.

Both leaned back, smiles breaking to the surface.

At least it gave them a place to start. If needed, she could go ask Jenna on her own, and if they could improve on this project, then she'd have to convince Weaver to make those changes and if not, she'd have to make a decision. He was right in that she didn't like making mistakes. She'd grown up crippled, her doubts exaggerated by severe punishments when she'd done something wrong. Now she asked a lot of questions early on so she understood what was required of her. Whereas, Weaver refused to be wrong – as if that mental leap was too much for him to handle.

Maybe the same end result. Just different methodologies. As long as they both managed to avoid triggering the memories of what happened to them when they were wrong, then it all worked.

But it also said that he had a lot more stuff going on in his history than he was willing to look at. Could she help him? Should she help him? Would he let her help him?

And how did that do anything for her? She was greedy. She wanted the progress for herself. Not necessarily for him unless she also progressed. She didn't want to slow anyone down, but neither did she want to be left behind. Her eagerness for this course had been all-encompassing and now here she was feeling flat and let down.

Once again it was like she'd asked for too much, hoped for too much, and reality, the bitch, had already let her down. Then again, what did she expect? There weren't any miracles in her life, remember? Miracles were only for people who deserved them.

Sean had found his miracle. Her brother Sean found Robin. Not that he'd say they were a hit right off. He'd seen how damaged Robin had been at the time and had moved forward *with* her.

Now it was Paris's turn, and she wanted a similar result. If not a partner, at least major growth. Could Jenna pull off magic a third time?

Dispirited, she looked around at the seminar room turned classroom and realized she didn't want to be here. She'd come with such high expectations, foolish ones, and foolish of her, but she'd been so wanting to be here and now that there was no sign of stardust in the air, she wanted to go home. Another one of her patterns. If she didn't like something, didn't look like it was going to lead her in the right direction, then she wanted to quit.

Why waste her time? She didn't have the laid back personality of her brother. She was driven to succeed. Driven to go after what she wanted in life. Whatever that was. Right now it was healing.

Was she just being impatient? After all, the workshop had just started, but it didn't feel like impatience. It felt like she'd taken a wrong turn somewhere, but she didn't know where.

Why wasn't it coming together for her?

PARIS WAS WIRED. Not the way he was wired internally, but wired as in needy and determined to get those needs filled. Because of that, sitting slumped with her eyes closed, he figured she was getting depressed.

Interesting mix again. The lack of direction in the report bugged her. He could understand that. No one wanted to waste time, but he doubted they were as anal about it as she appeared to be. Still, she was right. They didn't have time to redo the report if they were off on the wrong tangent.

How to make this work. He stared down at the notes he'd been so happy with earlier that now looked like shit. He hated that. "Okay, let's ask Jenna for more help."

Her gaze widened and she spun around to stare at him. "Really? Okay, let's catch her as she comes in."

"Uh…" But she was gone.

Holy crap. Not wanting to be excluded from anything, he forced himself up, smiled apologetically at the others, and walked over to where Paris waited. "This is hardly the time," he muttered.

"There is no time. The seminar is already in progress. We've been here one night already. We need to get on the ball."

The eagerness in her voice surprised him. Driven was one

thing, but this was a workshop. Sit back and relax, do a few assignments and carry on.

Not for her. And if he was going to get in her way, she'd run him over. "Why are you in such a hurry?"

She frowned at him. "You just don't get it, do you? We're all here for a reason. Each of us. Unlike you."

"Hey," he protested, "I'm here for a reason."

"Not one that is about healing or moving forward in your life." She snorted. "You're trying to climb the academic ladder rather than work on your life. That would be too hard. Much easier to hold your report up as an excuse instead of admitting that you have as much to work on as the rest of us."

Just then, she caught sight of Jenna and ran toward her, leaving Weaver in shock staring behind her. "How did she know that," he muttered to the empty hallway.

Only it wasn't empty. One of the women working at the hotel smiled at him as she walked past, her arms full of paper. "One of the things we've always seen here on Jenna's workshops," she said, "is transformation. People come here from one mindset and go home with another."

As her heels clicked down the sparkling hallway, he stared after her, his thoughts full of his earlier contemplations on the report. Transformation again.

The more he thought about it, he realized it didn't fit Paris. Because she wasn't waiting for transformation to happen, she was going to *make* it happen, and that didn't work in his mind. Transformation to him was something that happened inside. When you weren't looking. As if it were something that went on at very deep levels of consciousness and then when you turned around one day, you were at a completely different state of awareness.

Paris wasn't about that. There was an edge of desperation

to her actions. As if she was afraid that it wasn't going to happen. That whatever good could come out of this workshop would pass her by. That was not something she could live with. For her, it was time for change, any way she could get it.

As the last phrase slipped through his mental preamble, he realized that was the one that fit. There was an edge of righteousness to her actions. She deserved this. She'd worked for it. Been through a lot to get it, and now was afraid it wasn't there for her.

Or maybe she wanted to deserve it, but inside maybe she didn't really believe it. That's why the desperation.

He wondered if Jenna knew. That was one cagey woman. The insights she had into people's character was something he'd never seen and Weaver wondered, given his own blocks, if he ever would.

Paris made him feel a little ashamed. He didn't give a damn about moving forward. The place he was at right now was safe and he wanted to stay there.

Wow. Wincing, he figured that maybe they were a great pair after all.

He didn't want to move forward, and she couldn't stay where she was.

And they still had no plan of action.

Maybe that all related back to the transformation lesson again. Maybe they'd turn around and it would have happened at that inner level while they weren't looking. He'd love that. To move from where he sat to another major step without really knowing what he'd done, but in truth, life wasn't like that. These steps were painful. Huge and difficult. That's why he wasn't interested in going to another one – at least not right now.

Paris was too desperate. He understood that something

drove that desperation, but it made it hard to watch her. Great. Of course he had a whole week of being with her. Like it or not, Jenna had a reason for everything she did. And he doubted this pairing was any different.

And why the hell did Paris have to be so interesting?

A relationship with someone in therapy was a bad idea. Look where the last one had left him.

Alone and divorced.

There was no way he was going through that again.

Chapter 7

Paris bolted down the hallway toward Jenna. It seemed since she'd arrived this week she hadn't been able to walk anywhere. Something was always sending her forward at top speed, trying to get to where she was going and getting precisely nowhere. It was making her desperate and crazy.

"Jenna, we need help with this project."

Jenna stopped in the hallway, her gaze amused but calm. "Do you?"

"Yes." Paris nodded vigorously. "We do."

"We?"

Paris glanced behind her. Damn Weaver, where are you? "Sorry, I thought Weaver was coming to see you, too."

"Hmmm." Jenna studied Paris. "What part do you need help with?"

"The beginning." Paris hated the crippling feeling inside. That need to get it right. "I can't start," she said, then corrected her statement. "I don't know where to start."

"Did you come up with a theme?"

"Too many of them. Black and White. Right or Wrong. Justice. Transformation. That seems to be a major trigger point for both of us."

"Right and wrong, black and white, and Justice could be pretty much the same theme, so all of them could work."

Paris could feel the hot words bubbling up. "I don't want

something that *could* work. I want the *right* one. I need this to work," she cried. And then she gasped, falling silent, shocked at her own words.

After a long moment, she muttered, "I'm sorry."

"Don't be," Jenna said in a sober tone. "I think that was something that needed to come out for a long time." Jenna shifted the books in her arms and studied her closer. "This is an important issue. Remember, desperation often pushes away what you need most." She looked doubtful for a long moment, and Paris remembered the conversation where she'd damn near begged to be let into the seminar. Desperate then, too.

"I'm sorry. I'm sorry," she said, "I don't mean to be."

"No, but it's that very need inside you that needs to be addressed. You can't heal if you can't let go. So what do you need to let go of so you aren't so desperate to move forward?"

"Fear." The word popped out instantly. "Fear of not getting the same benefit out of the seminar that my brother did. Fear of..." she took a deep breath and let it fly. "Failing. Of once again not being good enough. Not good enough to be loved. To love. Being so horrible, so bad, so much a failure that no one will ever love me."

Her voice broke around her, the words splintering like icicles. Each hitting her skin like tiny pinpricks and making her bleed, and still the pain boiled over. "I tried so hard to be good. And I was never able to be good *enough*. He still beat on me every chance he got."

Tears flooded her eyes as the memories flooded her mind. This was not the place to break down. Not here. Not like this. Panicked to get away, she turned and ran.

Up the two flights of stairs, then down the hallway. The carpet in front of her was a blur. Instinct led her home. She made it to her room and got it unlocked, but it was a struggle. Moving at all was difficult. Inside her head, all she could hear were the words – *another failure.*

"Easy, Paris. You're fine. You're here at the hotel. No one else can see you."

Paris stiffened. It was Weaver.

Then she felt strong arms around her. She cringed, an instinctive reaction, still caught in the gray shadows of the memories.

His hands dropped away.

With tears in her eyes she waited, a sense of fatalism in her heart, knowing the blows that would come. He'd hit her next. Knock her to the ground and kick her until she couldn't get up again. She shuddered, feeling the film of sweat coating her skin. The waves of greasy pain ready to rise from her gut. And still nothing. Then she heard him beside her.

She shuddered again.

"I'm not going to hurt you," he whispered. "Never would I hit you."

The words rolled over her in a wave of disbelief as she shifted through time from her childhood to the seminar and the hallway where she stood like an idiot. Eyes shut tight, her body swaying in reaction, feeling flushed with realization. Oh Lord. It was Weaver next to her, not her father. Paralyzed, only a sob escaped.

Once again he wrapped his arm around her, turned her around, and tugged her up against his chest. She went stiff with fear. But this time he didn't let go. Her heart thumped. She knew better than to fight. But he just held her. Gently.

The gentleness was her undoing. The tears that burned her eyes burst forth and tumbled free, the waterfall gaining momentum as it poured down her cheeks and soaked his shirt.

Emotions washed through her, the onslaught so hard and fast, she couldn't move.

The primary emotion that beat as loudly as her heart was disbelief.

It had been a long time since she had had an episode like that. She'd hoped to never be crippled by those memories again. Somehow she'd failed. Somehow they'd snuck in from behind, waiting for her to fall to pieces.

And of course she had. With Jenna – her very words releasing the flood she'd worked so hard to keep dammed up.

Caught in the maelstrom, she didn't notice the soothing touch up and down her back for a long time. It was Weaver. Being nice. The only other person to treat her like this was Sean. Her beloved brother. Without him, she wouldn't have survived her childhood. She knew he felt that she'd returned the favor but she hadn't – not really.

"Feeling better?" Weaver's voice was deep...clogged.

Not wanting to show him her puffy face, she frowned and looked down. But he wouldn't let her hide. He tucked a finger under her chin and slowly lifted her face toward him.

She tried to pull free. He let her.

"You shouldn't hide your emotions, you know. They are honest and therefore beautiful," he said in such a pensive voice she couldn't take umbrage with him, but his words did startle a laugh out of her.

"Maybe honest, but also downright ugly." She pulled out of his arms and dashed into the bedroom then the bathroom to the side. There she stared into the big mirror. Red splotchy skin and eyes too big for her face. It went along with the equally large mouth. But her eyes glowed. Tear-rinsed and shiny, she wondered if the release of emotion might have made them look better.

"Maybe I should cry more often," she muttered. "Not." She took a moment to use the facilities then used cold water to rinse her face, hoping to ease back the puffiness. When she figured she'd waited long enough for him to have left, she opened the door and walked out.

He stepped up beside her.

Shit.

"No, don't avoid me, please."

She turned her face away.

He sighed. "You look fine now."

Laughter bubbled out from Paris's mouth. Weaver was delighted to realize it was real. He grinned. "Okay, let me amend that. You look great for having just been through a crying jag."

"That's better, I suppose," she muttered. "My face always looks so horrible when I've been crying."

"Well, it's over and time to fix the rest." At her honest smile, he added. "I don't suppose you'd like to tell me what brought tha—"

Before he could finish she was shaking her head, stopping his question. "No."

He lifted his shoulders in surrender. "I was just hoping to not trigger it again."

"You didn't," she said. "Jenna did."

"Oh." Well, that's what she was supposed to do, and likely it was a private matter that he was never going to know about. Damn it. Although he'd planned to stay detached and separated from everyone attending, he was finding that wasn't likely going to happen any time soon – not from Paris.

She wiped her eyes and said in a muffled voice, "I think

I'll stay in my room."

"Or we can go back to the seminar and get through the afternoon session like the trooper you are."

Her smile was still watery but it was normal. "I look like a mess."

"And you won't be alone. That's why we all came, remember?" He studied her, watching her gaze narrow and turn direct.

"Is that why you came?" she challenged. "I thought it was for your stupid publication."

"You forget, I'm damaged too. Whether this was my choice or not or whether the seminar works isn't the issue. One can't be here in a setting like this, with healing going on, without having change happen within your own psyche. Maybe I didn't come prepared with a big issue I was hoping to overcome, but I'm going to come up against issues regardless. Life is like that."

He might have forgotten that point too along the way but being here now like he was, watching her, dealing with the repercussions of his report, being around growth, well, he wouldn't be able to escape. He remembered that now. It really didn't matter. He'd move forward one painful step at a time – whether he liked it or not.

Chapter 8

The afternoon seminar moved quickly, being mostly group activities. They were easier to do and allowed Paris to pull back inside her shield so the world wasn't scraping her raw. There was a lot she could do to protect herself.

By the time they were almost done, Jenna called out, "For the next hour, work in pairs on your project."

She stood up. "Paris and Weaver, come up here please and we'll discuss yours."

"Oh finally." Paris bounded to her feet without looking to see if Weaver was coming or not. She stood in front of Jenna's desk. "Thanks."

Jenna smiled. "Take a seat, both of you."

That's when Paris noticed Weaver standing behind her. "Oh, sorry." She scooted to the side and sat down. Weaver sat in the other chair.

"Did you come up with a theme yet, you two?"

Paris shook her head. Weaver nodded.

Jenna smiled. "So one says yes and one says no. Interesting. Okay. Paris, have you heard what Weaver has come up with?"

Paris frowned at Weaver. "I don't think so."

Weaver shrugged. "No big deal. I was going to suggest transformation."

"Oh, I did hear that," Paris admitted.

There was silence as both women contemplated the theme.

"But what would we do with it?" Paris asked. "I'm not against that, I just don't understand how to use it for a report. Short of explaining how I've seen my life transformed."

She slid a sideways glance over at Jenna, who was moving a pen between her fingers, deep in thought.

That would be an easier project to do than some and would trigger a lot of memories. Some not so easy to deal with. That can of worms was better left unopened.

"Maybe we should define that more," Jenna said. "Not your life per se, but how one incident, a huge incident in your life, has affected every day you've lived since." Her gaze was direct, warm, caring and....shit....*determined* as she looked at Paris.

"In fact, I think it needs to be that really big white elephant each of us has in our lives that we don't want to talk about. That we don't want anyone in this room to know about." She waited a beat then added, "But that needs to come out."

"If we've acknowledged this incident as a problem, then sharing it with others is both unnecessary and painful," Weaver said.

"And can't happen," Paris blurted out. Jenna knew she couldn't deal with this. It wasn't possible for Paris to talk about it. She couldn't. The familiar tightening on her chest, her inability to breathe, these were more than feelings. They were real. Her eyes closed and she focused on the next breath. Just one. If she could get that one out – there – she did it. Then the next one, then the next one. By the time she opened her eyes, she realized that there was only silence around her as the others watched.

"It really sends you into a panic attack, doesn't it," Weaver asked.

She nodded.

"That's the big one then. You so have to let that go. The fear will kill you," he said seriously.

She gazed off into the distance. "But I know what it is, I know what happened, putting that into a project isn't going to help me – it will traumatize me. And I wasn't alone. I don't feel that I can share what happened without breaking a confidence in someone else. They need their privacy too."

"Use a different name?" Weaver suggested.

"No, he'd still be obvious. You'd know who he was." She thought about it. "And it's too big."

"Big is good," Weaver said. "It gives you lots to work with."

"No, like this is huge. I can't deal with this. It's too hard." Paris pleaded.

Silence.

Jenna spoke up, her voice warm and fuzzy, "Then deal with a layer on top. That will make the big issue a little easier for you to access, and yet you'll feel better for having gotten something done. Some level of pain gone."

"A top layer?"

"Yes." Jenna waited a moment. "How about the fear of not being good enough. Not deserving enough to get what you want in life."

That did it. Frozen again, her breath locked down. Jenna was referring to Paris's outburst this morning, when she'd almost lost it completely, and didn't it damn well figure that Jenna would pick up on that one horrible, crippling aspect. She struggled to take a breath, that oh-so-very necessary air into her lungs so she could take another breath – one that would allow her to fight the good fight and keep living for another day.

Heat radiated up her arm as she became aware of fingers gently stroking her skin, soothing her panic, easing back the rough edges of her control.

A gasping, raspy breath escaped.

"Sure," she heard herself mention sarcastically. "Like that isn't a big one."

"Good." Jenna stood up, deliberately misunderstanding her, and said, "That's settled. Find a way to visually express your transformation." And she collected her books and walked out, leaving Paris staring after her.

"Visually?" Weaver said. "Really?"

"That's what she said. Although how does one visually represent the fear of not being good enough? Not deserving enough have to do with anything?"

"I think she left us some latitude in there, but still."

Feeling more balanced, Paris shot a look around the room, but no one noticed. They were all packing up to leave. She planned to do that too. Just as soon as she could get her body to move.

WEAVER HAD SEEN several people have panic attacks but hadn't realized that Paris was crippled so severely by them. Jenna had certainly hit it on the head about what Paris's big dominating issue was. At least the one that was accessible. And she was right, one had to deal with the little bits and reduce the pain and fear around the big one until it was manageable.

Then when it least surprised you, that one opened up because you came from a position of strength now and it had been weakened. He could hope for such a breakthrough for her. She deserved it.

"What about at your work?" he asked curiously. "Is there anything there that would show you something visual in transforming? You deal with mothers and babies, correct?"

She nodded, a gentle smile on her face. "I do love my work. Helping the women yes, but seeing the babies, working with the ones that have a tough time and seeing them survive and thrive..." Her smile grew misty. "It's special."

"And the ones that don't survive?" he asked. How could she deal with the loss of babies like that? That would be too much for him, he was too big a softie.

"I cry," she said simply. "A lot. But never there. Never at work. I make it through my day – sad but functioning – then I go home and I cry for them. There's nothing else I can do. In many cases I have to wonder if it wasn't a blessing as the poor little things were in such pain and it wasn't going to get much better, but then I remember some that have struggled so hard and have done well..." she smiled, "and I remember that all we can do is fight. Sometimes we win and sometimes we lose."

"That's not a bad way to look at life in general." Weaver smiled. "Even now, today. We have a project to do. Let's apply that common sense to making it happen."

"I don't have a problem doing the work," Paris replied, "but once again I don't know where to start."

"That's always the hardest place," he said, "but the good thing is, in this case, you've already started!"

It took a moment for a small frown on her forehead to clear, and then she smiled. "That's true, but not very helpful."

He laughed. "Hey, whatever works. Sometimes I do the end of the report because I know that's where I'm going. I then backtrack to the beginning to lay down the steps required to get there."

"That's actually not a bad idea." Her face brightened. "I'll have to think about that."

"Good. In the meantime, how about a walk?" He could see the refusal forming on her face, he jumped in to add, "Nothing long, just out in the gardens or around the dock." He snagged her elbow. "Let's go."

Chapter 9

Paris had no desire to go out, to leave her safety net. Weaver wasn't giving her a choice. Before she understood what had happened, she was standing outside the hotel in downtown Vancouver, her jacket on, and staring up at the windy gray skies. It matched her mood. The emotions rocking her today were enough to make her tired, depressed. She hated the toll it was taking on her. It's like someone took all the stuffing out of her and just when she thought the bad stuff was all gone, she realized it was only a drop in the ocean of bad still waiting for her to deal with.

"I wonder if everyone has something major to deal with?"

"Everyone has *something* to deal with. The term 'major' is subjective. Trying to buy a new car and not sure how to could be construed as a major problem in some people's eyes."

She snorted. "I wish."

"Come on, let's walk."

It was the last thing she wanted to do, but her feet had a mind of their own and fell into step beside him. The air was cool for a September day. The moist, slightly salty air revitalized her spirits. Normally the spring and fall here were warm and stunningly beautiful with bright blue skies. Today offered the beautiful part, but it wasn't warm or blue. She stuffed her hands into her jacket pockets and let the world stroll by as she walked.

"We'll head towards the ocean."

"Wherever." She shrugged.

"Are you cold?" he asked in concern. "The breeze has a bite to it."

"I'm fine," she murmured. "It's cool but refreshing."

They walked in silence until the first glimpses of the sailboats popped into view. She broke into laughter. "They always look so bright and cheerful out there buffeted by the wind and waves."

"I don't know how cheerful they are today considering the beating they are taking."

The breeze that brushed by them was a strong wind out in the bay, but the people in the sailboats looked to be having the time of their lives. Then she caught sight of the kite surfers. "What a sport," she exclaimed.

"Looks like fun, but so not for me."

"Not into dangerous sports?" she asked, feeling shivers sliding over her skin. "I'm not either, but men generally like that sort of thing." Of course her brother didn't, but in their house, growing up had been a dangerous sport. She smiled, loving the reminder of her brother, and the shivers stopped.

"Not my style." He gave a harsh laugh and said, "I survived childhood. That was hard enough."

Shocked, she stopped all of a sudden, then turned to look at him. "I was just thinking the same thing."

With an understanding look, he moved closer to her. "Our daily life isn't like these people." He pointed out a particularly high-flying kite boarder. "He's happy to chase after excitement and danger. For most of us who grew up in a violent household, we are looking for the opposite. We want peace and safety now."

She couldn't have said it better. The insight into his life, his childhood, made her realize he really had been through the wringer – like the rest of them at the seminar. Holding her breath, she stayed silent, hoping he'd share more. One foot rested on the cement barricade between them and the water, the look on his face distant but calm. As if he'd come to terms with something behind him.

She wished.

There was a world of difference between his childhood and hers, she knew, but for the first time she realized there was also a lot in common.

"Maybe some of those people have been hurt so much they no longer care what happens to them?"

"That's the other side of the coin, isn't it?" He glanced at her. "Survival means different things to different people. Some say they survived, but inside they are dead and can't stand living. Some people do crazy stunts in the hope to kill themselves off because they aren't strong enough to do it themselves. Sounds horrible, but I've seen it."

"And in some cases, they are so angry inside they turn around and inflict the same abuse on others," Paris whispered, looking at the black mark his shoe scuffed into the cement barricade. Briefly letting her gaze follow the line of his foot up his leg, remembering how it felt when he had held her.

She didn't see the same rage in his demeanor or actions she'd seen in other men. He'd never hit anyone for fun. Was she right to trust that assumption? She didn't really know him. But she wanted to.

"Often those people feel that they have to get their own back. Or feel like if it happened to them, why should you be safe? I knew one male who figured it was his job to go around and attack women because then they wouldn't be so trusting. They'd take more precautions because now they understood life could be dangerous."

"Really? That's a little twisted, isn't it?" Startled, his words shook her out of her daze. She'd read about a lot of people and their odd reactions to stress and pain, but that was a new one on her.

"There are some very sad cases out there."

"And here," she muttered.

"As long as we do what we can."

"Everyone is doing what they can," she said quietly. "Even those still locked in that same horrible place they went to during the abuse. And they can't move out of there because it's either too painful or fear won't let them move. Either way, it's all they can do, too." Quiet, Paris wondered at what she'd started. What she'd inadvertently shared.

"You've been there?" Weaver questioned.

"All my childhood and teen years. I should have run away. Should have gotten help. I couldn't." Hands jammed in her pockets, she tried to still the shakes rattling her calm.

"It's easy to look back. Not so easy to avoid judging."

"Sometimes I think looking back is all about judging. What we could have done differently. What we should have done differently."

"Except…" Glancing down at her, their eyes met, "we have to make allowances for the age we were back then. The conditioning we were put through."

"And when we were older and still allowed the status quo to remain? Then what?" The bitterness in her voice was audible. She bit her lip "I stopped it – finally. I should have done it earlier."

"And how old were you when you stopped it?"

It took a long time for her to answer, and then with a sigh, she said, "Fifteen."

His shocked gasp made her look at him sharply, searching for the judgment she expected to see. And there was none. Still she felt she had to explain more, to justify herself. Her actions. "No, I wasn't very old, but I was old enough. And if I'd done something about it earlier, then someone else wouldn't have gotten so very badly hurt."

"You were a child. Before and during. The conditioning you were put through didn't give you the tools to handle resistance, to defend yourself or to stand up for someone else. We're usually so broken by the time we get there it takes a major turning point in our lives to make us change. In your case, maybe for this other person."

She gave him a hooded look. "More book learning?"

"No, life learning." And this time, it was him that turned away.

Something to think about. She sagged onto the railing and studied his averted face. "Life's a bitch, isn't it?"

That surprised a laugh out of him. "Isn't it though? Or maybe I should say, life used to be a bitch. Now it's much better."

"True." A young couple walked past them, holding hands and lost inside the joy of their young love. Jealousy rose up at the sight of them, and yet at the same time she wasn't sure she'd ever want to be so naive. She'd never been that innocent. Not like they were. And once you crossed a certain point, there was no going back. "Do you ever look at the people around us and wonder what we missed?" she asked.

"Yes." He studied the same couple as they passed by, murmuring with their heads close to together. "I'd like to look at it as what we still have waiting for us to experience."

"So not a missed opportunity, but rather in the future as something to look forward to?" The concept of not having missed anything wasn't something Paris had considered. But it was a much nicer way to look at the issue. "I can get on board with that."

The implication of what he'd said dawned on her. Her lips parted to ask him, then she realized how deeply personal a question it was. She closed her mouth.

"Go ahead and ask," he said simply. "I may or may not answer."

"That's fair enough. It's just what you said, the way you said it, while that couple walked by..."

"And..." His voice tightened just enough to let her know he sensed where she was going.

"Nothing." Losing the courage to go there, she shrugged and stood up. "Shall we keep walking?"

"Sure." They headed down the walkway in the opposite direction the couple had gone. Kinda like the way their lives had gone in the opposite direction.

"You were going to ask about the relationships in my life."

Startled, she glanced at him quickly then seeing his intent gaze, she switched to watching one sailboat trying to come back to shore, and a shiver crawled up her spine. Struggling but winning the war. Prophetic in many ways. "I guess I was. Just trying to figure out how trust works after there is none."

"It doesn't. That's why you have to start from scratch and build new trust in different things. When you've been hurt, then you try to avoid being hurt again. When you've been broken, you avoid anything that will take you down that path a second time."

Once again his words hit home. "So true. But that doesn't allow much room for trust."

"So you have to trust that people will be people. What you're really asking me is have I come to the point of trusting other people to not hurt me."

She winced. "It always comes back to being hurt."

"Sure. That's the big lesson in life – to go on even though we've been hurt. So trust in little bits. Trust your coworkers to treat you nicely. Trust your boss to be fair. Trust babies to be natural. Natural at that age is to be innocent, but they learn manipulation at a young age."

"They do at that." Paris smiled, thinking about the babies at work. "I love that about children. But when they hurt someone, they also feel bad."

"In most cases."

"But from there to becoming adults, people change. And that can be a different story."

"That is their issue. Remember, it's always about you and your issues."

"I want a family," she burst out. "Children."

Then went silent.

THE VEHEMENCE IN her voice startled him. "Surely that's not a bad thing?"

She bowed her head.

"I think that would be a dream many women would have," he offered gently, wondering where this was going.

"Sure they do." With a shrug of her shoulders, her tone bitter, she added, "But I'm not most women."

That's for sure, but he understood. "Maybe adopt if you don't feel the conventional way would work for you?"

"I'm considering it," she said slowly. "I've seen many single moms come through my ward. Most aren't in good shape either emotionally or financially. A few are strong and planned this journey to walk alone, but most aren't as they've come from recent breakups or relationships where they couldn't even remember the father."

"Not everything in life is so sad," he said.

"No," she whispered. "The babies are awesome. They are born so innocent and open to what life has to offer."

"Do you deal with a lower income level demographic that you see so many upsetting scenarios?"

"Not especially, and money doesn't protect you from breakups." Staring down at her hands, she sighed. "There is no guarantee that your relationship or your spouse will survive your children making it to adulthood. Few people go into a relationship expecting to become a single parent. Often they come with the disintegration of their own dreams, a major shift in their reality. Their circumstances." She raised her gaze. "And sometimes I envy them, regardless."

"Can't you have children?" Immediately he winced, wishing he held his tongue when her face paled to the whitest cloud in the sky and those huge eyes swelled with tears.

As she shook her head, he hated himself for not having read the signs. Hell, in her case, he hadn't been able to read any signs. Something about her blurred his usual logic and calm deference. He'd been lost on that highway like an idiot. "I'm so sorry."

Purposefully taking a breath, she nodded, sniffled, and then shrugged. "It's not news for me, I've known for a long time."

Moodily, he stared out over the water, recognizing that the storm clouds now looked to be ready to dump its load of rain on Vancouver. "So often it's that way, isn't it? When we really want something, we see others not giving value to what we want so badly."

"That's when my job is difficult. Although it's also joyful

and rewarding, it's painful," she admitted. "I've thought of changing jobs so I'm not around the babies all the time, but it's hard. I do love them and as I'm never going to be able to have one, at least this way I can be close to them."

"What about a surrogate? Although I guess that's not a guaranteed path of success either. Adoption is likely the best route. From another country maybe?"

Again he spoke off the top of his head, without his usual internal edit. He glanced at her, wondering if adoption was even an option. For many women, it wouldn't be.

"I've been looking into it," she said, "but that whole single motherhood thing is a problem again. Not an impossibility, but definitely a challenge."

"Is that why you're here?"

She turned to stare at him, her gaze flat, shuttered. "That's partly why I'm here. Anything that allows me to gain acceptance of this aspect of my life is always a benefit, but no, that's not the biggest thing." This time she winced and went quiet.

Really quiet.

Watching her, as her gaze remained fixated at her feet, he had no idea how to broach the silence. So far she'd been very open with him, and if he could just keep her talking, they'd have an easier time of it this week. But she wasn't giving him much in the way of openings.

Then again, neither had he told her about his life either.

"I was married once." Shit. Where had that come from? He hadn't planned on that, but the words just slipped out.

"Good for you," she said in a noncommittal voice, as if it didn't mean anything. And he guessed in the current world of relationships where a person was often married two or three times in their lifetime, maybe it didn't.

But for him, it had been major.

"It lasted six months."

She gasped and turned towards him. "What? Why?"

Angry with himself mentioning it, he shrugged and tried to look nonchalant. He'd done it now.

"I thought I could handle it. She thought she could handle it."

"And...?"

It was his turn to look down at his feet and he paused before replying. "We were both wrong."

And then she had to do it. She asked, "Handle what?"

CHAPTER 10

IT WAS MAJOR that he'd even brought up something so personal, and now she was dying with curiosity. That she'd spoken so openly said much about this conversation. Normally she'd never have said a word, but he was part of the week and somehow that made a difference. Besides, he obviously had problems himself.

Maybe he'd share them or maybe not, but he'd come a long ways already this morning. But oh Lord. Married for only six months?

"How long had you known each other?" Shit, she shouldn't have asked. It was none of her business. Seriously none of her business. Yet he'd brought it up and she was relieved to not be the one under scrutiny for a change.

"Months. But she was in therapy and hadn't progressed as far as I thought she had."

For some reason, that tone of his made her back go up. "And you?" she asked. "Had you progressed as far as you thought?"

His shoulders slumped, and for a long time she thought he wouldn't answer. "Obviously not. I couldn't persuade her to stay with me."

"Ouch," she murmured. "Well, at least you made it to the altar." Walking back to the hotel, her words surprised her and her cheeks flushed. "I never made it to bed."

She felt his startled response. Heard his strangled exclamation and ignored his question, "Really?"

He raced to keep up to her. "Why not?"

"For the same reason I can't have kids and the same reason I can't get past all the other lovely issues in my life."

There was a strong silence that almost made her smile. Hell, her honesty was making her smile. Normally she would never have let it all out. Maybe because she was at the workshop – and she wouldn't see Weaver again. That was what this whole week was all about, wasn't it?

She frowned. "How come I haven't seen you around Jenna's evening classes? Normally these workshops are full of her students."

"I haven't been to her evening sessions lately."

"Did she help you?"

There was pause before he answered, "Yes in that every person on our path helps each of us. She triggered a lot of issues. I met her after my wife and I broke up. So I needed the new perspective. The awareness that came from a few things she said."

"Yeah, she's good at that."

"I know this is intensely personal but I have to ask, do you mean to say you have never had a sexual relationship?"

This time she looked right at him. "The way you mean, no." She picked up the pace. The hotel should be around the corner. Not close enough, but it was her fault for bringing up the personal questions in the first place.

Glancing over at him, she could see him desperately wanting to ask more but not knowing how. "What you really want to know is what happened so I avoid men?" At his nod, she said, "I won't be sharing that until you're ready to share your mess. However, I was never raped, if that's what you're thinking, but there are things that can happen to you that are much worse."

Half shocked at what she said but mostly shocked at her ability to go there and still breathe, she turned, ready to bolt toward the hotel. When he grabbed her arm, she froze.

"Look, I'm sorry. Curiosity is natural, but it can also be destructive. I do understand that before growth comes the breaking down of barriers." Weaver said with a sigh and looked toward the hotel. "I only want you to tell me what you want to tell. I'm a good listener."

"But not necessarily someone who plans to grow past your own issues." With a tight smile, she pulled away from his grasp. "It's one thing to share and have sharing go both ways. It's another thing to talk to a therapist." She turned her back on him. "I have Jenna for the latter position already. Thanks though," she said with excruciating care. "I'll find someone else to do the sharing thing with."

Looking forward, she picked up her footsteps and ran.

Part of her never wanted to see him again. Yet part of her wanted him to follow. But why would he? He'd have to step up and be himself. A workshop participant was all about giving and taking. And she doubted he was up for much more of it.

Putting him firmly out of her mind, she rushed inside the front entrance, blind to the group milling about. There were so many she had to slip around people to get where she needed to go. She was getting hungry, but the restaurant was looking overwhelmingly full. Damn.

Why now?

Finally, she managed to reach the wall of elevators and came up against a huge billboard standing between the elevators. The boards were full of information, but her gaze was caught on the one word at the top. Justice.

Jesus. Like she needed more of that.

Her heart pounded and tears filled her eyes. She turned in slow motion to realize many of the people there were in uniform. Police uniforms. Some men wore suits, but all carried themselves the same way. The place was filled with cops. There was no room to stand, let alone breathe.

Then she caught sight of one man's profile. Her heart stalled then raced ahead as if trying to reach safety before the rest of her could. Please don't let it be him. Not now. Not here.

His features came up sharper. Dear God.

She closed her eyes and very slowly turned to face the elevators. Her feet were screaming at her to run. Now.

She bolted for the stairs.

Just as she disappeared around the corner, she heard someone call her name.

Blind, her only objective to get inside her room, alone, she ran. Faster.

WEAVER WATCHED PARIS disappear from sight.

Now what the hell was going on? Paris was continuing her confusing mix of personalities. Just when she began to open up and share, only when it got seriously interesting, she shut off the valve. And he really wanted to know the rest of it. It was not in him to leave a woman walking alone in Vancouver on the streets, and he'd kept up with her flight. Back at the hotel, he'd seen her make her way through the crowd. Being tall, he'd easily tracked her progress to the elevators. But he couldn't see the reason for her sudden bolt up the stairs. Was she claustrophobic? He hadn't seen signs of it before, but then again, the crowd here was intense.

Some kind of law enforcement seminar was going on. Cool.

He managed to find his way through the crowd to the stairs and followed her up.

There were others going ahead of him. He hated being worried about her, but there was something about that eager beaver attitude and wanting-to-make-her-life-happen innocence that was begging for trouble. She'd seen a lot in her life already, but damn he didn't want her to be hit with more.

Weaver followed her up to the fourth floor, but by the time he got up there, the hall was empty. She must have made it to the safety of her room already.

Inside his room, he tossed his light jacket over the back of his chair when someone knocked on his door. He went to answer it, only to find it hadn't been on his door but on the room across the hall. The older man in a police uniform turned to look. Weaver smiled and went to close the door.

The man called out, "Paris, are you in there? I know you likely don't remember me…"

Silence.

"I was hoping to meet you now that I know you are here."

More silence.

Weaver opened the door wider and said, "I think I saw her leave a little bit ago."

"Oh." The policemen looked at the door, then at him. "Okay. I thought she came here, but I'll check at the front desk and try calling her." He nodded to him. "Thanks."

Weaver waited until the man got onto the elevator and went downstairs. Should he knock on the door?

If he didn't try, he wouldn't know, but why would she answer him if she wouldn't answer the other man? The officer seemed to know her.

Still, he couldn't leave it. With his own door closed, he crossed the short distance to hers. The first rap yielded no response. He rapped again. "Paris, it's Weaver."

No response. He looked down the hallway and knocked again. Then he heard the heavy, gut-wrenching sobs within. Shit. Pounding on the door now, he insisted. "Paris, this is Weaver. Let me in."

"No," she cried from inside. "Go away."

"I need to know that you're okay."

"I'm fine," she said, her voice shaking. At the end, it broke, and so did a little bit of the stone around his heart. He'd tried letting his guard down once before in an attempt to lead a normal life. Have a normal marriage. It hadn't worked, so he'd put everything back up thicker and stronger than before. But there was something about Paris that brought it crumbling down again.

"I don't think so."

No answer.

"That policeman was trying to get a hold of you."

She gasped. Suddenly, the door was flung open and she stared at him in shock, her huge eyes terrified. "No, no. He can't find me." Wide-eyed and panicked, she looked down the hallway first one way then the other before grabbing his arm and pulling him inside.

"Why not? Are you running from the law?" he asked carefully. "Or are you just running from him?"

"I'm not running at all," she said crossly, wiping her eyes. "I don't want to see him. Ever."

"He looked harmless. In fact, he looked really earnest. Like he was hoping to talk to you."

"He's part of my past." Her voice quivered as she shook her head. "I can't see him again."

Wavering on her feet, Paris started shaking.

"Okay, easy." Immediately he reached for her and tugged her into his arms, wondering at this woman who spent so much of her time on his mind or in his arms when what he really wanted was to take her into his bed. The worst thing he could do – for himself and for her. Hell, he'd gone down that path once. So not a good idea. If he was going to be with someone again, it would have to be someone who'd dealt with all her shit. Not someone looking at him to fix her stuff.

As he knew all too well, he couldn't fix anything.

Her body relaxed against him for a long moment, neither of them moving, just resting, needing the peace of the moment. The only sound was their synchronized breathing.

All of a sudden, she pulled back. Never quite letting down her guard. Always aware of that line.

He found it – her – fascinating.

"I'm fine." She walked into the room and sat down on the small chair. "Honest, I am."

"Good. Then let's go get some dinner. I'm starving."

But her head was frantically sending her hair flying out. "No, I can't go down. I might see him."

At a loss for words, he asked. "What if he's here for more than just today?"

A visible shudder wracked down her slender frame. "Then I might just call this week a bad deal and go home."

"Oh boy. Okay, one thing at a time. If we don't want to go to the hotel restaurant and you're afraid to meet up with this person anywhere, I see two choices."

With her arms wrapped tightly around herself, she stared at him hopefully.

"I can either go out and pick us up something or we can order room service."

She blinked at him.

Chapter 11

THE THOUGHT OF pizza made her mouth water, but was there a place anywhere within walking distance? Was it fair to send him? No, it wasn't, and she really didn't give a damn right now. She needed to feel safe. But at the same time…she'd come here to push her boundaries. To get out of that safe world.

But she'd never expected to see that hateful person from her past. Someone who should have represented safety yet only brought up danger in her mind.

And sure enough, her brother's voice rolled through her mind. *Safe is no way to live. We have to experience new things and new people, otherwise our surviving was for nothing. If we choose to live, we must choose to live well, all in. No half measures allowed.* With a big breath, she pushed out the words, "Pizza. I want pizza."

Eyebrows raised, he replied. "Okay, pizza it is. I wonder if we can order one to be delivered here."

"No idea." She walked to the window. Damn it. She shouldn't be crippled by this. With everything she had been through, she should be stronger than that. Who knew Delaney would be here? Or that he'd recognize her? It had been so long and she had changed so much.

She'd grown up.

Or thought she had.

Facing Delaney though would be facing so much more than she could handle right now. She'd come to deal with her issues. But not the one involving him. That was too big. Too painful.

It wasn't possible.

But she might be able to do something. "Look, if we go out through the back of the hotel, I might go. We could slip out for pizza and sneak back in with no one the wiser."

"Like children playing hooky? There are evening sessions we're supposed to do, aren't there?"

Paris nodded. "Every evening there is something going on with Jenna. Although many are one-on-one private sessions with her as she checks in on everyone's progress."

A broken, painful sound escaped. "Right now there is no progress in my corner, just a horrible backward slide."

"And one you can change," he said firmly. "So what if you met someone from your past? He's in the past."

"Obviously not if he's here in my present too," she muttered. "I honestly never expected to see him again."

"That's why the shock then?"

Nodding, her stomach growled making the decision for her, she said, "I'll grab a sweater and we can go."

"If you're sure," he said doubtfully.

With a glare at his lack of support, she retorted. "It's now or never. I won't have the courage to go later."

"Now." He waited while she grabbed her light plum cardigan from the bed and walked out in front of him. "I need my jacket in case of rain again."

She followed him to his room, standing in the doorway while he picked up his jacket from the back of his chair. It was the same layout as hers.

With the hallway still empty but worried she couldn't get

out before that changed, she said, "It's clear. Let's go."

They walked quickly to the elevator and as he was going to push the button, she shook her head. "We'll take the stairs."

USED TO HER sudden requests, he shrugged and followed. Taking the stairs was no guarantee that they would miss the other man. Not when stairs were the healthy option these days. The stairwell was empty at the main floor, but she carried on to the parking garage level and walked out. Wow, she really meant to avoid this guy. Fair enough.

Outside, a light drizzle had started. He stood on the main street and looked both ways. Downtown offered a lot of food options in the daytime, but in the evening it didn't look as promising. "Any idea where to go?"

"There was a place over a couple of blocks. I haven't been there in years, but they used to have good food. Pizza was just one of the choices."

"Good enough." He tucked her arm into his and said, "Which way?"

She pointed left.

The walk was brisk and cool. It was hard to tell if she was walking so fast to escape the hotel or if she was cold and wanted to get where she was going quickly. At least she wasn't looking behind all the time to see if they were being followed. Afraid she was being chased.

Or afraid of being caught.

They were similar but also slightly different, and just different enough to make him ponder her actions.

That it was the policeman she was afraid of made him think she'd been involved in something illegal. Possibly she'd skirted around a crime or seen something. He knew he could speculate endlessly and still not be correct given the myriad of possible circumstances, but he couldn't stop his mind from working the issues.

"What made you go into nursing?" Was that a neutral enough topic to be safe to bring up?

"I love babies."

Good choice, as her voice softened as she answered.

"What's the hardest part of your job?" he asked again, hoping to keep her mind off the scenario back at the hotel.

"Mothers who don't appreciate what they have," she answered shortly.

He glanced over at her in surprise. "I thought it would be the sick babies or the ones that can't be saved, or the disabilities...infant deaths."

She nodded. "Those are all hard to deal with. And there are so many in different situations that you never get used to it as each baby has its own personality. Each mother has her own story, her own personality as well." She shrugged. "In a way, the babies are part of the circle of life. It's terrible and heartbreaking but almost understandable." Her voice hardened as she added, "But the mothers who didn't want their child, or who aren't happy with the sex of their child, or…" Stopping mid-sentence, then her voice quieted. "You get my meaning."

He did. "That's understandable. Especially as it's something you really want and can't have."

"Exactly. It also makes you wonder what kind of life those children are going to have if they are not wanted in the first place."

He peered closer at her, hearing a different note enter her voice. "Is that what happened to you? Were you and your brother not wanted?"

"Who knows?" She shrugged. "Our mother took off when we were little."

"Maybe there was good reason?"

"Sure." Paris gave a short hard laugh. "She was a victim of domestic abuse and was strong enough to get the hell out."

Oh hell. "But not strong enough to take you with her," he guessed.

"Nope. And with her gone, who do you think he turned to next?"

Shit. So much for trying to find a neutral topic.

He squeezed her arm in commiseration and pointed out a fancy old car parked on the other side of the road. Anything to get away from the dangerous memories of her past.

And his.

CHAPTER 12

Paris wanted to laugh. She was outside in Vancouver walking with a very attractive man, about to go and have dinner. Not exactly a date, but better than the guys that belonged to the gang at work going for lunch. It's not that she hadn't been able to date – she'd had lots of opportunities, but she hadn't been able to trust the men. So she'd brushed them off. Good men most likely, but because she was such a basket case, she hadn't been able to take that step. It would have been too difficult to explain any of her problems to them even if she wanted to. Here Weaver already knew she had problems – hell, it was a given in a workshop like this. And he had his own issues to deal with whether he was ready to acknowledge them or not.

That almost put them on equal ground. It removed that big elephant in the room when you went out on a date wondering how much you should explain. *I'm a virgin. I've been abused. I have father issues in the biggest way.* Or the steps that went way beyond that.

I'm terrified of the law. I'm terrified that it made a mistake. That it's waiting for me to screw up so it can get a second shot at me.

None of those were conversational starters. Yet she could likely say that to Weaver.

If he said things like that to her, she wouldn't have a

problem. She understood he probably shouldn't have mentioned the report to her but at the same time, she'd rather know now instead of later. What a betrayal it would've been if he hadn't said anything until later.

And maybe there was more betrayal to come. Anything was possible and she had no idea.

It was almost a given according to Sean. He'd been of the opinion that if you didn't get involved, then you didn't get hurt. At least that was his belief before he'd met Robin. That was funny to remember how much he'd changed. It was seriously a joy to watch how happy her brother was now. And…yes, she was jealous. She loved his partner, and that made it easier. If he'd dropped his sister in favor of a partner, that would have been very difficult for Paris. But he hadn't, and the bonds between the three of them had deepened.

Watching him grow gave her hope, and now her only concern was she didn't want to be left behind.

She wanted a partner too. Or at least know that there was the possibility of one in her life. Weaver wasn't it, and that was okay too, for the most part. He was his own person with his own needs and he had seen too much of her ugly side. He'd also been involved with someone from therapy before and wasn't looking for a repeat of that disaster. That was understandable. Likely it wouldn't be a good choice for her either.

Although it had worked out beautifully for Sean and Robin. Those two were made for each other.

So who the hell was she made for?

"Thoughts? You look so serious right now," he said, walking at her side.

"Just wondering if there is someone special out there for everyone or do some people miss out."

"I think there's more than one someone actually. There's likely to be a different someone depending on our stage of life and what we are looking for. Not all marriages last, and people move on. Not everyone is blessed with longevity, and those that lose a partner often find someone new to love. I think it's just a different love." That made her feel better. "I'd like to experience love once. In some way."

"You mentioned your brother – don't you love him?"

"I really love him," she said in surprise. "He attended a workshop with Jenna a couple of months ago and did phenomenally well out of it. He found someone special during the course. She had as many problems as he did, but they are a perfect match."

"Nice. You don't see that often." His voice sounded doubtful.

"Yeah, you'd have to know my brother to understand how difficult this was for him." She shook her head. "Trusting Robin to the extent he does – it's huge."

"Trusting anyone is huge."

They walked in silence.

"Are you going to tell my why you are avoiding that man?"

Conflicted, she shook her head. "It's not an easy thing."

"Really." He snorted. "What in all of this is easy?" He motioned to the city melding around them. "You left the hotel and came out in spite of him. That wasn't easy and you managed anyway."

She shrugged. "It was almost worse sitting there and waiting for him to come back. I saw him in the lobby earlier and hoped I'd been wrong. In all these years, I hadn't seen him, so why now?"

"If you believe that whole line about everything happens

for a reason..."

"Meaning I'm here at the workshop looking to move ahead and he shows up, so take that as a sign?" She turned to give him a hooded glance. "I had considered that. Then dismissed it."

There was his crooked grin again.

"Too bad life isn't quite so easy to dismiss."

There wasn't an answer to give so she stayed quiet, her arms wrapped tightly around herself.

"He's obviously a huge issue for you," Weaver added.

"Scary huge."

"So maybe see if you can get past it. It seems to me that this week is all about dealing with crap. This crap is what showed up – so deal with it. Maybe look at it as a gift."

"It's too big."

"How big?" he said quietly. "Big enough it impacts your ability to trust. Big enough to impact your ability to move on. Big enough to stop you," he paused for effect, "from moving on?"

He studied her intently. "Because if it is, this is so what you need to deal with right now. Forget the rest of the workshop lessons or what you are trying to make happen this week. This is a golden opportunity."

The thought made her shudder. No way could she handle that one. Not here, not right now. She needed someone to help her through this, not someone to toss her into the river and hope she could swim. As he gently grabbed her elbow and nudged her forward, she realized she'd come to a complete stop in the middle of the sidewalk. And was barely breathing. She gulped for air. And then again. Focusing on her breath and almost subconsciously on his touch, she pushed the panic deep inside.

Before she knew it, she was sitting down on a park bench, Weaver hovering at her side.

"Honestly, Paris, if it's this big...you need to deal with it. It's crippling you."

Tears welled up, and one big fat tear rolled down her cheek. "I know. But it's so big. Such a huge scary thing. I'm always afraid because of him. Always..."

"Then maybe that's what you need to do – face him. Tell him how he has crippled you. Tell him you need him to go away so you can get on with your life."

Her hair flew violently around her head as she shook her head like a dog shaking off water. "You don't understand. This is life-changing. I'll lose my job. My life as I know it will cease to exist."

"WHAT?" WEAVER SAT down beside the distraught woman. "How is that possible?"

"I can't tell you," she cried. "No one can ever know."

"No one?" He was confused and getting seriously worried. This was such a big fear in her life. He could see it was what she needed to deal with. That the opportunity for her was here and now with both Jenna and himself to help her through it. That was something he could do.

"My brother. Sean." She grabbed her cell phone and in between wiping her eyes and sobbing out loud, she sent her brother a text. He didn't want to pry but desperately wanted to know what she was saying. All he could see without obviously reading over her shoulder was *Constable Delaney*.

After hitting send, she slumped back as if that much effort had been too much. Now, looking around, the light lowering on the streets, the wind picking up, he was sorry they hadn't ordered room service. She'd been strong enough to leave but at the same time, they still didn't have food and she looked to be at the end of her rope.

Her cell phone beeped. She swiped across her phone, read the message, and cried out, "Talk to him. Sean, how can you say that?"

Weaver was starting to like the guy already. "It's what you need to do."

"I can't." Cold and dark, her tone of voice said this was a no brainer. She wasn't going there – ever.

She stood up. "I need food, then I need sleep."

And she started walking.

Weaver was lost and trying to catch up as she shifted from the weeping ineffectual woman to this coldly in-control female.

What the hell just happened? And who was the real Paris?

Chapter 13

THE BURNING QUESTIONS hung in the cool air around them. Didn't matter. She had no plans to answer them. There were things she could do and things she couldn't do. Talking to Delaney was on the second list. The other constable, whatever his name had been, might be a different story. He'd helped Sean in a way she'd never have been able to reach him. And that had made such a difference to her brother. Sean credited the man with saving him from a deep dark slide into the shadows of his soul and staying there.

But he hadn't had the same effect on her. Watching from the sidelines, covered in blankets but apart from the goings-on, she'd been in shock. And so much of what happened back then was a dim painful memory. To try and look at it closer was asking for a whole lot of pain. Who wanted to scrape their insides out again after it had finally healed? Not her.

Then again, that stupid little voice in her head said, *What if it never healed?*

It had to have healed. It had been over a decade. Surely that was long enough. But that same voice smiled and said, *If it was, you'd have no trouble taking a closer look. Because you won't even contemplate such an action, you know it hasn't. And won't if you can't deal with this stuff.*

"I can't," she snapped.

"What?" Weaver asked by her side.

She flushed then groaned. "Sorry, I was talking to myself."

"Arguing from the sounds of it," he said, his voice light and humorous. "Every time I do that, I lose."

Again she felt his light touch on the small of her back, and her heartbeat quickened. "I can't lose this one," she said resolutely. "It's not possible."

And that was all she was going to say on the topic. The pizza place was one storefront down from them. She hurried inside to get in out of the cold – in more ways than one.

Once back in her hotel room, she answered Sean's text. Her response was clear and simple. "No."

Of all people, he should understand. He'd watched her go to pieces at the time. In a different way than he had. In a different way since, but they'd both picked up the remnants of their life and carried on. It hadn't been easy, but they'd done it and she was always comforted by that fact. What she'd gone through afterwards had been so different than what Sean had gone through. That's where the understanding and mutual experiences diverted.

Her brother knew in theory what she'd been put through, but he hadn't been allowed to be by her side and she'd never been able to tell him. The police had questioned her for hours at the time. The process had damn near killed her. It took months for her to sleep again, afraid the cops were going to come any minute to haul her away. Afraid ever since that they'd made a mistake and someone was going to pick up that old file and remember what she'd done.

Her day of reckoning would come.

She was hell bent on making sure she wasn't the one who had to serve it.

And that meant avoiding all cops, especially the one she'd spoken to back then.

BACK IN HIS room, Weaver hesitated as to whether he should say something to Jenna about the cop being at the hotel and Paris's response. Was it tattling? Or was it in her best interests? He tried to think of it from the therapist's point of view in that he was there to help her heal. If Providence dropped a juicy opportunity like that into his patient's life, wouldn't he want to know?

Wouldn't he need to know? Her behavior was going to be off now — there's no way it couldn't be. And if Jenna didn't know what was going on, she couldn't help Paris deal with it.

The right thing to do was call her.

He opened his cell phone. "I need to meet you. Maybe the coffee shop if it isn't too late."

"Be there in five," she said cheerfully.

That was one thing about her that always blew him away. Not once had he met her in a bad mood. Always wide-awake and cheerful, she was ready to take on whatever the world tossed at her.

He left the hotel room and with a final glance at Paris's closed door, walked down to the coffee shop.

Chapter 14

Paris answered her phone. "Hi, Sean."

Silence.

"Are you okay?"

She burst into tears. In between her sobs, she managed to get out, "I'm..." sniffle... "fine."

His voice threaded with gentle loving humor, he said, "You don't sound it."

"Why is he here?" she cried. "Why now?"

"I don't know. Is he there alone?"

"No," she said, her voice rising in alarm, "The hotel is full of cops. Some kind of seminar. Talk about horrible timing."

"And maybe not," he said in that calm way of his. "You don't need to talk to him, but maybe by the end of the week, you could get to the point of not bolting every time you see a policeman."

Her mood lightened. "Well, so far it hasn't worked. I've bolted twice. Once inside to get away and once outside to get further away." She laughed.

"Of course you did." He chuckled. "And you might still do that for a while, but not all cops are bad. Remember that."

"I know he isn't bad. But not all are compassionate and caring. You hit the jackpot there. I didn't."

"No, you didn't, and I've always been so angry about that. I should have been there for you."

"No," she interrupted him. "Don't blame yourself. It's the system. We were victims first, and the system continued to make us victims."

"You more than I. We had a decent foster family for that last while, but they never quite knew how to handle you."

"Without you, I wouldn't have ended up mostly normal." She sighed. "The foster family was good to me. They were a rock when I was the storm. How they put up with me, I don't know."

"Well, it helped a lot that he was a psychologist." Sean's voice deepened. "Did you consider calling him?"

"No, I haven't dumped my problems on him in a long time." In truth, she never had. He'd been great at coaxing her back to the real world, but she'd been a lot of work. He had taken on several other kids after she'd moved out, although she didn't think any were as badly damaged as she'd been.

"Maybe you should let Jenna know."

Silence.

"I don't want to open it up," she said, her voice barely above a whisper. "And she's going to poke and pry and insist that the blood flow to cleanse the wound."

"So? You know it has to happen."

"So," she countered, using his own word. "Doesn't mean it has to happen here and now. Today or this week. It's not what I came for."

"Yes, it is." Again that calm manner and voice that had held him in good stead. "You went there to heal. We don't always get to choose *what* is going to heal."

Paris slumped on her bed and flopped backwards. "It's too hard to do all of this."

"Sure it is. That's why it's a good idea to bring Jenna on board so that you have the support you need. Think about it,

Paris. I know you went with other intentions, but this could be a huge gift. Deal with the cop. See him as the adult you are and not the traumatized young girl you'd been. He won't be the ogre you remember now because you are older and wiser."

"But it wasn't him as much as the power of the law that terrifies me," she reminded him.

"And that's just wrong," his voice rose in anger. "I've told you before. It's not your fault."

Her hand trembled as she brushed her hair off her forehead. Tears once again welled up at the corner of her eyes. "I know you say that..."

"I mean that. Anyone would tell you the same thing. Hell, dozens of people *have* told you the same thing," he said. "It's that asshole sitting at the damn hotel that's to blame for putting that doubt in your head." He made a half-strangled roar in the background. "I'm of a half mind to come down there and beat the crap out of him for what he did to you."

"No," she cried, "you can't."

Sobs broke free, and she couldn't hold them back anymore. "Besides, he didn't do anything other than his job."

"He was a hard ass to you and you didn't deserve it. You were traumatized. You needed support and counseling, not his heavy-handed warnings."

"But he was right. I started down a path and my actions have followed me ever since."

"Damn it, Paris. You escaped your past. You got an education, you got a life. We are both surviving and now I'm thriving. It's your turn."

Sniffling through the tears, she wished he was there to give her a hug. And then unexpectedly, an image of Weaver holding her close crept in, and she pushed it down. "I hope so," she whispered. "But I'm afraid it won't be in time."

"In time for what?" he asked, alarm making his voice rise.

"Before they haul me away."

There was an odd silence. "Why would they do that?" he asked in a low, controlled voice.

"Because he was right," she said, breaking down into heart-wrenching sobs. "I'd do it all over again."

She hung up the phone then threw herself across the bed, lost in the horrible memories of the night she'd killed her father.

THE COFFEE SHOP was mostly empty except for a few cops sitting in the far corner. Jenna wasn't here yet. He took a chair by the window with his back to the wall so he could watch for her. After ordering coffee for two, he waited, unsure if he was doing the right thing.

More cops came in and took a second table a few feet away from them. One was the man who'd knocked on Paris's door. Weaver frowned, wondering if he'd be able to overhear the conversation about to happen with Jenna.

As he looked up, Jenna walked toward him, smiling. As she approached, that one cop stood up and stopped her.

Curious, he tried to listen in, only to realize their voices were so low he couldn't hear what was being said. But they knew each other.

Suspicion settled inside. Had Jenna set this up?

He wouldn't put it past her.

Neither did he believe in coincidences.

These two were up to something. Jenna motioned toward Weaver and the cop nodded. He sat down again and Jenna continued on.

Now he didn't know what to do.

After she'd settled and her beautiful smiling face turned his way, the words spilled out. "Did you plan this?"

She raised an eyebrow. "Plan what?"

He nodded to the cop now busy joking with his friends. "Him."

Turning, she glanced back at the cop then turned to face him.

If he hadn't been watching so closely, he didn't know that he'd have caught it. Confusion, surprise, and maybe a little fear. But not the guilt he was expecting.

She shook her head. "I don't know what you're talking about."

After taking a sip of her coffee, her gaze never leaving his face, she asked, "Explain, please."

Stretching his long legs out in front of him under the table, Weaver sighed. "Paris has gone off the rails because of that man."

"What?" She stared at him, lowered the cup, and leaned forward. "What happened?"

Quickly he explained about finding this man knocking on Paris's door and her refusing to open it. About her crying jag. The escape to the pizza place followed by the little bits and pieces he'd managed to get out of Paris. "She's devastated over this," he finished. "I was hoping she could deal with it now that it's here in front of her, but she's adamant about not going in that direction."

"Of course. It's the shock. The sudden change in plans. When one is afraid, opportunity looks very scary."

She turned to look behind her. Weaver realized the group of men was getting up to leave.

"How do you know him?" Weaver asked.

"Through Child Services. I am working on a difficult case

right now. He's part of it."

That made sense. "Maybe that's how he knows Paris."

"Yes, most likely."

"But why would he want to talk to Paris?"

She smiled. "He's seen a lot. If he can, he likes to check in on his old cases and see how they are doing."

"Paris?"

"I don't know." She shrugged and sipped from her steaming mug. "Given her reaction, I'm going to say yes. However, her reaction is not one I've seen or would have expected to see." Her voice lowered as she added, "But in a way... it makes complete sense." She glanced at her watch. "I wonder if she's asleep."

"I doubt she'll sleep again."

Her gaze sharp, assessing, she asked, "Really?"

He nodded "She looked to be heading for a crying jag after we split up."

"That's not a bad thing."

"No, but not an easy one either."

"So what do you want to do?" she asked. "And how is this impacting you?"

Of course she'd turn it around to him. Leaning forward, his eyes narrowed. "I want you to fix this. Especially if you had something to do with bringing the cop here."

"I didn't," she interrupted.

"Good," he said, accepting that for the moment. "Then help her deal with this. This man is a huge issue in her life. Probably the biggest. If she could find a way to see him, talk to him, see that there's no reason to be afraid..."

Jenna nodded. "Did you consider that there might be a good reason she's afraid?"

No, he hadn't. Sitting back, he stared at her, Paris's weird reactions and her words – had she ever mentioned a reason for her fear? No, he didn't think so.

Still, he just couldn't believe she'd be guilty of anything. He shook his head. She so wasn't the kind.

"Remember," she said, her gaze gentle, her voice serious. "Under duress, each and every one of us is capable of doing the most horrible things."

Chapter 15

THE NEXT MORNING, Paris dragged herself from bed and straight into the shower. She didn't look in the mirror. She already knew how her face was going to look. The heat and tightness said volumes on their own. She stood under the pounding water and let it sluice down her face.

She'd barely gotten any sleep. Nightmare after nightmare dragged her up from the depths, only for her to fall under again from exhaustion. Now there was just exhaustion. This must be what it was like to live in hell. No. She already knew what hell was like.

There was another text from her brother waiting for her when she got out.

Did you think about it?

"Think about what?" she wondered aloud. But she knew. And she had thought about it. About the pain that cop had caused her. The fear she'd carried since forever. The nightmares he alone was responsible for.

Why would she be willing to talk to him?

Especially now.

As she looked at her first days at the workshop, she couldn't believe how much time had gone by and how little progress she'd made. The reason she'd come was to see something measurable. Something she could look back on and see the progress. She needed to see progress. Healing.

Inside it felt like she was doing the opposite.

That made her mad.

Why should this man pop into her life and destroy her like this? It wasn't fair. She'd been doing her best. Crossing her t's, dotting her i's for a long time, making sure there was never a reason for anyone in law enforcement to doubt her straight and narrow path.

And look what she got. The return of the one cop who'd destroyed her peace of mind since that lousy night. Before that night, there'd been a lot of lousy nights. A continuous stream of them. They'd been the norm.

She was an adult now. Not a child. Not a teen. Not a destroyed girl waiting for the good things in life to show up. For years she'd believed they would, then she grew older and she'd given up on them showing up. Now as an adult, she realized they *were* all there. One just had to look for them. And one couldn't focus on what was there before or else the bad things completely eclipsed the good things and redefined what 'good' things meant.

Like now.

Dry-eyed and tired, she sat wrapped in a towel on the end of her bed and wondered how she was going to get through the rest of this week.

She'd wanted to come since forever. Now she couldn't wait to go home to the point of considering that she should leave early.

Sad, drained of hope, she realized she wasn't going to find her miracle here.

WEAVER KNOCKED ON Paris's door, hoping to coax her down to the restaurant for breakfast. No answer. Feeling foolish, he knocked several more times. But she either wasn't there or wasn't planning on getting up anytime soon.

"Paris," he called out gently, "I'm going to the restaurant. Why don't you meet me down there?"

And he left. As he walked to the elevator, he turned to check to make sure she didn't open the door. But it stayed closed. After his talk with Jenna last night, he'd been feeling a little guilty. He was suspicious by nature, and Jenna's words had kept him up for hours last night.

Had Paris done something wrong? Was that why she was so afraid? He couldn't see it himself, but who knew what someone did? Especially a long time ago. She'd been abused. That much he knew. How long and how badly were details he could wish for but didn't see himself getting.

Taking the stairs helped him clear his mind before walking into the restaurant. As it had been busy last night, he half expected to see it the same way this morning. No, of course not. It was empty. He was early.

Maybe that's why Paris wasn't up. He took his usual seat and ordered coffee and opened his menu. Pancakes and eggs would be a great way to start the day. Closing the menu, he stared out the window. As he watched the few people rush by, he realized a long lean woman sat on a bench at the tiny corner garden. Damn it. That was Paris.

She sat so still, like a stone, he wondered how long she'd been there. She had to be cold. She wore a long gray sweater and had it wrapped around her, her fingers clutching the material together at the front as she stared at the flowers in front of her. He doubted she saw any of the beauty. Finally, she moved, standing up to stretch. Holding his breath, he waited, hoping she'd turn so he could wave at her. Instead, she sat back down in a different position.

Damn. His coffee arrived just then. He stared at it. Then at her.

Making a sudden decision, he called the waitress over and asked for a takeout cup for his coffee and a second one to go for Paris. Within minutes, he was striding out to the tiny city lot and the kaleidoscope of colors growing in the rough environment. Kinda like Paris.

She never heard him coming.

"Paris?"

Her back straightened and then slowly, as if afraid of who called her, she turned around. As her gaze landed on him, she smiled.

He grinned back, relief washing through him, his heart warming. At least it wasn't him she'd been trying to avoid. That it mattered should have worried him. Instead, he brushed it off as just concern for her. It was just part of the workshop, he told himself. She was struggling and he could help.

That he admired and respected her was normal. She was valiantly trying to find her way on a road that had shown her more rocks than flowers so far.

That she might help him never occurred to him – or rather it slipped in and out of his mind just as fast. This was not about him. He'd come out here to see if there was something he could do to help her.

"Here, you look like you could use this."

Her smile brightened as she accepted the cup. "Thanks."

"You're up early."

"Couldn't sleep."

"I hear you there." He sat down on the stone bench beside her. "It's another day, whether good or bad."

She snorted. "I spent my life saying bright and happy

things to cheer myself up. They weren't working this morning."

Weaver nodded, studying her. "Understandable. It takes time after a shock."

"Yeah, that's true. Time. Like lots of it."

There was an odd note in her voice.

"You don't sound like you're doing all that well this morning."

"Sure I am. Just had a difficult decision to make."

He waited, then curiosity got the better of him. "Oh? What decision?"

"Whether I stay and finish the week or check out this morning."

Chapter 16

So much for keeping that decision to herself. Telling him would just give him a chance to talk her out of it. Then again, maybe that's what she wanted. To be talked out of her decision. She didn't know anymore. She'd cried buckets this last day and she was so done with that. She'd never been a milksop, and just the thought of someone thinking of her as weak made her mad.

Waiting for him to tell her not to, she stiffened her back and her resolve. This was the right thing to do. Crawl away and come back another day. Sure, Jenna might not do a different workshop, and that would have to be okay, too. There were other people that could help her. Other people were skilled and caring. Jenna was right the first time when she let Sean in and not Paris. Paris wasn't ready. Not back then and maybe not now. Sad but true.

She realized that Weaver hadn't said a word. She slid a sideways glance his way, studying him as he studied his coffee. She traced his strong features visually before closing her eyes with a sigh. There was an urgency boiling up inside her, and in this confused state, she did not know how or why it involved him, but it was there. Waiting for her...

"You haven't said anything."

He looked up in surprise. "No. It's your choice. But I just realized I'm going to miss you."

His words shocked her. From the look on his face, his words shocked him, too. And that surprised her even more. Caring was something he obviously guarded against, and he hadn't recognized the sensation for what it was.

For her, the problem was she often cared too much and had been hoping to knock some of that back. Everyone at work always confided in her, told her their problems, looking for help in finding a way forward.

Here, she'd been the one with the problems. Weaver had helped her through the days. Only she didn't want to mistake gratitude for something else. He mattered too.

"I'll take that as a compliment," she said.

He was still staring at her in surprise. So much surprise it was almost insulting. "Am I that bad that you're so shocked to be missing me?" Her attempt at a light tone failed, her voice cracking with emotion.

Damn it. He could take that look off his face any time.

"No." He shook his head, a lopsided grin sliding out. "Not at all. But I didn't expect to get to know anyone here, and certainly not someone that fascinated me."

"Right, that damn report." She frowned. "Another reason to leave. I won't be in your report."

"You weren't going to be in it anyway," he said absently. Her breath sucked in. The shock and surprise he expressed had changed to an internal contemplation, or at least that's what she thought the distant inward look in his eyes meant. Hell, she didn't know anything about this man, so she shouldn't be making any assumptions where he was concerned. Still, he was a nice guy. Nicer now than at the beginning of the seminar. And warm, and sexy, and she so shouldn't be noticing. Except there was something appealing about that self-confidence. That hidden vulnerability she wasn't sure he was even aware of. But it was there. That he cared was a bonus. Hell, what was she talking about – it was a huge bonus. She liked him – a lot.

Before she went any further, she stood up and said, "I need food."

"About time." He bounded to his feet. "I was in the restaurant when I saw you out here."

"Ah," she teased. "So you're just trying to get me to go inside so you can eat."

"I could have eaten before," he said with a smile. "Still, it's much nicer to eat with someone else." He reached out a hand for her to take. "Like you."

She stared at it. It was likely the first time a man had done that. Why had he? Why now? And if she took his hand, was it a commitment? Because it sure felt like it.

WEAVER REACHED OUT and clasped her hand. She'd taken so long to decide he took the choice away from her. His ego could only stand so much. No one had ever called him an expert in women by any means, but he knew enough to know she was interested, or would be if this whole mess hadn't blown up in their faces. They'd had a rough beginning and then a rough middle. But when they touched, he could feel their warmth mingling into something new, something exciting. He figured if he could get her to stay for the rest of the week, they might have something worth trying to connect with after that.

But in order for that to happen, she had to take a few steps towards him. And he wasn't sure she could do that on her own.

Holding his hand could be construed as one of those and

proved his point.

Together, they walked back to the restaurant. Every once in a while, he caught her looking at their joined hands. Smiling, he used his other hand to push a strand of hair behind her ear. "Never held hands with a man before?"

When she didn't answer, he glanced over at her to see a rising tide of color on her neck and face.

"Actually, no," she replied, the honest pain evident in her quiet words. And still she held on.

Chapter 17

Paris felt the fool. Her own innate sense of honesty said she had to answer the question, but it felt odd. Just as odd as holding his hand. The heat from his much larger one surprised her. The firm, muscled pad. Large, lean fingers that dwarfed her own much smaller ones. Even his body radiated a warmth she hadn't expected. She was always cold. Inside and out. She thought it was that she was so skinny. And maybe it was, but he obviously had no problems there. Then, he too was lean, muscled.

She sighed.

"And more heavy sighs." He laughed, and damn if the sound wasn't carefree and young.

"Glad you're in a good mood." She looked at his laughing mouth and slid a little closer to him, wishing that sense of freedom would rub off.

"Hey, I'm walking with a pretty girl and heading for breakfast, my favorite meal of the day," he said with a lazy smile. "What's not to be happy about?"

"Men are so simple," she said, but she felt better. Lighter. Just a few words of acceptance. Of being wanted. Nice.

At the restaurant, he led her back to the same table where they'd sat before. "Order what you want," he said, "I'll be back in a few minutes."

As he headed to the men's room, she watched his long

easy strides. She'd have bet money that he was smiling. The waitress arrived with menus, so she ordered coffee for both of them.

"He's a cutie," the waitress said with a big grin. "As soon as he saw you outside this morning, he hopped up and grabbed the coffees and went right over."

The waitress left, but the envy in her voice had Paris smiling. Nice to think someone was jealous of her. Her own feelings toward Weaver were mixed. And confused. But definitely interested.

Maybe she didn't understand what she was feeling. This was new and it was something she hadn't ever felt it before...

Weaver represented something she didn't comprehend as she'd never been down this pathway before. He was also something she wanted. It was nice he was interested, but would he still be if he knew everything? Probably not. How could he? He'd said he was friends with a lot of cops. That meant he was okay with law enforcement and all they symbolize.

But he was also waiting for Justice.

Another sigh escaped her lips. She was too in many ways.

And she had nothing against cops in general. It was just this one.

The waitress walked back and deposited two cups of coffee on the table before walking away again. Paris barely noticed, lost as she was in her thoughts.

Weaver was right. This cop was the huge problem in her world. She stirred her coffee, staring in the depths, realizing something else she'd forgotten. Sean had been good at reminding her of small truths. Something he'd said a week ago stuck with her. He said, *Giving away your power made you powerless in the face of adversity. Call back your power so at least you are on equal footing.*

She *had* given away her power to this man.

He was just a man. He'd only ever been just a man.

She was the one who'd given him the elevated status of being the *bogey*man.

Having the force of the law behind him added to the effect. What she'd been through lent more power to it. She'd already been victimized. Thinking back, she realized she let herself be victimized ever since.

Not fair.

Weaver sat down in front of her. He reached over and clasped his hand over hers. That was when she realized she'd been stirring her black coffee – something that didn't need stirring – with enough force to make it slop up the sides of the cup. In fact, the saucer was full, too.

She sat back and stared at him. "I gave away my power."

His gaze widened, but he stayed quiet as if giving her comment due thought. Then he gave a clipped nod. "In a way, yes."

She dropped her gaze to the table. "It's a weird feeling looking back."

"Hindsight always is."

She laughed, but there was no humor in the sound. "It's also painful."

The waitress arrived to take their orders, but the mood had been broken. Paris didn't want to bring up the subject again. Though maybe she should speak to Jenna about it.

"Do me a favor," Weaver asked when the waitress left. "Before you check out, talk to Jenna first."

"Oh." She frowned. "I hadn't thought of that."

"She gave you a spot in the workshop, handpicked you for this, I suppose you might say. I think she'd appreciate the respect of hearing it from you firsthand."

Paris grimaced. That wouldn't go down well. Still, she'd subconsciously made the decision to stay but hadn't realized it until he brought it up.

"That would be the right thing to do."

"Yeah, it would," she said. "I will speak with her."

Satisfied, he sat back, looking pleased with himself. As if he believed Jenna would be able to talk her out of leaving, and true enough, she likely would. "I already decided to not leave the workshop."

Delight lit up his face, and damn it if that didn't warm her heart, filled some of the cold empty places inside. Maybe he really did care. She grinned, the weight on her chest easing. It was time for something good to happen in her life. Maybe he was the right one after all. Did she dare hope?

"Why?" he asked. "What made you change your mind?"

"You for one. It's nice to know I'm not totally alone in this. That you'd miss me. Thanks for that. My intuitive flash about having given away my power. Jenna – there's no way I'd want to have to tell her I wasn't strong enough to stay," she say wryly. "That woman is something else."

Weaver laughed and laughed. "Good reasons." He leaned forward, holding her hand firmly but gently in his. "Honestly, I wouldn't want to tell her either."

Just then their food arrived and they dug in, having moved on to a new step in their relationship.

WEAVER WONDERED AT the lightness inside. That sense of relief at her words. Why should he care so much? She was a stranger, really. But a fascinating one. And he was intrigued and attracted. Sure, some of it was professional, but a lot of it wasn't. It was like seeing an animal in pain and he might just be able to help her. She might hate him for it. This could end with her moving on like his wife had done. Afterwards, she might want nothing to do with him, seeing him only as a painful reminder. He'd helped his wife through a very difficult time and she'd been grateful – but then he'd become part of her negative memories and she needed to move past that.

He sighed. That was his garbage. Not hers and not Paris's.

"And here I thought you were happy. Instead, you're sounding depressed all of a sudden," she said, her gaze intense.

Their eyes met. He wondered if she felt insecure inside and afraid of having read a person wrong. If so…well, it was something he could relate to. Leaning back against the bench seat in a relaxed slump, she looked more at peace. Weaver pondered how far they had come. There were bags under her eyes and her skin missed that wonderful vitality of a good night's sleep, and yet she wasn't self-conscious. Or wary. It all seemed to have melted away.

He smiled gently at her. "I'm very happy. And I am proud of you," he admitted, seeing the flash of surprise in her eyes before she had a chance to cover it up.

"Wow, you're easily impressed," she mocked. "I was in the process of running away."

"But you didn't," he reminded her. "And that's huge."

Her laughter was light and genuine. Then she glanced at her watch and said, "We're going to be late if we don't get moving."

They stood up, paid the bill, and walked over toward the conference room. As they walked past the elevator, the doors opened to let half a dozen men exit. Law enforcement officers.

She gasped, averted her face, and picked up the pace.

They were going in the opposite direction so the men

passed them without even seeing her. Weaver couldn't see the man she was trying to avoid.

Still, she didn't run. Reaching up, he put a comforting hand on her shoulder and squeezed. Leaning into his touch, she tossed him a thankful grin back.

And damn if he didn't seem to need that as much as she did.

Chapter 18

Paris walked into the seminar and took her seat. Her insides were still shaking but as the incident had come and gone so fast without any kerfuffle, she felt like she'd just been spared a major confrontation. Now if her breathing would just calm down, she'd be fine.

Jenna arrived within minutes, and boy did she have a stack of paperwork in front of her. She smiled at the group at large.

"Homework," she said, holding the stack up amidst the outcry of groans. "Not hard, but thought-provoking. I want you to spend much of this evening thinking about your life, your past. Especially your future. Remember the questionnaire you answered on the first day? This moves forward based on the answers you gave back then. I'm going to hand those back to you, and you're going to use that one to help you fill out the second one."

Jenna ignored the groans erupting from the room. "Both are due back first thing in the morning."

One person piped up in the front, "That's a lot of homework, are we going to be given any time to work on it during the seminar?"

"No." Jenna shook her head. "But we will be doing intense thought-provoking workshops to help you start the process. It's important that you drop all the baggage you can from your life so that you can start as fresh and as powerful as possible as you move on to the next stage."

"What next stage?"

Paris didn't see who spoke. She was still remembering the paper she'd ripped to shreds and the piece she'd actually eaten. Lord, she wasn't going there. Yet, already her stomach heaved at the thought of someone seeing it.

"And are these answers going to be made public?"

Jenna shook her head. "They will be given to me only. This is, as always, confidential. Everything that happens in these seminars, the work you do, the stuff I see – it belongs between us – and only us."

There were a few nods, a couple of heavy sighs. And then silence as people waited for her to continue.

"So I'm going to hand these out later. Break into groups and get started."

Paris hated the group work, knowing it often triggered deep stuff publicly. So far it hadn't been that way, but the further they got into the workshop, the more likely it was to happen. Already she felt like she'd been through the spin cycle of a washing machine this morning. That meant her defenses were already low. Being tired made her more vulnerable than ever. Then there was the reminder of her first worksheet too.

It didn't forecast much good about the coming morning.

In fact, the morning was even worse than she feared. By the time the lunch break rolled around, Paris was exhausted. Dragging her tired, worn-out body upstairs, she headed for her hotel room. This day could not end fast enough. The delightful breakfast she had shared with Weaver seemed like ages ago. It wasn't that the exercises had been hard. Or that they had been intense. But it was difficult to listen to so many people deal with their own garbage. And in this scenario, the exercise amplified everyone's problems. There had been a lot of tears. A lot of breakdowns. A lot of hugs.

The surprise for Paris had been that there was no breakdown for her. But she was so weary. She needed some downtime – especially after no sleep last night – some time to distance from the emotional waves of energy.

Unlocking her door, Paris stepped into her hotel room. Without thinking about it, she set her keys on the desk and flattened out on her bed. She was asleep within minutes.

When she woke, disoriented, she had no concept of time. A knock sounded on her door. Weaver's voice called from the other side of the door. "Paris, are you okay? It's late. The afternoon session is due to start in a few minutes."

"Sorry, I fell asleep." She opened the door while still rubbing the sleep out of her eyes.

"Don't be sorry. You were exhausted." Weaver hesitated at the doorway.

Her heart still pounded, her skin clammy. She reached over and flicked on the light, blinking at the brightness. "I'll be just a few minutes. Go on ahead without me."

"Are you sure?" he asked.

She nodded firmly as she closed the door.

In the bathroom she washed her face, taking only a quick glance at the mirror. No change. Still the same tired, flat Paris that arrived here days ago.

A few minutes later, she walked into the restaurant and asked for a coffee to go. There were muffins on the back wall. Thinking of her own stomach and Weaver's, she ordered two to take with her. The waitress grinned and said, "Your boyfriend was just here. He ordered the same, only he had two coffees to go with it."

Boyfriend? Nice thought. A long ways from the truth, but

a nice thought.

Paris thanked her and walked away with her goodies, feeling ashamed. Had Weaver bought her a coffee and a muffin? She could share her muffins, had in fact, planned on it, but she hadn't thought to buy him a coffee. Thinking in twos had never before been necessary before.

In the seminar room, sure enough, he waited with a coffee for her. She sat down beside him and shook her bag of muffins. "Sorry, I didn't bring you a coffee."

He laughed. "Not an issue. I could use a second muffin, and I'm sure you can use a second coffee."

With a big grin, she replied. "True enough."

"Class," Jenna said, walking in just then. "We have a long hard afternoon as we're going to do the prep work on the worksheets now. So get into the groups you started with this morning and we're going to mix things up a bit."

Paris groaned but obediently shifted to the table on the far side. Jenna didn't like anyone working with the same group of people all the time. Her theory was that the comfort level became a hindrance. Paris didn't agree, but it didn't matter what she was thinking here. Jenna was the boss.

Still, it was rough. In the middle of the afternoon, Jenna walked by, handing out the worksheets. The ones they'd already filled out was stapled to the back so no one could see the answers but the owner of the papers. Paris did a quick check and winced. Yeah, that was hers all right. It had a big rip in the page and multiple folds from Weaver's origami. She hastily folded the paper and tucked it into her purse. If it was homework, then she'd do it later tonight. There was no way she was going to answer any questions on her old sheet's condition. As she glanced at the new homework sheet, she realized it had nothing to do with the old torn set of questions.

Weaver stared at her, one eyebrow raised.

"It's all good." She gave him a bright smile. He hadn't said anything, and she appreciated it. At the same time, she doubted he'd let her off the hook completely.

Just as the afternoon appeared endless from an emotional session where several people in her latest group had broken down and Paris knew she was on the verge of tears herself – the subject matter this afternoon being mothers – as if that wasn't enough to trigger something for everyone, there was a knock at the door. Expecting to see a hotel employee, she couldn't hold back the shocked gasp at the sight of Constable Barry Delaney.

Immediately, she hunkered down in her chair, her panicked gaze darting around the room looking for an escape. But there was only one way in or out. Unless she used the window. Panicked, she actually considered it for a long moment.

"Jenna," the constable asked, "Can I have a few minutes of your time?"

Jenna walked closer. "Sure. This session is almost done, then I have about an hour free."

"Perfect."

Jenna turned to the group. "You have your homework, so you're good to go for the evening. Those of you that are scheduled to meet with me tonight, please be prompt. The schedule is tight. The first appointment is in an hour, so please don't be late. There is time for dinner if you don't mind eating early. Other than that, I'll see you all tomorrow. Remember, worksheets are due first thing in the morning."

She walked to her desk and started to sort papers.

Chaos ensued throughout the room as everyone stood up to leave. Several small groups of people stood around discussing the latest of the projects while others formed, making plans for the evening.

Paris froze, her mind scrambling for an escape.

Weaver stood up and walked around so he was between the cop and her. "Come on."

In a blind panic, she shook her head vigorously. "He'll see me," she hissed, darting a look toward the doorway.

The constable wasn't looking her way, but he was gazing at the attendees as they packed up. Shit. He'd see her in a few minutes. There was no way he wouldn't.

"Not if you sneak out in the middle of the group," Weaver said calmly. "He hasn't seen you yet, so chances are he won't if we keep people between you and him."

"I'm scared," she whispered, clutching her purse against her chest, her fingers white as they gripped the leather.

"I know, but you're going to have to face him sooner or later. Better sooner."

"Better never," she muttered.

"Come on, let me help you out of here."

She stared at him, uncomprehending. Then got it. He was going to help her escape. Quickly scrambling to her feet, and seeing a half dozen people heading for the door, she realized that now was her chance. Keeping her head down, with Weaver between her and the cop, she raced toward the doorway.

Weaver grabbed her hand and stopped her headlong rush. With his calming presence, she made it to the door. The cop had moved out of the way as the group headed toward him. She was in the hallway in seconds, sweat pouring down her back, her breath locked in her chest. When she reached a point about six feet past him, she snuck a look behind her.

Delaney wasn't even looking her way.

Shuddering, she leaned into Weaver and let her pent up breath out. Oh Lord. She'd made it. She'd also caught a close up look of the man who'd brought her nightmares for the last decade. His face looked older. Sad maybe. Like he'd seen too much of life. She could emphasize. She had too.

She wished she had a chance to study his face without him knowing. So she could replace the childhood memory with the up-to-date one. Surely that would help. But then as if sensing her glance, he turned her way.

More relaxed now that they were out of the room, Weaver's grip had loosened. Up ahead she saw the stairwell and before either of the men had a chance to register her actions, she'd bolted up the stairs.

WEAVER FELT HER hand slip away, but she moved so fast he didn't have time to react until she was gone. He watched her take the stairs two at a time as she ran away. Should he go after her?

"Weaver."

Jenna's voice called out to him. Reluctantly, he turned and walked back to her. She was in conversation with the cop that Paris was trying to avoid.

Smiling as usual, she made the introductions. "This is Constable Barry Delaney. He specializes in cases with children at risk."

Weaver studied the man with interest. There was a calm steady look to the man. He reached out and shook his hand.

"I was hoping you could help me talk to Paris," the constable said. "I've been hoping for a chance since I saw her here. I can see she trusts you and I…" He stopped and shrugged. "I have a little unfinished business with her that I'd like to clear up."

Weaver didn't know what to say. Did he help Barry or did he help Paris? Were the issues one and the same? He didn't know. At a loss, he turned to Jenna. She stared at him, completely neutral. Really? Was she testing him somehow? He wanted to glare at her but knew that wasn't going to help.

The man seemed earnest, but the bottom line was simple. "Paris doesn't want to see you."

The man's shoulders deflated. Rubbing his face roughly with his hand, he nodded. "Understandable. I said something to her that I'd thought was appropriate at the time, but her words and reactions have eaten at me. I misjudged her then. I didn't know the extent of what she'd just been through. I was new to the department and had just come on to the case." He stared at the empty space between Jenna and Weaver, his gaze unfocused, distant. "When I learned the details, it was too late. She refused to talk to me again, and I never got a chance to fix it. I can't take back what I said…"

Forcing a smile, he continued. "I had hoped she'd moved on and done well for herself, but when I saw her here and she ran from me, I realized I had to clear the air."

Shit. Weaver stared at the man who appeared to be earnest and caring. If his words had hurt Paris unintentionally, then that was likely what Paris's issue with him was all about. She definitely needed to see him. But Weaver knew if he pushed it, she would hate him.

Yet, it was holding her back right now from having a full life.

Really shitty timing.

He glanced over at Jenna and this time, maybe she'd seen the change in his own stance. Maybe she'd been on that side since the beginning. But there was a decidedly positive look in her eyes as if to say, *You can do this, Weaver.*

It was true that he could, but he also felt like he was betraying Paris. How did he reconcile that?

He sighed. "What do you want me to do?"

Chapter 19

Paris stared up at the ceiling. She had her phone out and had already tried to call her brother several times. So far he hadn't answered even though she really needed him to.

Things were crashing here and her foundation was slipping. This was huge and when she said huge, she meant *huge*. Too huge. She couldn't handle it. But she just knew it was going to require handling.

That truth hit her stomach and came back up – with her coffee and muffin from lunch. She bolted for the bathroom and just made it as her stomach emptied.

On the floor, tears in her eyes, hating herself for hitting this point, she could feel herself unravel.

Somewhere along the way she should have grown up. She should have found a way to deal with this years ago. Not here and now when she was looking to move on. Moving on meant going forward, not dealing with these huge chains around her soul holding her back – well it did – but she hadn't realized how big and cumbersome the chains where. How ingrained the hurt was into her psyche. And if she couldn't walk through a doorway and see a person without puking up her lunch, they were bigger than she realized.

That bothered her more than anything.

Had she been so blind to not see the effect this man had on her every action? Had she just been so accustomed to her own reactions that they'd been commonplace and 'part' of her? So that nothing looked or felt different enough to be noticeable. Had this man's words controlled her reactions since? If they had that much power back then, how much effect had they had on her since? When she hadn't even realized they were there, like little marionette strings yanking her chain all these years.

Was she so weak? No. She wasn't.

Was she so powerless? No. Not now.

Was she so incapable of moving past this she couldn't function? At the moment...yes.

And that couldn't continue. What had happened, had happened a long time ago. She'd done the best she could in a really shitty situation. Where survival had been the goal. Her brother had survived. She had survived.

Her father had not.

It was her fault, and at the same time it wasn't her fault.

Her own fear had brought her down this pathway. Her survival instincts had been right on. She'd been traumatized, then the cop had traumatized her more.

Now her own future was dependent on her accepting this. Not just accepting, but acknowledging her actions. By saving her brother's life and her own, she had to live with the consequences of her actions. Only she hadn't.

Trying to build a life. Trying to get through each day without letting her history define her present and not affect her future.

But what about the cop's words? Said in warning. Taken as a threat. She'd internalized his words and held them up as the one fight she still had to win. Yet did she? Still?

All these years. She was still living with a victim's mentality.

Had she made no progress at all?

Dry-eyed now, she stared down the long history of her life. At the damage her childhood had on her. The impact her actions had played in her life. The effect the others around her had on her then, and now.

Being a victim, in her case, had meant not showing any kind of reaction, just locking everything inside. In her early years, she learned quickly that to show a reaction was to take a beating if she showed the wrong one at the wrong time. Her father never left clues as to what was right or wrong, and she'd been beaten regularly. She'd always gotten back up. In fact, it had been a point of pride. Maybe not at the time, like Sean had, but later after the danger had passed. She'd gotten up again and carried on.

She thought she'd grown out of it, changed her attitude, and become stronger. Now as she considered how she'd let the constable impact her life, she realized she was – at least in his case – still in victim mode.

In many areas she had moved forward. After going to school, she had a good career and loved her work and the people she worked with. Always went when called in. Always stayed late when needed. Always worked hard. Not because she wanted to but because she was afraid not to.

Sadly, still in victim mode, still afraid of the consequences of saying the wrong thing. Of saying "no."

Truly she'd gotten nowhere. All of the goals and dreams she had, and yet she hadn't taken the steps to fulfill them. She hadn't put in an application for adoption because she was sure she would not be accepted. Nor had she tried relationships because she was sure it would go bad. If she didn't try, she didn't fail. But maybe that was because the right person hadn't come along yet.

Weaver was here and interested — she didn't even know how interested because she hadn't given him that opening. Every corner of her life, she held back just in case she did it wrong and got beat back down. Instead of living, she was waiting for the other shoe to drop, waiting for something to go wrong.

Victim mode.

WEAVER FELT LIKE he was betraying Paris. "I don't want to do anything that will make her feel ganged up on," he said to Jenna and Delaney. Jenna had been mostly quiet through this exchange, but he had a strong sense that she wanted his help. That it was fine to help, but they might not understand the long-term impact this man had on Paris.

"No, of course not," Jenna said. "We'd like her to be happy to meet Barry, but if that isn't going to happen, we need to give him a chance to say what he needs to say to her before she runs. Maybe then she'll have time to process the words."

His head was already shaking. "She's going to run as soon as she sees him. There's no way she won't."

Jenna frowned, and then turned her head to see if maybe Paris had come up behind her. "I'll talk to her."

"Good," Weaver said. "You do that. I'm all for helping her, but not for hurting her."

"And you know she has a lot of hurt to go through to get to the help?" Jenna watched him, as if looking for a chink in that armor of his.

Nodding, he felt defensive. "She's already had a lot of hurt, and I don't even know the full story. I don't want her to feel betrayed by us and have all that hurt magnified."

Constable Delaney spoke up. "I had no idea I hurt her

that badly." He looked devastated.

As much as he wouldn't mind letting the man suffer for all the fear Paris had been through these last many years, he couldn't let the man suffer more as well. "It's a combination I think. There was a lot going on before you and whatever you did compounded it." He shrugged. "I'd love to know the history of this but as she won't tell me, I'm kind of in the dark here."

"And it's not my confidence to share."

Jenna looked over at Barry. "Let me talk to her first. See if I can get her to see reason here."

With a sad look, the constable nodded and turned away. "Make sure you tell her that I don't want to hurt her. I never wanted to hurt her. I just want to apologize."

And he left, heading in the direction of the restaurant and bar. If Weaver were a betting man, he would put his money on the bar.

"Thank you, Weaver."

Startled, it took a couple seconds for Jenna's words to soak in. "Thanks for what? I didn't exactly agree to your plan."

She smiled again, and damn, he was going to lose himself in the depth and compassion in her eyes if he wasn't careful and he forgot his focus. "You did what was right for you. That's all we can ask of anyone." Her gaze intensified. "How are you doing this week?"

He thought about it. "I don't know. I'm a bit lost actually. The seminar is what, half over? Almost half over and I haven't written the report on the workshop or even started the project in the workshop."

"Life isn't just about the academic side of things. There are a lot of emotions flying around here. How are you handling that?"

"Trying to stay separate and detached is difficult," he admitted. "I don't know how you manage it. I'm not sure I could do something like this."

"You don't have to." She laughed. "There are many fields where your expertise and input would be welcome."

"Well, I don't feel that I have any expertise," he said, "and I haven't had much to input anywhere yet." That note of chagrin in his voice had her grin deepening.

"Yes, the joys of being a student. We know everything one minute and we know nothing the next."

"Exactly."

"How are you getting along with Paris?"

That question slid in so smoothly he'd already reacted before he could answer. And he knew that sharp gaze of hers caught every nuance. He decided to be honest. "I'm getting along fine with her. She fascinates me," he admitted. "She's so strong and in control one moment then so broken in the next. She has amazing defenses in place, and if Delaney hadn't shown up, it's quite likely she'd have blazed through this workshop without a dent to that cool, blasé control she shows to the outside world."

"Yet you see inside?"

He nodded. "I'm seeing inside. Just not sure I'm seeing very *far* inside. She's very complex," he said in what he hoped was a neutral tone of voice. At her knowing look, he realized he'd failed. A tide of color washed up his neck.

"It's not like that."

She nodded, but her smile didn't dim. "Good."

Already looking for the elevator, he stopped and said, "Good?"

"Well, if it's not like that, then you won't toy with her

affections."

He blinked. "Sorry?"

"If it were like that, then you'd be interested and she might be interested back. As you're not interested, then she won't get hurt more."

Blinking again, he stepped toward her. "Am I missing something?"

She shrugged. "I don't know. Are you?"

"Damn it, Jenna," he snapped. "Don't play games."

"I'm not. You just said you're not interested."

"No, I didn't. I said it's not like that," he corrected. "*She's* not interested."

Now she gave him a fat smile. "You need glasses. You don't seem to be seeing too clearly."

Then she walked past him to the restaurant. He stood there and stared at her in bewilderment. Was Paris interested? He had been getting mixed vibes from her all week. Then she was a huge mix of all emotions. He didn't think it was very healthy to start a relationship under these conditions.

Then he stopped once again. And groaned.

Hell, one way or another, he was already in a relationship with her.

Chapter 20

Paris knew what she wanted to do. But she wasn't sure she could. She had to think about it carefully. Failure was not an option. There were many times in her life she'd said something similar, but this time she knew the consequences would be horrific.

But she'd always been a survivor.

She had to take the chance. Had to.

Right?

No. It was a choice, but one she needed to make.

God, this was going to destroy her. She flopped backwards on the bed once again, confused and upset. Torn. What she thought and felt seemed to change every few minutes. She was an idiot who couldn't even make up her own mind on what to do. How to do this.

The conference was wearing her down. She knew it was deliberate on Jenna's part. They started with little exercises to take the top layer off, leaving everyone feeling a little exposed. A little vulnerable. Then they started digging at the newly exposed tissue, trying to open another level of pain. Of hurt.

Her stomach growled, putting her focus on more mundane issues.

Damn, lunch had been a long time ago.

She glanced over at the clock. It was almost seven. Was her one-on-one session with Jenna tonight? She couldn't remember if it was. No. If so, she'd cancel. Postpone it. Panic once again rose at the thought of meeting Jenna. Another layer, or ten, would be ripped away. Something that was supposed to happen, but the pain and fear she was going through right now was excruciating. And then there was the panic. That immediate response to the stressor that said, *No. Run. Hide.*

Shuddering, she climbed further into the blankets and buried her face.

Someone knocked on the door. She froze. Was it the cop? She leaned over to make sure she'd locked the door, then she curled up in a tiny ball and just rocked herself gently on the bed. Whoever it was, they'd go away. Soon. Surely.

Instead, she heard Weaver's voice. "Paris, open the door. I brought dinner."

In a low voice, she protested. "What if I'm not hungry?"

But she was. She was starved. And Weaver wouldn't give up as easily as another man. He didn't look like he had much give in him at all.

"Open up, Paris. It's Greek."

"What if I don't like Greek?" she called out as she walked toward the door, wiping her eyes, knowing she looked a mess. Well, that should send him away if nothing else. But she really liked the guy. Knew he liked her, but there wasn't any way they would get together. At least not permanently. She was good with that. And having Weaver in her room would be a distraction. His warm laugh, piercing eyes and muscular physique would be a welcome change to the gnawing uncertainty that wracked her thoughts.

She opened the door to see Weaver, wearing an aura of concern, standing and holding a large takeout bag of Greek food. His muscles bunched as he held the bag, and he frowned when he saw her. It made her smile.

Maybe she wasn't good with that.

"You're making me crazy," she said, pushing the door open wider and letting him in. Turning back inside, she tried to calm the rolling emotions in her head, stomach, and damn it — her heart. She didn't want to care about him. She didn't want to care about anyone. She'd be opening herself to a world of hurt. And him with his lopsided grin and light-hearted manner, what if it was all a game to him? A fleeting thing. She didn't know that she could do that.

She really just wanted to do what she wanted to do and forget the rest. *Liar,* her head whispered. *You want what Sean has. You want someone special. You want to see where the warmth of his touch will take you.*

He's not special though. He's arrogant, rude, ignorant and...caring, compassionate, sexy as all hell and...so very nice to look at.

She groaned. "You really are going to make me nuts."

"I'm making you crazy? I haven't done anything to you," he protested, following her inside. "What are you talking about?"

"Oh, nothing," she said with a snort. "One minute you're looking gorgeous and happy and the next you act like a gargoyle, then you're back to looking gorgeous again," she said crossly.

"WHAT?" HE DIDN'T know what to say, and his mind went from gargoyle to gorgeous. Did those two words even belong in the same sentence? He couldn't see it. "Gargoyle?"

She snorted. "What is it about men that they pick up on a single word like that?"

Walking to the small coffee table that sat in front of her couch, he set the bag of food down. "You'd rather I ask about gorgeous?" he asked dryly. He sat down beside her, watching as she worked efficiently without asking him about it, dividing up the food onto two plates and handing him one.

Without a word she took her seat, picked up her plate, and proceeded to eat with a vengeance.

He ate much slower, keeping an eye on her, noting the red eyes and the pale cheeks, the hair that was brushed back off her face impatiently several times. "You worked up an appetite?"

Her glare would have melted glass if there'd been any heat behind it. He laughed. "Okay, so a tough afternoon, but we're here, eating, and that's good, right?"

She shrugged and kept eating.

Not knowing what to say, he was still stunned at her gargoyle and gorgeous comment. Had Jenna been right? Did she like him? Was she interested in him? Damn, he felt like a school kid again trying to sort out matters of the heart. He'd been much older when he learned there was no understanding them.

Now he was right back to being confused. He sighed and stared down at the delicious Greek potatoes on his plate. His appetite was gone. Why was she suddenly so important to him? This last outburst from her seemed so open and honest, and heat rose within him.

"Don't you like it?" she asked in between bites, eyeing his still half-full plate.

"Are you trying to steal my food?" he asked mischievously.

Smirking, she said in a crafty voice, "If you give it to me, I'm not technically stealing it." Putting down her own empty plate, she waited expectantly.

"Wow." He split the rest of his meal in half and pushed one half onto her plate. She snatched it up and settled back to eat again.

"How can you eat so much?"

"Nerves," she said. "Always been high-strung."

"I can see that. You're very slim." Weaver replied, looking her up and down.

"Add boyish, slim as a board, pancake. It's okay, I've heard it all."

He raised his head and said mildly, "I wasn't thinking in terms of your chest size."

"Good thing as I don't have one." She smirked and popped a big chunk of potato into her mouth. "The nice thing is I can run without those things flying in my face, too." And damn if she didn't make a comical face that had him shouting with laughter.

Another side of her he hadn't seen before. If she could laugh at her physical body, maybe she'd get to the point where she could laugh at her other problems too. It was great to see.

"See, I knew I could bring out the other side of you." She picked up another bite.

"What other side of me?" As her words had mirrored his thoughts, he was confused for a moment. "What are you talking about?"

"You're too serious," she said. "You rarely laugh. And never at yourself."

"How would you know?"

She grinned. "As I do it all the time, I recognize it in others – or the lack of it."

"Maybe I'm just not comfortable enough around you to do that."

"Maybe," she said cheerfully. "And maybe you're just not comfortable around yourself."

Damn.

Chapter 21

WHERE HAD THIS great mood come from? But saying what she wanted to Weaver without fear of repercussion was huge. So freeing. Having him here in her room, felt comfortable, and so much more…

"I'm really glad I can say anything to you. It's given me such a sense of freedom."

He nodded, but there was a distance to his gaze, as if he'd turned inward. And he likely had.

Still, she polished off the last of her meal. "Thanks for dinner by the way."

He slowly reached over and put his plate down on the coffee table then sat back. He said, "Care to clarify that comment about gorgeous and gargoyle?"

With her eyebrows raised, she said, "Hell no. Figure it out yourself."

"I was working on it. Just not sure where you were going with it. See, I really like you. I'd love to see you when this week is over. Maybe go to a movie, have a pizza, and take it to the beach," he said with a light shrug. "Take it slow. Nothing too pressuring."

"What if I want pressure?" she asked, her words shocking both of them. Instantly, she could feel her blood pounding in her veins as she sat breathless for a second. Who the hell was this talking? Surely it wasn't her. Fear had always stopped her from being so open, so... flirty.

He sat up and tilted his eye sideways as he assessed her closer. "Meaning?"

"There's that academic side of you, looking for answers." Paris avoided his question, not really knowing the answer herself. Wanting to touch him, to feel him touch her as they shared their innermost secrets with each other, washing themselves of their past. Shaking her head, she looked up.

"And there's that side of you that darts forward, drops a bomb, and then retreats in case it blows up and you're caught in the backlash."

"Oh," she said in a small voice. "Does that make me a tease?"

This time it was his eyebrows that shot up. "If you do it sexually as an advance and retreat, yes, that would make you a tease." He shrugged. "I wasn't seeing or saying that. I'm seeing more of a baby deer darting forward in life excited and carefree but gets out a little too far and remembers mother's warning so it dashes back to safety." Now his voice was warm and caring again.

"Nice. I think I like that analogy. Except the mother part," she added, thinking of her own mother. "You'd have to have a mother who cared enough to warn you. I barely remember mine. She walked out a long time ago."

"Ever tried to look for her?"

Her headshake was so violent her hair flew out in all directions. "No. And can't see myself ever wanting to." Besides, she'd be tempted to punish the woman like she'd been punished. And that wasn't going to end well.

For anyone.

The joyous lightness inside dropped as she contemplated her mother and her instinctive response to his question.

Maybe that damn constable had been right after all. What did that say about her?

"Hey, why so serious? I'm sorry I brought up your mother." Leaning forward, he placed a gentle hand on her leg.

She watched his fingers close around her kneecap and squeeze gently. A man's touch that wasn't out to cause pain or humiliation. How about that?

If she sat there much longer, she might just ask him to take her to bed and prove all men weren't assholes when they had a woman vulnerable in their grasp.

But so not the way to have a relationship. As an experiment yes, relationship not.

At the word experiment, she froze. That's what he'd been doing in this class. Right.

"Am I an experiment for you?" she said before she let herself double question the sensibility of asking. "Cause I don't think I could stand that." She scrambled to her feet.

"What?" he asked, shaking his head as if to question her sudden switch in conversation. "No. Hell no."

She glared at him. "Damn well better not be."

Walking closer, not sure what she was going to do herself, she leaned over and...kissed him.

SHOCKED AND A little overwhelmed at the suddenness of her actions, Weaver was afraid to respond in case she bolted. He didn't mind being an experiment for her but would prefer to understand exactly where he stood in this study. Not that she'd let him know. As she eased back, a gentle sigh on her lips, he leaned forward, following her retreat.

"My turn," he whispered and tugged her onto his lap. She made a startled sound, but he covered her mouth with his own and teased her lips open for him. Smooth and dark, he deepened the kiss until she sagged in his arms. He lifted his head, wondering at the shakiness inside himself.

With her head against his shoulder, she whispered, "Nice."

He grinned. Finally they had found something they agreed upon.

Chapter 22

Actually very nice, but she didn't want to make too big a deal over a kiss. Except…it was a big deal. She'd been kissed before. Even in ardor, but it hadn't done anything for her. She'd participated to see if it was something she *could* do.

She could. Just why would she? Previously, she hadn't felt anything. It had been wet and sweaty and awkward and hell no. It was not something she had wanted to repeat.

For her partner at the time, well, they'd been friends and that had been more of a *hey, we've gone out a time or two it's past time for a goodbye kiss*. For her, it had just ended that whole sex thing.

After all, why do it if it didn't feel good?

Now Weaver's kiss – yeah, that had felt good. Dry and warm and caressing, his kiss had made her feel cosseted, safe, cared for. He'd been compassionate, yet there'd been heat under there. A banked heat that also said he was in control. And it left her wanting more…

Like she'd said, "Nice."

And now what? Did she just lie here and wait? Wait for what?

"Glad you think so," he said, humor lacing his voice. "I thought it was nice too."

Lifting her head, she gazed at him suspiciously. His smile

deepened.

"Are you laughing at me?" she accused him, pushing up to look up at his face.

His grin widened and he snatched her back into his arms. "Absolutely not."

"Hmm." Then he lowered his head, and damn if she didn't reach up to meet him halfway.

So this was what you were supposed to feel? She wanted to analyze the sensations but his hands stroked across her back, her shoulders, distracting her. The gentleness of his touch, the soothing stroke so unlike anything she was used to. The warmth flowed between them, erasing all the hurt of the day, melting them together.

When he lifted his head the second time, she curled up against his chest, closed her eyes, and relaxed.

It had been a tough couple of days. There was a feeling that the seminar was over – almost over – a winding down in some regards. The workshops had been helpful. She'd seen a few of her problems. She just didn't know how to deal with the big one in her face.

What was she supposed to do with that?

Usually she'd call Sean and talk it over but ever since he'd hooked up with Robin, she'd tried to give him more space. If he could be there for her, he would. She almost wanted him to swing by. Maybe stand by her side while she pondered the possibility of seeing Constable Delaney.

Delaney. A coldness whispered through her. He'd become a blockage she couldn't get around. He was an issue that she *had* to get past. So far she'd managed to avoid him, but she knew that wasn't the answer.

If only she could figure out how to go about it.

Neither did she want to turn around to find him standing

there. She needed to be prepared for the confrontation.

"Thoughts?"

The sound of his voice rumbled up his chest under her ear.

With a pained voice, she said, "I'm thinking about the cop I'm avoiding."

"Hmmm." Non-judgmental, listening, waiting. Nice.

"I know I should face him, but I don't want to."

"Sometimes we have to do what we don't want to do," he said. "And often what we think is a huge deal before and turns out to be nothing afterwards. We can see it had only been big in our minds. Is this man likely to hurt you today? No. It's still the child in you that sees him as a big bogeyman."

"I don't know," she said, her voice barely audible. "I might still be a child when I see him, in my mind at least, but the fear is real." Her chest tightened. "The panic is there, the inability to breathe."

"Right. To be expected. Even now at the thought of talking to him, your mind is recreating the same panic it had when you were a little girl. Although you realize he's not going to hurt you, or haul you away, or any other number of ugly scenarios, your mind doesn't want to let go. It's too locked onto that belief."

Abruptly, she pulled away from him. He held her back for a moment then reluctantly let her go.

"It's just really hard." There was a long pause as she stared at him, considering his words.

"Yes, it absolutely is." He waited a moment then admitted, "But it's so worth doing. This man is crippling you. He's stopping you from being the person you want to be. From having the life you want to live. Is that what you want? Is that who you want to be?"

Shaking his head, he continued before she could protest. "I haven't known you for very long, but I already know that's not what you want for yourself. Not what you want to be able to tell your kids down the road when you've recovered even further and look back on this stage."

"That doesn't make it all doable though." She settled sideways on his lap, hating that her breath was still hiccupping in her chest and her blood flowed too quickly in her veins.

"Everything is doable. Just in small doses." He grinned. "Kinda like that worksheet."

She frowned at him. "What worksheet?"

"The one from the first day...the one you tried to erase then ripped, balled up, and finally ended up swallowing."

The memory of her chaotic panic had her scrunching up her face in disgust. Though she had come a long ways since then.

He laughed and pulled her close to him again.

"Oh, *that* worksheet," she muttered.

"Are you ready to tell me what the answer was that you felt so strongly about?"

She shook her head violently. "No."

LEANING BACK, IT was his turn to sigh as he tried to not let the disappointment choke him. He knew it was about trust. Another big issue for her.

Maybe one she could handle and maybe not. Maybe if he took the first step...shared something he kept private...

After all, he had his own issues. Lord did he have issues.

"My father was murdered," he said suddenly.

She gasped and spun around to face him, "What?" she cried. "When? How?"

Hating his own instinctive physical withdrawal that happened anytime he remembered that incident in his life, he just stared at her. "I don't normally tell anyone that." In fact, he wasn't sure when was the last time he brought it up. The sympathetic looks and sideways glances people gave made him uncomfortable, made the situation worse.

"Wait...I thought you'd been abused as a child?"

He could understand the confusion in her voice, her words. "After my father was killed, my mother fell to pieces. She took to the bottle. But along with the bottle came the rage, the sorrow, and the complete inability to deal with life ever after."

"She's the one who beat you."

He nodded. "For being home late. For being home early. For not getting up on time. Because the dishes weren't done. Because she didn't have any money. Because she didn't have a bottle in her hand." Wondering at the ease with which he spoke, he shrugged. It was easy to talk to Paris, especially with her so close. "I think the alcohol let her release the rage about my father's untimely death in a way she couldn't do sober. She was always apologetic afterwards, but then she was never sober anymore so there were never any breaks when she was nice."

"Is she still alive?"

He nodded. "She's been in and out of rehab for a while now. It got really bad until I grew up enough to fight back. The trick is to fight back just enough but not do any damage or the cops look at you like you've done something wrong."

Frozen in shock, she stared at him and finally managed to strangle out, "That's very true." Several times her mouth opened and always closed as if to add something, only she couldn't get the words out.

Curious, he waited for her to speak.

Finally, she gave up. Then out of the blue she said, "I'm sorry for your mother and you." She looked at him, "How did your father die?"

"It was stupid. It was a carjacking and my dad resisted. He was slammed to the ground and stomped on before the assailants took off in our car. My mom and I were standing on the side of the road while it happened. We'd done what we were told to do. He, on the other hand, had loved that car. He hadn't wanted to give it up so easily."

"And they killed him?" She gasped.

"Yes, he had internal bleeding in the brain. It was hours before he got medical attention and the doctors did their best, but he didn't make it. I was six at the time and he was only thirty. My mom a couple of years younger."

"Ouch, that's tough."

He shrugged. "Everyone's got tough stories. Sometimes we can get past them and for others…it takes time."

"And for some people, it's never over. Instead, it becomes a living, breathing thing inside, ready to flare up. Ready to demolish your hard won calm and make you realize that, in fact, nothing has changed."

"I know that feeling too," he said. "After my mother spent months at a time drunk, it was tough to see any point in surviving. I had nowhere to go. At ten, I'd thought of running away, but where would I go? I had no other family. Didn't have many friends, because living with a drunk keeps those numbers down. Hell, I couldn't have friends over and hadn't had a birthday celebration or party since losing my father. My life didn't fit the same life other kids were living. Then again, I wasn't living. I was surviving.

"The killers were never caught. Are not likely to ever be caught." After all these years, he still felt an ache in his heart.

"The police figure the man who actually did the damage was part of a gang. Chances are good he's never going to pay for what he did."

"I'm so sorry."

"Like Jenna said, Justice is an issue for me. There's a big part of me that wants to make that asshole pay. And another part of me that says I need to just move on. Move forward and let it go. But saying that and doing that are two different things."

Chapter 23

Paris stared at him. They were so different. For him, Justice was something he wanted, and she was afraid Justice wanted her.

She slipped off his lap and moved over to the chair on the side. It wasn't that she wanted to put any distance between them…but she wanted to put distance between them. This was getting intense quickly.

"That must have been difficult growing up," she said quietly.

For long seconds he was silent, then he opened up a little more. "For years, I hated my father. Hated him for dying. Hated that he'd been more concerned about his car than his family, but I've come to understand. I doubt he was thinking at all at the time. He likely just reacted and paid a high price for his resistance."

"I'll say," she said with feeling, hating what he'd been through. "And your mother, did she blame him too?"

"Absolutely. That made it harder for me. As she was so angry, it was hard not to get angry at him as well. She was a good woman. One who, once she slid into the dark side of life, could never get back to the right side again."

"That's very sad," Paris said. In his eyes, she saw the sadness of a little boy who had been through unthinkable tragedy.

"The trouble with any kind of dependency is it becomes a

crutch. She could always find forgetfulness in a bottle. The anger came when there was no bottle and reality slapped her in the face."

"I imagine those scenes would have been tough."

Her father never drank. Said it made fools of men. And he was no fool. No one and nothing was going to have that type of control over him. Never. He was bigger and better than that and always would be. But inside, he was a raging ball of anger with extreme hated of his own father and he despised his mother. But his uncle, just mention that man's name and her father went ballistic. Her father had been one scary dude.

It was years later when she heard him muttering about the kiddy pedophile uncle of his that she realized her father had likely been a victim, too.

This was the first time in a long time she had thought about these things. She'd forgotten a lot of family history lessons in life, probably on purpose. The ones she remembered hadn't been pleasant. Of her mother's family, she knew nothing. Maybe she never would. Now though she no longer hated her mother for leaving them. It was highly likely that she had been abused as well. Too bad she hadn't taken her children with her when she finally escaped. Paris's childhood would have been very different if she had.

"Life is a bitch sometimes," Paris said.

"Yes it is, but when you hang around with people in therapy, you realize we all have stories to tell but many of us don't want to share. Why would we?" He shrugged. "We've already lived through it. We just want to move on."

"Do you feel you've dealt with it all, or do you give Jenna a pat answer to those uncomfortable questions, knowing inside that you're lying?"

He gave a bark of laughter. "You do that too, do you?"

"Absolutely. I figure she must know."

Nodding, he continued solemnly. "I think I've dealt with a lot of stuff, but I'm still struggling in some ways."

"Such as..."

"Jenna thinks I should go see my mother." He winced. "I haven't seen her in ten years."

"That's a long time to go without a mother." She should know. Would she want to meet hers after all this time? Or would she just be angry – even now?

"Not really. It's hard to look her in the face and accept that my life sucked in a big way because of her."

"Interesting. Any remorse for her? Sadness? Any hope she'd make a better life for herself?"

"Sure, but I don't want to be involved in the process. I haven't forgiven her. Better to just let her be and see if she's strong enough to get out of the cage she built herself."

"But cold for her and maybe lonely for you?"

He gazed off into the distance. "Loneliness is an issue for people like us, isn't it? Before we can share, we have to know our secrets will be safe. Otherwise, we can't really be ourselves, and the trouble is compounded when you hook up with someone going through therapy too. Your partner will be dealing with their own stuff and that can be just as difficult."

"Was that the problem with your wife?"

"Something like that. She desperately wanted to get married. To not be alone. But once married, it took her only a few months to figure it's what she'd needed but no longer what she wanted. If that makes any sense. I'm still trying to sort my way through it all. And likely will never get an answer." His voice had taken on a weary tone, as if he'd trashed this one to the end and back and still had no idea.

"Do you still see her?"

He shook his head. "No," he said. "She moved back east to be closer to her family." Then, rolling his eyes, he explained, "She said something about how I'm part of her past and she didn't want to be reminded of me and our short life together so it was better this way."

Paris laughed. "Too bad she didn't figure that out before the nuptials."

"So true." He grinned. "Still, it's nice to be able to laugh now, but at the time..."

"Everything hurts when it happens."

"That's for sure." Looking over at Paris, he smiled. "I do tend to avoid women with baggage. So many have issues."

"No," she snickered, "you're looking at this all wrong." Her smile widened. "You're actually seeing women who are trying to deal with their shit, instead of women who aren't even acknowledging it *is* shit!"

His laughter rolled free before dying away to a comfortable silence.

Now what? She didn't know how to proceed. What to say? But she did feel like she knew him a lot better. Liked him a lot better and felt closer to him. Her mind wandered back to that kiss. Maybe too much so.

Certainly he had been through a lot in life.

Why the hell had Jenna put them together again? And that brought up the damn report. She stood up again, intent on walking to the window. He held out his hand. Letting him tug her back down onto his lap, she tried for nonchalance and asked, "So how do we take all this and turn it into a visual project for Jenna?"

HAPPY TO HAVE her back in his arms, he tried to focus on her question. Visual? Interesting directive from Jenna. He wasn't a painter or artist of any kind, but there was one thing he'd done a lot of over the years. He asked her, "Can you paint or do some kind of art?"

Paris gave a quick headshake. "I do stick men."

"Good to know." He laughed. "Well, maybe we'll have to cut magazine pictures and create a collage of some kind."

At the look of surprise on her face, he realized she likely hadn't done anything like that. Like him, she'd had a poor childhood. School would have been an escape if she'd had a way to stay there after hours. It certainly had been that way for him.

But maybe that hadn't been an option for her. If her father had demanded she return right at the end of the school day, then she wouldn't have gone against that.

Once he'd grown too big for his mother to hit, life had changed for him. He'd done whatever he wanted to do and whenever. Not that the change had been a good thing, and it certainly hadn't stopped the abuse. Just the physical beatings. In a way, he'd almost become the parent in that relationship.

Paris hadn't had that choice. She'd been younger and with her father being the abuser, well, it would have been damn hard to have protected herself from him.

Weaver would love to show her life wasn't always so hard. That there were good people in it. She had been through school and nursing training. Most of the time she related well to people, but there was that inherit lack of trust with men specifically. Big men. Understood. But he was gentle. Or at least he could be gentle if that was required. And in this case, it was definitely required.

Holding her in his arms, he kissed her gently, thinking about the simplicity of the moment in contrast to the complex reality of their lives. It would be easy to stay cocooned with one another. His eyes drifted over to the bed and he took a breath.

How to proceed? Because he really wanted to spend time with her. Sex was one thing, but this…this could be so much more.

But she had to want it as much as he did, and she wasn't even close.

CHAPTER 24

"WE'RE SUCH A mess."

That shot his eyebrows into his hairline. "I *was* a mess. Sometimes I'm still a mess, but lots of times, I'd like to think I have my crap together, thank you very much."

Lifting her head, she smiled. "You're also very nice."

Kissing her upturned forehead, he tilted his head in acknowledgment. "Thank you. I like you too."

Snuggling in closer, she dropped her head onto his shoulder and nuzzled his neck. "Would you like to go to bed?"

Instead of getting a laugh or shocking him, he froze.

This time, it was her turn to see if he had stopped breathing there for a moment. A kind of hiccup escaped his lips, then he answered, "I'd love to go to bed."

And he didn't say any more.

So had he meant to go back to sleep? In which case, was she keeping him up? She pulled back and looked at him warily. "Does that mean you're sleepy? Or…"

He grinned. "Or…"

Her cheeks flushed with heat and she turned to look out the window. "Ha." Wishing she'd kept her big mouth shut, she backtracked quickly. "We're strangers. Aren't you supposed to do that with someone you love?"

His eyebrows shot way up. "Really. How about someone you like a lot? Someone you're interested in getting to know better. Someone you might like to spend a lot of time with."

Her cheeks were hot, but her gaze was steady as she stared at him, still snuggled close to him, their hearts beating in unison, the heat rising between them.

"Your big issue is trust," he said, looking at her with big eyes.

She dropped her gaze and slowly nodded. "I've never really been interested in anyone before. So it hasn't really come up. I'm essentially a novice, and that's always intimidating."

A laugh lit up his face. "It's also reassuring."

She frowned at him, loving the lighthearted laughter in his voice, and wanting to be able to make the move her body was urging her to, she asked. "Why does every guy want to be the first?"

"I couldn't care less." He shrugged. "It's just nice to know that you don't spend all your time hopping in and out of men's beds."

"What if it was women's beds?" she teased.

"There is something almost appealing about that."

She laughed. "Men are so simple. Sex, sex, and sex."

"Hey, this is the first time the subject has come up between us. We've known each other a whole three to four days."

Instantly she gasped and said, "Oh my, that's right. That's so not long enough."

"Not long enough for what?" he cried in a mock-pitiful voice. "If it's right, it's right, and time doesn't come into it."

"I'm not holding out for the church wedding and white picket fence, remember." She smiled. "I'm actually looking to adopt as a single parent. I didn't write men off, just thought it wasn't likely to happen to me."

He tugged her upward into his arms and lowered his

mouth to hers. Kissing her gently but thoroughly, his hands stroked her back before reaching around to hug her close. When he lifted his head, it was her pulling him back in for more. Breathless, they looked at each other.

In a voice deep and low, he said, "Well, maybe you should rethink that."

THE CONFUSED CLOUDINESS in her gaze was a total come on. He'd done that to her. And although it was arrogant of him, he was also damn happy he'd been the man to put it there. All he could think about was her. He wanted her more every minute. A mix of confusing sides, she was hard to read. How she'd survived was beyond him, but she had, and she was sweet and caring and had so much to give. He could see that she'd poured all that love into her patients. Those lucky babies. And given the strength and power of love, he couldn't help but think those babies must have responded beautifully.

He lowered his head again and closed his eyes, gently savoring the sweetness of her lips. The tenderness of her touch, the softness of her hair. The acceptance as she lay in his arms. He'd had several relationships. His own childhood abuse, not having had a sexual content to it, had geared him more to being disdainful of women. Tarring them all with the same brush. But he could never see this woman the same way. There is no way she would turn to the bottle to forget or abuse a child because she was so full of anger.

Paris had spent years working to heal. Trying so hard to adapt. To be strong and to survive. She'd done it at great cost – emotionally and spiritually. But she'd done it, and that was important.

She wasn't like his wife. And he had to remember that.

Paris was her own person, and she'd be damned if she'd allow anyone to compare her to someone else.

Good thing – he didn't want anyone else.

Just her.

Chapter 25

THE TASTE AND touch of his kiss…the feeling of those strong fingers slowly rubbing her back, exploring her ribs and caressing her skin. Nice. Addictive. She'd always wondered. Always wanted to have someone to hold her. Especially after seeing Robin with her brother. Seeing the affection and caring, how love bound them together.

And it had started here.

Like her relationship.

Was it possible? Could miracles hit twice in the same location? Third time if they counted Robin's friend Tania. And maybe more. Jenna's workshops were legendary. Who knew how many relationships started with them? And she had to wonder how many lasted.

This wasn't about having a forever perfection – although like every woman, she certainly wanted such a thing if it existed. But she'd take little bits and pieces of wonderful goodness for now. Weaver was extraordinarily kind. He'd been looking out for her in the same way Sean had done for decades. Maybe that was the attraction. But it was more than that, it was his touch, his smell, the way he would not back down but was gentle at the same time. It gave her hope.

"What are you thinking?" Weaver asked, the heat of his breath sliding down her cheek to her neck as he trailed a line of kisses across her face.

"You remind me of my brother," she said honestly, tilting her head to give him better access.

He froze, lifted his head, and said, "I don't feel brotherly toward you."

And this time when he kissed her, it was as if he wanted to erase the thought from her mind, stamping his personality on her soul, taking possession of her needs and wants and spiking them higher and higher.

Heat coursed through her, feelings she'd never experienced before making her shiver – with want, with expectation, with need. She'd missed out on this in life. It felt so good. So right. She wanted to see where it could go.

Wrapping her arms around his neck and pressing closer, she was willing to see what more there was. What more he could show her. Make her feel and forget. To enjoy this moment.

He shuddered then shifted and she found herself lying flat on the couch beneath him.

The weight of him on top felt so natural, so good. She loved the rapid thud of his heartbeat. The red flush on his neck and face. The glitter to his eyes. She wasn't scared of him.

And though it shocked her, she trusted him.

With a sexy smile, she murmured as she placed tiny kisses at the corner of his mouth, "Take me to bed, Weaver."

WEAVER DROPPED HIS forehead to rest on hers. He closed his eyes. He wanted this. He really wanted this. But he needed to know she was okay with it – regardless of her words. Or maybe in spite of it.

He opened his mouth, and she placed a finger against his

lips, telling him to stop.

"Don't ask if I'm sure. I'm sure. Don't ask if this is what I want. It's what I want. I know this pushes my boundaries and yours. But I can do this. I want to do this. Besides…"

The little catch in her voice was barely audible but he heard as she added, "Besides, I trust you."

His heart overflowed. For many guys, they wouldn't care about that. For him, it was major.

"Thank you," he whispered. Slipping off the couch, he grinned at her wide-eyed confusion. "No, you didn't say anything wrong." He held out his hand. "I figured the bed would be a whole lot more comfortable."

With a startled laugh, she stood up with him, already walking backwards to the edge of the bed, his gaze intent, searching. He wanted her to be there inside – right there with him – and maybe she was, but he was going to give her every chance to back off if she needed to.

It might kill him…but she needed to be in control. At the edge of the bed, he flicked off his shirt and tossed it back on the couch then unbuckled his belt while slipping off his shoes. Seeing her gaze widen, he leaned forward to kiss her. She shook her head and stayed just out of reach.

Uncertain, he watched her retreat. Only she grabbed her own shirt and pulled it over her head and tossed it onto the couch with his. With a bark of laughter and sheer joy, he quickly divested himself of the rest of his clothing.

He stood in front of her, nude, aroused, and comfortable in his skin, waiting, watching as she did the same, matching him step by step.

When they were only a foot apart, both nude, she swayed toward him. He tugged her close, feeling her shock as heated skin met hot skin. God, he wanted her. His need was something he couldn't hide. Lord was she beautiful. Long, lean, muscled, but gently rounded everywhere.

"Are you—"

Her mouth latched onto his, silencing him as she began to explore his body.

Yeah, he'd have to say…she was sure.

Chapter 26

She'd been shocked at the sight of his aroused body. Not at the physiology of an aroused man. Anyone with access to the Internet got more than they ever wanted to see there. No, her shock was at the proof that he wanted her. Something she'd never expected to see.

Briefly she considered that when he saw her rib and hipbones sticking out, he'd be turned off. Instead, there'd been a stronger reaction, as if he was pleased with what he saw. Like go figure.

Then he'd opened his mouth, and she'd wanted to stop the question again from coming up. Maybe she didn't want to be given a choice. To be given a second chance to wonder. To doubt.

It wasn't that she *needed* to do this. There'd been so much in life she'd needed to do – just to survive, to function in that crazy world of life after being a victim.

This she *wanted* to do for herself.

Clumsily, she'd kissed him, trying to express the feeling roiling through her. And again, he hadn't seemed to notice her lack of experience or her roughness. He was so damn accepting and so damn sexy, she wanted to explore, to touch every inch of his body.

And she loved that he seemed to authentically care about her. For the first time, she realized how far she'd come this week. Who'd have thought she'd be standing here with him right now?

As he pulled back slightly, she didn't let him go.

That same lopsided grin came out and chased the worry away. "Just a minute," he whispered.

He stepped around her, grabbed the bedding, and pulled it down to the end of the bed. Then while she was still figuring out what she was supposed to do, she was scooped up into the air, a tiny shriek escaping, and tossed into the middle of the white sheets. The cold bedding hit her skin, making her gasp, only to have that sensation followed by his long muscled body coming down on top of her to chase away the chill. In fact, she was now surrounded by an inferno. Inside and out.

Her body woke up in a big way. In a way she'd never known was possible, but she'd gone from being slightly cool, slightly uncomfortable, to being hot and twisting beneath him, wanting so much more.

She knew the mechanics but hadn't expected the emotion. The heat or...the overwhelming need and the connection, the power of touch.

Lowering his head, he proceeded to show her all she'd been missing. And she let him. Acquiescing, she followed where he led and he didn't disappoint. A whole new world of experience opened up for her.

As he stroked her ribs and kissed the old scars she'd completely forgotten about, her hands felt their way along his broad shoulders. His fingers stroked and caressed her small plump breasts before taking the nipple into his mouth and suckling. She arched her back in surprise, wondrous at the surge of sensation not only at her breast but between her legs. This was almost pain...yet so pleasurable it was a feeling she did not want to end. She was so confused and overwhelmed as he caressed and explored, awaking nerve endings she never knew existed.

When he slid two fingers into the curls at the juncture of her thighs, she cried out in joy, almost weeping as pleasure washed through her.

"You're so responsive," he whispered, kissing her navel and licking his way below, past the long scar and multiple little ones.

She twisted and cried, whimpering when his tongue slid over her nub, her body open and desperate for release. Lifting her hips, she tossed her head and gripped him with her body. Her fingers dragged through the dark curls on his head. She didn't know if she wanted to pull him up to her or push him lower. She couldn't think – just feel.

Then he slid lower.

And he tasted her, licking her as if she was the best ice cream cone. When he slid two fingers deep inside, she cried out, her hips arching up and away from his maddening touch.

Until something twisted inside her.

He grabbed her hips, held her down, withdrew his fingers, then slid his fingers in again.

She exploded.

A kaleidoscope of colors matched the rolling waves of sensations driving through her body. She'd whimper if she could. She'd laugh in joy if she could. Instead, she could only lie there and shudder.

Waves upon waves of…joy washed over her, around her. She was in the center of the vortex. Sensations so freeing and wonderful she just lay still in delight and let it happen.

Weaver kissed his way back up, stopping to taste her navel, her nipples, before giving her a deep drugging kiss that pushed her deeper into the center of the vortex. It was barely noticeable when he shifted her position, making a place for himself, like he belonged there.

He lifted her hips and in one sure stroke settled himself deep inside her core.

Gasping, her pelvis, with a mind of its own, softened. Accepting, caring, welcoming him, reaching up for him.

There was no pain. Just a newness. A sense of rightness.

She sighed. How could anyone stand this? It felt so good. So *right*. So full. So much more than she'd ever thought it could be. It was…perfect.

Then he started to move.

And she realized it was happening all over again. The pressure built up quickly, and she couldn't do anything as the sensations buffeted her from one side to the other. It was going so fast, all she could do was hang on for the ride.

She opened her eyes to see him, his own eyes closed, the cords on his neck tight and hard as he drove toward something only he could see.

Then he gave a long groan, his body arching backwards, and she could feel his release inside her. So deep inside. So special. With him in a togetherness she did not know was possible. And damn if she didn't come apart again.

He collapsed beside her, their bodies slick with sweat, and he tucked her up close. She lay curled up at his side, wide-eyed yet exhausted. Her body hummed. Her emotions spun and her mind…it couldn't believe what she'd just experienced.

No wonder everyone spent so much time thinking about sex. Where to get it, how to get it, having it, and who with. Holy crap.

She was a convert.

His chest rose and shuddered unevenly as he took a big gasping sigh and let it out, his breathing settling right down.

She grinned. Lifted herself up on her elbow so she could look down at him, and said, "Now that you've recovered, ready to go again?"

HIS GAZE WIDENED in shock, a startled laugh escaping.

He cuddled her close. "Anytime, any place," he said.

She snickered and relaxed down beside him.

He was so damn grateful for this moment, he just wanted to squeeze her harder. She'd been...well, he was speechless. In trying to make it good for her, trying to make it special, and he'd been so surprised at the depth of his own need, his own response, hell, it had ended up...perfect.

"Thank you." That gentle voice floated up from within his arms. He had to question that he'd really heard them. He twisted slightly so that he could see her face and the look on her eyes.

"For what?" he murmured. Now what was she worrying about inside that pretty head of hers?

"For making it good for me."

Leaning over her, Weaver stared down at her in astonishment. "My pleasure," he whispered, dropping a kiss on the corner of her mouth. "This isn't a one-person activity. Both should be just as involved."

She gave a tiny shrug, but the matching smile on her lips caught his eye. "That might be true, but we also know it's not always that way. I'm not sure I could have had that same experience with another man."

He pulled back slightly. "Hell, I don't want to think of you with another man," he said, "But I can't allow you to think that. There are many men in the world, and many are very experienced and good lovers," he admitted. "With way more experience than I—"

"Experience has nothing to do with it," she whispered. "It has to do with caring. With wanting me to be happy. To find pleasure. You helped me reach through a very difficult thing. The first time for any woman can be traumatizing. In my case, it was a mix of issues. Thank you for being you. I managed to trust you enough to do this and…" That beautiful smile of hers deepened. "And you gave me so much more than I expected."

Her words were lovely, the tone perfect. The sincerity…well, he'd never been thanked for doing something he'd wanted to do so badly. But he remembered that there'd been no pain. No hymen to break. He wondered about mentioning it then decided it wasn't the time. Later, when she was more comfortable, then maybe she'd share. Right now he was just so damn glad to be where he was. He wanted her to come back to this point in time and remember it with joy, not heartache.

She looked so lovely in his arms, such a perfect fit, his heart swelled. He gave her a tiny grin. "Yeah? Well in that case, let's see what we can do for round two."

And he lowered his head, gratified to find her lips already reaching up for him.

This woman was all about giving.

He'd never met anyone quite like her.

Then he couldn't think as her hand slid down his back to his buttocks and squeezed. Her toes slowly climbed his calves, and he realized she hadn't just enjoyed the first time around. She had learned. As she slid her hand between them to find him, his eyes crossed.

"Christ," he whispered as her fingers closed around him, her body sliding lower and lower.

She'd learned a hell of a lot.

Chapter 27

THE NEXT MORNING Paris woke slowly, confused by the aches and pains mixed with the delicious sensations throughout her body. She lay quiet for a long moment until the memories of last night filtered into place. Weaver. She smirked. A beautiful name. He'd woven a beautiful experience together for her. A night to never forget. A memory to cherish forever.

Hoping they had many more to come, she smiled at the thought of them as a pair.

She rolled over to find his side of the bed empty, the bedding thrown back as if in a hurry. She sat up, pushing her tousled hair back and looking around. She caught sight of her reflection in the massive television screen. Even in there, she looked well loved.

For the first time, she realized that's exactly what she was. Loved.

She hopped out of bed to look for a note or something to explain where Weaver had gone. Nothing. Hating the building worry that he'd walked away, she stepped into a hot shower and soaped herself all over. She'd have loved to have Weaver in there with her right now. Maybe later tonight. It was her last night here.

That reminder slowed her strokes as she used the washcloth on her skin. Her face. She had some decisions to make.

They weren't something she could make so easily.

But time was running out.

Back in her room, she realized there was still no sign of Weaver. It was almost time for the seminar. She'd forgotten to check the time before going into the shower and now she was late.

She quickly dressed, then raced down to the restaurant, grabbed two coffees, and hurried toward the conference room. There was a group of law enforcement off to one side. She skirted around them, keeping her head down and going around the centerpiece in the lobby. When she figured it was safe, she went to turn back and heard a voice that made her smile. Weaver.

Glancing in his direction, she almost dropped her coffee. He was speaking with Delaney. She froze, trying to assimilate what she was seeing. And couldn't find any reason that made her feel good. She turned and ran into the seminar room. Shit. Standing in the middle of the room she didn't know what to do. With stricken eyes, she searched the place she normally sat to find two coffees sitting there, waiting. She proceeded slowly, her heart desperate for an explanation but her mind coming up blank.

Weaver knew how devastating that man's presence was to her.

Was he trying to do something for her? Against her? A small shudder went down her long frame. She sat down before her legs gave out, but...

"Hey, are you all right? You look like you've had a horrible shock," a man sitting in front of her asked.

She tried for a smile. "I did actually. But I'm okay."

Busying herself with trying to organize all the cups on the table, she tried to reorganize the thoughts in her mind.

All she could see was the word *betrayal* flashing in neon colors in her mind.

Again.

WEAVER, ANGRY AND disturbed, slipped into class. He saw Paris already in her seat, and his smile bloomed fully when he saw the double set of cups on the table. He loved that about her. She rarely thought about herself and was always looking about to help others. He imagined nursing to be one of the best professions for her.

"Hey," he murmured to her bent head as he sat down.

He'd expected a wide grin, even a shy blush.

But she kept her head down and said, "Hey back."

He stared at her bent head in dismay. Damn. He hadn't wanted to leave her in bed this morning. He'd planned to wake her up in a special way, but he'd gotten a call from Jenna. Against his better judgment, he'd left the bedroom. And left her.

Alone.

He tried to see her face, but she had her head down enough that her hair fell to cover her features. Reaching across, he squeezed her shoulders and tried to make contact. She stiffened but didn't look at him.

Shit. He eased his hand back and turned to snag up one of the coffees. Hating that he felt like he was in the wrong, he took a drink and tried to pay attention. Jenna was setting up for a special set of exercises. The dynamic way she held the audience was inspiring. The way they all paid attention, as if she had the answers to life in the palm of her hand. Maybe she did.

It would be nice if she could share some of that smoothness. Especially with Paris. But circumstances kept him separated from her all morning and although he tried to catch a glimpse of her, she never looked his way. Was she regretting their night together?

With his heart sinking, he wondered how badly he'd screwed up. Then he got mad because if leaving her this morning was a deal breaker, then she should have let him know ahead of time.

Then again, she'd never been in this situation. She might not have any idea how etiquette worked.

Or maybe she was regretting last night.

Wouldn't that be his luck, the best night in his life and she wanted nothing more to do with him? Damn it. If that happened, life *was* a bitch.

Just then he was forced to put his focus elsewhere as his group ended up being the first to take on Jenna's exercises and for the next few hours, he didn't have time to think about last night or Paris's odd behavior. In fact, there wasn't much time to do anything. When they finally did break for lunch, he turned to find her and instead realized she was leaving with her group. Uncertainly, he watched her leave the hotel with them, willing her to look back and check on him.

She kept on walking.

"Come on, Weaver. You're coming for lunch with us. There's a lovely Japanese restaurant around the corner."

Japanese food was the last thing he wanted, but they wouldn't accept his excuses. And maybe he was better off not alone. Confused and angry now, he couldn't imagine what would happen if he let himself travel further down that path.

What the hell had he done?

Chapter 28

It was hard to reconcile the Weaver she'd known intimately last night with the man listening to Constable Delaney this morning. Her euphoria over the wonderful loving she'd received had turned to dust in her mouth. She didn't have a clue what to say to him now. She wished it was Friday and the workshop was over so she could leave. But it wasn't. She had one more night. This morning she'd have done anything to have that last night with him.

Now she couldn't get away fast enough. Although sitting at a restaurant with a group that didn't include him was the best she could do at the moment.

At the same time, a part of her said that wasn't fair. Until she talked to him, she couldn't know for sure that he'd betrayed her.

Since she'd trusted him last night, she wanted to trust him today.

If she hadn't seen the two men talking, then her day would be so different. Now she could barely look at him and when she did, it was to assess him. Study him. To look for that strip of character that said her trust wasn't misplaced.

Of course, she was well on her way to loving this man. To caring for him in a way she'd never cared for anyone before. And it terrified her and confused her, because it was all so new.

And if she was wrong in her interpretation of what she'd seen – then he had every right to be seriously angry with her. Tired of the mental ramble in her head, she rubbed her sore temple, wishing she could escape to her room. But it wasn't to be. She had said she'd come for lunch and looking around the Japanese restaurant, she realized the change would be good for her. She loved group lunches at work. They were fun and interactive. Not personal.

Right now, that's just what she needed.

The door blew open, letting another group into the restaurant. And damn if it wasn't Weaver's group. With a sense of inevitability, she watched Weaver walk in. He stood there, tall, cool, composed – personally she preferred the man who'd come apart in her arms – but there was no doubt this man had a presence. Her mind flashed to the previous night, their bodies in sync with one another.

Then his gaze caught hers. Locked and held hers captive. He strode toward her.

Frowning at him, she debated fleeing.

She hated public arguments. He'd better not start anything right now.

Her mouth opened to say something first, only he reached her, scooped her up, and sealed the words bubbling out of her mouth with a hot, rousing kiss.

She sagged against him, and her anger melted away as she dimly heard the cheers rolling through the restaurant all around them. He released her and with his breath warm against her ears, he whispered. "I don't know what the problem is, but this distance between us is over. I'd never...do anything to hurt you."

Calmly, he sat her back down on her chair. Then he snagged an empty chair from another table and created a space for himself right beside her.

WHEN SHE MELTED in his arms, he'd known he made the right decision. It had been a spontaneous decision. He hated to think he was as primitive as his ancestors, but it had felt like staking a claim. Her response had made the agreement public.

God, he'd loved how quickly her shock had turned to enthusiasm and straight into complete surrender. It was that honesty he needed in his life. To know he could trust that response. People often lied with their words, but their bodies showed the truth.

And he loved her truth.

He'd stunned her and likely the whole workshop group, but everyone loved a happy ending, and damn, he was determined that would be their story. Sure, they had issues. The workshop and the cop for two of them, but after tomorrow, both would be over. Both impediments to their future gone. He just had to hang in there until…

He was sure they could do that.

He looked down at her and realized she appeared very distracted, out of it. Leaning back, staring down at their entwined fingers, his protective instincts rose to the surface. Dropping a gentle kiss on her forehead, when the waitress came around the table to his side, he quickly ordered for them both. He knew she had to be hungry. Whatever had been churning inside had to be eating at her. Time for her to fill up and give all the stress something else to work on.

She was an amazing person and she'd been doing so well.

He wanted to do anything he could to help her.

A thought struck him. He'd been so focused on helping Paris, he'd forgotten about his own needs. Then he stopped.

No.

Originally he *had* been looking at his next professional step. While he hadn't thought to be lucky enough to find a partner anytime soon, when he'd turned around – there she was.

Now all he had to do was keep her there.

Paris was his. No ifs, ands, or buts. She just had to wake up and see the same thing he saw – they were meant for each other.

Seriously satisfied, he tucked her more comfortably against him and turned his attention to the others.

Chapter 29

Her head still singing, her heart still stuttering in her shock, her body hummed with joy and expectation over what was hopefully going to happen next.... Paris just sat, tucked up against Weaver's side, his arm wrapped around her shoulders, as the bubbly conversation flowed around them.

The duality of the situation presented itself as she wanted to stay there like a limp attachment and never let go, yet she also wanted to smack him. Then ask him what the hell he'd been doing talking to *that* cop.

And she realized that's where she'd gone wrong; judging him and walking away, not letting him back into her space until he'd *taken* his spot back. She'd never asked him about what she'd seen.

Never given him a chance to explain. So scared and panicked, she'd just sort of locked down inside until he'd taken matters into his own hands. It never occurred to her that any man would care for her enough to do that.

Thank heavens. She nestled into him, relishing his familiar smell and warmth.

The lunch arrived with a more than normal set of confusion with the double tables now combined and people no longer in their original seats. As a plate was set down in front of her, she started in surprise. She actually didn't remember ordering.

"Hope this is okay," Weaver said. "I ordered for both of us."

How very controlling of him. No. She stopped and took a deep breath. How very caring. She was obviously still out of everything mentally, and he'd done what he could to smooth over any awkward moments. That was something she loved about him.

And then it hit her. Oh Lord. What if he'd been telling the cop to leave her alone?

Pulling back, she stared at him in stricken silence. Had she made such a big mistake against someone who'd only shown her kindness?

His gaze darkened as he caught her glance. Opening her mouth to say something, she suddenly became aware of their huge audience. She closed her mouth and pleaded for forgiveness with her eyes.

He opened his arm and tugged her back up close. Against her hair, he whispered, "Whatever it is that's wrong, we'll fix it. It's okay."

A shudder rippled down her back, an uncontrollable reaction to knowing she hadn't blown something so special.

"Did you hear me?"

She nodded, but the movement was stifled by the fact she was wedged up against his chest.

"Good. Then let's eat and keep the attention we're attracting to a minimum."

Right. She was making a spectacle of herself. She took a deep breath and straightened, then turned to face the others watching her curiously. She glanced down at her heaping plate then over at everyone else's normal side plate and said, "Let me guess, Weaver ordered for me."

Laughter broke out across the table.

"Hey, I know this girl," Weaver said. "And boy, can she eat."

Feeling blessed and once again back to normal, Paris picked up the first bite of the California roll and popped it into her mouth. Her world was good.

WELL, THANK HEAVENS for that. He'd been trying to figure out how to get back into her good graces, and it looked like he'd managed it.

For the moment.

For Paris, he'd do a lot to keep the peace. Relationships were filled with ups and downs, but they needed a foundation to be able to weather the changing tide. A couple of days in a workshop and one night of hot sex was not a foundation. It was, however, a starting point, and he'd take it. Last night had been an eye-opener for him. About himself and about her. The freedom she'd shown, the lack of restraint – she'd been wild – for her own joy and for his.

He'd never made love before.

That's what was different. At least he thought so. It would take some more thinking about. He'd had sex before. Had been in several relationships, but he wasn't sure that depth of emotion had ever been there. He'd been good friends with his wife, but the relationship had been comfortable, not passionate. The memories of last night swirled through him, making it hard to keep his mind on the lunch before him. Keeping her left hand in his right hand while they ate left him only his left hand to eat with. Something he wasn't being very good at. But he'd rather look awkward and ridiculous than lose that physical contact.

"Here, try this." As he turned to face her, he saw a sample

of something coming toward him. She laughed, her beautiful eyes twinkling as she popped the morsel into his mouth.

"It looked like you were starving."

His lips quirked and he squeezed her hand. "In that case, feel free to feed me."

"Ha, that would mean sharing, and you know how great I am at that."

He snorted. "You're just plowing through your lunch and hoping to be done fast so you can polish off my plate," he joked, loving the camaraderie. He caught several looks from the other attendees and a few were curious, but more were envious. And he realized how special this week had been. It wasn't over, but it was damn close. Things were winding down. Tonight was the one-on-one for him with Jenna and likely for Paris as she hadn't had one yet. Then tomorrow were projects followed by other speakers and wind-up sessions. Jenna always concluded on a Friday so the participants had the weekend to recuperate at home before they had to rejoin the real world. Smart strategy.

After today, he was feeling on the worn-out side himself. The emotional roller coaster had been brutal and he wasn't off yet. Might not get onto a stable platform for a long time.

And he wouldn't want it any other way. Not if Paris was that platform. He needed her. Her joy. Her insecurity. Her hope.

As he got to know her more, he realized in many ways she had done a better job of recuperating than he had.

She could show him a thing or two.

And after last night, he was dying to show her a few more things. He grinned and gave up on utensils with his left hand. He used his fingers and started to make a decent inroad into the various rice rolls on his plate.

Chapter 30

Paris finished her plate, happy and content. She watched, a smirk on her face, as Weaver gave up on decorum and let hunger rule. No one said anything as he used his fingers. It was working for him, so she didn't have a problem keeping his hand clasped in hers.

In fact, she wasn't sure she could let him go. It was that nice. That important to keep that connection there. She needed it, and she needed him. They fit together in a way she had never anticipated being possible.

In her heart she knew he was right, they could work this out.

As he finished lunch, she got a text from Jenna confirming the time for her evening session. She responded, giving her an affirmative. It was going to be at seven-thirty tonight. A bit late, but doable. Jenna's schedule was brutal, she knew. And she was lucky to have made as much progress as she had before her session with Jenna. It wouldn't have made sense to have her session early in the week. She'd still be floundering.

Though she still was in many ways, she had come further than she'd expected thanks to Weaver. It was shocking how his gentle persistence had won her over.

When was his session with Jenna? Maybe it would be around the same time so they could be together afterwards.

The group finished their meals, paid their bills in a mess

of laughter and confusion, and stood up. She let go of his hand and murmured something about going to the ladies' room.

In the small room she stared at her face, seeing the fatigue from the night with little sleep and the hated confused emotions that had been rolling through her all morning. Using the facilities, she washed up, taking a moment to slap cold water on her cheeks and burning eyes. She still had the afternoon to get through.

Somehow, knowing she had Weaver at her side again, she knew she'd make it.

A text came in as she was walking back to the front door. Sean.

She smiled and read the simple question asking how she was doing.

He was a special brother. She responded, telling him she was much better and now looking forward to getting through the rest of the workshop.

His instant response took some of the joy out of the communication.

Did you talk to Delaney?

It was her first reaction not to answer, but she knew he would not leave it alone. She gave him a short answer. *No.* Then in a separate text she added, *I can't.*

Though he might be disappointed, he wouldn't judge her. She hated disappointing him though. As far as she'd come in life, he'd been there rooting for her the whole time. Knowing more than anyone what she had been through, he wanted her to see this guy. Deal with it and move on. Just the thought was setting the bile in her gut seething. Talk about a big issue.

Her footsteps slowed as she walked through the restaurant. After all she had learned this week, she wanted to be big enough to handle this. She needed to be. Maybe she could set a date down the road, like in six months' time. Time to prepare for the meeting. Time to adjust.

Time to panic and find ways of getting out of it.

She sighed. Confused and depressed suddenly by her own lack of resolve, she opened the front door and walked into the sunshine. Outside, she joined the group and found Weaver waiting for her.

He searched her face. "Tired?"

She nodded and turned to fall into step behind the other attendees heading back to the hotel. "A little."

"Looks more like life is hitting you a little sideways."

"True enough." But she wasn't ready to share her problem and the gut-wrenching decision she needed to make. So much in her life had been hard. How hard could this one be? Or maybe a better question was if she were to look back on her life in a year, would she be happy? She'd been strong enough to make this step and ashamed she'd been so weak. Once again incapable of doing what she needed to do. A failure.

Just that word made her cringe.

Instead of sharing, she said, "What's it going to take to have you move past needing Justice for your father?"

He stared at her, as if he hadn't been expecting the change in topic. There was silence for a long time. She winced. "Sorry, I shouldn't have brought it up."

"You're entitled. We're doing a lot of pushing boundaries just because we're here but also because we're involved," he said calmly. "But you made me realize something I hadn't considered before." Their eyes locked and their hands clasped together. "It's not that I'm not willing to share, I'm just not sure where all this revelation leaves me in this situation."

"Oh, well maybe that's a good thing then." She smiled.

"It would be nice to see you grow through this workshop too."

"I'm growing more than I thought possible," he admitted with a smile. "Maybe that's why I'm stuck for an answer. It seems to me my instinctive response has changed and I need to think about it."

"Good enough," she said lightly. "When you figure it out, will you let me know?"

HE SQUEEZED HER hand. "Sure. It's an important issue for you, isn't it?"

She gave him a serious nod. "It is."

Interesting. Curious, but also a little confused, he stayed quiet trying to work through it. He knew Justice was a big one for her. It was for him too. But maybe not as big as it had been in the past.

And why was that?

He'd held that up as a flag in front of him for a long time. It had been very important. As if he could solve that and that would give him peace over the issue. Make peace with his past. Make peace with his childhood. Have someone to blame. The killer. If he'd not taken his father away, then Weaver's childhood wouldn't have been so horrible. So if he had someone to blame, then he wouldn't have to take on any of the responsibility himself. Then why should he? He'd been a child and he'd done what he could to survive.

And he'd done that part quite well. Sure, there'd been a lot of hiccups. But in many ways, it had been smooth sailing forward. So why was he hanging on to that issue as if to say it still made a difference? Yes, he'd like to see his father's killer caught and pay the price. Was it likely to happen? Maybe and maybe not. Did he want to hang onto all that emotion and energy that was pulling him down?

But it wasn't pulling him down. He didn't feel like there was any weight there. No emotional tug as he considered the missing man in his life. Not anymore.

Why?

As he walked, it became clear that he'd already let it go. Somewhere in the last few years, he'd come to realize that his father had died young and it was a horrible shame for all involved. Including his mother. She'd been unable to move on, and he'd taken her methodology as his own and held up his father's death as a major roadblock in his life. Except, in the intervening years, he'd formed his own methods of dealing with his life. Ones that suited him.

Not hers that kept her locked up in a crumpled-up space of time and emotion.

But ones that freed him from those bonds.

A child learned from his or her parents. That was the way of the world. He knew that. He'd been taught that, he'd seen it over and over again and knew it well. But at one point in time, a child also had to determine when and how he wanted to relate to the world around him as an individual. Either he further developed the tools his parents gave him or he learned his own coping skills.

If the latter, at one point the original coping skills became redundant and fell away from disuse.

Just like his had.

After a while, he'd learned to look at life differently. All the patients he'd seen and interacted with through grad school and had been blessed to have been a part of their process had taught him something even if it had taken him until now to understand. Maybe nothing major in the sense of an aha moment, but they'd slowly built up to show him what he wanted for himself and what he didn't want for himself.

His own wife had done the same thing. But he hadn't seen it. It had been her intense purpose to get married as she'd needed that security. That foundation. She hadn't been able to go forward with their relationship until that happened. Being ambivalent about the legal side of marriage, he'd agreed.

When after six months, she'd turned and said, "Thank you, I can move past this stage now," he'd been literally stunned.

And angry. Very angry. He'd been happy married to her. Thought she'd been happy. And she had, until she realized that it wasn't marriage she was looking for as much as having *been* married. So she had caught up to where everyone else in her world was at for her age level. She'd been so afraid that marriage would slip past her, be an old maid so to speak, and she'd been sure that being married would make her happy.

Only to realize she not only didn't want to be married but didn't really want to be with him at all.

After he'd gotten over the hurt and anger, he realized she'd also been a good lesson for him. She'd done what she needed to do and moved on. Regardless of whom she hurt.

For him, he had not moved on because he hadn't wanted to hurt or be hurt. His wife had tramped around in his life for a good year and by the time it was over, he could see she was doing much better having understood where her own issues had been at.

As she had explained to him, "You're part of my past now. And I'm ready to leave all that garbage behind."

Not nice.

To find he'd been part of the 'garbage' hurt. But it wasn't the same thing as to find his love unrequited. Because he hadn't really loved her in the first place. There was an attraction for sure and he'd cared for her a lot. More, he'd been content. Hadn't cared to get married as he'd seen no need. That meant a further commitment that wasn't required – wasn't wanted, he realized now.

His fault. He hadn't looked at his motives. Or hers. They hadn't discussed why the marriage. They hadn't really done anything but take the step she felt she needed to "feel secure." That she didn't miss out on something she thought was important until she was married.

Now he understood it. Even though it had been painful, he learned to look at relationships differently. He'd been avoiding anyone in therapy so to avoid a second scenario like his wife.

And he hadn't come to the workshop to do anything other than take notes for his paper.

And while he hadn't been looking, Paris had shown up.

And blown him away.

Therapy might not be done for her and she might need help again in the future, but her self-awareness was amazing. It was clear to her why she should do something and why she couldn't do something.

He couldn't argue with that.

She was doing the best she could.

Chapter 31

THE AFTERNOON WAS traumatic. Paris watched one woman break down completely and require help to leave the room. She felt close to tears many times as they dealt with the term *dreams*. Dreams they held and dreams they felt they could never have.

And how to modify those dreams to be something they could have.

By the time Jenna called the end of the day, there was a film of sweat over Paris's skin and her eyes burned with unshed tears. The emotional workout had been harder than anything she'd expected to have. Just the thought of packing up her stuff and making her way to her room made her want to just roll over and die.

Weaver stepped in front of her.

Gazing up at him, she was not ready or willing to stand up. And realized he looked about the same. She held out a hand and he clasped it, helping her up. "I think the rooms are too far away," she murmured.

He nodded. "Today they are."

But his voice was gritty, strained.

"Hard afternoon for you too, huh?"

Wide-eyed and serious, his head drooped, and damn if there wasn't a brightness to his eyes she'd not seen before. She squeezed his hand in commiseration and grabbed her purse.

"I'm ready."

After leading her out into the lobby, he stopped and said, "Which way?"

"Outside," she said suddenly. "Fresh air and flowers. Sunshine and new growth."

Gaze brightening, he nodded. Together they walked out into the sunshine, the hustle and bustle of the busy city streets. The sheer normality of their surroundings.

Not talking, they walked, automatically heading to the water and the boats they'd seen earlier. It was a ten-minute walk, but its curative effects were wonderful. She could feel the constriction around her chest easing and the bands knotting her stomach breaking up. By the time they found a bench to sit on and watch the world on the water, she could breathe normally.

"How does she do that?" she asked in a low voice. "This is the last full day and there were so many things happening, so many people breaking down. Stuff coming up for everyone. I've never been through anything so intense."

"And that's still going to continue. Tonight, overnight, and all day tomorrow. I don't know if they are all like this but with this level of intensity, it's no wonder her workshops get such wonderful results."

"It's not what I expected when I started a few days ago," she murmured. She wasn't even sure what had happened today. Lots of father stuff. Stuff about value. Having value. Deserving to be valued. Lots of emotional letting go of the bonds she'd carried for so long. "The stuff we do and did, the stuff we believed, a lot of it is so stupid."

"Only now that you can look back and see what it's like as an adult," Weaver said. "As a child, a teen, it's impossible. We absorb the environment around us. We learn from those abusing us. We grow based on everything – one direction or another."

Quietly contemplative, Paris sat for a moment then said, "Do you know my father told me I was the reason my mother left? And I believed him? Didn't think I was worthy of love. Didn't think I could be a mother because my mother had walked out on us, so what if I did the same? Figured that if I had been a 'good girl,' my father would forgive me for forcing her to leave and he'd love me too."

Weaver growled by her side. "That's what I mean. A child just wants to be loved, and they are so open to all influences. It's amazing that any of us can make it through childhood with our sanity intact."

That made her smile. "Maybe that's why so many of us are screwed up."

"You're not screwed up," he said instantly. "You're busy trying to unscrew all the twists and turns and emotional blackmail your father put you through. Not your fault."

"No, maybe not, but I still don't feel quite normal."

"There is no normal for anyone. That's a myth." He smiled down at her. "The trick is to find a *normal* that suits you."

She liked the sound of that. "You'd make a great psychologist. I'm glad you've gone in that direction."

"Ha." The sound he made had a little humor behind it, but was sadder. She turned to look at him. "I mean it. You're a great listener and you understand how all this works. You will be great."

He didn't look convinced. "I don't think I'm ready. I still have so much of my own crap to deal with. And I am affected by the growth of those around me."

Her gaze widened. "Why are either of those impediments?"

"They just are." He shrugged.

"No, that's your insecurity talking. Sure, you might not be ready to do this full-time today, or tomorrow even. Maybe you need to go back to school or do a practicum." She threw an arm out wide. "I don't know how this works, but it seems to me you'd be a natural. I think that's why Jenna was willing to help you with your paper. She saw the potential in you as well."

He studied her closely, as if wondering if her words had merit. "I doubt it, but thanks. And there isn't going to be a paper on the workshop. I couldn't do it. I became too attached to what was happening."

"What? But that was important to you."

"Jenna seemed to think publications would help me, so maybe she's willing to consider a different topic."

"But I thought that's why you came here this week."

"It was, but it's not why I stayed." He twisted on the bench seat until he could look at her. "I stayed because of you."

"I like the sound of that." She smiled at him. "And I'm glad you stayed, but I wish you'd been able to do the paper too."

"I needed something else from this week, and that was of more value."

"Maybe, but it seems like a waste to miss out on publishing credits."

He shrugged. "Maybe, but right now my mind is overwhelmed, and when I'm learning and growing as much as I am, it's hard to be detached."

"So leave it a week and write up something. It will be more personal. It will be your own story and referenced to those of us who were here – without names or personal information – but still valid."

The rhythmic lapping of the water drew her gaze, then he said, "We'll see. Today isn't over yet. And could still be difficult."

"I know. I have my session with Jenna tonight."

"So do I."

"What time?"

"Six-thirty."

"Oh, I'm at seven-thirty. I'd rather be earlier," she said, staring out across the water. It was glassy and calm with nary a breeze. So different from the last time she watched the boats fight against the waves. Now in contrast, sailboats lulled in the ocean, not moving, just sitting there.

She wondered at their sluggish movements. They must have motors onboard to be able to get home in weather like this. Otherwise they were stuck.

Kinda like she'd been on the first day of the course. Weaver had been her engine. He'd gotten her moving in all kinds of directions.

"We could switch if you want. Just show up with me at my time and we'll ask her." There was an odd tone in his voice. She stared at him, but he was staring moodily across the water at the same floating sailboat she had been watching earlier.

"Sure, that sounds good." And it did. She wanted it over with so she could go to her room and know this tough day was over. Being peeled from the inside out was brutal.

It hurt to have an open, constantly oozing type of wound. Then you actually gave permission for someone like Jenna to go in there and scrape out a little more. Talk about pain.

"So, food first then?" she asked, wondering if she was even

hungry. If she really wanted to be bothered. She was just so tired. And with more to come, she knew the tears would flow. Her stomach always ached then.

"Afterward," he said. "That afternoon ran really late today. It's already six o'clock. We've been sitting here like zombies for forty minutes already."

"Zombies – good term." And it made sense to eat afterward. She was a little worried about him though. There was something else bothering him and he seemed really depressed. She reached out and held his hand. "Thanks for being there today."

It crossed her mind to bring up Delaney, but at the same time she didn't. Why ruin the moment? And they were both so tired that if things got out of hand, they'd say things they would both regret. Not a good scenario. Get through tonight. Then tomorrow was the project. A project they hadn't done. She hadn't even done today's homework. She was pretty sure Weaver was in the same boat. They'd been a little too preoccupied last night to even consider homework. Now the project faced them. And she had no idea what to do about that. She kept hoping for a miracle. Some insight that would give them a quick and easy answer.

The sailboat was still wallowing on the horizon. Like she'd been doing. And like her, until that wind came along, it wasn't going anywhere.

She sighed.

Turning her into him for a hug, he asked, "You okay?"

She nodded. "I will be. I just want tonight over with."

"Me too. Let's head back. I could use another coffee."

She laughed. "We drink too much of that stuff."

"True, but it keeps me going. Especially now."

Slowly, as neither had the energy to move quickly, they

made their way back to the hotel. At the restaurant, she took a look at the food behind the counter and realized she'd had enough muffins for the day. Likely for the week. They took their coffees and meandered through the hotel until they came to the small room Jenna had been using for her one-on-one sessions.

They were early. The room was empty.

"I'm so tired I just want to sleep," she said, collapsing into a chair.

"Understandable." There was a pause then he said, "Given last night and everything else going on around here, it's amazing you are still functioning."

"True enough," she said, wondering about the sensibility of her upcoming session. "I wonder if I should try to cancel Jenna's session."

He looked at her in surprise. "Why would you do that?"

"Because I'm so tired. Because my defenses are down. Because she's likely to see way more than I want her to see."

"Isn't that a good thing?"

A laugh burbled out. "Maybe, but I still have to be strong enough to deal with the aftermath."

"True." He gave a sad sigh. "Oh so true. And tonight being the last night, it's likely to be harder than ever."

"Exactly."

There was a commotion at the door. She turned, noticing that Weaver stared straight ahead, a grim look on his face.

And watched Jenna walk in.

With Constable Delaney.

She gasped in shock and turned to face Weaver, pleading for help. But he closed his eyes and slumped into his chair.

Shit.

He already knew.

She'd been ambushed.
Betrayed.

HE WASN'T READY for this. Finally, he had found something precious and he was going to lose it. Why him? Why couldn't they have done this without him? He'd only agreed to bring her here. If she wanted to walk, they had to let her walk. Was she ready? He doubted it. But he was going to be there for her regardless. If she'd let him.

He figured she'd turn, slap him, and walk away.

And he'd lose her.

Why would she trust him after this?

He stood up and faced the other two. He nodded a greeting.

"She gets to leave if she wants to," he said in a hard voice. Yet contradicting his own words, he held Paris's hand in a tight grip. She tried to tug her hand free. He wouldn't let her. Her touch was essential. He needed the contact, even if she was unwilling. He heard her gasp and felt her shock but didn't dare look at her. Desperately, he willed her to have the strength to do this. And yet if she couldn't, he wanted her to have the opportunity to walk out.

Jenna walked forward, a lovely smile on her beautiful face. "Hi, Paris."

Paris shook her head and shuffled backward a half step. Weaver felt the movement.

He looked down at her, seeing the shakes already racking her body, and said, "This has to be her choice."

Chapter 32

JENNA SAID IN a quiet voice, "Sometimes there is more than one person who needs healing in a certain situation."

Paris froze. Weaver's hand gripped hers securely. She didn't think she could run if she tried. Had he set her up? He'd had some part in it. Is that why he'd looked so defeated? So tired?

She didn't want to be here. She didn't want to face him. Hell, she didn't want to face any of them.

But as Jenna talked, Paris realized that although the panic was at her throat and her breath refused to cooperate, her hand was gripping Weaver's as hard as his was gripping hers. She was holding on to him. Her rock.

But what if he had set her up?

It *should* matter.

Then Jenna's words hit home. Slowly, she raised her head to stare at her. She knew she looked confused and terrified. There was no way she didn't, but Jenna, outside of the very gentleness in her voice, didn't seem to care.

"And sometimes, crossing that barrier can be the hardest thing we've ever done," Jenna said. "For both parties."

Paris shook her head. What was she talking about? There weren't two parties involved. There was just her…

She dared not look at the constable.

"Constable Delaney needs to talk to you. You need to talk

to him. I'm here to facilitate that conversation if both parties are willing to let it happen. I'm not here to force it. This has to be your choice."

Tears welled up in Paris's eyes. How was any of this a choice?

"Just remember," Jenna said. "You are loved, and people want to see you through this. No matter how hard it can be."

"Hard," Paris cried. "Do you know *how* hard this is?" She still refused to look at the constable.

"No, I don't. And I can't until you tell me." Jenna was so comfortable, so calm, coming from such a heart position, it was damn hard to get mad at her for being the guardian angel of their souls whether Paris liked it or not.

"I'm sorry." That muttered, almost gruff voice came from the doorway, slightly behind Jenna. A voice from her past.

Sorry? She was so confused. Why was he sorry? Why was he even here? He was stalking her. Surely he should be in trouble for that. But no, the cops got away with murder. At that thought, her shoulders slumped and she collapsed to the chair, her hand still clutching Weaver's. No, she'd been the one to get away with murder.

The voice continued. "Years ago when I met you, I'd just joined the team and was actually brand new to your case. The rest of the team would have been better off talking to you. I know that now. Back then, I didn't. I wasn't used to talking to traumatized teens. Hadn't expected to see what I saw."

Her shoulders and chest seemed to sink in on themselves and her eyes closed tightly as memories pulled her back in time. A time when life hadn't held rainbows or unicorns. There'd only been pain and darkness.

"I said some things I shouldn't have."

He stopped for a moment, and then said. "In another circumstance the words might have been appropriate, but I read you wrong. I read the situation wrong." He took a deep breath and said, "For that, I'm sorry."

"What did you say?" Weaver asked in a hard voice.

The constable hesitated, then said, "I warned her not to do it again. That she'd liked it too much and it would become something she craved."

"It?"

"It's not my tale to tell," Delaney said. "I'd hoped to see that she'd become a wonderful adult and human being, that she'd moved past my words without a problem. But when I realized that she wouldn't see me, or acknowledge me, and worse, she ran from me – I knew my own fears had been correct."

For the first time, Paris turned to face him. The man who'd given her nightmares. The man who'd made her afraid of the one thing she'd never been afraid of before – herself.

"Paris?" Weaver asked in a hard voice. There was no arguing with that tone. He wanted to know what was going on, and he wanted to know now.

"I killed my father," she said.

She waited a beat, but there was only silence from Weaver. Silence from the other two. In a dull voice, she continued, "He beat me every day of my life. Sometimes for fun, sometimes because he was bored. Sometimes because he loved to hear me scream. And often to just punish my brother." She heard Weaver's subdued groan, but she was staring at the squiggly random pattern on the floor as her whole life had been a seemingly random pattern.

She dropped his hand and clenched her fists in her lap, the knuckles white. Weaver wouldn't want anything to do with her now. Knowing the truth, he'd know that she wasn't worthy. She didn't deserve him.

She lifted her gaze, her head was heavy with emotion, pain. "He was killing my brother, you know," she said in a calm, reasonable voice. "Daring me to do something about it. A favorite game of his. He'd beat one and yell at the other to fight him. Then he could turn and beat the second one down. Sean had been trying to save me when our father turned on him. He beat us often. Once so badly, he damaged my insides so I can't have children. In fact, surgery was required and I lost half my reproductive organs." She heard the shocked gasps from the others.

"But I'd have survived the physical damage, survived the emotional damage, except for one cop who warned me about liking it too much. That he saw how much I'd enjoyed the killing. That there was something inside of me that I needed to keep an eye on."

Delaney winced. Weaver moved forward, anger radiating from him.

"And you were right," she said calmly, her eyes shadowed with memories. "I did enjoy it. I did love knowing that he was taking his last breath while I stabbed him over and over again. I saved my brother – and likely myself."

She lifted her chin and stared defiantly at Delaney. "But you were the reason I lost sleep over and over again throughout the years. I enjoyed killing him because I'd been a beaten animal, desperate to live and to save the only other decent human being I knew in this world. I didn't enjoy the killing – I enjoyed killing *him*. Stopping him from hurting my brother. Hurting me. Over and over again. He never stopped. He was *never* going to stop."

Delaney nodded, an understanding on his face she hadn't expected to see. But the dam had been broken.

"All these years, I was afraid that I'd kill again. I went into nursing to try and help people. To absolve myself of the guilt of my actions. I love babies because I can never have them, thanks to that man who called himself my father. But more than that, a part of me was glad because it meant his evil genes couldn't be passed down through me. I was going to adopt, but that fear was always there in the back of my mind. What if I lost it and killed my own child? What if my father's evil lives in me – which it does – right?" she added in a hard mocking tone. "Because I've already killed once."

He opened his mouth to speak.

"And no," she said, steamrolling right over him. "I have no regrets – not really. I'd kill the bastard a dozen times over to save my brother. I never did it to save myself. I did it to save him."

Silence.

Then she added, "And I'd do it again." Her smile was glacier sharp, her eyes bright, hard. "And I'd enjoy it each and every time."

WEAVER STARED AT her, feeling his chest lock down and his gut slammed with pain. This was what was behind all her fears. She had killed her father.

He'd spent his lifetime looking for his father's murderer.

In stark contrast, she spent her lifetime looking at herself as her father's murderer.

Oh Jesus.

He couldn't imagine.

The room was silent. Paris stood up, tall and defiant, but he could see the thread of shivers continuously running through her. She was standing through guts alone. Then, that was Paris.

Waiting for a verdict, she stood silently. A judge and jury to take her away as she'd always suspected she deserved, or to be given a pass and would even then always wonder if she'd gotten off too lightly.

The defiance radiated from her, but not as an attitude. As a defense. She expected to be hauled out of here in handcuffs. All her life she really thought she'd done something wrong. That there was something wrong with her.

There wasn't. And to have spent a lifetime, first because of her father, then by her actions and the words of this cop – terrified of being defective – now that was criminal.

Glancing at Jenna's face, Weaver saw only compassion and maybe a hint of relief. He could relate. He was so proud of Paris.

A mixture of emotions crossed Delaney's face. Pain, regret, guilt.

Good.

The tableau had frozen and Paris's trembling increased. He knew she was heading for a complete breakdown. Calmly, steadily, he stepped to her side and hauled her up against his chest, his warmth slowing her shaking. In a voice loud enough for the rest to hear but especially so that there was no way she couldn't, he said. "And I'm glad you did."

Her back stiffened.

"Your father was a rabid animal out of control and had been for a long time. He was going to kill your brother and you eventually if you hadn't stopped him." Gently he massaged her hard, terrified muscles, hoping to find the right words to unlock a decade of fear and make it okay. "It's called self-defense for a reason."

Shaking her head, she tried twisting away from him. He

grabbed her hand back. "Not the enjoyment. I'm sick. Inside. All I could ever think of was a life without him. A life where I didn't have to be afraid. A life of peace."

She broke off as her voice broke down. Then she pulled herself back slightly and regained control. "Other people kill in self-defense if they are attacked by a home invader or something similar. Not like I did."

"No," Jenna said, her tone oozing compassion, so gentle he thought surely it would bring Paris to tears. "They hadn't spent a lifetime being beaten by the one person who was supposed to care for them. They didn't spend hours and days watching those they loved getting beaten over and over again, and neither did they have the reason to do what you did. You know he wouldn't have stopped. You knew someone would have to kill him to make him stop."

"But why me?" she cried out brokenly. "It was the best thing to have happened yet I feel so guilty. Surely there was another way?" She turned slightly away.

"Maybe," Jenna said. "But most likely not. It would have been you or Sean. You know that because no one else was there. No one else was ever there. You two fought with this man every single day, but you didn't tell anyone, did you?"

When Paris shook her head, Jenna continued. "You did what you had to do to survive. You can say you did it to save Sean, and I believe you, but you also did it to save yourself. He'd have killed you next. Eventually he would have had to. He couldn't let you live to tell anyone what he'd done, could he?"

Paris gazed at her. Weaver stood by her side, his arm around her shoulders, holding her close. He'd be damned if she was going to think she was all alone here. She wasn't.

"I'm glad you had Sean all those years," he said gently.

"You helped each other survive."

"I'd do anything for him," she whispered.

"You already did. You need to let that go."

She shook her head violently. "You can't just let something go. It's with me every single day. There isn't a day when I don't wonder if I'll ever do it again. If I might abuse a child of my own. If I might kill again."

"And that's normal and healthy," Jenna said. "We can't live with major events in our life without wondering about scenarios like that. Any more than you could sit there and wonder 'what if' you hadn't saved Sean that day? What if your mother hadn't run away? How different would your life be?"

At an odd sound beside her, she turned to Delaney.

"Barry? Do you have something to add to that point?"

He hesitated, then plunged in. "I had no idea your mother was missing. I thought she was deceased."

Paris stared at him. Weaver stared from her to him. "Do you know if she is?"

"No, I don't know, but I thought there was something in the files." He frowned. "I'm sorry. I'd have to look it up."

"She's missing," Paris said. "That's all I know. She walked away without warning."

"And who told you that?" Delaney asked.

"He did. He said she didn't want to be a mother anymore and she'd left. Pulled out in the middle of the night so she wouldn't have to face us and went back east."

The pain in her voice made Weaver want to snatch her back into his arms and take her away. But she needed to stand there and do this on her own for as long as she could.

"Did you have any communication afterwards?" Delaney asked, his voice calm, professional.

Weaver looked at him sharply then switched his gaze to

Jenna. Did they know something?

Paris shook her head. "No, my birthday was the following week, and I'd hoped she'd contact me for that. She'd made plans for a small celebration, just the three of us, but then she ran," she said bitterly. "I never saw her again."

"What kind of celebration?" Jenna asked curiously.

"I don't really know. She said I couldn't mention it ever, but that we'd have a wonderful celebration, just the three of us."

There was a long silence.

"And did you see any of her stuff after she left?"

"I saw my father bagging up her clothes and personal belongings. He threw them into the truck and we hauled it away to the dump." Now tears glistened. "I wanted to keep a few things and he laughed at me. Told me she was gone and I'd never see her again. To throw all that shit away and forget about it. And her."

"He said that you'd never see her again?"

Paris nodded and wiped at the corner of her eyes. "Yes, he said it all the time as if to torment us. She'd hated us so much she couldn't stand the thought of being around us. I figure she found her chance to run and took it. For whatever reason, she couldn't take us or didn't want to take us with her."

And finally Weaver got it.

He winced. "You think her father killed her mother, don't you?"

Chapter 33

Paris gasped, her gaze going from Weaver's to lock onto Delaney's face.

The constable shrugged. "I don't know for sure, but we certainly see that scenario over and over again in abuse situations. She might have been planning to leave with you – that might have been your birthday celebration – but he got wind of it. Tell me, were the beatings any worse afterwards?"

Paris found it hard to breathe. She remembered her mother as a gentle soul. She'd often fantasized that her mother had escaped the torture they'd all been through, but when there was never any contact, she'd lost that hope. Figured her mother had made a new life for herself. Maybe had more children.

And as the mind was wont to do, she'd considered her mother might have died, but she hadn't had any reason to believe it either way. It was easier to think she'd died in an accident and couldn't come back for them than to accept that she *wouldn't* come back.

"Is there any way to find out?" she asked. "With my father dead, we aren't likely to ever know for sure."

"Unless she's in our database as a Jane Doe."

Automatically, she nodded. There were too many shocks to know how to respond. She could only react. It hurt so much to consider her mother might be lying in a cold drawer or buried in an unmarked grave, unloved and unidentified.

"I'd like to do whatever I can to make sure she's not there."

"It's just a DNA test." He splayed out his hands. "The labs are all overworked, so there won't be any answers for a long time."

"I haven't had any answers up to now. If one day I get one, then that would bring closure."

"It might, but it's not the real issue here, Paris," Jenna spoke up. "The issue is you right now. You know your father needed to be stopped…"

"I know," Paris whispered, "But it's not easy to look at yourself and realize that you are capable of killing."

"We are all capable of killing," Jenna said, her voice a steady beacon in the storm. "And it's that much easier if you are trying to save loved ones. You aren't guilty of murder. You know that in the eyes of the law. But you are still afraid, aren't you."

Paris nodded. "What if they made a mistake?"

"They didn't," Delaney said. "The law was very clear in your case. You weren't let off the hook because you were *never* on the hook."

"And the things you said," she asked, getting more backbone into her voice. She glared at the man whose words had tormented her since forever. "You believed them."

"I did at the time – at least, I worried that they might be true." He hesitated then plunged in. "I'd just come off a particularly difficult case where a young man had murdered his entire family, including an eighteen-month-old sister. In that case, he had enjoyed it. He'd enjoyed killing each and every one of them."

At her gasp, he nodded. "So when I saw you, having just

killed your own father, I was afraid it was a similar situation, just that side of you hadn't been developed as much as this other kid. I didn't want it to be true. I could see something in there, inside of you, but didn't know what I was seeing. I warned you to be careful and not let that feeling be something you chased. Because once you start killing for your highs in life, there's no way to stop."

She shook her head violently. "There was no high. I was sick for days. I couldn't keep food down and I couldn't stop shaking."

"Shock," Jenna said, "and to be expected. And before we gloss over this, it's important to understand that at that moment in time when you were saving Sean, you did enjoy it. You enjoyed finally being able to take control. Finally, you could do something about the pain and torment."

"I didn't enjoy it as much as I was so damn glad that I'd done it. That I'd picked up that knife and stopped him. I didn't think, honestly. I just reacted." Tears started pouring down her cheeks. "I kept telling him to stop, that he was killing him. He answered, 'Perfect. Good riddance to another one.'"

"Another?" asked Delaney. "Don't you see? In all likelihood, he killed your mother before you. You'd have been dead next."

She stared at him, hating the words, the concept, but realizing that he might be right. Relief bloomed ever so lightly inside. Like a tiny unfurling bit of hope. Maybe her mother hadn't abandoned her. "Maybe that's why she never came back for me."

Weaver squeezed her shoulder, making her aware for the first time that she'd spoken out loud. "She'd have come back if she could, you know that."

"I want to know that," she corrected. "But chances are, we'll never know for sure."

"I'd have to check out the files back then. See if a missing person's report was filed."

"He wouldn't have filed it," Paris said. "He wanted her gone. At least, he often made comments afterwards." Rubbing her pounding temple, she couldn't remember anything clearly anymore.

"I always knew she was gone for good." She was exhausted and worn out, but she realized what she'd always known inside. Her mother wasn't *ever* coming back. She couldn't. She was dead. Her childhood dreams of her mother escaping to a better life, maybe coming back to save her and Sean, were just that – dreams. Happier stories to help her get through the days.

"He killed her." She crumpled into a chair, her legs too weak to let her stand. "I think I always knew inside."

"Most likely he did. It would fit the pattern," Delaney said. "And given that, knowing he killed your mother, do you still think you did wrong? That you'd kill heedlessly in the future?"

Dazed, she stared at him, trying to assimilate what she knew now to her life, her thoughts, and her pain. Her future.

She shook her head. "Never." She held up a hand. "Unless someone was hurting those I love."

Weaver, the constable, and Jenna all spoke up at the same time and said the same word.

"Exactly."

Her gaze went from one to the other, hoping, searching, wanting to see the truth of their words.

And saw what she needed to see – her heart exploded with relief.

And she burst into tears.

WEAVER SNAGGED HER up and squeezed her tight. That she went into his arms so easily bruised his heart. She'd been through so much. Her and her brother. He closed his eyes and held her close, breathing deeply at all he had just learned. In the background, he could hear the cop speaking with Jenna. There was something about checking when the cop got back to the office. Weaver doubted that they'd find anything about Paris's mother after all this time. After all, look at his father's case. It was still open. However, she could now open a missing person's file on her mother and they'd learn what there was to learn. It was something.

If it wasn't enough, then he could help her deal with that.

That was a truth he'd been living for a long time.

If they did find out the truth, good or bad, he could help her deal with those issues too. In fact, he'd just like to be there to help her in whatever way he could. She'd helped him. He'd moved past many issues. Just from being around her, seeing her perspective.

And updating his own. That had been his problem – hanging onto the hurt. Paris had been badly hurt and had made it her goal to stuff it deep inside and go on in spite of it. In his case, he'd let the hurt stop him. He could have had relationships since his wife walked out. But he hadn't. It was easier not to. He had a tough childhood, but even his mother had been working on cleaning up her act.

He hadn't.

He didn't know if he believed it or not, but that was his past conditioning judging her. It was time to release that. Let it go and let her go. She was trying – that was all anyone could wish for.

Maybe he could check in on her. See if she wanted to see him. See if she wanted the connection. See if there was a connection to build on.

If not, nothing changed. But if there was, then like Paris said, he'd done without a mother for a long time.

Maybe it was time to change that.

Chapter 34

Paris stood in the circle of Weaver's arms. The stuffing was gone from her insides. If he hadn't been holding her up, she'd have slid to the floor a long time ago.

She didn't know where to go from here. Her history, her interpretation of events, the hurts, the pain, the sense of abandonment. Everything had changed. All of this information rolled around inside her head. Think about things – or maybe not think, just let sensations rise and fall. Let the lies fall away. The emotions rise and dissipate. Her life was changing from this point forward.

Thank heavens.

As if understanding, Weaver tightened his grip around her. Had he been a part of this? She figured he had. Was she upset about that? She had been earlier. Now... now she understood... maybe. Except her mind couldn't reconcile betrayal and helping. When did one become the other?

Then she heard voices in the background. Constable Delaney.

Should she let *him* off the hook? She understood now what he'd gone through. Where he'd been at in his life when he'd spoken to her. What his mental process had been coming in.

She'd been terrified back then. Had been looking for bogeymen in her world and with her father gone, she'd placed

Delaney in his spot. Especially with the power of the law he wielded firmly behind him.

He hadn't deserved it. He'd been trying to warn her, to keep her on the straight and narrow. To be good for the rest of her life. He hadn't meant to terrify her. Okay, maybe he had, but not to panic her.

Not to have her question everything she did in light of his warning. But she had.

If he hadn't warned her, what would she have done differently? She'd still be afraid that she was too much like her own father. She'd still be worried that she wouldn't be a good parent. The conflict over not being able to have children would remain.

As if he heard the mess in her head, Constable Delaney said to Jenna, "She'd been badly hurt for years. But a month or two prior to the final blow, she'd been hospitalized with internal injuries."

Those memories washed through her. The pain. The shock. The dismay at learning she'd never have children.

The conversation still threaded through the air around them, and she knew she had to finish this. Gathering up her courage, she stepped back from Weaver's arms and turned to face the cop. Her hand entwined with Weaver's, a reassuring contact that she wasn't alone.

"I don't blame you for what you said that day." Her tone was harsher than she wanted it to be. Her words sharper.

With a sigh, she tried again. "I was so traumatized back then that your words just added to the rest of the nightmare in my life," she said. "I survived that childhood by learning to hold everything inside. So on the outside I looked calm and in control, cold even, whereas on the inside I was waiting for my world to blow up." She paused, adding, "I knew I'd done something horribly wrong in the eyes of society, so even though everyone at the time said I'd done what I needed to do and wouldn't be charged, I couldn't believe them. Your words aligned closer to the fears inside and meant you were more likely to be right than the others."

Weaver squeezed her hand. She smiled, staring down at their linked fingers, "So your words were the ones I remembered the most."

Delaney nodded. "It was that calm that worried me." He waited then added, "And I'm sorry for adding to your pain back then. You'd been through enough already. If I had a chance to do it all over again, I'd have approached the case very differently," he said, his tone apologetic yet sincere. "You've been on my mind since. I worried about you. When I saw you here...well, I'd hoped to clear the air."

For the first time, a natural smile crossed her lips. "And you did. Thank you for being persistent enough to push this. I wouldn't have done it without that." She slid a sideways look at Weaver. "I caught sight of you and Weaver speaking together this morning. I got quite a jolt."

She felt Weaver start, and then he squeezed her hand again.

"Has he been plotting this meeting then?" she asked.

"No," Delaney said. "I'd been trying to convince him to talk you into seeing me." The older man smiled. "He refused to do anything out of your comfort zone and wouldn't do anything to hurt you. He's been very protective."

"But I did know they'd be here tonight," Weaver said heavily. "I'm sorry, but this was something you had to do. An opportunity to deal with a huge issue."

She nodded absently, remembering the sadness in his voice, the sense of finality she remembered. As if the workshop was coming to an end, and so was their relationship.

Maybe it was at that. She was confused and overwhelmed, as if her past had been rewritten. But along with that crazy array of emotions was a lot of confusion over her feelings for him and his involvement.

Last night was too special. Today's ups and downs – traumatic.

So much had happened in such a short time she didn't know what she should feel no matter what she *did* feel. And could she trust any of it given the tumultuous events?

"As much as I don't appreciate the collaborative effort – I do appreciate it," she said quietly. "I wasn't strong enough to get here on my own."

"I didn't want to deceive you."

"But you had to." She nodded. "Got it."

But she dropped his hand, unable to reconcile the issue. She stared down at the floor, confusion and heartache twisting her up inside. Was it a good thing what he'd done? It was time to let this all go. But could she? Was it a betrayal? Yes. Did she want to forgive him? Hell yes. Could she? She had no idea.

The whole mess was exhausting. From the bad day, now the evening. She'd planned on dinner with Weaver and spending the night with him but had no idea where all of this left her. Left them.

Did he want to move forward, or was this over for him? Was this his goodbye? Not that it made any sense, but then nothing did right now.

Glancing over at Jenna, she saw her conversing quietly with Delaney. Paris didn't know if she was supposed to stay for her session tonight or if this was it. She hoped it was done – as in she was too tired for more analyzing. Especially her own psyche.

She needed to leave.

She needed to sort out the confusion going on.

She needed...she didn't know what.

Then she saw exactly what she needed. She burst into tears and ran.

Into the arms of the man who stood in the doorway.

Sean.

WEAVER WATCHED PARIS bolt and throw herself into the arms of a stranger.

Or maybe not. The two looked close enough to be family. And he knew. This was her brother Sean. The one whose life she saved.

He studied the man carefully, but all he really needed to see was the naked love in his face. This man cared about Paris like Weaver hadn't ever seen anyone care before.

Weaver's childhood had been shitty. But for these two, well, there were no words.

They'd been close during the abuse trying to help each other, and now that bond was even stronger today. He didn't know if Sean had come on his own or if he'd been called. For Paris's case, it was a good thing. But it also reminded him of his role in this. She'd turned away from him.

She'd gone running to Sean.

She didn't know or trust him.

She trusted and loved her brother.

He wasn't jealous of the bond between the siblings. But he'd love to be inside that inner circle. Unfortunately, the bond between family members, in this case brothers and sisters, often wasn't elastic enough to let others inside. This insight into the family unit hurt. It made him feel like a kid again when he hadn't belonged anywhere. Not even with his wife. She'd gone back to her family and left him behind. Now here, again, he was on the outside looking in.

Not that there wasn't room for him in the circle. But as yet, he hadn't been invited in.

Then he watched Paris take a step back, her face streaming with tears but smiling and laughing. She opened her arms to a woman standing just to the side. A woman whose face was badly disfigured, but her smile was stunning, showing the beauty within. From Paris's conversation, he realized this must be Robin. The woman Sean had met here at the seminar.

If there was a way to leave quietly, he'd slip out and go to his room. Leave Paris her privacy. Something he'd like right now, but there was no way to escape.

He felt disconnected. Uncomfortable. Unsure. Watching the tableau in front of him, he settled into a wider stance, crossed his arms, and waited.

CHAPTER 35

PARIS'S HEART SWELLED to bursting and then washed clean. A river of emotions flowed through her. So much pain. So much heartache. So much fear and so much love. For Weaver for making her do this. For Jenna who'd helped make this happen. For Sean who'd shown up to help her. She didn't know if he'd been called in to help her or if he'd instinctively known she was struggling to the point of no return.

And then there was Robin. That she'd come to support her was huge.

She had no idea how they'd been able to get in, but she was damn grateful they were here. Even more grateful that she could say, "I'm okay."

Sean, his hands clamped on her shoulders, held her back slightly so he could look into her eyes. Whatever he saw there made him smile. He tugged her closer and hugged her hard. "I'm very glad to hear that."

"Did you come down to try and talk me into seeing Delaney?"

Sean nodded. "Absolutely. This was *the* biggie in your world, and I would have done anything to help you get past it."

She wiped the tears from her eyes, gulping in fresh air. "Thank you."

"Don't thank me," he said easily. "I can't ever thank you

enough for what you did."

"No thanks necessary." Smiling up mistily at her brother, she hugged him close. "I'm just sorry I didn't do it before he beat you so badly."

Sean shook his head. "It's over. We need to move on. We're good at that."

His gaze lifted and he surveyed the few people in the room. She could tell who he was looking at by the way his gaze changed. It softened when he came to Jenna, hardened when he glanced at Delaney, and widened when his all-too-perceptive gaze landed on Weaver.

Sean slanted a questioning gaze at her.

And damn if she didn't blush.

His grin was wide enough to split his face. "Jenna's magic maybe?"

"Maybe," she muttered in a low voice. "But maybe not. He was part of this."

"Good. I like him already."

She gasped and slapped him lightly. "That's not fair."

"Doing what needs to be done regardless of the personal cost to him is huge. And don't kid yourself about a huge personal cost in this case because there was – still is from the look on his face. As if he'd like to be a million miles away."

She stiffened and turned to face Weaver, but he was staring at Jenna and Delaney, an odd look on his face.

And she realized Sean was right. If he cared…he'd taken a huge risk of losing her if it ended up that his actions were so big she couldn't get over it.

"It's the betrayal," she murmured to her brother. "Aren't you supposed to support someone by not turning them in?"

"Unless turning them in is the only way for them to move forward. In this case, you weren't going to see Delaney on your own. You needed to do this," he said seriously. "And doing what needs to be done is painful, and it's also painful for those around you."

"It could have backfired on him," she said, studying the cold detached look on his face.

"It did backfire on him."

She spun to look at her brother. "Why do you say that?"

"Because he's standing over there all alone. You're here with me, wondering what to do about him."

"I'm just still in shock... confused maybe," she protested, "I guess. I don't know. So much stuff has just happened that he's mixed up in that mess in my mind."

"Then separate him from that. He did what you weren't strong enough to do. That is worth so much. And if he's here, he's got his own problems and you're going to be triggering those."

Shit. She flinched, remembering his ex-wife who'd decided he was part of her past and she'd grown past him. Paris had just *done* something similar.

Her brother spoke quietly to her. "Now that I know you're going to be okay, I'm taking Robin out for dinner. Go talk to him."

She stepped forward and hugged him. "Thank you," she whispered. With a misty smile, she reached up and kissed him on the cheek then stepped back. "Best brother ever."

"Then go deal with the next problem."

Robin grinned at his side. "Then bring him for dinner on Sunday. We'd love to meet him."

Paris's gaze widened over the easy acceptance on their part. And she realized there was no guarantee about this outcome. "We'll see if I can fix this."

Sean's smile was breathtakingly full of love. "You can fix

this. If you want to. You already know you'll do anything to save someone you love."

He took Robin's hand in his and with a gentle smile, they turned and walked out.

Delaney stepped forward and held out his hand. "You've become a beautiful woman inside and out. You always had that potential, but now you've grown into that promise. Congratulations, and I'm so sorry for my part that hurt you, scared you, or caused you any discomfort since we met." He shook her hand, gave her a sad smile, and walked out.

Now she had to face Jenna.

"Did you call Sean?" she asked Jenna.

"No." Jenna shook her head. "He's always known when you needed him. The same as you knew when he needed you, didn't you?"

Surprised, Paris thought back to that fateful day when she'd come running to her brother's aid. "I hadn't thought of it that way."

"Well, it is that way, and the good thing is you didn't need him this time. By the time he understood you were in trouble and the time it took for him to get here, you'd dealt with it." Her lips curled into a delighted smile. "I'm proud of you."

Paris started. "I'm not proud of me. I should have done this a long time ago," she muttered.

Jenna's beautiful laugh rang free. "Hindsight is always a gift. You weren't capable of doing anything about it before. You are now."

"And thanks for that."

"You owe Weaver thanks for that, too." She reached out a hand and clasped Paris on the shoulder. "We'd asked him earlier to help you and he refused. He didn't think you were ready and didn't want to do anything to hurt you."

Paris stared at her numbly. "He did?"

"He did. Today he knew you were running out of time, and he refused to do anything other than ask you to come – it was his condition that you be allowed to leave if you still weren't ready." Jenna stepped to the side. "So keep that in mind when you go to speak to him."

Paris was still standing in shock and dismay as Jenna walked around her and left the room. Paris spun around to face Weaver, wondering what to say. What could she say?

Only to realize she was alone. He'd already walked out.

WEAVER TOOK THE opportunity when she was busy talking to Delaney to slip away. He'd been walked out on before – not nice. There was no way he would stay there and wait for Paris's rejection. The awkward explanations. Difficult good byes. Been there and done that. What was that lesson he'd not learned? Oh yeah, don't fall for women who were in therapy.

Too bad he couldn't seem to remember that lesson before he got involved.

Pissed and hurt and afraid to look at his future, he made his way out the door and just kept walking. For hours. He needed to give her time. Anything less wasn't fair. But he didn't have to like it. Neither did he want to say goodbye.

He'd let her off easy. There had been enough heartache and trouble in her life already. Hell, she'd probably already let him go.

It was the way of healing. She'd moved on now.

Except they still had tomorrow to get through.

Tonight was a write off. Glancing at this watch, he was not surprised to see it was after nine already. He wished it were after midnight. Then he could go to bed. Not that he'd sleep. There was no way to get the thoughts of her out of his mind.

He'd hurt her.

There was no way around that. She'd consider it a betrayal. It wasn't. He'd done it because he cared about her. Knew she had to take this step. Felt like he had no choice if they wanted a future together. But damn, that was arrogant of him. It was her life. She had a right to take the steps she needed to take on her own time. In her own way.

He'd overstepped his boundaries. He'd been worried about that. That she'd blame him. But Jenna had convinced him otherwise. Still, he'd made sure she had the choice.

Only really – what choice did she have?

When there in the room, cornered by everyone – had she had a choice? Yes. But not much of one. And not an easy one to exercise. She'd not had access to the doorway to be able to leave, Jenna and Delaney had filled it.

Paris had to face them.

So she'd been coerced.

And he'd been a part of it.

Not liking himself very much at the moment, he sat dry-eyed on the same bench they'd sat on earlier today as the wind picked up around him. Leaving him cold – inside and out.

He had to trust she'd see his point of view. Believe in him. Believe in what they had.

Because really – given the choice – he'd do it all over again.

Because she was special.

He was... less so.

He'd learned more than he thought possible about himself – and her – during this workshop. Arriving with a pompous attitude and superior sense of self, he'd thought he was comfortable here at this place in his life. After all, he'd already done a ton of work on himself. To a certain point he was. But this workshop had shown him that he had further to go than he'd thought. Some of those steps he'd taken unknowingly.

Some of them lay before him.

He'd always felt unloved. That was his childhood speaking again. Memories rippled through his mind...maybe if his father had cared more for his son than that damn car, he wouldn't have gotten himself killed. If he'd been more lovable, then his mother would have preferred him to her bottle. Then there was his wife. She'd obviously not loved him either. Not if he had been a stepping stone to what she'd really wanted in life.

Up until now, he hadn't realized how much he'd tried to keep people at a distance so he wouldn't get hurt if they rejected him. He could have walked over to Paris's brother and introduced himself. Instead...he'd been the one to walk away. Escape rather than face them.

Like a little boy who had been rejected so many times, he was hell bent on rejecting everyone else first so he didn't have to deal with the pain again. He hadn't given them a chance to love him because he'd already assumed they wouldn't.

Hadn't he grown up at all? Why was he still giving that little boy so much credit for who he was now? Especially when he'd thought he'd walked away from that type of behavior a long time ago.

And what the hell was he going to do about it now?

Chapter 36

Paris shifted her position. The hallway floor was damn uncomfortable. She'd been waiting for hours. Her coffee cup was long empty. Then again, so was the one she brought for Weaver. It was after midnight and there was no sign of him.

She didn't know what to think. Had he left the workshop? Gone somewhere else for the night? If so – where? And was he coming back?

This couldn't end like this. She owed him an apology and if she were honest – a thank you. Sure it had been a shock and a tough thing to wrap her mind around, but now that she was on the other side of the meeting, she was emotionally drained but in a good way. It was a good thing he had done for her. But then he was going into the same profession as Jenna, so it made sense that he would.

Now that she'd gotten over her shock and come to understand, she wanted to be adult about all of this. But it wasn't going to happen if she couldn't connect with him. They still had to do a stupid project. And she had no idea what to do about that. She'd been hoping he'd have a miracle tucked up his sleeve that would save both their asses.

At this point, she was so exhausted, she figured she'd tell Jenna that she'd come up blank and had no project to hand in. What could Jenna do after all?

The hard floor woke her first. And movement. She groaned as she straightened, slowly getting to her feet.

And realized she wasn't alone.

Weaver stood frowning down at her.

She swayed. He grabbed her, holding her upright.

"Sorry, didn't meant to fall asleep," she whispered. "So tired."

"Shh." He unlocked his door and pushed the door open. "You should be in bed."

She closed her eyes and tried to open them again when the world went spinning out of control. She was lifted and carried into the bedroom, briefly put back on her feet, then laid down on the cool sheets.

"Need to talk," she murmured, shivering.

A blanket was tossed over her shoulders, and Weaver's deep voice said, "Sleep. We'll talk in the morning."

She slept.

With a smile on her face.

WEAVER STARED DOWN at her with mixed emotions. In the beginning, he'd tried to detach and had given that up early on when he realized he was already involved. Opening up to caring was painful. With her here in his bed, their future unsure – it was even more painful. "What the hell am I going to do with you," he murmured.

"Love me," she answered, but the words were so faint, her voice so low he thought he dreamt it. Wishful thinking on his part.

"I got that part covered," he whispered, his heart overflowing with emotions.

There were huge black circles under her eyes, and even

under the blankets he could see the shivers making her thin frame shake. With a muttered curse, he quickly undressed and got in on the other side. She immediately rolled over and cuddled close.

As dawn crept forward, he realized he'd have to wake early and be ready for that talk they desperately needed to have.

They should have done it tonight – earlier. He'd do it now, but emotions were still hot and they were both exhausted. He doubted he could wake her enough to be cognizant at this point. No, risky as it was, he'd hold her close to his heart all night and hope that they could work through this in the morning.

He had a lot to think about. A lot of himself to assess. She'd done so much. Achieved so much. She'd shown him how to step up. He wasn't proud of his own actions. His own thoughts. But he knew he could change. Do what needed to be done to move forward. He wasn't a little kid anymore. It was time to leave all that hurt behind. Sure, it would rear up from time to time, but he didn't have to let the pain and fear control him.

Not any longer.

As he thought about the workshop and all he'd been through, both as an attendee and an observer, he thought again about the paper he'd planned to write.

Paris was right. He should do it.

But not about her. Not about the others.

But about him. She was right about that too. His experiences. His personal journey. His personal transformation.

Because that's what this week had been all about. He needed to let the image of who he was fall away, acknowledging that the hurt little boy still lived inside but no longer allowing him to rule his adult self.

And let his authentic self step forward.
What he had found with Paris was unique.
He'd do whatever he could to keep her in his life.
What they had together… it was so worth fighting for.

Chapter 37

Paris woke slowly. Heat from a furnace blasted all around her. It felt deliciously wonderful. She sighed and shifted, wincing at something digging into her side. Her bra strap?

She came aware in an instant. She lay in the unfamiliar room long enough to reorient herself and realize that Weaver slept beside her, his arm around her waist even now keeping her close, protecting her.

Again.

She hadn't done anything for him.

How sad. Relationships were supposed to be partnerships. She hadn't contributed anything.

Shifting, she groaned as the waistband of her pants tugged at her skin. Her dry, irritated skin. Shower time. She felt like crap, her eyelids heavy and caked with sleep. She slipped out of the bed and winced. Sleeping in clothes sucked.

Her shoes were on the floor by the bed. Quietly, she put them on and snuck her way to the door. This was not how she wanted him to see her. She looked and felt disgusting.

With a last glance, she realized he was sleeping heavily. She was instantly jealous. She'd tossed and turned all night.

Back in her room, she stripped and stepped under the hot running water, groaning in joy as her sore aching body eased back and her tender flesh shifted and moved freely. After a long soak and several washes of her hair, she turned off the water, better prepared to start the day.

Inside, she still felt like someone had reefed her insides out, put them under a microscope for a closer look, then stuffed them back in again.

Yesterday's session had been brutal. Last night's session…well, there weren't words.

But it was over.

And she'd survived.

Now to make it through today and she'd be good. This workshop had been intensive, deadly, and so worthwhile, but she wanted one more thing from it.

She wanted Weaver.

They needed to talk. If they had talked last night, it would have been better. Instead, he'd disappeared and she'd been exhausted – inside and out – and after searching, had parked herself outside his door waiting for him to come back. She'd wanted to spend the night with him – and she had, but not the way she intended.

It was also lousy to go to bed with her clothes on and wake up the same way.

Dressed, she checked the time. He needed to be woken up to get downstairs in time for the morning. If he cared to go. She also had to check out of the hotel. Did he? She packed up quickly and grabbed her card key. She'd leave her bag at the front desk while in the morning session.

Outside at the hallway, she walked across and knocked on Weaver's doorway. No answer.

"Weaver? We're late. Time to get moving."

No answer. Damn.

She picked up her bag and walked to the elevator. Maybe she could call him from the front desk. After she finished paying for her hotel room and left her bag with them, she tried to call his room and got no answer.

Not sure what else to do, she walked to the restaurant and grabbed two coffees and two muffins for the last time, carrying them to the conference room.

There were a few people working hard on filling out the last of the worksheets, ones she hadn't done either. The others worked on their projects. Something else she hadn't done. A hell of a morning.

Setting her load down, she grabbed her homework, quickly finished the first sheet, then came to her original ripped up, folded up mess of a sheet from the first day here.

The one she'd written on about killing her father.

And realized how far she'd come. The dreams she'd now be able to create and the pain she'd released.

Reading through the questions on her worksheet, she grinned. This one she might be able to do something with.

She quickly filled in the blanks and finished that part of her homework.

Then she pulled out her sheet with notes on the project. There was essentially nothing there. No instructions. Just something visual.

She sighed. Great. She could sing a song, do a dance, and draw little stick figures. Anything else? Hell no.

As she sat there frowning at the last assignment and in truth the biggest one, she was at a loss. She had no idea what to do.

All she could do was tell Jenna.

As she pondered the effects of actually not doing something for once, of failing…Jenna walked in. And Paris's stomach knotted.

Her mind whispered through all the past conditioning of

failing, and she realized that it no longer mattered. Sure, failing and doing something wrong might give her some grief depending on the situation, but it wasn't going to get her a beating. Jenna might not be happy with her, but she wasn't going to hurt her over it.

In fact...

She might actually be fine with it.

Feeling lighter and easier and happier than she had been in a long time, she took a sip of coffee and realized the second cup of coffee was missing. Somehow, Weaver had slipped into his place beside her without her noticing.

Her whole body lit up. She smiled up at him. "Hey," she whispered, "I didn't see you come in."

His gaze was steady and searching. "You were deep in contemplation mode."

"Yeah, a lot of that going on this morning."

"And how are you?"

"Fine." She straightened, wanting to break down the strangeness between them. "Actually better than fine. I feel good. Younger. Freer."

"Good. That's the way it's supposed to be."

Jenna spoke up then, taking the attention off them and back to the program. They'd be given an hour to finish up their projects as several were done already and she'd be speaking with them at the back. Mid-morning, she had guest speakers coming in to talk to the group. There'd be a final lecture and time for questions, then they were free to go.

"What the hell are we going to do about this project?" she muttered. "I'm of half a mind to not do it."

He laughed. "I hear you. But I think that it's supposed to be an important step for our growth."

"Great, another one. So not. So, suggestions." She gave

him a wry look. "We have less than an hour."

He grinned. "I do. It's more me doing something."

"Hey, I'm good with that," she joked.

"Okay, so let's ask you. I need a sheet of paper that has some of the toughest things written down on it. Something that you wish you didn't have to write, but they are honest and true and painful."

"Like Jenna's lovely worksheets?"

"Sure, that would be perfect."

She dug into her class assignments and pulled out three that had been ugly to do. "Will these work?" she asked.

"Yes, and this one…" he snagged up the ripped up sheet. "I gather the thing you wished you'd never done and ripped out of here was killing your father."

She sighed and nodded.

"Good." He stood up. "Have your coffee. I got this."

And he took her worksheets and walked out of the room.

She watched him leave until he turned down the hallway. She didn't have a clue what to do now. Normally she was the one who did everything. Even double-checking that everything was done correctly. Instead, this time she sat there and let him do everything.

As she sat, she realized *she* had transformed in the last five days. Even if Weaver was doing the final project for them both, Paris felt she should do something too. But nothing came to mind. No, Jenna had said *visual*. How the hell did a non-artistic person do something visual? Maybe she'd actually fail this part of the workshop.

She didn't have a picture of Delaney anywhere that she could use right now but if she had, she'd glue Weaver's face over the top.

Although that was an insult to Weaver.

Instead of making her cringe, she was okay with that. So maybe with this project she wasn't going to do well. That was all right too. She'd already done phenomenally well.

She'd have to take what she could get. Besides, she was well satisfied with her progress. Delighted actually.

An hour passed.

And another half an hour. No Weaver, and so far Paris hadn't been called to the back.

Good thing.

Then Jenna walked toward her. "Paris and Weaver – your turn."

Paris stood up and walked to the far corner where Jenna had set up a space for the projects. She took a glance around the room. No Weaver.

Okay, here it went. She took a deep breath and said, "I didn't do the final project."

Jenna's gaze widened, but not in shock. Surprise and then…joy shone in that gaze. As if Paris had done something wonderful.

She motioned for Paris to sit. "Now tell me how you feel."

"Like I didn't do what I was supposed to do," she confessed. "I don't feel like I failed, but that I should have tried harder."

"And when were you going to do that?" Jenna joked. "You've been through a lot lately."

"True, and honestly I owe my transformation to Weaver," she said. "He's been working on me since the beginning of the week. I know about the paper that he set aside for me. It caused me a lot of trouble at the beginning, but then I forgot about it. He was there when I needed him and often when I didn't. He didn't let me wallow or hide away even when I wanted to."

She gazed down at the files sitting in front of Jenna on the table. Hers and Weaver's folders both with photos clipped to the top. An idea came to her.

Someone called to Jenna. She stood up and excused herself for a moment and walked across the room.

Perfect.

Paris grinned, leaned forward, and snagged up both photos. Grabbing a pair of scissors sitting in a container with pens, she quickly cut what she'd wanted to and with the glue stick found in the same container, she glued the cut pieces together. Feeling like a kid in primary school but having fun anyway, she quickly created her visual.

There.

"Weaver..." Jenna said from behind her. "There you are."

"Sorry, it took me a little longer to do this right."

Paris looked up and gasped. "Oh my."

Weaver had created dozens of tiny origami birds from her worksheets and tied a fine string – dental floss, maybe, to each one. They hung from several coffee cups glued together as a hanging mobile.

"That is...beautiful." And it was. Delicate, imaginative, and so very appropriate.

"Stupid," he said. "But the theme was transformation. So I took her worksheets. The ones she'd worked hard on, cried tears over, and generally worked her ass off to do and transformed them to the wishes and dreams she'd hoped for and was working toward. Created these tiny birds to remind her of those dreams and all the hard work she'd put in to get here...and that she had the ability to make them take off and be something."

Paris barely heard, her eyes glued on the brilliant art piece.

The birds were tiny, maybe an inch across and created from folded paper done so well that she had a hard time seeing the details until she looked closer. He'd written little words on their wings. Children. Family. Freedom.

She sat back, stunned.

"That is amazing." She laughed, tears forming in the corner of her eyes. "And the best use of those damn worksheets I'd ever seen."

Jenna looked pained. "Hey, I worked hard to create those for you guys."

"And you did a great job. They are intensive, deep, and painful. But this..." Paris put her hand to her breast. "This is the best thing ever."

Impulsively, Paris jumped up and threw her arms around Weaver and kissed him. "Thank you."

With his free arm, he hugged her close. "Don't thank me. You lived this transformation." He gave the art piece a little shake. "But I watched it happen. So it was very visual for me."

Misty-eyed, she pulled him close. "Thanks. For being here all week. It was a tough time."

"But you got through it," he said firmly, "and you are in a much better place now."

She nodded, but sensing a distancing from him, she tightened her grasp and looked him in the eye. "True. And I couldn't have done it without you." At his head shake, she grinned. "Sure, I *might* have done this without you, but I'm glad I didn't have to. I'm glad you were there and that you stood by me. I know I put you in a tough spot, and so did Jenna and Delaney. I understand that you're afraid I'm like your ex-wife and will walk away when I grow past this issue." At his widening gaze, she shook her head and said, "But you're wrong. I know what I want. I always have. I know how to get it most times, too."

She paused, remembered what she had in her hands, and chuckled. "And just in case you thought that I am making this up, maybe you should see the corny amateur project I was about to hand over."

"What?"

She handed him her project – upside down.

He glanced over at Jenna, who shrugged her shoulders as she hadn't seen it yet, then slowly turned it over.

She'd taken both photos and glued them together and cut as they were, they were in the shape of a heart, both halves mostly complete but overlapping in a way that made them one.

"See," she whispered, "You're not in this alone. I'm here too."

And she reached up and clasped his hand that held the photos.

He gazed at the photos, his throat moving, then slowly lifted his gaze to her. The moist brightness in them made her heart squeeze tight. He went to say something, only he couldn't get the words out.

Snatching her up into his arms, he buried his head in her hair.

"You win," he whispered. "Your project is the best."

"No," she whispered right back. "We both win. Because we found each other."

And she pulled back to look up at him, adding, "Thank heavens."

And with the photo crushed between them, he lowered his head and kissed her.

Author's Note

Thank you for reading Broken but… Mending! If you enjoyed the book, please take a moment and leave a short review.

Dear reader,

I love to hear from readers, and you can contact me at my website: www.dalemayer.com or at my Facebook author page. To be informed of new releases and special offers, sign up for my newsletter. And if you are interested in joining Dale Mayer's Fan Club, here is the Facebook sign up page.

Cheers,
Dale Mayer

If you'd like to read about other books I've written, please turn the page.

Your Free Book Awaits!

KILL OR BE KILLED

Part of an elite SEAL team, Mason takes on the dangerous jobs no one else wants to do – or can do. When he's on a mission, he's focused and dedicated. When he's not, he plays as hard as he fights.

Until he meets a woman he can't have but can't forget. Software developer, Tesla lost her brother in combat and has no intention of getting close to someone else in the military. Determined to save other US soldiers from a similar fate, she's created a program that could save lives. But other countries know about the program, and they won't stop until they get it – and get her.

Time is running out ... For her ... For him ... For them ...

DOWNLOAD a *complimentary* copy of MASON? Just tell me where to send it!

http://dalemayer.com/sealsmason/

Previews

Second Chances – Book 1!

Go ahead. Take Charge of your life. Move forward...if you can...

Changing her future means letting go of her past. Karina heads to a weekend seminar and discovers the speaker is the person she needs to move on from. But she soon realizes bigger issues are facing her...

Brian has moved on, at least he'd believed he had... until he sees Karina in his audience...and realizes he's been lying to himself.

Passion pulls them together, love binds them together, but a revengeful enemy determines to keep the two apart...and destroy them both.

Second Chances Sample

Chapter 1

HER HEART RACING, Karina pushed open the glass double doors and walked into the almost deserted pub. Her breath quickened as she searched the faces of the few patrons inside. *Had he left already?* Or was Brian Saunders somewhere here, drowning his sorrows? Wendy, Brian's girlfriend of two years, had broken up with him and taken off for Europe, or some such thing. Karina knew she should feel sorry for him, but instead her mind wouldn't stop pestering her.

Here's your chance. One last shot to make him notice you before you go home and never see him again.

That the timing sucked wouldn't stop her.

Besides, if anyone asked, she was just here having a drink. And she could use one. Her last exam was done. She'd finally finished school and damn if she didn't feel like crying instead of cheering.

"Hey, Karina, thought you'd have booked it by now."

She waved at one of several friends having a good time at a nearby table. Most of the students who'd finished exams had already left, and the few stragglers writing tomorrow were either cramming or here trying to forget about writing in the morning.

"Nah. Leaving in the morning. It's a long drive and I *so*

don't want to deal with that tonight. Or the ferry."

That elicited several nods. Anyone who lived on Vancouver Island knew about ferry woes to the mainland. She'd tossed around the idea of staying on the island, had even looked for work, but nothing had come of it, so she was heading home to Vancouver. Victoria, and the university in particular, would stay a happy memory. And, in some ways, a tough one.

She ordered a draft at the bar and turned around to take another look. Maybe she'd missed Brian in her first skim.

Shit. Ian Blackburn was here, too. And he'd seen her. Shit, shit, and triple shit. He'd always been super friendly to her, but there was something about him that gave her the creeps. And then last week she'd seen another side of him altogether. A professor in one of the classes they'd been in together had given Ian a poor grade on an assignment. Ian had lost it…big time. Someone had even called campus security to get him out of the lecture hall. He'd turned into something that terrified her and probably every other student there. She shuddered at the memory.

Karina turned around and glanced the other way, deliberately putting her back to Ian.

And there he was. *Brian.*

Her heart sighed even as it started to pound. She should go over to him. He looked sad, like he'd lost his best friend. Which, after the end of a two-year relationship, she guessed he had. But Karina told herself she was still a friend, right? Albeit a casual one, but still… They'd had classes together, the odd beer-and-pizza night as part of a group. That kind of thing. He had no idea that she'd been in love with him for a long time. She'd been careful to keep her feelings hidden. He hadn't been free and she wasn't the type to break up relationships.

She checked out the other half of the bar before her gaze zinged back to Brian. He lifted his beer bottle and poured the remaining golden liquid down his throat. Slamming the empty down, he reached for the spare, waiting. Damn, she hated to see him like this.

All right. She was going to go over there. Just a sip of beer for courage, first. She raised her glass to her lips.

"Karina. I'm glad you're here. I was hoping to see you before you left. May I sit?"

Ian. Shit. He'd somehow evaded her awareness and seated himself on the barstool next to her without her knowing. This was what she got for being nice and polite to a guy who mistook it for encouragement and, frankly, gave her the willies.

She attempted a smile behind her glass as she drowned a big gulp. She had to get away. Now.

"Sorry, I came here to meet someone." She said it lightly, dismissively. She'd planned to wait another minute or two before approaching Brian, but Ian's crowding was forcing her hand. "Oh, there he is. Brian."

She got up and waved in Brian's direction, tossing a good-bye smile at Ian.

His brows came together in a dark vee and his lips thinned, the expression causing her smile to falter and her stomach to heave. His thick nose and heavy brows might indicate a Mediterranean ancestry, but the darkness in his eyes gave her the spooks.

"I hadn't realized."

Keeping her face averted she took another big step and cast a glance back, relief washing over her when he didn't follow, but instead walked back to his seat.

Well, she'd started down this road, so…

"Hey." She slapped a bright, friendly smile on her face and sat down across from Brian. Now that she was safely seated her unease over Ian abated, even while her heart lurched at the deep unhappiness on Brian's face.

He looked up at her, a lopsided attempt at a smile peeking out. "Hi, Karina. I'm not good company right now."

"Oh." She didn't know what to say. His pain was a palpable thing. Impulsively, she reached across the table and laid her hand on his. "I heard and I'm sorry."

Surprise lit the dark depths of his chocolate eyes.

When he didn't say anything, she stood. She'd intruded on his private pain, and that wasn't right. She turned to leave.

"Wait." His husky voice reached out to her. "Please, don't go."

She smiled warmly at him and sat back down.

She stayed there for several more rounds as they talked deep into the night. Once or twice she glanced over at Ian. Every time she looked he appeared to be seething with anger as he stared toward her and Brian. She shuddered.

"This place is closing soon." She tugged Brian to his feet. "Come on, you look ready to drop."

"I'm not that bad," he protested, but allowed himself to be shuffled out the door. The cool night air hit them and snapped some of the buzz away. Karina looked at the stars, her heart full and happy. Not exactly a dream date, but it was Brian…and her…alone.

"Let's go to my place. I think I have a bottle of wine," he suggested.

"You're going to fall asleep before you ever get it open," she scoffed as she fell into step beside him.

He looked at her, his little-boy expression pleading that it couldn't possibly be bedtime already. "I don't want to be alone tonight," he admitted softly. "Please come share a bottle of wine with me." There was only a slight slur to his voice and she'd had just enough to drink to feel the same.

Besides, she didn't want the night to end either. It might not be the wisest move but she couldn't come up with any convincing reasons why she shouldn't spend the last few hours with him.

She gave in.

He grinned at her, wrapping an arm around her shoulders. "How come we didn't do this before?" His sloppy grin made her heart laugh. "We should have. I've always liked you."

Magical words.

They walked toward his room, arms around each other, talking, murmuring in low voices. The heat of his voice, the tenor of his words, the glow of moonlight, Brian's touch – it was magic. And she wanted more. She wanted it all. Tonight.

THE COUPLE WALKED down the path, sliding in and out of view. He'd hidden in the trees thinking to see where Brian was taking Karina. And hoping his instinctive guess was wrong.

But no; there she was. Ian thought he'd missed her leaving. But no, she'd left with Brian. Why? *Why Brian?* Brian was nothing. And he had a girlfriend. Or he'd had a girlfriend. According to the gossip, he'd just been dumped.

How could Karina do such a thing? It's not like Brian was in any shape to enter another relationship right now. Had she no respect. For him? Or for herself?

He stood in the shadows of the trees that darkened the path and watched them make their way to Brian's dorm.

Anger simmered inside.

Brian had many girls fawning all over him. He didn't need Karina. He'd only cast her off later.

Karina deserved better. If she weren't so blinded by Brian's flashy looks, she'd realize it. She'd be sorry later.

Damn Brian to hell.

SATISFACTION THRUMMED THROUGH Karina's body as she collapsed beside Brian in the wee hours of the morning. Her skin was damp and her body buzzed from their heated lovemaking. "Who'd have thought?" she whispered into the darkness.

A deep rumble rolled out from his chest as he attempted to speak but couldn't. She grinned. She'd brought him to this. She'd been the one he'd turned to tonight. Not Wendy, but her – Karina. Maybe she shouldn't have jumped at the opportunity…but she'd needed the chance to show him how good they could be together. How perfect.

And given that exams were over and all students going their separate ways, it had been now or never.

It seemed she'd loved him for so long. Always an acquaintance, never quite a friend and always superficial, kept on the outside…the last place she wanted to be.

She could no more stop blurting the words than she could stop the tidal wave of love that swept through her, giving the words their freedom.

"I love you," she whispered and dropped a kiss on his bare chest, before nestling her head on his shoulder and falling asleep.

MORNING DAWNED BRIGHT and clear. Karina woke slowly, her body still warm and achy from the night's activities. She bolted upright as memories flooded back. *Brian.* She'd had the most wonderful night of her life. She grinned and bounded out of bed.

Wrapping herself in the sheet, she walked out to the communal room, grateful that Brian's roomies had already left. *Empty.* She stood in the middle of the room, dread forming a sinking ball of steel in her stomach. An engine started outside.

She raced over to the glass doors, stepping out onto the small verandah in time to see Brian's car disappearing down the drive at a good clip. *He was coming back, wasn't he?* She stood there, waiting, for a long time after his car disappeared from view. As her heart broke into a dozen tiny pieces, hope faded away. The small sedan was gone.

And he hadn't once looked back.

TO BE CONTINUED…

This ends the preview of Second Chances. Part 1 of the book is available. Part 2 is also available.

Second Chances…at Love Series

Second Chances – Part 1
Second Chances – Part 2
Second Chances – complete book (Parts 1 & 2)

Touched by Death
Adult RS/thriller

Death had touched anthropologist Jade Hansen in Haiti once before, costing her an unborn child and perhaps her very sanity.

A year later, determined to face her own issues, she returns to Haiti with a mortuary team to recover the bodies of an American family from a mass grave. Visiting his brother after the quake, independent contractor Dane Carter puts his life on hold to help the sleepy town of Jacmel rebuild. But he finds it hard to like his brother's pregnant wife or her family. He wants to go home, until he meets Jade – and realizes what's missing in his own life. When the mortuary team begins work, it's as if malevolence has been released from the earth. Instead of laying her ghosts to rest, Jade finds herself confronting death and terror again.

And the man who unexpectedly awakens her heart – is right in the middle of it all.

This book is available. Sample chapter is next...

Touched by Death Sample

Prologue

IN PERFECT SYMPHONY the clouds swayed in the sky, wrapping the moon in protective cotton wool as the ground shook and trembled beneath the sleepy town of Jacmel in the south of Haiti.

Mother Earth growled and raged over and over again as if she knew the secrets long kept hidden in the hills behind the small town. As if she knew about the injustices done. As if she knew this had to stop. She gave one last mighty shove and the earth cracked open.

Trees toppled, their roots ripped from the ground in hapless destruction. Large rocks tumbled as their foundations were wiped out from below. Everything fell to the force of Mother Nature – at long last exposing old secrets to the light.

When she was finally satisfied, the clouds slipped back from their protective stance, letting the moon glare upon the result of Mother Earth's game of fifty-two pickup with the Devil. The rays shone on bones long picked clean – now newly exposed to the sky.

The ground undulated one last time. The surrounding hillside shuddered, sending a light dusting of earth and rock to rebury the gruesome evidence. As if the sins of man were too much for even the moon to see.

FIVE DAYS LATER, a tractor, hastily called into service, with a bucket on the front, groaned as it carried yet another load of the town's dead to a large grave. Herman, the tractor driver, was beyond pain and grief and death. He focused on the gritty details of plain survival. Five days of heat and exposure hadn't been kind to the dead – or to the living. Survival had become a grim business and rotting bodies needed to be buried or disease would crush them further. So many dead. No money. No time. No help.

No choice.

His neighbor, John, lifted the last small corpse from the dump truck load on the ground to the loader's bucket. He pulled off one work glove, straightened the bandana tied around his mouth and nose and shouted, "Good to go!"

Herman popped the gear shift forward, swore and prayed that Bertha would survive the job given her. He trundled forward. "Come on girl." He patted the stick shift in his hand. "I need you to get it done. If you quit on me, I ain't gonna make it through this." And that was no joke. He knew for damn sure that he wouldn't if ol' Bertha didn't. *Bad business this.* He had respect for the dead. Every one of his family and friends had received a proper send off, a decent burial – as was fitting. Until this earthquake.

Pain clutched his heart and squeezed. So many dead.

He'd lost his wife, one son and two grandkids this last week. Sex and age hadn't mattered here. Mother Nature hadn't cared. She'd wiped them all out.

John, the only other person who'd stepped up to help, had been lucky. His young wife and her family had survived the devastation. Living out of town had helped. That also contributed to his motivation to help out. This grave butted against his wife's family's land so it made sense for John to make sure this grave was closed over right and proper. There could be many people trekking to the grave on All Soul's Day, as families came to honor their dead. Then again, complete families had been buried together. There might not be anyone left to mourn.

He would come and visit. There were too many people here to forget.

Herman tugged at the old t-shirt tied around his nose and mouth, his black skin blending with the poor light. Nothing kept the smell out. He'd already gone through a half dozen pairs of gloves. But without the makeshift bandana the breath caught in his chest, making him gag. His clothes would have to be burned after this. There would be no way to clean them.

Bertha struggled forward. Darkness hid the evidence of what they were doing. What he'd done. He only hoped he wouldn't have too many more loads to haul.

In the aftermath of the earthquake, everyone had been numb, in shock or frozen with grief. No one had been able to make decisions. There'd been no army to take care of the problem. The government buildings and staff had been as decimated as the rest of the population.

Herman hadn't been able to leave his people lying exposed like that. Determined to do what he could he'd taken command and had done something. Something so awful, he couldn't close his eyes without seeing the stares of the dead – blaming him.

So far, close to sixty people had gone into this pit. The natural depression, a ready-made burial spot, was a godsend to the desperate survivors, a fast answer to the bloated dead rotting on the sidewalks. He didn't know how many more were to come, maybe hundreds. Later, much later, if someone cared, they could open this mass grave and do the right thing. But not now. Now they had to get on with the business of survival.

Mother Nature was a bitch.

Chapter 1

One year later…

JADE HANSEN TWISTED in the cool sheets. Her sweaty panicked body searched for a way out of the endless nightmare of bloated bodies, desperate people and cries for help – pleas that would never get answered. She turned in the fog as one more person, caught among the fallen rocks, cried out to her. She came face to face with a woman – blood congealed in her hair and streaked down the side of her face, a chunk of concrete crushing her legs. She begged for Jade to find her son.

Screaming, Jade took off to the safety of the tent, the tent filled with the dead…and the living that searched for their families.

She couldn't help them all.

She couldn't help any of them.

She couldn't even help herself.

With tears streaming down her face, Jade woke in a panic as if the demons of her nightmare had followed her into the present.

Shuddering, she recognized the hanging lamp overhead as the one in her apartment. The Aztec print couch she'd fallen asleep on was hers, a gift from her brother. And she finally understood that the evening's in-depth television coverage of a small earthquake in Haiti had been the trigger for her nightmare.

Jade curled into a ball, pulling her throw higher up on her neck. She winced at the images still flashing on the news. Another earthquake in Haiti. Only a little one this time. Not that the size mattered. The memories of her one and only humanitarian trip to that area, after the major earthquake almost a year ago, had etched themselves permanently into her brain. A horrible time, a-praying-on-your-knees-for-help kind of horrible time. In Haiti, nightmares had destroyed her sleep. The shortage of food for those suffering had destroyed her appetite.

She'd lost weight over there, but nothing compared to the pounds that had slipped off after her return home. Sure, that had been almost a year ago. It didn't matter. With the nightmare fresh in her mind it felt like only two days.

So much pain and suffering. *So much torment.* She couldn't stop it. She couldn't even begin to make it right. There'd been nothing she could do to help – or so little relative to the scope of the problem, it might as well have been nothing. If she'd been offered a ride out of that hell on any given day, she'd have jumped over her colleagues to grab it.

She wasn't proud of that.

In fact, it made her feel small and ashamed. Her colleagues had done so much better.

She'd wanted to be better. She'd tried to be better.

She'd failed. Failed her colleagues. The victims. And herself.

The memories still haunted her.

She had her nice safe lab job back in Seattle. She drove to work every day in a nice car and returned home every night to her clean safe apartment with running water, heat and electricity. All the comforts denied the Haitians still struggling through the devastation.

After she'd locked her front door behind her that first day home, the tears had started to pour. It seemed she'd been crying ever since.

Her life had gone from bad to worse for a while before she'd picked up – somewhat.

And now another earthquake.

If a small one like that triggered her memories what was the reality doing to all those poor people still living the horror?

The phone rang.

She ignored it.

It wouldn't quit. Finally, she couldn't stand it so picked up the receiver. She didn't even bother to check the caller ID. Duncan called every night at nine.

"I'm fine, Duncan."

"Hey, Kitten." Her brother's pet name for her made her smile as he'd probably intended. She used to be like him. Upbeat, funny and carefree. Until life had dumped her on her ass at the top of the slide and given her a hard kick downhill. She wasn't sure she'd hit bottom now either.

"I've got a job proposition for you."

His cheerful voice made her want to smile. The job proposition didn't. "I don't want to hear it."

He laughed, a buoyant sound that rang around the room. He never failed to raise her spirits. The effect just didn't hang around after his calls. "Maybe you don't, but maybe you do. How will you know if you don't hear it? It's a good one."

His wheedling tone made her smile in spite of her horrible mood. "Not if I don't want to hear it."

"You don't know what you want."

Jade groaned. "If I don't know, then how do you?"

That laughter pealed again. She shook her head and felt the lightness – the joyful spirit that was her brother – ease the ache in her soul. "I know you keep trying to save me, Duncan, but I'm fine."

The laughter and joy cut off suddenly. Duncan's voice, sober and sad, whispered, "No. No, you're not."

Tears choked her. She rubbed her eyes. She wasn't going to cry, damn it. Not tonight. Not *again* tonight.

"This has to stop, Jade. You're going to collapse and I don't want that to happen." Love slipped through the phone receiver making it harder to hold back the tears. Jade didn't trust herself to speak. She sniffled ever so slightly.

"I know you're hurting inside. I feel it and I hurt for you."

"I know," she whispered, starting to shake, knowing she had to stop – only she didn't know how. And once again – couldn't deal with it. "Look, I'm really tired. I need to get to bed. I'll talk to you tomorrow."

She didn't give him a chance to say good-bye and hung up instead. As soon as the receiver clicked down, the tears rolled. Hot and steady, they streamed down her cheeks. She snuggled back into the couch and let them run.

The point of stopping them was long gone – besides she no longer knew how.

"HEY DANE. THAT guy called again." John called out.

"Yeah, which guy?" Dane walked over to stand beside his stepbrother who'd stopped by the site for a visit.

Dane tugged his hard hat off to wipe the sweat running down his forehead. Christ it was hot and humid here. He surveyed the hospital construction site in front of them. Not bad at all. They were ahead of schedule, but completion of the new wing was still months away. Jacmel hadn't recovered from the last big earthquake and with smaller ones continually causing setbacks, the country would be years getting back on its feet.

It had taken weeks to convince John to let him come over after the quake. When he'd realized how badly in need the town was, Dane had stepped in. But John had refused Dane's help to fix John's small engine repair shop that had been decimated in one of the smaller more recent earthquakes. John said he wanted to fix things himself.

"The guy about the grave." John said, "Remember they want to open it and retrieve some guy's family?"

Dane glanced over at his brother. There were only the two of them left in the family. Both stubborn. Independent. And family oriented. It had only taken one phone call with something odd in John's voice to catch Dane's attention. He'd put his Seattle construction business in the hands of his capable foreman, an old school friend, and without his brother's invite, he'd flown to Haiti two days later. That had been months ago.

Shielding his eyes from the hot sun, Dane said, "I have to admit, never-ending sunshine and warm, dry weather is hardly a hardship. Of course we haven't hit the humid summer season, yet."

"See? Isn't this much better than the wet misery of the coast? Seattle is probably still buried in snow – even in March." John grinned with satisfaction.

Dane couldn't argue that. His foreman had been complaining of just that in the last phone call. "Not everyone hates the rain like you do."

"Come on, admit it." John reached over and smacked Dane's shoulder. A cloud of dust rose, making him step back hurriedly. "You love it here."

"I love visiting you and of course, I adore Tasha." Dane grinned over his white lie. There was no arguing that Tasha obviously adored his brother so that was good enough for him. It had, after all, been the call of family that had brought Dane here.

John had a terrible history with relationships. His long-time high school sweetheart had walked out the door of her home one day just weeks before graduation and had never returned. A few years later, John had married the witchy Elise. That marriage had been a walking disaster right from the wedding reception. Dane hadn't been able to stand the woman and the feeling had been mutual. John was just a big teddy bear who attracted unscrupulous people.

After that fiasco, John disappeared for years before finally setting up housekeeping with Tasha in Haiti. Dane's antennae went off at that and given the past, he could be forgiven for worrying about his brother. Only John appeared to have stabilized, was flourishing even. Dane had been delighted.

The major earthquake had changed all that, sending John back into the same morose angry man as before.

"Hey, are you in there?"

Dane started.

John smirked at him, a sign his light-hearted kid brother was showing through the more cynical angry one of recent years. "What's the matter; Felice getting to you?"

Heat washed over Dane's throat. Felice was too hot, too willing and way too young. She was also the daughter of one of Tasha's friends who'd visited yesterday. He didn't know the specific laws in Haiti relating to that sort of thing, still he was pretty damn sure he'd get jail time back home and that was deterrent enough for him.

"She needs to be locked away for a few years."

"Not here. Girls her age are often married and pregnant." John added thoughtfully, "And not likely in that order."

Dane shook his head. "As long as it's not to me."

John changed the subject abruptly. "What am I going to do about the call...about this guy's request for help at the mass gravesite? Sounds crazy to me."

Easily following the lightning shift of his brother's mind, Dane said, "What's to do – he's a grieving man. His request isn't unreasonable. And it's done all the time."

John visibly shuddered. "I never expected to feel so strongly about it, but after that earthquake... I don't know Dane. I saw too much death. More than I should have – more than anyone should have. It seems wrong to dig up those poor earthquake victims again."

"You've been living here too long. Some weird Haitian's beliefs are rubbing off on you."

John snickered, making Dane laugh. "Or not long enough. According to Tasha, Mother Earth claimed them and she won't be happy if she's forced to give them up again."

With a sigh of disgust, Dane said, "That's crazy talk. This guy lost his family. He wants to take the three of them home to Seattle and bury them properly. He needs closure. That's all. What's so wrong about that?"

John kicked a stray rock in the dirt. "I don't know that anything is wrong with it. I guess if it were me and mine, I'd want to take them home, too. But it's a mass grave. There are other bodies to consider. Other families who will be hurt."

"Really?" Dane stared at him. "Like *how mass?*"

John shot him a look before grimacing and staring off in the horizon. "I stopped counting at sixty. We did what we had to do. The dead...they were everywhere. Herman, our old neighbor, used his loader...Christ it was bad."

Dane scrunched his face. John rushed to explain.

"God, there were children playing beside bloated bodies. They'd become dulled to them; there were so many. Oh don't blame the children. They stayed close to the people they knew because they had no one else. That a dead mother or sibling lay within a few feet didn't seem to matter. Even dead, they were a comfort."

Dane closed his eyes as terrible images flooded his mind. He couldn't imagine the horror. "I wasn't judging. I just can't envision what you went through. And to think of children sitting there, so lost and alone… Well…it's a terrible thought."

Shadows darkened John's eyes. Dane was sorry for what John had been through. "That's the thing about family." Dane patted John on the shoulder and noticed his brother cringe.

"So you think this guy should be allowed to come in and remove his kin?" John wasn't backing away from this one.

"I don't have any say in this. I wasn't aware that you did, either. I'm sure this man has already gone through the authorities. I'd suggest that you accept that this is going to happen whether you want it to or not. The team of specialists is going to be here soon. When they arrive, be nice to them. Helpful. They will probably be there for a day or two, a week or two max. Then they'll be gone, leaving the others to rest in peace."

"It's not that easy."

"I know. There are other people with loved ones in that grave. Maybe someone should suggest that all the victims be identified and even…" Dane pursed his lips and nodded his head, pleased with his idea. "Reburied properly. This guy has money. Maybe some of it should be put toward assisting the community to help them deal with disaster."

John shook his head. "You don't understand the full scope of the problem here. There could be hundreds of bodies there. We just kept putting them in then piling dirt and rocks on top to make sure they weren't disturbed. We probably went overboard on that part."

Dane blanched. "Hundreds?" He swallowed heavily. "Okay so maybe the team will need a little longer. Still something could be done for the other remains." Dane winced. "Or at least the remains they can find and identify while they search for the ones they are shipping back to Seattle."

John stared at him, and gulped. "That's not helping."

"Yeah. I know. Sorry about that."

The two men stared at the half-completed building in front of them. Dane took an involuntary step back. Right now the damn thing resembled a skeleton reaching out of the ground.

TO BE CONTINUED…

Touched by Death – Part 1 is available.
Part 2 is also available now.

By Death Series

Touched by Death – Part 1
Touched by Death – Part 2
Touched by Death – Parts 1&2
Haunted by Death
Chilled by Death
By Death Books 1–3

Tuesday's Child

What she doesn't want…is exactly what he needs.

Shunned and ridiculed all her life for something she can't control, Samantha Blair hides her psychic abilities and lives on the fringes of society. Against her will, however, she's tapped into a killer – or rather, his victims. Each woman's murder, blow-by-blow, ravages her mind until their death releases her back to her body. Sam knows she must go to the authorities, but will the rugged, no-nonsense detective in charge of tracking down the killer believe her?

Detective Brandt Sutherland only trusts hard evidence, yet Sam's visions offer clues he needs to catch a killer. The more he learns about her incredible abilities, however, the clearer it becomes that Sam's visions have put her in the killer's line of fire. Now Brandt must save her from something he cannot see or understand…and risk losing his heart in the process.

As danger and desire collide, passion raises the stakes in a game Sam and Brandt don't dare lose.

Broken Protocols

Romantic comedy & suspense

Dani's been through a year of hell...

Just as it's getting better, she's tossed forward through time with her orange Persian cat, Charmin Marvin, clutched in her arms. They're dropped into a few centuries into the future. There's nothing she can do to stop it, and it's impossible to go back.

And then it gets worse...

A year of government regulation is easing, and Levi Blackburn is feeling back in control. If he can keep his reckless brother in check, everything will be perfect. But while he's been protecting Milo from the government, Milo's been busy working on a present for him...

The present is Dani, only she comes with a snarky cat who suddenly starts talking...and doesn't know when to shut up.

In an age where breaking protocols have severe consequences, things go wrong, putting them all in danger...

It's a Dog's Life

Romantic comedy & suspense

It's the first day of Ninna's job in the local animal shelter...and a dog is talking to her. Not just any dog...a fat, old, smart-alecky Basset Hound who says his name is Mosey.

She can't quit, she needs this job. And then there's the yummy vet. Who turns out to live across the street from her in a much bigger house than her tiny house. Big enough to hold a few animals – including the mouthy Mosey. With all this going on, she doesn't have time to worry about the rash of break-ins and the sense of being watched. She's too busy worrying that she's nuts.

When Ninna agrees to dog sit for the cute vet from work, she sees it as a trial at being a pet owner and a way to build on her budding relationship with the vet. For Mosey, this weekend means time to get to know each other.

For the stalker who's tracking Ninna's movements, it means...opportunity.

About the Author

Dale Mayer is a USA Today bestselling author best known for her Psychic Visions and Family Blood Ties series. Her contemporary romances are raw and full of passion and emotion (Second Chances, SKIN), her thrillers will keep you guessing (By Death series), and her romantic comedies will keep you giggling (It's a Dog's Life and Charmin Marvin Romantic Comedy series).

She honors the stories that come to her – and some of them are crazy and break all the rules and cross multiple genres!

To go with her fiction, she also writes nonfiction in many different fields with books available on resume writing, companion gardening and the US mortgage system. She has recently published her Career Essentials Series. All her books are available in print and ebook format.

Connect with Dale Mayer Online

Dale's Website – www.dalemayer.com
Twitter – @DaleMayer
Facebook – facebook.com/DaleMayer.author

Also by Dale Mayer

Published Adult Books:

Psychic Vision Series
Tuesday's Child
Hide'n Go Seek
Maddy's Floor
Garden of Sorrow
Knock, Knock…
Rare Find
Eyes to the Soul
Now You See Her
Shattered
Into the Night…
Psychic Visions Books 1–3
Psychic Visions Books 4–6
Psychic Visions Books 7–9

By Death Series
Touched by Death – Part 1
Touched by Death – Part 2
Touched by Death – Parts 1&2
Haunted by Death
Chilled by Death
By Death Books 1–3

Second Chances...at Love Series
Second Chances – Part 1
Second Chances – Part 2
Second Chances – complete book (Parts 1 & 2)

Charmin Marvin Romantic Comedy Series
Broken Protocols
Broken Protocols 2
Broken Protocols 3
Broken Protocols 3.5
Broken Protocols 1-3

Broken and... Mending
Skin
Scars
Scales (of Justice)
Broken but... Mending 1-3

Glory
Genesis
Tori
Celeste
Glory Trilogy

Biker Blues
Biker Blues: Morgan, Part 1
Biker Blues: Morgan, Part 2
Biker Blues: Morgan, Part 3
Biker Baby Blues: Morgan, Part 4
Biker Blues: Morgan, Full Set
Biker Blues: Salvation, Part 1

Biker Blues: Salvation, Part 2
Biker Blues: Salvation, Part 3
Biker Blues: Salvation, Full Set

SEALs of Honor
Mason: SEALs of Honor, Book 1
Hawk: SEALs of Honor, Book 2
Dane: SEALs of Honor, Book 3
Swede: SEALs of Honor, Book 4
Shadow: SEALs of Honor, Book 5
Cooper: SEALs of Honor, Book 6
Markus: SEALs of Honor, Book 7
Evan: SEALs of Honor, Book 8
Chase: SEALs of Honor, Book 9
Brett: SEALs of Honor, Book 10
SEALs of Honor, Books 1–3

Collections
Dare to Be You…
Dare to Love…
Dare to be Strong…
RomanceX3

Standalone Novellas
It's a Dog's Life
Riana's Revenge

Published Young Adult Books:

Family Blood Ties Series
Vampire in Denial
Vampire in Distress

Vampire in Design
Vampire in Deceit
Vampire in Defiance
Vampire in Conflict
Vampire in Chaos
Vampire in Crisis
Vampire in Control
Vampire in Charge
Family Blood Ties Set 1–3
Family Blood Ties Set 1–5
Family Blood Ties Set 4–6
Family Blood Ties Set 7–9
Sian's Solution – A Family Blood Ties Short Story

Design series
Dangerous Designs
Deadly Designs
Darkest Designs
Design Series Trilogy

Standalone
In Cassie's Corner
Gem Stone (a Gemma Stone Mystery)
Time Thieves

Published Non-Fiction Books:

Career Essentials
Career Essentials: The Résumé
Career Essentials: The Cover Letter
Career Essentials: The Interview
Career Essentials: 3 in 1

Made in the USA
Charleston, SC
27 August 2016